"WHAT EXACTLY IS IT YOU NEED MY HELP WITH?"

He'd been lethal enough to her libido when barefoot, wearing paint-spattered jeans. Standing there all intense and enigmatic, framed by his prowling roadster only intensified things. If that were possible. "Fantasy dates."

"Fantasy dates," he repeated as he eased the car out of the garage.

She risked a glance at him. He wasn't exactly smiling, but there was a distinct air of amusement about him. "Yes."

"A little fun indeed," he murmured.

Any reply she might have made was lost on her sudden gasp as he floored the gas pedal and sent the little sports car rocketing down the rear drive. When she looked at him again, he was grinning. And a fiercer thing she'd never witnessed in her entire life.

Dear God, she'd unleashed a monster.

The Great Scot

DONNA KAUFFMAN

KENSINGTON PUBLISHING CORP.
http://www.kensingtonbooks.com

BRAVA BOOKS are published by

Kensington Publishing Corp.
850 Third Avenue
New York, NY 10022

All Kensington titles, imprints, and distributed lines are available at special quantity discounts for bulk purchases for sales promotion, premiums, fund-raising, educational, or institutional use.

Special book excerpts or customized printings can also be created to fit specific needs. For details, write or phone the office of the Kensington Special Sales Manager: Attn. Special Sales Department. Kensington Publishing Corp., 850 Third Avenue, New York, NY 10022. Phone: 1-800-221-2647.

ISBN-13: 978-0-7582-1202-3
ISBN-10: 0-7582-1202-X

First Brava Books Mass-Market Printing: February 2009
First Brava Books Trade Paperback Printing: March 2007
10 9 8 7 6 5 4 3 2 1

Printed in the United States of America

Chapter 1

Dozens of sheep surged across the single track road and surrounded Erin MacGregor's car, pushing the tiny rental to and fro, bleating and carrying on as if the event was one giant sheep rave. They leapt in hordes over the low stone wall on the opposite side of the road, apparently dying to discover if, in fact, the grass was greener on the other side. Erin could have told them that was impossible. As it was, the grass in Scotland already looked like Astroturf.

Her forward progress temporarily halted, Erin used the break to once again study the directions given to her by Brodie Chisholm, the pub owner back in Glenbuie. She'd already gone past the family-owned Chisholm distillery, driven through endless stretches of Chisholm-owned farmland, and was finally nearing the mountains north of the little highland village. During the time she'd spent nursing a pint of ale at Hagg's and chatting up the locals, she'd learned, among other things, that the Chisholm whisky label was the backbone of Glenbuie's economy and had been for several centuries. "Well, just maybe I can add to that bottom line a little," she explained to the sheep, who paid the announcement little attention; quite unlike the villagers, however, when she'd mentioned the same thing to them.

She drummed her fingers steadily on the steering wheel, no longer cringing as, one after the other, the sheep banged around her car. She'd already learned that the horn didn't faze them in the least. The first time the little bleaters had suddenly gone from being innocent woolly bystanders to abruptly leaping over the stone wall directly in front of her car in an apparent mass suicide attempt, she'd screamed and slammed on the brakes, terrified she might hit one of the adorable little black-faced darlings. One hour and four sheep-jackings later, her humanitarian instincts had rapidly receded. One of them gave her wheel well a thump as it passed, and she made a mental note to try the lamb before she left the country.

She nudged the car slowly forward, earning a few sheep glares, but was finally able to move past them. Minutes later the valley was behind her and no longer in sight, her rear view swallowed up by towering pines as she wound her way into the mountains. *Almost there.*

"Please, please, please be what I'm looking for," she prayed, downshifting as the climb grew steadily steeper. She'd scouted locations a million times, confronting language barriers, cultural differences, and any one of a number of complicated obstacles, and usually got what she wanted. So there was no reason to feel nervous or edgy. Yet, she did.

When their London site burned to the ground ten days ago, it had been Erin's bright idea to go to Scotland. She'd first gone to Edinburgh, convinced she'd find something in the ancient city to suit their purposes, but nothing had really grabbed her. So, this morning she'd headed north, intending on Inverness, and its proximity to both the mountains and the sea, but had gotten sidetracked the instant she'd wound her way into the tiny village of Glenbuie. It didn't have the cosmopolitan feel they usually went for—the "class factor" as her boss, Tommy, termed it—but what it lacked in urbane sophistication, it more than made up for with its intimate charm and romantic appeal. Glenbuie was like Brigadoon come to life.

She rounded the tight turn near the peak and found herself facing a narrow rock strewn lane, fronted by two, massive stacked stone pillars. There was a small brass plaque on one of them, long since oxidized green from exposure. She rolled to a stop and read the raised lettering. *Glenshire*. She was here.

Low, stone boundary walls jutted out from the pillars and disappeared up into the rocky hills, but as they were mostly covered with ivy, and backed by more thick stands of towering pines, she couldn't see how far they extended, or any of the property that lay beyond. She drove slowly up the rutted lane, thankful there was not one sheep in sight, and automatically began making mental notes about what would have to be done to make the entrance accessible and camera-ready. She doubted the owner would mind the upgrade.

The narrow drive wound upward almost another full kilometer before finally topping out on another hairpin turn. All thoughts of pre-production prep work fled her mind completely as she let the car roll to a stop. That familiar, much-wanted rush of adrenaline punched into her system as she hungrily took in the vision before her. *Wow. And double wow.*

So, Brodie hadn't been kidding. In fact, he'd undersold the place. She sat at the entrance to a circular cobbled driveway. The centerpiece was a huge, beautifully sculpted fountain that had seen obvious repairs, but was all the more remarkable because of its age. Beyond the fountain rose Glenshire itself. Not a fairytale castle by any stretch, nothing so Disneyesque as that. No, this place had true character. It was a rather immense, battle worn pile of bricks, but with the ivy covering the walls and the crenellated trim that ran along the rooftop edge, it was impressive. She could only imagine the history those walls had endured.

The central section sported a huge double door entry with a massive iron and glass light fixture strung up on heavy chains above it, all of it appearing to have been there since the original mortar was mixed. It was imposing, and made the estate even more interesting and inviting. The double doors were framed by tall, narrow windows. The steeply peaked roof was inset with a pair of gabled windows, their glass panes gleaming brightly in the just setting sun.

Two-story wings jutted from either side of the three-story central section, the stone a slightly darker color brown, with the odd black brick here and there throughout. Each had a row of wide, double-casement windows along the bottom, and smaller inset windows along the top. Those had flower boxes beneath, each overflowing with a gorgeous array of pink and white blossoms that Erin, who had a black thumb and only had to think about planting something to kill it, couldn't have named if her life depended on it, but was envious of their vitality nonetheless. The bright spot of color, along with the neatly trimmed box hedges that ran beneath the lower windows, and the topiary trees set on either side of the front door, all leant the place a rather magical glow.

She could easily picture a horse drawn carriage circling the cobbled driveway and made another mental note to tell the production staff to consider using one in the opening sequence. Maybe Greg could come prancing in on some fine stallion when he met the women for the first time. She sighed just a little, framing the shot in her mind.

There were no cars in the drive, so she pulled all the way around to the front of the house. Only then did she see the view from the house itself. She'd wound her way so far into the mountains she'd lost her bearings, but she'd assumed, this being the Chisholm clan stronghold, and perched on the peak as it was, that it would look out over the valley that ran between the village and the mountains, allowing the clan chief to look down over his domain. She'd expected to see Glenbuie and the distillery dotting the vista below.

The view was altogether different, however, but equally majestic and commanding. She climbed out of her rental car and turned, shading her face with her hand against the sun. Standing in front of the house looking out, her view was straight down the mountain range. An endless ripple of deep blue and green peaks, contrasted to the plum and rose hues of the early evening sky. The peak on which she stood was clearly the highest, providing her with an awe-inspiring outlook.

She walked over to the part of the circular driveway that edged along the steep drop off. It was railed off and quite safe, but the way it jutted outward, stepping to the railing felt like stepping off a cliff. Her heart caught in her chest as she looked down at the tops of trees that soared stories high. The dense stand of pines were so thick she couldn't quite make out any of the winding mountain road below. She looked out across the narrow drop to the rise of the next mountain, then the peak beyond it, and on and on, as far as the eye could see. It was definitely a rush, like standing head and shoulders above the world. She could only imagine what it would be like to stand here during a wild storm, or when the mountains were cloaked with mist and fog.

The canals of Venice, the Eiffel Tower, the Leaning Tower of Pisa . . . each had been backdrops for previous seasons of the show. Glenshire was so completely different from anything they'd used before, far more remote, without a famous historical landmark as a marketing tie-in. But standing there with the warm, late afternoon breeze whipping at the tips of her hair, she couldn't think of a more fitting setting for their next Prince Charming happily-ever-after story. Glenshire was earthy and bold, ancient and imperfect . . . and utterly romantic.

"The view is something, is it no'?"

Erin let out a little yelp. The unexpected voice had come from quite close behind her. A very deep, beautifully melodic, male voice. She made a grab at the railing when her feet slipped on the cobblestones as she whipped around to face him. She was rarely caught off guard, her internal radar having become highly developed by, oh, around age four. Being raised in a state home did that to a person. No one snuck up on her.

Disconcerted by so swiftly losing the upper hand, she plastered a self-deprecating grin on her face even before she found her balance. "So much for my grand entrance," she quipped, even as he moved swiftly to take her arm and help her regain her footing.

"The stones get a bit slick when the evening mist comes in."

The sun had just begun lowering in the sky and there wasn't so much as a hint of mist in the air, but she welcomed the gentlemanly offer of an excuse. "Yes, thank you." She slid her arm free from his unsettling touch and leaned back against the railing, gripping it with both hands, just as a precaution. Her knees had gone a bit wonky when she'd gotten her first full tilt look at him.

Earthy and bold, yet utterly romantic.

Her words to describe Glenshire could easily be used to describe its owner. Back in the village, they'd affectionately referred to him as The Great Scot. She'd never gotten around to asking why.

Now she didn't have to.

He was tall, more than a head-and-a-half taller than her own five-foot-seven, forcing her to look up to see him properly. Way up. Like his younger brother, Brodie, Dylan Chisholm had a gorgeous mane of thick, dark hair, but the family resemblance ended there. His was straighter, and he wore it more on the long side. It fell across his forehead in a rakish sweep and brushed well below his collar in the back, which only added to the overall Heathcliffian effect. She doubted it had seen a brush in some time, but looked as if it had been repeatedly raked through by his own hand. Made a woman want to sink her fingers into it and tousle it a bit more. Her grip tightened on the railing as she realized she wanted to be that woman.

Her gaze lifted to his, and she noticed his eyes were a dark gray, fringed with dreamboat-thick lashes. All that lush beauty was offset by high, aristocratic cheek bones, a strong nose, and a hard jaw shadowed by a hint of a beard. It was an incongruous jumble of angles, not a classic profile by any stretch, and yet arresting for its imperfection. But it was his mouth that snagged the best of her attention.

His lips were firm, but slightly full, as if they'd been chiseled on an Italian Renaissance statue. Even more compelling were those deeply grooved lines on either side of his mouth that hinted at dimples, yet his expression was far too serious to truly believe him capable of it. And when you added his accent into the mix? Well, what warm-blooded female wouldn't have gotten a bit wonky-kneed? If she had indeed seen any mist, she could be easily convinced it was just a cloud of pheromones wafting around him.

She belatedly realized she was standing there, all but ogling him. And he was letting her, with nary a flicker of amusement or consternation filtering into his steady expression. Although she couldn't be too sure on that last part. He was rather hard to read. And it wasn't like her to get so caught up in appearances. Far from it, in fact. Working in Hollywood had long since inured her to dreamboat good looks.

So why was it that this one made her want to fluff her hair and check her teeth for leftover bits of parsley? That was about as foreign a concept to Erin as wearing makeup or worrying about what outfit to wear. And yet, she had to resist the urge to run her tongue over her teeth and suck in her tummy a little.

She made herself release her death grip on the railing long enough to stab her hand toward him. "Dylan Chisholm, I presume? I'm Erin MacGregor. Your brother, Brodie, was supposed to call and tell you I was coming." Which, from the totally blank look on his face, she could only assume hadn't happened. Great. Strike two.

He took her hand, in a quick, business-like shake. His palms were wide, a bit work roughened, he had long fingers, warm skin and . . . and why in the hell was she noticing that? She jerked her attention back to his face, which didn't help all that much. "I'm guessing you missed his call."

"Apparently," he said. "So . . . what exactly am I missing?"

Not the flirty question it could have been, despite the hint of amusement that had crept into his tone. In her experience, men who looked like Dylan generally didn't make innuendo-laden, sexually suggestive small talk with women who looked like Erin. Which was to say average. Dead average.

And up until right that second, she'd been perfectly

okay with dead average. Average was non-threatening and it enabled her to get what she wanted more often than not. As long as what she wanted was a production location and not . . . well, what she found herself suddenly wanting right at the moment.

"I'm interested in booking Glenshire. I understand you've turned part of it into a bed and breakfast." She forced a steady, confident smile, when she, surprisingly, felt anything but.

"Ah, I see." As understanding dawned in his eyes, he seemed to relax a bit. "I appreciate the interest. I'll have to thank my brother for sending business my way, but I'm afraid we dinnae open for guests for another fortnight."

"Oh, I know. That's okay. Preferable really."

He quirked one eyebrow and frowned a little, somehow managing to look even hotter doing so. "I'm afraid, as much as I'd like to accommodate you, I'm no' ready for guests as yet." There was the slightest twitch at the corners of his mouth, teasing at those intriguing creases, but the smile didn't emerge. "Still more work to be done before we're presentable."

Erin grinned. "I don't think you understand. I want to rent out your *entire* bed and breakfast. For the next two months."

Chapter 2

"I beg your pardon?" Dylan couldn't have heard the Yank properly. One of his brothers was having a go with him again, no doubt. "Did Brodie put you up to this? Because his humor can be found a bit wanting at times."

"I'm perfectly serious." The young woman stuck her hand inside her jacket pocket, fished around, came up empty, then patted down her other pockets, before smiling at him and pulling a card from the rear pocket of her jeans. "Sorry. I apparently handed out all my other ones in Glenbuie. I have more in the car."

She'd handed out cards? He took the somewhat dog-eared business card and glanced down at it. "Erin MacGregor. Location Coordinator. Thomas Marchand Productions." He looked back at her. "Wha' exactly would ye be coordinating?"

"I'm scouting sites for one of America's top-rated television shows. Perhaps you've heard of it? *Your Prince Charming.* We're getting ready to film our eighth season."

Your prince what? "I don't watch much of the telly, sorry."

"We're not syndicated over here," she hurried on to say, "but we're talked about in print and online all over the world. We've used locations in Italy and France, Brussels, Sweden. It's a watercooler show." When he frowned, she added, "You know, the show everyone talks about the morning after it airs? At work? We score very well with the broadest demographics. Advertisers love us."

He handed the card back to her. "Well done, I'm sure. I'm sorry to say, however, that it won't be possible to stage part of your show here. There is still work to be done and I'm booked up in less than a fortnight."

Her smile didn't falter. "Glenshire has been in your family for centuries, is that true?"

What was she on about now? "Aye, that it has." Why was he still standing there, talking to her? There was more work to do than a battalion of laborers could tackle, and he was presently an army of one.

She stepped past him and walked a few paces toward the house, her stride confident, as if she was certain he'd follow. A determined sort, this Erin MacGregor.

She stopped next to the fountain, her gaze taking in the house in its entirety, her expression one of both awe and almost palpable excitement. "It's amazing. I don't know how you manage it."

"Mostly I don't." He had no business standing about, having a chat, yet he made no move to dismiss her. Five minutes ago he'd been wrestling with a particularly stubborn spot of plumbing, before noting his visitor from the central window above. He still wasn't entirely certain this wasn't one of his brother's practical jokes. Or worse, another matchmaking scheme. "Mostly it manages me."

"I can well imagine. Quite the restoration project. Brodie told me," she added by way of explanation. "Which, I understand, is partly why you're opening the bed and breakfast."

Dylan scowled. Didn't his brother have anything better to do than flirt with Yankee lasses? The man was newly married, and shouldnae be consorting about. Of course Dylan knew full well that Brodie was naturally gregarious and equally affable with all who entered his pub, and totally besotted with his new wife. But that didn't give the man license to spout on about personal family business with every straggler who wandered in the door, now did it?

She glanced over at him. "You're the oldest, right? The clan chief?"

"Aye, that I am," he answered absently, his thoughts momentarily diverted by the lecture he was plotting to deliver to all three of his younger brothers the first chance he got. It was one thing to nudge their lone, solitary sibling back into the land of the living, and, truly, he had arrived there some time ago now, but it was up to him when and if he chose to delve into a new relationship. They had no business tossing women in his path, no matter how well intended. Not that any lecture he delivered would likely stop them. Or any of the villagers for that matter. *Bloody hell.* He just wanted to be left alone to get the place into shape for his upcoming guests. Was that so much to ask? He looked at the smiling face of the woman before him. Apparently it was.

"I can't imagine what it's like," she went on, "being responsible for maintaining the collective assets of your entire ancestry."

"If ye only knew the half of it," Dylan muttered. He stared at the crumbling heap, trying to see it as she must, and no doubt failing.

He'd grown up inside those moldering walls, feeling the pressure of all those eyes staring down at him from the endless rows of portraits hung in every available nook and cranny, knowing very early on that no matter what he did during his lifetime, the place would never be restored fully. Though his grandfather, Finny, had done his best to maintain a positive outlook, the burden would overwhelm even the most optimistic of souls. He'd tried to teach Dylan how he focused only on the most dire of Glenshire's maintenance needs, and no' the whole pile at once, or it would drive a man mad.

Unfortunately, Dylan had never been good at compartmentalizing. Perhaps he'd have been a better partner, a better husband, had that been the case. Perhaps he'd have better handled the sudden loss, too.

He swallowed a weary sigh, knowing it was indeed a talent he still sorely lacked. Exhausting as his birthright was, he'd long since come to the conclusion that maintaining the physical remnants of the Chisholm clan legacy was still a whole hell of a lot easier than overseeing the human element that came along with the title of clan chief. Which was more truthfully why he avoided the latter on most occasions.

"I know nothing about my ancestry," she said, still taking the measure of the place.

Her easy confession startled him out of his ponderous musings. "Never traced your heritage?" As unimaginable as his burden was to her, likewise he couldn't imagine that kind of absolute freedom.

"Nothing to trace," she said with a shake of her head, causing her hair to dance a little in the early evening breeze.

He generally wasn't a fan of short hair on women, nor did he care much for that messy just-out-of-bed-look. Sleek and elegant, with an eye toward sophistication, had always been what turned his head. Not that it mattered. If she really was who she said she was, she wasn't here to turn his head. Which suited him just fine.

"I'm sorry to hear that," he said, more as a polite response, so he was surprised to discover he meant it. He might envy her freedom a wee bit, aye, but at the same time, he couldn't quite imagine not knowing where he came from, who his people were.

She shrugged, smiled, her green eyes alight with a gleam that could only be described as impish. How was it he hadn't noticed them earlier? They were quite striking, actually, enlivening her otherwise plain face.

"Don't be," she assured him. "I didn't tell you that to play on your sympathy, I was just trying to convey how otherworldly this seems to me."

He hadn't forgotten she wanted something from him—his home, to be exact—so it would bode him well not to let her charm him in any way. He doubted that she'd forgotten for one second why she was here, and moreover, he was fairly certain despite her claim to the contrary, that this was all a rather calculated attempt to soften him up, or at least get him to let her linger long enough so she could make another sales pitch.

"When I was younger, I used to make up stories about my family," she went on. "But even on a really good day, I could have never come up with something like this." She turned back to the house, but not before he saw something that looked like yearning in her eyes. "Would it—?" She broke off, shook her head.

"What?" he asked, despite knowing he should end this now.

"I was going to ask if I could at least look inside." She waved a hand, silencing whatever his response might have been. "But I should let you get back to . . . whatever it was you were doing. I would say I'm sorry I intruded." She glanced up at the house one last time and a smile stole across her face that snagged his attention in a way a pleading speech never would have. "But I'm not." She pressed the card back in his hand. "If you change your mind, I'm going to stay in town tonight.

Please contact me." The sharp gleam returned to her eyes. "The lease agreement we'd offer would top whatever your guests would be paying. And we'd happily absorb the cost of relocating those who aren't willing to reschedule until after we're done shooting. Of course, it goes without saying the free publicity will likely keep you booked up for some time to come after the show airs."

He took the card without thinking. She was really something. And it hadn't escaped him that she'd gotten her sales pitch in anyway.

"Thanks again," she said, then turned and walked back to her car with a last glance at the house, but not at him. He watched her, his attention split between being somewhat dumbfounded by her moxie . . . and the way her rolling gait made her hips sway in a manner that wasn't remotely enticing, especially in the baggy khakis she wore, but had his full attention, regardless. Forthright and determined, if not overtly feminine. So why he found himself wondering just what the curve of her bum looked like beneath those shapeless trousers, he had no earthly idea.

She paused just before rounding the front of her little car and looked back at him. "Oh, and thank you for the rescue earlier."

He lifted a hand, gave her a nod . . . and wondered at exactly what moment he'd lost his mind. Because it took considerable control not to issue the invitation that was presently sitting on the tip of his tongue. He didn't realize he was holding his breath, waiting to see what she'd say next, until she waved and climbed in her car without another word. And, on a short sigh, he realized he was disappointed.

Maybe his brothers were right after all, he thought, watching her depart. Maybe it was time he got out, socialized a bit more. He'd been back almost two years now. But it wasn't as if he wasn't holed up out here, still wallowing in grief, much as they all suspected. There was simply too much work to be done to waste time frittering about in town. He'd get to that again. At some point. After the B & B was up and running most likely. It wasn't as if he didn't know how. He hadn't always been Dylan Chisholm, grudging clan chief and widower. Back in Edinburgh, he'd been Dylan Chisholm, stock trader, society darling, husband. Aye, and in that order, unfortunately. Of course, Maribel's priorities had been laid out much the same. But that was nobody's business but theirs.

He was back now, that was all that mattered. And he took his role quite seriously. He hadn't been in favor of throwing the doors of Glenshire open to paying guests, but he hadn't had a better idea, either. So it had come down either giving it a go, or being the one to lose the family heritage after four centuries of steady ownership. So he was giving it a go.

Dylan watched as Erin's taillights disappeared down the drive, then turned his back on her and her interesting, if completely insane proposition, and trudged back into the house.

Hours later he was still wedged under the sink, swearing quite creatively while trying to loosen an ancient, rusted-over pipe fitting, when the phone rang. He debated the relative merits of letting the machine pick up the call, but decided he could use the break. It was that or take the wrench to the entire project like a cricket bat.

He made it out onto the third floor landing where the phone table was positioned for use by the guests who'd be put in the upper floor dormer rooms, and snatched up the receiver on the fourth ring. "Hallo," he barked, then immediately followed with a slightly less caustic, "Glenshire, may I help you?" They'd been taking bookings for the past several months and he still had a devil of a time answering his own damn phone like the receptionist in a bloody hotel.

"Ye can start by tellin' me why you didnae at least give our lovely lass Erin here the chance to tell you how many bloomin' zeroes were goin' tae be on that check you so blithely turned down. Ye foofin' arse."

Oh, for Christ sake. Getting chewed out by his brother was about the last thing he was in the mood for at the moment. "I'm doin' the work of ten men here and have little time for your dramatics, Brodie. Tell Ms. MacGregor that if she'd like tae lease the place in the fall or winter when bookings are slim, we'd love to reconsider. Now, if we want our guests to be able to take a piss while they're stayin' here, I need to get back to replacing the pipes in the loo."

"No need to get, well, pissy," Brodie said, far more amused than abashed by his eldest brother's outburst. Damn his perennial jovial heart to hell.

"Glad I can entertain. If ye'd really like tae help, get Marta to take over the bar and get your foofin' arse out here. Preferably with a wrench in your hand." He hung up the phone without waiting for a reply. It wasn't entirely fair to jump Brodie like that, he and Reese had pitched in more than their share when they could get away from their own businesses, as had Tristan, when they could drag him in from the fields. But Dylan wasn't much in the mood to be fair and impartial at the moment.

He stomped back into the WC, forcibly pushing aside any concern save the recalcitrant pipes he was trying to replace, and once again positioned himself beneath the sink. Only to find his thoughts wandering immediately to a pair of dancing green eyes and a lively, confident smile. Other than being a female, of which he'd seen few enough of late, there was nothing particularly fetching about the Yank. Ms. Baggy Bum, with that off-kilter gait and hair cut off all short and shapeless.

He sighed and positioned the wrench back around the offending fitting. But when he bent his will back to the job at hand, it was exactly those khaki clad hips that refused to leave his thoughts. And then there was the way her mouth kicked up at the corners, as if she was in on some amusing bit of news of which he was the last to know.

Frustrated by his inability to shut the Yank from his thoughts, he vented his ire a bit too heavily and snapped the corroded section clean in two, sending a spatter of rusty gunk spraying across his face and neck, and a stream of foul language spewing from his mouth.

"My, my. Have a bar of soap handy? Looks like your face and mouth could both use a good swipe."

Dylan squeezed his eyes shut and worked mightily to keep his tongue under control as well. Through clenched teeth, he said, "Hallo, Mrs. Dalrymple. I didnae hear you come in. My apologies. These pipes are proving a wee bit of a test."

"So, I see. I rang, but with all the clanging and swearing going on, 'tisn't a wonder you didn't hear me. I didnae want to drag ye away from your work, so I thought I'd let myself in."

I just bet you did, he thought unkindly, not particularly sorry for the sour sentiment. Letitia Dalrymple ran the bakery in the village with her daughter, Sally. Letitia and her good friend, Doris, who, along with her husband ran the butcher shop just off the square, were two of the busiest bodies in Glenbuie. They'd formed a knitting club some time ago with several other women of their generation—more of a gossip club if you asked him—and no one in Glenbuie had had a moment's peace since. He'd only had to deal with it for the past two years, and that with the added buffer of living way out here. Through a miracle of patience, Brodie and Reese handled the lot of them without much concern and he'd as soon leave them to it.

But with all three of his brothers either newly married or about to become so, Letty and her cackling horde had set their sights on him. The *puir* widower Chisholm. Naturally Reese, Brodie, and Tristan found this highly amusing and did their best to assist the women in their endeavors whenever possible.

Letty scooped a rag from his tool chest and dangled it over his head. He forced a tight smile as he took it and wiped it over his face and neck. "Thank you." He shoved himself out from under the sink. At this point he'd have to tear the whole damn thing out, which he'd been afraid of, the cost of which he'd been hoping to avert with a few replacement parts. Why he'd thought anything he might do around here would actually save a few pounds, rather than cost him a whole pocketful more of them, he had no idea. It never seemed to work that way. Now he was out valuable time as well as money.

He rolled to his feet and wiped his hands off on his pants. "What brings you out this way?" *Other than just having to stick your nose into everybody else's business, namely mine.*

Standing as she was in the hall, she cast her gaze through the open door opposite the loo and took a look about. There were two large dormer-style rooms up here on the third floor of the central section of the house. One dormer was ready for guests, but naturally the room Letty was examining still needed some finishing work. He hadn't been planning on getting that one completed in time for the opening, but had to get the WC functioning as he had a party of four booked into the finished dormer.

"It's quite the mission you've undertaken here, Dylan."

"Aye, that it is."

"More than a man alone could hope to complete, but I see you've put yourself fully to the task." She shifted her gaze back to him, and that dreaded look of affectionate concern clouded her expression. If there was one thing he hated more than the villagers poking their nose into his business, it was their collective concern over his bachelor status. Her bottom lip pursed as she tilted her head slightly and said, "I would imagine all the hard physical labor you've put into this place since your return has been somewhat therapeutic for you."

Here we go. "I suppose it has been," he responded honestly, knowing his return home had been both therapeutic and cathartic for him. Just not for the exact reasons Mrs. Dalrymple assumed. "Is there anything specific I can do for ye?" he asked, striving to sound patient. He gestured to the broken pipe. "As you can see, I have my hands full, and with less than a fortnight until my first guests arrive, I—"

"What did you think of that nice Erin MacGregor? Wasn't she a breath of fresh air?"

Dylan swallowed a groan, and perhaps a few more swear words as well. It was a vain wish indeed that the villagers would leave him alone. "She seemed very pleasant, but I—"

"Pleasant? Why she seemed a wee bit more than simply pleasant, wouldn't you agree?" She gestured to his face. "Ye've a bit of something still on your cheek there."

Sighing, Dylan shifted to look in the mirror, ignoring the rather frightful sight of himself as he dutifully cleaned off the rest of the splattered gunk. But it was hard to ignore the weary fatigue etched on his face. It was no wonder his sudden appearance had startled Ms. MacGregor so badly. Och, but he needed to rid himself of her image, and of the busybody, Letitia Dalrymple, and get back to the task at hand. "I appreciate you stopping by," he said, turning toward the stairs, hoping she'd take the not-so-subtle hint.

"Why didnae ye take her up on her offer? A man out here alone, under such an immense burden, and here she was, bright and lovely as a spring day, offering you a solution to your woes."

Dylan's gaze narrowed, but he refrained from asking her just exactly what woes she was referring to. "I appreciate your concern, but the bed and breakfast will open as projected and we'll do just fine without her offer."

Letty was not so easily swayed. "She was such a bright young thing, don't you think? With all the younger generation heading off to Edinburgh or Inverness, it was refreshing to have a lovely new face in town."

Dylan tried not to grind his teeth as he forced a smile. "Be that as it may, as you can see, I'm quite busy with the demands here. I've no time to have my head turned."

"Darling lad, every man has the time for that. You can't lock yourself up in this monstrosity forever." Letty placed a hand on his arm. "I know how difficult it must be, starting over. Why I was just telling Doris the other day how hard it must have been for you to come back here and start over all alone, having had such an exciting and fulfilling life end with such tragedy." She patted his sleeve. "But move on we must. You canno' pour all your heart into this place, Dylan. She's a demanding mistress, aye, but she canno' keep ye warm on the long winter nights. Dinnae close yourself off so. We're all here to help, ye ken. We've only your best interests at heart."

Dylan briefly covered her hand on his arm, then gently freed himself from her grasp, trying to remind himself that she really did mean well. He just didn't understand why it was that everyone assumed he needed a woman in his life in order to be happy once again. Not that he minded the concept. Someday. But when the time came, he'd like to think he could handle that particular endeavor on his own. Not as some kind of pathetic village project.

"I appreciate the care and concern, I do, but rest assured that I'm quite content dealing with my concerns here." He gently ushered her towards the stairs. "Thank you for stopping by," he went on, following her down the stairs. "Please give my best to Doris and the rest."

Not one to be steamrolled, Letty halted their progress in the grand foyer. "Perhaps you should come into town. As a businessman now, not to mention our chief, it wouldnae hurt you any to be seen more about the village."

It was a gentle rebuke, but one he took to heart. Because she was right. He should be a more visible leader, even if the position of clan chief was largely figurative at this point. From a business standpoint alone, it behooved him to be on friendly terms with the villagers. His guests would be spending time in the village shops, and he'd be wise to encourage the shop owners to talk up the bed and breakfast to other passers-through as well. "I'll do my best."

Her smile softened and she patted his arm again. "We all want ye tae succeed, Dylan. We know how hard all four of ye work, maintaining Glenshire and all that the Chisholms have worked so hard for. Glenbuie prospers because of your efforts. And it's with that in mind that I want you to listen to what I have to say about this offer ye've so hastily turned down."

Just when he'd thought this particular skirmish was over. He reined in his impatience, and forced a smile onto his face. "Have yer say then."

"Only that we'd all benefit from your agreeing to it.

In fact, I've never seen the town quite so excited about any prospect. It was rather unifying."

When hadn't the villagers been a unified lot, Dylan wanted to know, but wisely didn't give voice to the question. Letty was on a roll now, and obviously on a mission as well. Best to let her say her piece, if he had any hope of getting more work done this day.

"Letting Miss Erin move her television show into Glenshire would be a great boon to us all. Think of the economic boost we'd all receive from such publicity."

Apparently the villagers were no more immune to the Yank's charm than he'd been. Fortunately he was the one making the decision here. "Ye canno' honestly wish to have them descend upon us like a pack of jackals, turning our lives inside out, and all to broadcast us on some crass American—"

"Och, now ye sound like the city snob we all feared ye'd become from too many years spent falutin' about with all your posh friends. I know better, Dylan. You just want to hide out here and lick yer wounds." She lifted a hand. "I'm no' meaning any insensitivity, I've only your well-being in mind when I say this, but perhaps it's time to think on a grander scale, and put the needs of the town, your villagers, your clansmen, before your own." She squeezed his arm. "More important, though, I think throwing your doors open to Erin's crew might do you a world of good, yourself." She finally released him and stepped through the front door he was presently holding open for her. Just outside, she paused and looked back, a soft smile on her face, and a steely glint in her eyes. "She'll be in town until morning. Do the right thing. For us. And for yourself."

Chapter 3

"No, I haven't given up, Tommy. Yes, I know minutes are money. Yes, this place is worth the extra twelve hours, I promise. I'll have it sewn up by tomorrow." *Please don't make a liar out of me, Dylan Chisholm.*

Erin disconnected the call with her boss and tossed her phone on the bed, then went to stand in front of the window of her hotel room. From the top floor, she had a lovely view across the village square. The sun had finally set an hour ago but between calls to her assistant and the one from her boss, Erin had missed it. She raked her fingers through her hair and massaged her temples as she watched the people below. So many of them, out enjoying the early summer evening as the moon climbed higher in the starry night sky, strolling hand in hand, pausing now and again to chat with others out enjoying the evening as well. She wondered what it would be like, living in such a place. No pressure, no traffic, no harried phone calls and pre-production lists of demands. It was a Tuesday night and no one appeared to have anything better to do than amble about and make small talk.

"Must be nice," she muttered, then turned away and dug a fresh shirt out of her luggage. She unrolled it, shook it out, debated on the relative merits of tracking down an iron, but that would mean actually using one, so she tugged it on as is, smoothed it as best as she could, then grabbed her satchel and headed for the door. Her plan for the evening was to head over to Hagg's, but it wasn't a social call. She was on a mission to chat up the locals some more. The pub seemed to be the social center of the small village and given how open and encouraging everyone had been earlier today in the lunch crowd, her hope was they'd be even more amenable this evening, their work day over.

Of course, there was the little matter of Brodie and his failure to call his brother about her business proposition. She didn't think he'd just been humoring her, nor did she think that of the locals, either. He'd probably just gotten busy and hadn't gotten to it before she'd arrived. She'd stopped by the local sandwich shop to grab a bite on her way back into town and the few people she'd come across had all asked her how her meeting with Dylan had gone. And here she thought L.A. had a good gossip loop. They'd each seemed sincerely disappointed when she couldn't report that an agreement had been reached.

She hoped that buzz had spread. Maybe if she was really lucky, by the time she reached Hagg's, they'd have already formed some kind of plan, or committee or something. She took the elevator down and found herself slowing down her usual pace a little, sauntering a bit as she crossed the square to the pub. She took a few precious seconds to enjoy the warm breeze and the relaxed vibe of the town. If she ever took a vacation, this place would be perfect, she found herself thinking, then smiled at the thought. She loved her job. It took her all over the world. She didn't need a vacation.

She reached Hagg's and pushed open the heavy oak door to the pub and quickly apologized when the door bumped into someone on the other side. The older gentleman shifted quickly out of the way and sketched a light bow as he held the door open for her. "Come on in."

"Wow," she said, squeezing herself into the place. It was jam packed. On a Tuesday. "Busy place."

"We've a bit of entertainment tonight."

"Ah." She realized everyone was facing the rear of the bar, so she raised up on her tiptoes trying to see over their heads. "Music?" she asked, thinking it would be nice to see one of the local *ceilidhs* she'd heard about. Once she landed Glenshire, she'd have to scout additional locations for Greg's dates. On her list was possibly incorporating the traditional Scottish folk music and dance into one of those dates.

"Not tonight," the older man said. "Not yet anyway." He faced her and stuck out his hand. "I'm Alastair, by the way," he said. "I run the repair shop across the way with my daughter. Brodie, here, is my son-in-law."

There was no mistaking the pride in his lovely blue eyes and Erin found herself smiling and shaking his hand with sincere pleasure. "I've heard nice things about them both, all well deserved, I'm sure. I'm Erin—"

"MacGregor, aye," he finished for her.

Erin lifted a brow, but his smile only brightened.

"Small villages have big ears. The whole place is buzzing with news of your visit to Hagg's and Glenshire."

Erin smiled. She couldn't have hoped for better. And it looked like she might have Alastair on her side. Someone with an actual direct tie to the family, who was also a business owner, and didn't appear at all put out by her presence in town. If anyone could get to Dylan, make him understand what a great opportunity he was passing up, it was quite possibly this man. She cranked up her smile, and hopefully her charm, and said, "Is it good buzz, or bad buzz?"

"Quite good." His eyes twinkled. "But then, it's no' often we get a fetching lass from across the pond visiting our modest little village."

So, she thought, he was seduced by the whole Hollywood thing, too. Because fetching she was not. Whatever worked. "So you know why I'm here, then. Could I buy you an ale, perhaps? Bend your ear? I have some questions I was hoping to get answered and I think you're just the man to help me."

Alastair's laugh was rich and infectious. "The man with the answers? I dinnae know so much as all that, but I'll never turn down an offer of an ale." He began to expertly weave his way through the standing-room-only crowd. "Follow me, stay close."

"What's the hubbub all about?" she asked as she steered behind him, raising her voice to be heard over the sudden cheer that went up, starting somewhere in the back of the pub.

"Dart contest."

"Ah. I'm guessing you take that pretty seriously then."

"Of course. My daughter is the reigning champion, you know." He shuffled them around the side of the bar and miraculously wrangled her a stool. But then, most everyone was standing and craning their necks to watch the dart contest. He gestured her to take the seat.

"I didn't know that. That's great. Oh, thanks, but I can stand."

He waved her to sit. "You're buying, I'll stand."

She laughed with him and began to relax a little. Maybe it was all the bubbling energy inside the small pub, or being bodily swallowed up in the easy camaraderie of the crowd, but her anxiety about getting the job done was easing a bit. She waved at Marta who was working behind the bar and signaled for two ales. Earlier today Marta had been working back in the kitchen, preparing some of the best beef stew Erin had ever tasted. But she didn't see Brodie anywhere tonight, so perhaps Marta was pulling double duty.

Another cheer went up, and she shifted around on her stool to see what was going on now. The cheer was followed by hoots and catcalls. She turned back to Alastair, his smile rueful now.

"Och, but the lad should have known better than to tangle with my Kat. She doesn't play to lose." He shook his head. "Even when it might be in all of our best interests if she did."

Marta slid two ales onto the bar in front of them and Erin picked hers up and took a sip. "Who? Brodie?" She thought it was rather sweet that Brodie's wife came to the pub after work and played darts with him. Even more charming that the entire village enjoyed the apparently heated battle between the newlyweds.

Alastair shook his head. "Dylan."

Erin almost sprayed her sip of ale. She surreptitiously wiped her chin with her sleeve and tried to adopt a casual mien. "Really? I thought I heard earlier today that he wasn't much of a joiner when it came to village activities. In fact, the locals made it seem as if he never came down off the mountain."

Alastair enjoyed a long sip of his ale, then nodded. "Aye, 'tis true. Why do you think this place is packed on a Tuesday night?"

She didn't know what to make of that. Coincidence? "So, he suddenly decided to come down and play darts?"

Alastair shrugged. "Apparently. But he might never again if Kat doesn't play nice." He sighed again, but Erin wasn't paying attention.

What were the chances Dylan had suddenly come to

town the same day she'd shown up on his doorstep, talking about leasing his place? Had Brodie talked to him after all? She'd hoped to bend Brodie's ear this evening, but with the crowd, she doubted she'd have the chance. Of course, with the Great Scot himself on the premises, she could just go directly to the source. First, she needed a plan. She pictured those enigmatic eyes of his, the set angle of his jaw as he'd turned her down flat and took another sip of ale. A little fortification couldn't hurt, either.

Another whoop went up and Alastair excused himself. "I suppose I should go make sure she doesn't single-handedly destroy the goodwill we've spent the past year or two establishing with the poor lad. Bad enough Letty and her gaggle spend all their estimable free time planning his future, complete with new wife and, if they have their way, probably a half dozen wee Chisholms to boot. Let his brothers take on the task of creating heirs, I told them, be happy he's back home. Do they listen to me?" He motioned Marta to top off his ale, then hefted the glass and squeezed past Erin. "Knowing Kat, we'll be lucky if he's no' packed up and heading back to Edinburgh by morning." He patted her shoulder. "Back in a blink."

Erin was still trying to absorb that latest tidbit of information. New wife? Meaning there had been an old one. She'd sort of suspected as much, given the meaningful looks shared between the locals when referring to Dylan, as if he'd come home under less than fortunate circumstances. She was still trying to figure out how to use that to her advantage when Brodie suddenly burst through the wall of people and bodily lifted her off the stool with a big hand on her arm.

"There ye are!" he boomed, his jovial smile in place as always. "Come, lass, we need help settlin' a sporting question and you're the only one who's qualified to judge."

Erin wasted a precious second or two juggling her glass of ale, trying not to dump it on herself or anyone else, and lost her window of opportunity to stop him. By the time she got her wits about her, she'd been tugged into the small, cleared area in the back of the pub where the dartboard was located. *Think fast, think fast.* She wasn't prepared to see Dylan quite yet.

And then there he was, large as life. Larger, really. Great Scot indeed. In a room filled with people, he dominated the space easily. Big and broad at the shoulder, with all that hair and hard jawline. But it was more than his physical presence that commanded attention, it was that ever present enigmatic demeanor of his, still every bit as tightly held, she noted, even though he was supposedly surrounded by family and friends.

Or maybe he'd been smiling and relaxed until she'd been dragged into the picture. Hard to tell. But he didn't seem thrilled to see her, that much was clear.

Then Brodie was tugging her forward again and their locked gaze was abruptly disconnected as he turned her to face the dartboard. "Okay, here's the thing. My wife's dart." He motioned to a gorgeous, antique, hand-carved wooden dart flocked with what appeared to be real feathers. "My brother's dart." He motioned to the other dart, also handsomely made, if not as spectacularly as the first, wedged into the very same hole. "What say you?"

"I'm not sure I'm the one who should—"

"Nay, you're the only one in the room who can be impartial."

Erin noticed the room had fallen completely silent as everyone waited for her to make her pronouncement. She dared to scan the sea of faces crowding the dartboard area, but couldn't read the lay of the land. She only had Alastair's comment on the village wanting to court the goodwill of their apparently recalcitrant chief . . .

and the knowledge that the other contestant was the wife of the man who owned the establishment. Lovely. The trick was going to be how not to piss off anyone and still have a chance in hell of getting what she wanted. What she had to have. And from the looks of things, she had about five seconds to figure it out.

She chanced a quick glance at Alastair, hoping maybe he could signal her somehow, but he had his head bent toward a fresh-faced, younger woman dressed in dungarees and a pub T-shirt—Kat Chisholm, she could only presume—and didn't see Erin's silent plea for a rescue. She'd have to suck it up and go for it.

Turning away from the crowd and very purposefully not looking at Dylan, she turned the brightest smile she could conjure at Brodie. "I don't know the rules, but it looks like a tie to me. Can't you have a do-over?"

The crowd erupted in raucous cheering and debate and Erin wasn't sure, but it appeared that by trying to be as fair and impartial as possible, she'd pissed everyone off. How had she so thoroughly lost control of her only mission? Then Brodie was stalking to the dartboard and plucking out the darts, proclaiming, "You heard the lass, we'll have a 'do-over'."

Then Kat was stepping forward and motioning to Erin. "Come here, then."

Erin had been thinking she'd slink back into the crowd and make a mad dash for the exit, but Kat was motioning her to come over to where she and Dylan stood, and before she could decide for herself, the crowd nudged her forward. "Yes?" she said, spying Dylan in her peripheral vision and deciding now was really not a good time for her nipples to go painfully hard, but there they were, right at attention. What was it about that man anyway?

What wasn't it about him? her little voice offered. He stood there scowling in his T-shirt and jeans, but he might as well have been wearing the plaid with a claymore strapped to his hip for all he exuded the whole rogue highlander thing. She really had to get a grip. She turned her head and focused exclusively on Kat, who, she belatedly noticed, hadn't missed a thing in Erin's momentary little distraction. Even scarier, she smiled. Broadly.

"Okay, do-over it is," she announced, quite jovially. She turned her laser beam smile on Erin. "But you'll stay." She nudged her a step or two closer to Dylan. "Right there." She smiled very prettily up at Dylan, but only a fool would take that as a sign of friendship and goodwill. "You don't mind, do ye now?"

It was as if the entire room took a breath and held it. Only when Dylan nodded, once, did the tension ebb, if only for a moment. "Ladies first," he announced.

And just the sound of that voice sent a little tingle of awareness through Erin that only served to keep her body on point. Two of them, to be exact. She folded her arms across her chest, then realized she was still holding her ale. She impulsively chugged the rest of it and set the empty glass down on one of the tall tables lining the wall behind them. She tried to shrink back slightly, out of the center-of-attention spot, but Kat was having none of it.

"It was all quite amusing when you thought to distract me with my charming husband here. Well, two can play at that. Erin, be a darling and stay directly in Dylan's line of vision for me."

From the instant reaction of the crowd, it was easy to understand what kind of distraction they wanted her to provide. Completely nonplussed, Erin automatically pointed at herself. "Me?" Had they not actually looked at her? She was hardly eye candy material. Her gaze tracked to Dylan, completely without her authority, but he looked neither nonplussed nor repulsed. In fact, it was hard to tell what he was thinking. So what else was new?

The crowd was chanting her name now and she saw her entire career taking a fast nosedive in the middle of Nowhere, Scotland. Why hadn't she stayed in London? Why?

Seemingly satisfied with the situation, Kat took her darts, very lovingly handed to her by her husband, who then proceeded to hold her around the waist, dip her back over his arm and kiss her deeply, much to the delight of the villagers. Kat swatted him when he set her upright again, but the pink in her cheeks and the twinkle in her eye belied her annoyance. Erin sighed a little inside. They were wonderful together.

Then, very swiftly, and with deadly precision, Kat buried both of her darts dead center on the board. She curtsied to Dylan, then snagged her husband, pushed him back against the nearest pool table and returned his earlier favor. Of course, it ended with her smacking his hands away as he tried to pull her up onto the table. Everyone was laughing, tankards were raised and more rounds of ale poured.

And then it was Dylan's turn.

She was jostled closer to him, brushing up against his arm before moving back. She looked up at him and mouthed, "I'm sorry," hoping he understood it was for all of it, not just the inadvertent contact. He held her gaze for what seemed like an eternity. Erin spent the next couple seconds being partly terrified and mostly ridiculously turned on, wondering if they were supposed to somehow match Brodie and Kat's antics. But just when another hush was starting to descend over the crowd, Dylan merely stepped past her and planted himself on the hash mark branded into the wooden pub flooring. Part of the crowd began chanting her name, the other half tried to shush them. Apparently they weren't sure how far to push their fearless leader, either.

All she knew was that she should have stayed in her hotel room.

She watched as Dylan, with absolutely steady hands, tossed both darts in quick succession, knocking one of Kat's darts to the floor and pinning the board right next to the other one. A cheer went up as both Dylan and Kat looked to Brodie, who, in turn, looked at Erin. Who took the coward's way out and shrugged. It was smart business, she told herself.

"Where did you learn to throw like that, anyway?" Brodie wanted to know from Dylan.

"They do have pubs in Edinburgh, you know."

"Of course, I do. I just never thought you spent time in any of them."

There was a slight gathering of breath amongst the natives, and Erin wondered why that would be a touchy subject. Certainly Brodie didn't really think it was a betrayal for his brother to patronize other pubs. Clearly he was kidding, anyway. Every word out of Brodie's mouth was accompanied by that charming smile of his. She found her gaze drawn back to Dylan, much like a tennis match. Ball in his court.

"You'd have been surprised then." He glanced at the dartboard and, if she wasn't mistaken, a rather mischievous light entered his eyes, if only briefly. "Clearly."

Laughter filled the warm room and some half-hearted calls for Brodie to claim a winner resumed.

Brodie and Kat began to debate the rules, encouraging the villagers to good-naturedly chant for more, but before it could go any further, Dylan raised his hand and said, "I think I've caused enough of a stir." He sketched a short bow. "I appreciate your support, especially against such an engaging and worthy opponent."

Kat struck an exaggerated curtsy, which looked all

the more incongruous given that she was still in her mechanic's overalls, and tankards of ale were lifted all around once again amidst continued chatter.

"Surely somebody has a fiddle." This from Alastair. "I say we work off this collective energy with some dancing!"

Erin instinctively took a step toward the door. She knew she should stay, her mission was far from complete, but she was happy at the moment to end the evening with a chance to continue her pursuit another day. She didn't understand the politics at play here and it would be wise to step back and regroup before making another move. She still had every intention of leasing Glenshire, but she was smart enough to know she had, at best, one more shot at it, then it was game over. And there had been enough game playing tonight as it was.

She turned, looking for Alastair, thinking it was only polite to let him know she was leaving, as their chat earlier had been aborted by the dart game, only to find herself swung around by the arm as music filled the warm, yeasty-smelling air. "Come on, lass!"

"But I don't know how—"

The rest of her protest was swallowed up, as was she, by the sea of bodies she was tugged into. She had no idea who her partner was, other than he was middle-aged, nice enough looking, hopefully patient. And wearing solid shoes.

He spun her expertly through the crowd and when she finally got her bearings, she realized it was an organized line dance of sorts. Then she noticed the looks everyone was giving each other, little smiles of anticipation or something. Almost like everyone was in on some secret except for—"Oh!"

She'd paused a beat too long when she spun through the last turn and found herself unexpectedly flat up against a very hard male chest. She knew who it was before she met his gaze. Or her body knew, anyway. "Sorry," she choked out.

He'd already taken hold of her arms, but almost, it seemed to balance himself rather than her. "We seem to have a wee bit of a problem with this," he said. If he'd been smiling, she could have assured herself he was teasing her. As it was, she wasn't quite sure. So what else was new?

Taking a quick glance around as the other dancers closed ranks behind them, subtly shifting them to the periphery of the makeshift dance floor, she noted their expressions hadn't changed much. Only now, in addition to the quick exchange of private smiles, there was a bit of elbowing going on and chins jerking meaningfully in their general direction as the dancers whirled by. And all Erin could think was, were they so hard up to find their clan chief a woman that they'd picked her? Surely she was reading this wrong.

"Don't mind them," Dylan said, tipping his chin toward the passersby and their hopeful expressions. "They mean well."

Okay, so maybe she wasn't. "Mean well about what, exactly?"

"They have it in their heads that I should socialize more. Dinnae worry, they're a harmless lot."

Erin had no idea what to say to that. A first. "Uh, good." *Make small talk,* she admonished herself. She really needed to take advantage of this portentous occasion. *Business, think business*. She wished she'd had a bit longer with Alastair. She needed something, anything, to use as an approach.

"You two going to stand about when there's music playing?" Alastair called out, an attractive older woman on his arm, who had nothing but stars in her eyes for him as they swung expertly by.

Erin tensed all over again, but Dylan merely nodded. She wasn't sure she could handle actual direct physical contact without being rendered a complete, drooling idiot. The idea of his hands intentionally making prolonged contact with any part of her body . . . She crossed her arms over her chest. Just as a precaution, of course. Although a quick glance down told her she'd perhaps been extra-prescient on the matter.

"Dinnae fash yerself, lass. I believe I've socialized enough for one evening," Dylan said, his tone a bit tight. "I'll be taking my leave now." He sketched a quick bow and started to turn away.

Seeing her one and only opportunity slip from her grasp before she'd even made a stab at it, Erin acted impulsively and grabbed at his arm. "Surely you can manage one dance?" *What on earth was she doing?* By some miracle she managed to pull off a semi-natural looking smile. "Keep the natives happy and keep me from being abandoned to the wolves." Which was a joke. If the men here had looked twice at her, it was because they'd heard why she was in town. "Maybe you can manage to work us closer to the door and we can both make our escape." She told herself that would give her more time, just the two of them, away from the noise and prying eyes of the villagers, to talk business.

Tell that to her nipples though.

Dylan, being a gentleman, and confronted with an audience that somehow managed to dance wildly about the crowded floor while paying almost rapt attention to their leader, could do little but comply with her request.

"I'm not very good," she told him, having to raise her voice to be heard as they edged into the crowd.

"No' a problem, neither am I," he replied, and for a second there, she thought she caught a hint of a dry smile.

But then his hands were on her and all rational thought took flight.

* * *

What the bloody hell did he think he was doing? Dylan stared down into Erin's moss green eyes and wondered when, exactly, he'd lost complete control of his life. He wasn't entirely certain, but it seemed to coincide with her arrival in town.

He'd hardly gotten any work done all day for thinking about the disruptive Yank. So he'd let Letitia's guilt trip send him into town. Anything for a distraction, he'd told himself. He'd foolishly challenged Brodie's wife, known far and wide as a dart shark, to a match, and had succeeded in diverting the entire village's attention. Then he'd surprised himself by almost having a good time. But just when he'd thought maybe he could mix and mingle and be one of the crowd after all, she'd shown up.

And within minutes, the crowd had shifted, en masse, back into matchmaking mode. Although, to be fair, he wasn't entirely certain if their interest in matching him up with Erin was for his personal gain, or for the betterment of the village. He'd been surprised to hear how enthusiastic everyone seemed to be about her little mission.

So, he'd dance with her. Once. Make everyone happy. Then he was going home. He'd come back to town after she'd moved on to scouting her next location. Looking at her, he told himself he couldn't remember why he'd been so distracted by her anyway.

Then he put his hands on her, and she immediately tripped over her own feet, then over his, and looked up at him with laughter in her eyes and a quick apology on her lips . . . and he found his own lips curving. And his hold on her tightening. And his body responded when she tightened her own as well.

Good thing she really was a remarkably bad dancer.

More for his own safety and that of his toes than

anything else, he maneuvered them closer to the pub door. Of course, he was well aware that the village would be buzzing if they left together, but he thought that might work to his benefit. Maybe they'd back off a little if they saw him actually showing interest in the opposite sex. Maybe he could convince them he could take it from there, and they'd ease up a little, stop looking at him with that dread mix of determination and pity. Especially that last part. *Och, the puir widower Chisholm.* He felt like such a fraud.

Several people noticed his trajectory and tried to intercept, but fortunately Dylan was able to catch Alastair's eye. The auld mechanic was still pretty spry and managed to twirl himself and his partner expertly into the path of the interlopers. Now Dylan knew why he admired and respected his new sister-in-law. She got her smarts from a good man.

He didn't waste any time taking advantage of what little edge he had. He maneuvered Erin in front of him and they were out and closing the door behind them before the song came to an end.

They both came to a staggering halt just at the edge of the sidewalk. He was careful to steady her before finally letting her go and taking a sanity-restoring step back himself. He was quite ready to head around back, hop in his lorry, and drive straight back to hearth and home. If he had his way, he'd stay there. Preferably till the next millennium. But the situation demanded that he at least be a gentleman. "You staying at the hotel?" It didn't come out sounding quite as polite as he'd intended, judging by the way her smile faltered, before making a swift, if forced encore.

"Yes, but I can see myself home. Thank you for the rescue. Again." Her smile relaxed a bit. "I'm sorry if my presence in there ruined your evening. I—I didn't know—I mean, I never thought they'd . . . you know . . ."

Her voice trailed off and even under the lamplight he could see the pink that stained her cheeks.

She was an interesting duck. So confident about some things, yet very disconcerted about others. "No' to worry. Feel free to head back in. Now that I'm gone, you'll likely have a better time of it." He wanted to smack himself the instant the suggestion left his lips. All he needed was to give her any more time to persuade anyone else what a great idea it would be to invade their peaceful village with television cameras and crew.

"Oh, I think I've done enough for one day." She stuck her hand out. "It was a pleasure meeting you."

Nonplussed by the gesture—he'd been sure she was going to hit him up again on her offer—he shook her hand without thinking. So he was taken quite off guard by the warmth and strength he found there. So much so he dropped her hand a bit abruptly. What was this effect she had on him anyway? He either needed to get out a great deal more . . . or never leave home. "You certain you don't need an escort?"

"I'm thinking crime is probably not high on the list of problems in your little burg. I'm betting I can safely cross the square. But I appreciate the offer. Good-night." She lifted her hand, then paused for just a second, staring at him. Then her cheeks went pink again and she abruptly turned and headed off in a straight line toward the hotel. She didn't look back.

"Good-night," he responded, only realizing when she disappeared inside the front hotel doors that he'd stood there watching her the entire way, much as he had earlier today when she'd driven out of his life. Or so he'd thought. Shaking his head, he turned and made the trek around the pub to the rear lot. "Curious bird," he murmured, then vowed to put her out of his mind. He heard the music pulsing inside the pub, and was surprised by the sudden urge he had to step back inside. He'd made the decision to come down tonight to assuage the Lettys of the village—hiding from them hadn't worked out too well, so perhaps it was better to join them—and also because he'd wanted to make sure they weren't working themselves into some frenzy over the idea of being on the American telly.

For the most part, he'd enjoyed himself. Enough so, that he looked forward to making it a more regular event. But if he went back in there now, he'd be hounded about Erin, or worse, thrown at somebody local who wouldn't be checking out of her hotel room and leaving town in the morning. Better to let them have their hopes and dreams, at least for the remainder of the evening. It was a small enough town. They'd all know soon enough that Erin had checked back into her hotel room immediately. Alone.

And by then he'd be safely back on his mountain. When he descended into town again, they'd all have long forgotten about the crazy American. Once calmer heads had prevailed, they'd see he'd been right to turn her down. Glenbuie did not need to be turned into an American reality show spectacle to remain economically sound. They were doing just fine, and would continue to do so. Just as soon as he got that bed and breakfast open.

His mind mercifully turned to the list of jobs he had lined up for tomorrow, starting with calls to track down the parts needed to fix the loo. His mind wandered down the list, mentally adding on to it, but as he drove around the square and past the hotel, he couldn't keep from glancing up at the windows . . . and wondering which room she was in. Was she dressing for bed? Was she already, right now, naked in the shower? His mind immediately flashed on that image, and for a split second, he was sorry he'd been so quick to dismiss her.

His body stirred again at the idea of where the evening could have gone instead, and he couldn't lie to himself and say it wouldn't have felt damn good. She might not be a head turner, but she had intrigued him. He'd turned into something of a recluse while getting Glenshire up and running, but he wasn't a monk. He just lived like one. For now. Small towns made anonymous flings impossible and he didn't have the time or energy to run into the city for anything other than plumbing supplies.

He slowed, glanced up at the only window that was lit up, the one on the top floor. She'd likely gotten his attention only because she'd been available and not a local. Even monks had needs. He pressed down on the gas and drove out of the village and toward home before he could do something really foolish. She might be leaving in the morning, but she wanted something from him that he wasn't willing to give. And no way was he giving her another shot at convincing him, especially in that kind of situation. He hadn't spent much time with her, but enough to know she was a determined sort. Determined enough to swap sex for a favor? He couldn't say.

Miles of moonlit green fields and stacked stone boundary walls passed by him in a blur as his thoughts stubbornly refused to abandon the track he'd stupidly put them on. So fine, he let his mind wander. No harm in that. He'd be home shortly, where there was a cold shower waiting for him. He smiled. Or maybe a hot one, with a lot of slippery soap. Like he'd said, even monks had needs. He might have to embellish reality a bit to get the job done, but she'd never have to know.

He thought it was pretty funny actually . . . here she'd come to Glenshire looking for something from him, only to go away empty-handed. While, this evening anyway, he was going to be anything but empty-handed.

Chapter 4

Erin had just climbed out of the shower, where she'd spent a very unsuccessful thirty minutes trying to get Dylan Chisholm, hot Scot, out of her mind, and back on Dylan Chisholm, manor owner and sole obstacle to her keeping her job, back into it. Perhaps she shouldn't have been standing there with hot, steamy water streaming over her body as she rubbed lavender-scented soap all over her skin. "Yeah, that might have helped," she muttered, rubbing her hair dry with another towel, then shaking it out. "Or not." She sighed and pulled on her gray boxer shorts and faded Lakers shirt. She glanced at the bedside clock. One in the morning. Check out was at eleven. Didn't give her much time to develop a battle plan.

At the moment, her plan was to track down Daisy MacDonnell in the morning at her stationery store. She was both a fellow American and Reese Chisholm's fiancée. Erin had met her earlier today during her first visit to Hagg's. Daisy was a former advertising guru who'd escaped the rat race in the States upon inheriting her aunt's shop. She hadn't left her career behind, though. She'd brought the internet to Glenbuie and had been successful in putting up websites for the distillery, along with a number of the village shops, as well as one advertising Glenshire as a bed and breakfast. In fact, she'd been the one who'd first brought up the idea of Erin checking out Glenshire for her show when they'd all been sitting at the bar eating Marta's stew.

Seeing as how Daisy had worked with Dylan in creating the website, Erin hoped maybe she had some insight on what other kind of approach to take. Other than going back to Brodie, or one of the other Chisholm brothers—and they seemed more interested in getting their brother laid than anything else—she wasn't sure what else to do.

She was just about to climb into bed when there was a knock on the door. Startled, she immediately looked around for something else to pull on. Could Dylan have come back? It was a small enough village that everyone in it probably knew what room the American was staying in.

"Front desk with a message," came a lilting female voice on the other side.

Erin rolled her eyes. "You only think you're in Brigadoon," she muttered. "You're still Cinderella before the ball and there's no fairy godmother in sight." Clearly needing to get over herself, she walked to the door in her boxers and T-shirt, because, honestly, who cared? She opened the door to find a young woman named Amelia standing there, according to her hotel name badge, anyway.

She gave Erin a bright, but apologetic smile. "Sorry to disturb, but the light was still on, and I thought you might be wantin' this." She handed Erin a folded piece of stationery.

"Thanks." Erin took the note, then patted her gym

shorts for change she immediately realized she wasn't carrying. "Wait, let me get you—"

"Oh, that won't be necessary," Amelia said, cheerfully waving away the tip. "We'll prosper well enough when the camera crews arrive."

Oh god. Erin opened her mouth to warn the perky Amelia not to count her chickens, but the young woman had already gone merrily off, back down the hallway toward the elevators. Erin watched her depart, thinking she'd have been only half surprised to see the young clerk suddenly burst into song and perform a perfectly choreographed dance routine down the carpeted corridor, quite naturally involving the two maids and one bellman she passed along the way. Brigadoon indeed.

Erin clicked the door shut and thought it was a good thing Dana wasn't here. Her assistant would be having a field day if she only knew how ridiculous Erin was being about this place. "Ah, bite me," she said, to the room at large, and her assistant in absentia, somewhat comforted by the sound of her own sardonic tone. See? She wasn't that far gone. She still had her edge.

She opened the note and read it as she crossed the room, back to her bed. There was a single scrawled line, more of a slash really, across the middle. She read it out loud. "Come out to Glenshire in the morning at 8 A.M. Just you. Dylan." Her eyebrows arched high on her forehead. "Wow. Surprise, surprise."

She tapped the note against her chin, wondering what had happened to change his mind. Had he gone back in the pub maybe? Or had Brodie said something to finally convince him to hear her out? Not that she was going to look a gift horse in the mouth. Hell, she'd head up there right now if she thought it would make a difference.

Visions of getting Dylan out of bed, seeing what he looked like half naked, hair all tousled. Or maybe all the way naked. He probably slept in the buff. She shut that track down immediately. Well, almost immediately.

"Get a grip," she schooled herself. She had to see him again in less than seven hours and she needed to be on her utmost professional behavior. Whatever the reason was he'd agreed to see her, it wasn't because he'd suddenly decided she was a raving beauty. More like she was a raving loon, with her crazy American reality show. She didn't think that opinion had miraculously changed, especially after she'd tromped all over his feet during their two whole minutes of dancing.

She wasted another minute reliving those glorious two minutes. Well, glorious for her, anyway. Outside of being very self-conscious of her clumsiness and the fact that everyone was watching them, she had rather enjoyed the way his hand had engulfed hers, and how the other had rested so confidently on her waist, guiding her through the crowd. She'd half wished the crowd would have jostled them together, so she could feel what it would be like to be held against that broad chest.

"And just how pathetic are you?" she murmured, then read the note again, still not quite believing her good fortune. Good business fortune. "Just you," she repeated. *Hmm. Where had that come from?* Did he think she'd show up with half the village in tow? Maybe he thought she already had a whole camera crew stashed here in town or something and would take any sign of capitulation on his part as a reason to show up in full force. He didn't know she was a force to be reckoned with all by herself. She grinned and tossed the note on the nightstand. "But he will."

She climbed into bed and reached for the lamp, but instead picked up the note again. The writing was decidedly masculine, but it was likely just the hand of whoever had taken the message. Except, as far as she knew, the desk clerks were all women. Meaning he'd come into the hotel tonight. Why not just ask to see her, or at least have them ring her room? Of course, it was pretty late . . .

She put the note aside once more, shut off the light, then lay there, staring at the ceiling, her thoughts refusing to stray from the man she'd be seeing again in a few short hours.

Interesting how the village was playing matchmaker for him. Although they were getting desperate if they were going after passers-through. Of course, maybe it had nothing to do with matchmaking. Maybe they'd hoped if the two of them had struck sparks, he'd agree to the filming. Could an entire town be so mercenary?

Erin snuggled more deeply into the soft, down bed. She almost felt sorry for Dylan, even though she could see he was perfectly capable of taking care of himself. She knew what a pain it was just having one well-meaning person climbing all over her social life. And Dana only wanted her to get laid regularly. She couldn't imagine having a family nosing about her love life, much less an entire village. She didn't blame him for wanting to get out of there tonight, although it would have been nice if he'd at least pretended he wasn't just as anxious to get away from her.

She forced a mental shift back to business. How was she going to present her case? She wondered briefly if losing his wife was yet another roadblock to having a show based on finding true love filmed right in his own home. It would certainly be understandable. Definitely better to talk money and economy over love and romance. Sleep claimed her as she mulled over her options.

Which did nothing to explain why the images that wound their way into her dreams had absolutely nothing to do with profit margins and ratings spikes, and everything to do with other things . . . spiking.

* * *

The following morning, as she headed back out to Glenshire, the skies were a stunning robin's egg blue, not a cloud on the horizon, and the valley was such a vibrant, verdant green she still swore that the grass had to be genetically engineered. Even the sheep seemed especially perky and cute that morning.

She, however, was not. It had taken a hot shower, followed by a cold one, followed by two cups of espresso and a big, sticky pastry from the tray in the lobby before Erin had finally, mercifully managed to push aside every detail of last night's hot and sweaty dreams—and wasn't it amazing how the more she wanted to forget, the more details she recalled? She gripped the steering wheel more tightly. But she was fully focused on her job now. Dylan was merely a means to an end. One that didn't have anything to do with either of their ends getting naked.

Nope. Business, business, business. She wouldn't even imagine him in bed. Much less naked. In the bed. Or in the shower. Hot, steamy water running all over his slick skin. Nope. Not even imagining that. Not if she could absolutely help it anyway. So what if he was that perfect tragic figure who appealed to her secret romantic soul? The reclusive, wounded hero, burying himself in his work to push aside the pain of losing the woman he'd given his heart to? To her he was a business opportunity, nothing more, nothing less. Besides, he didn't seem all that wounded anymore. Mostly he just seemed annoyed.

Which suited her fine. She was relieved, in fact, that she seemed to be the only one suffering from delusions of infatuation. Thankful, even. It would make her job that much easier.

Liar.

She swallowed against a suddenly dry throat as she

rolled to a stop in front of Glenshire's massive front door and put her car into park. If anything, the place was even more impressive and perfect in its romantic decay by morning sunrise than it had been in the late afternoon light.

She got out of the car, smoothed her pants, then her hair, before she realized what she was doing and stopped instantly. She'd bet a full ratings share that the only thing that mattered to Dylan where Erin MacGregor was concerned was how big an offer she was bringing to the negotiation table.

Which didn't explain why she slipped her lip balm out of her jacket pocket and ran it quickly across her lips. "Damn Brigadoon," she swore under her breath as she made her way to the front door.

She looked for a buzzer, and, not finding one, lifted the heavy brass knocker instead. Shaped like a boar's head, it was shining brass and weighed a ton. She rapped once, heard the ominous echoing sound it made, and decided that was enough. She shifted her weight back and forth as she waited, refusing to smooth her hair again, or check her teeth in the newly polished knocker. Her pulse rate had kicked up a few notches in anticipation. Not of seeing Dylan again, of course. She was simply excited to finally be getting a peek inside her newest location. And she would prevail. He had a price, she just had to find out what it was.

She was leaning in, looking at her warped reflection as she pushed her hair from her face—only because there was a wayward strand poking her in the eye, of course—when the door suddenly swung open. An instant later she was eyeball to impressive pectorals with the object of her midnight fantasies.

"You're back," he said flatly.

She quickly stepped back and smiled, not at all liking how this meeting was starting. Taking in the full impact of Dylan's impressive frame didn't exactly help matters. He was dressed in loose jeans that hung low on his hips and a paint-spattered, Glenbuie Distillery sweatshirt that had clearly seen better days. Eons of them, judging by the hacked-off sleeves and tattered neckline. His arms were impressively muscled and surprisingly tanned. Apparently all of the work on the house hadn't been indoors.

"Why?" he asked, dipping his chin just slightly to snag her wayward gaze.

Caught staring, and confused by his less than cordial greeting, she faltered. "I'm—" She stopped, looked down at her watch to check the time, and absently noticed he was barefoot, which for some reason struck her as incredibly sexy. Apparently any naked part of him was enough to send her vivid imagination on a detailed romp, so she countered by shifting her gaze swiftly back up to his face. Bigger mistake. He was even more imposing today, hard as that was to believe.

He was standing in a doorframe that would, in any other setting, be considered massive. Yet, somehow he managed to fill that empty space quite commandingly and that with cream-colored paint tipping the ends of his shaggy hair and a swipe of baby blue across his unshaven jaw. And really, what a jawline, huh? The camera would love him, all of him really, from that hard, stubbled curve to those defined biceps, and—and she realized where her thoughts were going and quickly reined them in. If only it were so easy to do the same with her jackrabbit pulse.

She drew on every last bit of her extensive under-Tommy's-fire training and mustered her brightest smile. She didn't know exactly what was going on, but in her experience it was always better to go with the supposed program until someone else derailed it.

"It's eight o'clock," she said brightly. "I'm right on time."

His frown deepened, if that were possible. "For what?"

And it was at that moment Erin realized why she'd looked twice at the handwriting on the note last night. She'd seen it before, only she hadn't realized it at the time. On the chalkboard at Hagg's, toting the dart scores. Brodie Chisholm's handwriting, to be exact. "I can't believe it. He set us up. Again."

"I beg your pardon?"

She looked back at Dylan. "When was the last time you talked to your brother? Brodie, I mean."

"Before we left the pub last night, why?"

"You didn't go back inside after I left?"

Dylan folded his arms over his chest, which only served to point out just how divinely muscular his shoulders were, too. "No. Why?"

"I should have known you didn't send that note." Why hadn't she had this little handwriting epiphany last night when it might have done her some good? But oh no, she was far too busy running hot, sexcapade scenarios through her fevered brain. Now she'd barged in and bungled the one final chance she had.

"What note?"

"I got a message at the hotel last night, ostensibly from you, requesting I meet you here, alone, at eight A.M." And she hadn't brought it with her, dammit, the one piece of proof she had. But why would she?

"I thought I made myself quite clear yesterday."

"Oh, you did. I thought perhaps Brodie had talked to you, or anyone back in the pub, maybe Alastair," she added, playing her only ace. And she wasn't even sure he was one. "I thought maybe he'd changed your mind. Made you realize that the good of the village and your family bank balance would be worth inconveniencing yourself for a little while."

"Inconvenience? Is that what you call it? And for 'a

little while' is it? I believe you mentioned eight weeks. Have you no idea what all must be done to ready this place? And that's the mere tip of it. I've guests booked. An inn to run. I canno' walk away from the place for so long a time."

This was so not going how she'd envisioned it. She hadn't even gotten inside the place yet. Tommy was going to kill her. Unless Dylan tossed her off the cliff located conveniently a hundred yards behind her and saved her boss the trouble. Her heart sank. This place was so prime, so perfect, and she'd taken her eye off the damn ball. "What if we worked it out so you could stay here?" she blurted, desperate. Tommy would never go for it. And even if he did, the network's legal beagles would have a stroke. They'd learned that particular lesson the hard way on season one when a tiff with the owner had ended in a nasty lawsuit.

But when Dylan didn't immediately close the door in her face, Erin finally, mercifully, flipped into negotiator mode and pushed her tiny advantage. Even a tiny crack had the chance to become a wall-crumbling fissure if the right pressure was applied in exactly the right place. All she had to do was find that precise spot . . . and push.

Visions of soft spots and just what could be pushing on them punched with ridiculous ease through her tough combatant armor. She'd never really believed in Dana's whole "you just need to get laid" theory, but she was beginning to think maybe there was some merit to it after all.

"The lease offer will compensate you above the business loss. And, as I told you, we'll gladly pay to relocate whatever guests can't rebook for a future date, not to mention that from the exposure you'll get, you'll replace those guests with many, many more. You'll book up—"

"Far and away into the future, aye," he grumbled. "So ye've said. Do you have statistical proof of that claim? How many bed and breakfasts or hotels have you used in the past?"

Exactly none, was the answer. They usually used privately owned property with little to no public access. But she wasn't completely unarmed. "I have documented proof that the communities we've been located in have always experienced an extended, noticeable economic surge. In fact—"

"Will you back up that claim with a written guarantee? If I lose business, or if I have to shut down in order to repair any damage done, will you guarantee I'll be fully compensated to my complete satisfaction?"

Erin's heart rate kicked into overdrive. He was negotiating. He might not realize it, given he was still scowling and his arms were banded across his chest like they were barring entry to a fortress with a pair of broad beams, but he was talking. He wasn't shutting the door in her face.

"We return every alteration to its original state, and we always repair anything that might suffer any unforeseen damage. You will have that in writing." Seeing the shrewd gleam in his eyes, she added, "We run a videography of the entire location before and after, so any alterations and repairs are easily determined by both you and the production crew. There's no way to hide anything." Which worked both ways as it also kept owners from claiming damage or repairs already needed before the crew ever set foot on the property. "If, for whatever reason, anything is irretrievably broken, altered, or damaged, we would, of course, be responsible for settling with you on an appropriate reimbursement." She tugged her satchel around and slipped the catch open. "I have the entire agreement here. Perhaps I could come in and we could discuss it in more detail? You can have your attorney look it over as well if you'd like."

It had been her experience that most people were so flattered and eager to have anything they owned be connected with a television show, they often signed without the hassle and delay of getting lawyers directly involved. She didn't think Dylan fell into that category. She could only pray his lawyer was local. And reasonable. They didn't have time for an extended review period.

"I'm no' exactly at a place in my work load where I can stop and sit. In fact, I need to get back to it." He shifted his weight and unfolded his arms and she went from hopeful to panicked all over again.

"I'll be glad to help." She really had to learn some impulse control around this man. But never let it be said that Erin MacGregor didn't go the distance to get what she wanted. "With . . . whatever it is you're doing."

"You're offering to help me paint?"

She nodded immediately. "Sure. I'd like to look around the place anyway. Maybe you can give me the nickel tour on the way to . . . wherever it is you're painting. And we can talk while we work. You can ask me about whatever concerns you might have. And when we're done, we can sit down and look over the agreement specifically."

His gaze narrowed and he was far from smiling, but if she wasn't mistaken, the light that had entered his eyes now was one of faint amusement. Or maybe bemusement was a better word. It didn't matter, as long as he let her in the door. A step forward was a step closer to a signed agreement.

She held his gaze directly, keeping a confident, sunny smile in place. As if she did this kind of thing all the time to placate her clients.

After what seemed like an eternity, he stepped back and waved a paint flecked forearm in front of her. "Come in, then."

Not the heartiest of welcomes, but beggars couldn't be choosers, now could they? Erin stepped past him through the door and with one look knew she'd do a hell of a lot more than paint walls if it meant getting his signature on that lease agreement. The foyer area was extensive, opening upward two stories, dominated by a wide staircase leading to the second floor landing, and accentuated with a stunning, sparkling chandelier. The floor beneath her feet was slightly uneven hand-laid stone, most of it covered by multiple layers of heavy, ancient Persian rugs that were all the more interesting for how worn the coloring was in the intricately patterned design. She wondered how many generations of Chisholms had walked across them.

"Impressive," she said, never more sincere, as she slowly turned around and took it all in. Only when she got back around to facing the staircase did she realize Dylan was already halfway up, assuming she was right behind him. Swallowing the myriad questions that were already springing to mind, she turned her attention back to more immediate matters. Namely her host. And her newest job. Painting.

Dylan didn't wait for her at the second story landing either, and she had to hurry to keep up with him. And it was a good thing she did, as he turned left at the top of the second flight and disappeared through one of two sets of double doors just as she topped the last riser. Apparently each wing of the house was deep enough to have two parallel hallways running the length of them. Both sides of each hallway were lined with doors, though not evenly spaced apart, meaning some rooms were larger than others. The heck with a bed and breakfast, he could have opened a freaking hotel in this place.

The hallway was wide, carpeted with throw rugs, much the same as the foyer, which would be a nightmare for mobility with the cameras and crew people. It was lit with smaller chandelier fixtures hanging down in regular intervals and a massive window at the very end. More lighting would be required, she noted, looking at the paintings, mirrors, and wall sconces, some more ornate and gaudy than others, that filled the wall space between each door.

The whole effect was rather overwhelming, and she stood there, all but gaping as she took it all in. No wonder they had a hard time maintaining the place. Just this one hallway alone was a monster, and there were four of them on this side of the house alone, two upper, and two lower. Plus the rooms in the central part. She couldn't imagine one family, much less one man, maintaining all of it. One thing was for certain, though, depending on the condition of the rooms behind those doors, there was no question the place was quite big enough to house their entire production.

She almost missed it when Dylan made a sharp turn and didn't enter either hallway, but opened a door and began climbing yet another set of stairs that led, presumably, up to the third floor of the central section of the house. This staircase was far more narrow, straight up, with closed walls on either side. However her attention wasn't on the walls, the jumble of paintings hung all over them, or the fact that the stairs were dimly lit with wall sconces only, no overhead lighting. No, her attention was pretty much riveted on the very fine backside of a certain Scotsman climbing the stairs in front of her, said backside showcased quite nicely in faded denim. He must do a lot of stair climbing, she thought, admiring the flex and play of his hamstring muscles as he charged up the stairs.

So intent was her focus, when he stopped short just

at the top, she was unable to halt her forward motion in time and wobbled precariously on the next-to-top stair, grabbing for the hand-railing to keep from toppling backward.

Before that could happen, he caught her by the arms and pulled her up next to him, wedging them both in the narrow doorway at the top. Suddenly short of breath, she tried for a laugh, but it came out sounding far more like a soft little moan. Probably because it was.

"You seem to have a wee problem with balance," he said, that intent gaze of his directly on hers, but no hint of expression otherwise.

"I—I'm normally not such a klutz, really. I even went to college on a sports scholarship. Honest. Team captain." She was babbling when she should be extricating herself from his arms, and from the tight space they were presently sharing . . . but her body wasn't exactly following her brain's orders. Of course, that could be because her brain wasn't entirely certain she should be going anywhere, either, especially since there were all kinds of benefits to staying right where she was.

Like the way the hard length of him felt so incredibly good against the not-so-hard length of her. Better than she'd imagined, better than that brief moment in the pub. He was solid, and strong, and she felt absurdly safe and in absolute danger all at the same time. Her heart was pounding . . . and she realized he wasn't making any attempt to move either.

"Your clothes," he said, at length.

"Yes?" she breathed, barely managing to get the words out, as images of him tearing them off and—

"Ye'll get paint on them."

"I—oh. Right."

"I'll lend you an auld shirt of mine to cover up."

"Yes, that, that would be great. Super. Thanks." She made a valiant attempt at an insouciant smile. Of *course* he wasn't thinking of tearing her clothes off. It was far more typical of a man to want to cover her up. In fact, he was probably wondering why he hadn't just let her tumble back down the stairs. Probably afraid of the lawsuit she'd file.

"Come on," he said, and stepped into a short hallway, disappearing into one of the two rooms on the left. As if he hadn't been remotely affected by their little moment.

Because he wasn't affected, you idiot. You're the only affected one here. She sighed. "Afflicted is more like it," she muttered.

"I beg your pardon?"

She looked up to find him standing in front of her once more, a paint splattered, white dress shirt dangling from his fingers. Would she ever not look like a complete fool in front of this man? She took the shirt from him. "Thanks." She felt the quality of the linen and glanced back up at him. "Nice work shirts you have."

He shrugged. "No other use for them now." He turned and walked into one of the two rooms that had paint buckets sitting in the middle of the floor. "Let's get to it then."

She slipped the shirt on over her own and rolled up the sleeves. *Yes*, she thought, *let's get over your fixation with the hot Scot and get back to business.* She surreptitiously lifted her arm so she could breathe in his scent from the linen.

And she would. Any minute now.

Just as soon as she figured out how.

Chapter 5

The instant he had a spare minute to call his own, his brother was going to hear from him and quite loudly. Not that he hadn't thought of contacting Erin himself. But he'd like to think that was his conclusion, drawn after a long, sleepless night of deep contemplation about the business ramifications of her offer. But the truth was, he'd had a hard time putting her out of his mind.

It was bad enough he'd had to turn even a portion of his family's ancestral home into an inn. He had zero desire to turn Glenshire over to some American film crew. After all the blood, sweat, and tears he'd literally poured into both restoration and renovation, they'd come storming in, setting up all their cameras and cables, causing untold damage in the process. No. He'd accepted the commercialization of their Chisholm heritage. He wouldn't further sell out their integrity by allowing it to be used as a backdrop to some crass dating show.

But the devil on his other shoulder wouldn't stop whispering that if the check was big enough, and they agreed in writing to repair anything they damaged, how could he not at least hear her out? And, though it felt unseemly, there was no getting around the fact that the promotion for future bookings was something to consider in getting the bed and breakfast off the ground. Even with Daisy's marketing savvy, Glenbuie wasn't exactly a hotbed of tourism. The television show could change all that.

He'd fallen asleep last night with the battle still waging, only to have Ms. MacGregor play a starring role in his dreams. Which had nothing whatsoever to do with television programming or keeping four hundred years of Chisholm history from crumbling to dust, and far more to do with the images he'd wrestled with most of the way home last night. Images that followed him into sleep if the rock hard state of his body when he woke up was any indication.

So he'd steamed those confusing images of Erin's ready smile, her spontaneous laughter, her natural joie de vivre from his mind with a long morning shower, intent on putting his thoughts back into focus. In the end, however, one thing had led to another and it had taken a bit more creative use of soap and suds, taking the matter in hand, so to speak, to finally make that happen. He should have just done that the night before as he'd planned. Maybe then he'd have at least gotten a good night's sleep.

Then, bang, there she was again, right on his doorstep, first thing in the morning, lease agreement clutched in hand, and an entirely too cheerful smile on her pixie face. He hadn't blushed since he was a very young lad, but it had taken a considerable toll on his willpower to hold her gaze steadily for more than one second and not flame up, as he was incapable of not thinking about the very different version of her he'd been envisioning a mere hour or so earlier, while he'd been . . . doing what he'd been doing.

Hell, even now his body was stirring just thinking about it. He angled himself more toward the wall. Just in case. What the bloody hell had gotten into him anyway? He'd all but run up the stairs in front of her just to get enough distance between them to will himself back under control. Only to get trapped with her all but plastered against him back there in the doorway. She hadn't seemed to have the least clue of the rather insanely bawdy direction his thoughts had taken, but then he'd been so disconcerted by the whole thing, he'd all but shoved one of his old shirts in her face and escaped to his paint brush and drip tray.

His sole concern was supposed to be what to do about the bloody lease offer, which was the only thing he should be considering leasing out. He slapped the brush against the wall and dragged his recalcitrant thoughts back to the real business at hand.

"Oh!" came a surprised gasp from behind him.

He turned to find her looking quite put out. Though, given the rather large splotch of pale blue paint presently oozing its way into the open neckline of his dress shirt, and between her breasts, he couldn't say he blamed her.

She looked down, then up at him, but rather than complain, she laughed and sort of thrust her chest out in an exaggerated fashion pose. "And blue is so not my color."

Dylan found his lips twitching. She was just so . . . real. His gaze was drawn back to the splotch. "I don't know," he said, considering, then immediately bit back the rest of what he'd been about to say, which would have sounded suspiciously like flirting. He didn't flirt. Or hadn't, anyway, in a very long time. He certainly had no business being compelled now. Erin was an obstacle of sorts, and witty banter of any fashion was not the way to clear that particular hurdle. She already had more of an edge than she realized. He'd be a fool to give so much as a toehold more when there was negotiating to be done.

Belatedly realizing he was still staring, he grabbed a rag from the pile on the floor. "Here. If you get it off now, likely it won't leave a mark."

She took the rag and plucked his shirt away from her skin so she could scrape off the offending blob. It was only after several moments of watching her dab at the spot between her breasts that he realized he was still staring. He quickly jerked his attention back to his own paint brush and the stretch of window trim awaiting his attention.

"How long have you been working on renovating the place?"

Yes, innocuous banter. Good. Anything to distract him from the fact that he'd noticed that while she might not have a sexy swing to her hips, she had far more of a curve to her bosom than he'd have suspected. And if the nipples pressing against his old shirt were any indication, quite perky, too. He cleared his throat and stared at the wall. "I'm fairly certain a Chisholm has been renovating some part of this place since the moment they laid the final stone." He glanced in her direction, testing himself. "Perhaps even before that."

She shot him a grin before turning back to her section of wall. There was a blue smear across her cheek, her hair stuck out at odd angles, apparently on purpose as it had been much the same yesterday, and she seemed entirely unconcerned with how she came off. Appearance-wise anyway. He was already quite certain when it came to her business mien, she was more than concerned. Or she wouldn't be wearing his shirt and slopping paint all over herself.

And looking somehow quite charming doing so. *Get hold of yourself, lad.*

"How much of the place, overall, are you turning into the B & B?"

Her questions seemed casually asked, but he knew they were anything but. Calculating her offer most likely. "The upstairs wing on the north side—that was the hallway we entered earlier—and these three central loft rooms. Fourteen rooms all total. Various sizes."

She made a noncommittal noise and didn't look up, focusing instead on keeping the brush steady as she drew it down alongside the trim. He saw that when she was really concentrating, she bit the corner of her bottom lip. Which was entirely alluring. On the right kind of woman, of course.

She turned and caught him looking at her, but didn't react in any overt way. "What about the other first floor on this side? Any plans to expand further if things go well? Do you plan to use anything downstairs?"

So many questions. All of them about business. He should have been happier about that. He attacked his trim with renewed determination. "The rooms along the second upper hallway are in various stages of renovation, one whole section has been completely shut off for years. I don't foresee the need to add them to the list of available rooms, but I suppose if I were to change my mind, I'd start with the more readily available rooms there. The first floor in this wing has only one common hallway. The rooms below are considerably larger, meant for social gatherings, some in better shape than others. The plan is to open the main parlor, situated near the front of the wing, closest to the central part of the house. The kitchens are located in the central rear, so serving breakfast there makes the most sense."

"No dining room, then?"

He paused, looked over his shoulder, but she was

concentrating on the sill now. "We have several, the smallest of which seats a modest thirty—or would if there were furnishings in it. At present, it's closed off. Sagging walls, sinking floors. A common problem with a lot of older structures and this one is no different. Anyway, I felt the parlor had a more intimate ambience, suitable to a bed and breakfast, with several small tables set up for a more private atmosphere. Guests can also take their morning meal on the side portico with a view of the mountain range."

"It all sounds lovely," she said, sounding quite sincere and likely she was. Yet he easily imagined her mental calculator busily toting up numbers in her head.

"Across from the parlor there is also a library, more of a study really, but on a rather larger scale comparatively speaking, that has been put to rights. It will be available during the day should anyone care to sit and read, play a hand of cards, or whatnot. But otherwise, the other rooms in the lower part of the north wing will remain off view. As will the entire south wing."

"That is the family wing, I take it?"

"It's where I reside, if that's what you're asking, aye. However, most of it has been likewise shut off. There is no way to tackle the entirety of Glenshire, so we preserve what we can, and seal off, at least temporarily, what we canno'. It's the only way to keep her afloat."

"I know I said it before, but it's such a huge undertaking for one person." She let out a small laugh. "I guess that's the understatement of the century."

His lips quirked, but he kept to his work. "Aye. Several of them, in fact."

They spent a few moments in companionable silence, and he was surprised at the urge he had to fill that silence with some questions of his own. He was equally surprised to discover that, inquisition notwithstanding, he was rather enjoying this particular disruption of his work day, much as he had his trip into town last night. It felt . . . good to have someone around. Someone who wasn't Letty Dalrymple, anyway.

"So, when you open your doors to guests, will you bring someone in to help with the cooking and room cleaning?"

He turned. "Rather sexist, don't you think?"

Appearing honestly surprised, she stopped as well, and blew her hair off her forehead. One wispy lock had adhered itself to a spatter of paint and didn't budge. She was going on about something to do with how she was a woman in a man's field and the last person who'd ever pigeonhole anybody, but he wasn't really listening. He found himself too distracted by the sudden urge to go over there and free those muck and mired strands.

"My guests won't go hungry," he interjected finally, more to get himself back on track—again—than to shut her up. "And they'll have fresh linens."

Erin broke off, smiled, then, without skipping a beat, said, "Hard to imagine a place this size ever being fully utilized just by family and staff."

She'd said it sounding more practical-minded than dreamy romantic. Made him wonder if there was a romantic heart beating beneath her all-business exterior. Given the brand of television show she was touting it seemed she should be a bit more of that happily-ever-after sort than she appeared to be. But what did he know?

"The sheer history of it, the centuries it has endured, it really makes this place quite a draw. And then there's that awe-inspiring view. I imagine you'll have no problem filling those rooms."

Aye, a businesswoman, then, through and through. She was right about Glenshire's rather gothic ambience being its main selling point. He'd always thought of the crumbling decay as being more eyesore than particularly romantic or attractive, but Reese's fiancée, Daisy, had taken the same view as Erin. In fact, she'd made that the focal point of the website she'd created as an adjunct to the site she'd developed for the distillery. She'd packaged Glenbuie distillery tours, with village shop discounts and a stay in Glenshire's bed and breakfast, and lo and behold, though it had taken some time to get the bookings started, over time it had worked. Maybe it was some kind of Yankee sensibility, though the two women couldn't be more different.

"You're not too keen on the whole idea, though, I take it."

Dylan lifted his gaze to hers, realizing once again he'd trailed off into his own thoughts. He'd been out here on his own for so long now, he wasn't used to being observed by anyone, much less having to concern himself with whether anyone could interpret his thoughts or expression. "I thought I made my stance on that clear yesterday."

"Though you're reconsidering now," she said, that impish light back in her eyes. She waggled her brush at him, splattering paint on the dropcloth. "But that's not what I meant. I meant you're not too keen on the whole bed and breakfast plan, either."

"What would make you say that?"

Erin laughed. "Let's just say you don't exactly have the temperament of an innkeeper. You talk about Glenshire with a combination of pride and weary acceptance, but there is a guardedness to it, like a brother who can talk smack about his own siblings, but dare someone else do the same and they'll get a fist in their face. You're protective of her," she said with a softer smile. "And maybe a bit resentful of her demands. But you don't really want to share her with anyone, do you?"

Dylan said nothing in response. He was a little disconcerted by her insight. Maybe more than a little. Because she was right. And he'd wondered more often than he cared to admit whether, despite his commitment to the joint decision made with his brothers to go ahead with the bed and breakfast scheme, if he'd be truly up to the actual task of running it when the time came. Putting the place to rights was one thing. Planning the room layout, the breakfast menus, the pricing structure, taking reservations, he'd done all of those things, the things an innkeeper would do. And yet, other than the occasional laborer or subcontractor, he hadn't had to deal with actual people yet. Not a paying guest anyway. And he'd be lying if he said that that part of this whole deal didn't have him a little nervous.

Because, as she'd so rightly pointed out, he wasn't exactly innkeeper material. And if she'd picked up on that inside of thirty minutes spent together . . . what chance did he have with the paying guests? He argued the point anyway, maybe more to convince himself than her. "I've devoted two years of my life readying this place for that exact eventuality, what makes you think I'm not wholly invested in the idea?"

She lifted a shoulder and scrubbed the back of her hand across her nose, leaving more paint as she did so. "What did you do for a living when you lived in the city?"

"What does that have to do with anything?" He had to curl his fingers inward against the renewed urge to cross the room and rub the paint off the tip of that pixie-like, upturned nose of hers. "And how did you know I lived in the city?"

"Brodie mentioned it, or maybe it was Alastair." She waved her brush. "It's common knowledge. And I'm just curious. I'm trying to adjust my view of you."

Why it mattered what her view was, he had no idea.

But he found himself answering anyway. "I traded stocks. Why do you look so surprised?"

She lifted her shoulders again. "I have no idea, really. Actually, that occupation seems to suit you."

"You don't even know me."

"You know what I mean, your general demeanor. You seem more suited to the hustle and bustle of big city life, I guess is what I'm saying. You're very . . . intense. Stock trading is an intense occupation. That's all."

So she thought him intense, did she? He recalled that moment on the dance floor when she'd first bumped against him. Then again, just now, at the top of the stairs, when they'd been wedged in the doorframe. It had been a rather charged moment, but he assumed it was his own folly, given the fresh memories of his morning shower activities.

"So," Erin went on, "what is it about opening Glenshire's doors that bothers you most?"

"Who said it bothered me?"

She just gave him a stop kidding yourself look and continued. "Are you afraid she'll come up lacking? Or is it a heritage issue, beneath the family name to take in boarders, that kind of thing?"

"I'm no' afraid of what people will think of Glenshire," he responded truthfully. He was a wee bit more concerned what his guests would think of him, but only because he needed their patronage to keep the place from complete ruin. Were it up to him, he'd have far rather continued managing his stock portfolio, investing as wisely as possible, and repairing the place as the funds became available. But while his personal portfolio had benefited them all over the years, the market was too unpredictable to trust their fortunes exclusively to his investment prowess, no matter that he was still largely successful at it.

And, frankly, sitting in this drafty auld place, tapping away at a computer terminal as years passed by, wasn't exactly an enticing future for him to contemplate either. "As to opening her doors, it's no' beneath us. It's far from the first time Chisholms have taken on the role of host within these walls." It was the first time they'd charged money for the privilege, but she was far too nosey for her own good. No need to give her any more information than was necessary.

She bent and dipped her brush in the pan, and he couldn't help but notice the way her pants pulled tight across her bum. Huh, he thought. Not much of one there, as it turned out. Her legs were a bit on the spindly side, too, though she wasn't all that narrow of hip or waist. Add to that her long arms, which gave her the appearance of being taller than she really was. She straightened and turned back to the trim work, reaching above her head. She wasn't skinny, more gangly, like a baby giraffe, all stick limbs, blocky torso, and slender neck.

No, not at all his type. There wasn't a sleek, sophisticated bone in her, nor the curves to make up for their absence. He shook his head slightly and returned to his own spot of trim. And thought about his morning shower. And started to get hard all over again. *Christ.*

"So you're doing it for family, then. Clan leader, oldest son commitment," she commented after a few minutes had passed, as if there hadn't been a break in their conversational flow.

He wondered if she had any inkling of how keenly aware he was of her. She didn't seem conscious of her impact much at all, to be honest. Maybe because she typically didn't make one, not of the sort he was thinking about anyway. And why was he thinking like that? He really had to reconsider the whole monk thing. And he would. Just as soon as she left town. "Like all that came before me, we do what we must to maintain the family assets," he said, at length.

She finished carefully running her brush along the inside edge of the sill, before turning to face him once again. "But that doesn't mean you have to like it."

He stopped and looked at her. "No, no it doesn't." He found it impossible to be anything other than candid in the face of her own easy frankness. And yet, he wondered how she would respond if he were the interrogator and she the object of his inquisition?

She propped her brush on the pan and wiped her fingers on the edges of his increasingly paint-spattered loaner shirt, then grinned at him. "So, why don't you let me get you away from all of this?" She gestured to the room as if she were a game show presenter. "An eight week, all expenses paid vacation. You'll come home to a place in better shape than when you left it, starting with us finishing up all this detail work and including any reworking and refinishing necessary for our production, and with the added bonus of a nice check to put in the bank as well." Her grin broadened. "A win-win proposition. I don't see how you could turn it down."

Standing there like that, all twinkly eyed, cocksure smile, and paint-spattered cheeks, he was having a hard time remembering why he was fighting this so hard himself. A chance to get away for eight minutes would have been more than welcome at this point. Had he anywhere to go. He missed the city in some ways, but not the drama that went along with it. Too many ghosts there, not to mention Maribel's family and friends, who were well meaning, but suffocating. Even a short visit would allow them to drag him right back into the emotional birl he'd spent the past two years successfully working his way out of. But he hadn't exactly found an even footing yet in Glenbuie, either. He was living in a sort of surreal limbo.

So Erin's offer to escape the life he'd somehow

found himself inhabiting was far more attractive than even she could have known. And she never would. Surreal or not, fulfilling or not, his commitment was here. And if his marriage had proven anything, it was that when he made a commitment, he stuck with it. No matter what.

The fly in the ointment here was the money. He needed it. Or more to the point, Glenshire needed it. But he couldn't, wouldn't, relinquish the place to a cordon of strangers, and allow them the kind of unfettered access they'd likely demand. He couldn't risk his heritage in that way for any amount of money or accidental repair riders attached to the contract. Some things weren't reparable. However . . . perhaps there was room for a compromise.

"So, what do you say?" she said, cocking her head to one side as he continued his silent regard of her.

"I canno' vacate the premises here," he stated flatly.

Her entire body seemed to vibrate then. She'd sensed victory within her grasp. But her voice when she spoke was calm, even. "I promise, we would ensure that any—"

He held up his hand. "I'll no' vacate the premises."

To her credit, she said nothing. She wasn't a fool, far from it from what she'd displayed so far.

"As noted previously, the other wing of the house is off limits to guests. I'll need to see exactly what you're offering me in terms of compensation for relocating or rebooking my guests. And I'd also need to discuss in detail exactly what adjustments your crew would make to my home in order to set up shop here."

"We have resources that you don't. I could have a team of people in here less than twenty-four hours from now. We could finish a lot of this type of—"

Again he silenced her with a raised hand, or brush, as was the case. "I'll need a free flow of communication throughout the production." He could see that didn't set well with her at all. He completely understood her reluctance to have the owner underfoot, but she'd learn he wouldn't be swayed on that point. "To that end, will you be staying for the duration of the filming?"

She looked surprised by the question. "Why do you ask?"

"I realize you'd prefer me not to get in the way of your filming, and I'd definitely prefer to steer as clear of the entire endeavor as possible."

"So let us put you up in town, then," she offered quickly, banked excitement in her tone now. "We would pick up the tab, of course, and I'd work it out for you to get frequent reports and updates, addressing any concerns you might have. We've done this for seven seasons, now. Trust me, we know what we're doing."

"Be that as it may, I'm responsible for the welfare of my family's heritage. We've done so for over four centuries now, and we're quite good at it as well."

She gave him a rueful smile. "Point taken. Surely we can come up with some kind of compromise that will ease your concerns and make the entire event as easy on both sides as possible."

She'd used the word event, but he'd heard the word ordeal. It would be both, of that he was certain. "I've already come up with such a plan. But you hav'nae answered my question."

"About me staying on? I'm usually on site through pre-production, scouting out the various local spots we'll use for some of the outings taken by our contestants, but once everything is in place, I'll be heading back to the States. We've been picked up for another season already because we shoot two a year, so I'll be working on scouting the next location while they're filming this one."

He frowned. "That will be a bit of a problem then."

She frowned, too. "Why is that? I'll make certain

they set up a direct line of communication with a production assistant before I—"

"We communicate well enough. You understand my concerns here. I don't see the need to develop another association when this one is working just fine."

"But—"

"I won't be relocating to town, Erin."

"It would be so much easier for you, trust me. You'll see that—"

"Why don't we cut to the chase here, as you Yanks say."

It was her turn to look wary now. "Okay."

"How badly do you want to lease Glenshire?"

Like any good businesswoman, she said nothing, but her folded arms and set stance spoke for her.

"In exchange for my staying here and giving advance approval on all improvements or adjustments, I will agree not to interfere with any of the filming." Her rigid stance relaxed somewhat at that. "However," he added, "that is only if you agree to stay and be my direct line of communication from the production crew."

"But anyone can—"

"You strike me as a very straightforward person."

"I'd like to think so."

"Then I trust you'll continue to be that way throughout. If I'm to turn over four centuries of my heritage to be bandied about by a crew full of camera jockeys who could hardly appreciate the unique history of what they're dealing with, then the very least you can provide me is the utilization of the one person I've developed any sort of trust with." He put his paintbrush down and stepped around the pans on the floor until he was directly in front of her. "Barring any unforeseen glitches that might arise in the actual contract and require further discussion, do we have a deal?" He stuck out his hand.

She looked from him, to his hand, then back to him again. "Nothing is set in stone until you sign."

It was clear on her face she still thought to bargain with him and get her way on certain matters. Little did she know who she was dealing with. "Deal?"

To her credit, she held his gaze directly as she took his hand in a surprisingly firm shake. "Deal."

He gestured for her to leave the room before him. "Then let the deliberations begin."

Chapter 6

"Good work on this, MacGregor. I knew I could count on you."

Erin accepted the rather hearty thump on the side of her arm with as much grace as possible, struggling not to drop her boss' bags as she helped him unload them in front of the hotel. Unfortunately Tommy had grabbed an earlier flight than expected out of London, so she'd missed the chance to pick him up at the airport in Inverness, thereby also missing her one chance to fill him in on Dylan's little contract stipulation while they weren't surrounded by a million other people. She liked to get yelled at with the smallest audience possible.

"Thanks, but there are some details we need to talk about. I had to make a few concessions."

Tommy heaved the last duffel bag onto the pile. He was fifty-five years of age, a short man who came eye-to-chin level with her. If she were barefoot at the time. He had vivid blue eyes, a wide mouth stocked with more teeth than seemed humanly possible, and a shock of white hair that ringed his otherwise tanned head. His voice was gruff with both bark and bite, made all the more ominous by his thick, bushy eyebrows, still heavily peppered with the original black hair, all of which served to complete the deranged leprechaun look he sported most of the time. "What kind of concessions?" he demanded, slamming the door shut and moving around to the driver side of the vehicle.

Erin took a step behind him. "Well—"

One of the many production assistants who had invaded Glenbuie in the last forty-eight hours since they'd begun moving the production up from London raced around the car. "I can get that for you, Mr. Marchand. We have a lot reserved in the back of the hotel for you."

"More money, right? Bastards always want more money." Tommy barely glanced at the assistant. "Keys are in it. Make sure they get back to me or Tanya, a.s.a.p."

The young P.A. nodded and all but leapt into the leased Range Rover, but Tommy wasn't paying him any attention. "The exposure his little inn will get from our involvement will keep him booked up for years, but no, they always want more money."

Erin didn't bother to point out that it was no "little" inn. Tommy had seen the exterior shots she'd taken. "Actually, he accepted our initial lease offer."

Tommy paused, then started looking around for someone to start moving his mound of baggage. "Good. Where's Tanya?" he demanded, already distracted. He snagged the arm of the nearest person he could reach. "Find Tanya for me. She was supposed to meet me in the lobby at one."

Erin could have mentioned that he'd just barked orders at a hotel employee, not a staffer, but there was no point in it. Besides, the hotel was small enough that she assumed the bellman probably knew where Tommy's number one assistant was anyway. Especially given that she'd probably been the one barking orders at them until now.

"This place better be worth the hassle, MacGregor, or your ass is the first one I'm selling down the river to the suits." His satellite phone chirped to life. He ignored it. "I want to hear about these concessions. The isolation of this location from any major city support puts a major cramp on our already constrained budget. And I don't need to remind you how far behind schedule we are."

"Glenshire can easily house the cast and site crew. And I've worked out an agreement with the hotel in Glenbuie to accommodate the rest.

"Fine, fine." Once Tommy agreed to something, he didn't want any additional info. In typical fashion, he moved directly to his next point. "I need at least two trailers on set, in addition to the production trailers. Did you work that out?"

Erin mentally scrambled to figure out how to meet that demand. "It will be a bit cramped for space, but there is a rear utility entrance and courtyard. It means having production trucks a little closer to the house, but there isn't any other space. You'll have to be creative with camera angles in terms of shooting around them, but there isn't much back there that you'd likely want to use on camera anyway."

Tommy nodded, satisfied. For now. His phone went off again and he ignored it again. "Concessions. What did we give in on?"

Erin forced herself to stay relaxed, calm, as if this were no big deal. Hard to do when she knew damn well he was likely to pop an artery. "Mr. Chisholm is going to stay on property." She lifted a fast hand. "I did everything in my power to get him to agree to move off site. And it isn't to say that we won't get him to change his mind once he sees what it's like living with the chaos." Though, privately, she doubted anything would budge him. She was a tough negotiator, but he'd been tougher. "He didn't ask for more money, so we banked there. But he stood firm on this. I fought him on it, but it was clear this was a deal breaker. He's protecting four hundred years of his heritage and there is no way he's—"

"You know I hate having to contend with the owner, Erin. It wastes considerable time and money. We can't be babysitting him and still—"

"Well, see, you won't have to." Where was Tanya when she needed a good interruption anyway?

"Meaning?"

"He doesn't want to be directly involved in the actual process any more than you want him to be. He just wants a clear line of communication."

"He certainly doesn't need to be on site for that. Everything is outlined in the standard agreement and the rest can be handled via phone, fax, or e-mail. If they have such a thing in this godforsaken outback."

"He won't budge on this, but I've worked out a line of communication with him that will relieve you and the immediate crew from any contact—"

"You gave him an assistant, didn't you?" Tommy slapped his thigh, then barked at another assistant to find Tanya. "Do you know what that's going to cost me?" he shouted, turning his attention back to her. "Fine, then. We'll just give him yours."

"Actually—"

"You think you can just freely disperse my already over-extended manpower? You'll have to make the sacrifice. Dana will have to handle it."

"It's me," she said. "He'll only work with me."

"*What?*" It was amazing how much emotion a small man like Tommy could pack into a single word.

"I'm going to be on site for at least the next two weeks anyway," she hurriedly said, before he completely imploded. "I'll have time to get him used to the process, build his trust. Hopefully by then he'll be so sick of dealing with everything we can get him moved off site completely."

"You're killing me here, MacGregor."

"If worse comes to worse, I'll leave Dana here to handle him, but I really don't think it will come to that." Privately, Erin knew her assistant would be thrilled with that little assignment if it came to pass. But Erin had far too much to do, and needed Dana's assistance too much to let that happen. She pasted on a big, confident grin. "I'll make it all work. I've never let you down so far, have I?"

Tanya chose that moment to come rushing out of the hotel. "So sorry, I've been tied up—"

"See that you do make it work," Tommy instructed Erin, then took Tanya by the arm and hustled her into the hotel.

Erin waited until Tommy was out of sight before heaving a deep sigh of relief and heading inside. *Well. That hadn't been too bad.* She stepped over piles of luggage and scooted over to an unoccupied corner before pulling out her binder and scanning her notes. She had a meeting at three with Daisy to go over date location ideas. Dana wouldn't be coming in for another couple of days, as Erin had assigned her to scout the final weekend excursion site in Paris. Erin had been looking forward to scoping out that particular location, but thanks to Dylan's demands, she couldn't risk leaving before Tommy arrived and was brought up to speed. Dana was ready to take on more responsibility anyway, and this date event was a good, hands-on place for her to start. Still, Erin couldn't help but think that she could be wandering the Champs Élysées at the moment, and not dealing with the insane accelerated schedule Tanya had just thrust on them in their first team meeting earlier this morning.

"Oh thank god, there you are!" Another of Tommy's personal assistants pushed his way through the cluster trying to check in, waving a stack of little pink slips. "Will you please talk to him already?"

"Talk to who? Tommy? I just spoke to—"

He looked both bedraggled and bewildered. Not unusual when you worked for Tommy. He shoved the stack of slips into Erin's hand. "Make this go away," was all he said, then disappeared into the clamoring throng once again.

Erin fanned through the crumpled stash, her attention immediately snagging on the one common thread in each note. The name in the "From" box at the top of each slip. Dylan Chisholm. She'd sent word to him yesterday, along with the bare outlines of the new production schedule, and told him she'd be in touch sometime today to go over details and personally answer any questions he had, as they'd agreed. Apparently Dylan hadn't been patiently waiting for her to find time to call. She flipped quickly through the rest of the pile, but the message was the same on each. "Have Erin MacGregor contact me a.s.a.p."

"Great." She sighed, checked her watch, before glancing longingly at the lobby stairs that led to the upper floors . . . and her room. Her nice, quiet room, away from the mob, away from the madness. Where she'd hoped to spend a whole forty-five minutes in peace before tackling the new pile of work Tanya had just thrust in her lap. She hadn't liked two of the four date locations, or either of Erin's backup sites, which meant working overtime to come up with alternate locales. Hence her meeting with Daisy.

She gave a final longing look at the staircase and the

nice warm bath she wasn't going to get—again—then resolutely pushed her way through the crowd and out the back of the hotel to the tiny car lot where her rental was parked. She'd wanted to set the damn show in Brigadoon, she could hardly complain now that she'd gotten her way. Shoving her pink slips into her satchel, she tossed it on the passenger seat, and pointed her car in the direction of Glenshire.

Halfway there, she had a little brainstorm. If Dylan were going to make himself a general pain in her ass, which, clearly, he was going to, then she might as well find a way to make it work for her, right? He wanted to stick his nose in? Well, she was about to let him.

By the time she pulled into Glenshire's rear service entrance, which was already clogged with a stream of vans and crew trucks, she had a plan firmly in place. She absently nodded and waved at the guys who were presently streaming in and out of the house, running miles of cable, toting lighting fixtures, barking orders. It all looked completely normal to her, but she knew it was quite the opposite for Dylan. She pretended not to see the men's aggrieved expressions as she ducked past on her way through the central part of the house.

It didn't take long to find him. In fact, she heard him seconds after hitting the second floor landing.

"I dinnae much care what the contract stipulates. There's no need to go stringing lights and mounting cameras in every bloody corner!" Dylan's bark echoed through the halls. "That plaster isn't going to hold those brackets. One good tap and the whole face will crumble down upon your Charming Prince's pretty head. I'm savin' ye from a certain lawsuit."

"Erin!" The poor crewman who was the target of Dylan's current tirade all but leaped upon her the second she turned the corner into one of the two main upstairs hallways where four men were mounting cameras and installing lighting. "Thank god, you're here." His fingertips dug into Erin's arm as he all but dragged her to his side. Jaw clenched into a sorry facsimile of a smile, he said, "Mr. Chisholm has been expressing some doubt regarding the installation process. Perhaps you could discuss this with him privately while I get back to directing the crew?"

She wasn't given any time to answer, but was instead all but thrust directly in front of Dylan. "Um, sure," she said, pasting on her own bright smile. "In fact, I need to talk to Mr. Chisholm anyway." The relief on the faces of the workers was so complete, she was surprised they didn't do the wave. She turned to Dylan. His jaw was set, his legs braced apart, arms folded across his chest, every bit the Great Scot. "We need to talk." She cast a quick glance over her shoulder. "In private, if you don't mind."

He shifted his intent gaze from her, to the crew who had paused in their banging and drilling, then back to her again. His jaw flexed and a vein pulsed along his temple. It was only when, after what felt like an eternity, he finally gave her a curt nod, that she realized she'd been holding her breath.

Trying not to release it so fast that she became lightheaded, she cautiously motioned for him to lead them both out of the hallway.

"I want nothing more done in this hall until I've had a chance to discuss things with Ms. MacGregor," he ordered, sounding exactly like the clan chief that he was. He stepped over power cords and shifted around the ladders and dollies with surprising grace for someone his size.

Something she had no business noticing at the moment. It was bad enough he still snuck into her dreams at night.

"Erin," the crew leader pleaded.

She tore her gaze off Dylan's muscled backside and shot the young man a quick, placating smile. "Just give me a few minutes," she said, loudly enough for Dylan to hear, but as she hurried to keep up with his long-legged strides, she made a hand motion behind her back for the crew to continue on after she and Dylan were gone.

From the looks of things, they were well behind the new pre-production schedule. Somehow she suspected Dylan was likely at least partially responsible for that. If word got back to Tommy, her ass would be chewed into tiny little leprechaun bits. It was exactly what she'd promised him wouldn't happen. What Dylan had also promised her he wouldn't let happen. Which was the first thing she planned on reminding him about. Just as soon as she got him away from the house.

She caught up to him at the top of the central staircase. "Would it be okay if we took a short drive?"

"A drive?" He stopped and looked back at her. "Why? Where?"

She managed a light laugh and placed her hand on his arm. Big mistake. It was like touching a live wire with a wet hand. It took considerable control not to jump at the jolt it delivered straight to her libido. "Don't worry, I'm not kidnapping you." Although the images that scenario sent springing to mind didn't help matters any.

"I dinnae feel comfortable leaving here just now." His tone was tight, his voice deeper even than usual, his accent more pronounced.

"You signed the agreement," she reminded him as gently as possible. "You're not even supposed to be in this part of the house."

"Something I'm regretting with every passing second."

"We agreed to return everything to its original state or better. Why can't you trust me on that?"

"Agreeing is one thing. Seeing with my own eyes the havoc they're wreaking is making me less than confident of yer claims."

"I can assure you your fears are unfounded. And you'll be far less stressed out about it if you'd just stay in your part of the house like you agreed to. You know, it's not too late to let us put you up in town. The hotel is booked and frankly overrun with crew anyway, but we have a few private homes lined up for overflow—or maybe you could stay with one of your brothers."

Another worker banged up the stairs just then, a ladder balanced on his back, forcing Dylan to pull Erin closer as he backed up to allow the man to pass. "Come on," he commanded. "We'll discuss this downstairs. I have an office, we'll talk there."

Erin was momentarily incapable of speech. Dylan's hands were on her again, his chest was brushing up against hers, and she could feel the warmth of his breath on her cheek. If she tipped her head back and lifted up on her tiptoes, her lips would brush across his chin, so close to his mouth, so close to—"I—I need you to show me something," she blurted, self-preservation mercifully kicking in. She quickly untangled herself from his grasp. "My car is just out back. It won't take long, I promise."

He cocked one brow and didn't budge one inch. "What could I possibly have to show you? I'm no' a fool, Ms. MacGregor. You're wanting me off my property so your crews can finish their systematic demolition of my home."

"Partly," she said, thinking that, where Dylan was concerned, she might get farther by just being frank. "But I do really need your help. We can go over exactly what they're doing and why, and what kind of processes we use to restore things on the drive. And please, by now, it's Erin." He'd only used her first name once before.

Two days ago, standing on a paint-spattered drop cloth. She remembered it quite clearly, the sound of her name on his lips. Foolish really. But if they were going to get through this, it was silly to continue to stand on business formalities.

And if he was at all swayed by her polished little speech, his autocratic features didn't reveal it.

"We won't be gone long," she promised. "Come on. Give me an hour. You'll be back bullying the crew and disrupting everything in no time, promise."

"This isn't a joke to me, Erin."

She wasn't sure which thing got to her most. The implacable tone, or the way he said her name. Even spoken so sharply, just like last time, it did something funny to her insides. Maybe strictly business-like wasn't such a bad idea. It was that damned accent. Made everything sound sexy. "It's not a joke to me, either," she told him, as serious now as he was. "And I know this isn't easy to watch. It never is. I tried to get you to bunk elsewhere. Now you know why. There's nothing else I can say that I haven't already. But Glenshire has weathered far worse battles than this, I'd wager."

"Except, in the past she's typically been attacked from without. Not from within. Some of the walls they are so handily drilling and hammering were last restored over a hundred years ago. It's no' always a matter of putting up a new bit of plaster, ye ken?"

"I understand, I do." Just as she understood that no amount of arguing or haranguing on his part was going to alter the crew's course of action. There was no turning back now. She had a legally binding agreement backing her up, and Dylan was quite well educated enough to realize that, too. He was just trying to bully his way past it. And her.

It wasn't going to work. This season's cast was due to arrive in seventy-two hours, with filming slated to start the following Monday. From what little she'd witnessed, it looked as if they'd need twice that long to get the place into shape. "We have a contract," she said quietly. "You can't stop things now, Dylan."

She'd used his given name intentionally, hoping to create a sense of camaraderie, remind him he supposedly trusted her. The result was that his gaze settled exclusively and quite intently on her. If she wasn't completely mistaken, he seemed as caught off guard hearing her speak his name as she'd been in hearing him speak her own. Of course that was complete and utter nonsense, but still . . . when he looked at her like that, well, it made utter nonsense seem a lot less . . . nonsensical.

But the way he was looking at her made her skin heat up and muscles tighten in the most interesting places. "In addition to being your communication director, I still have a job to do." His pupils expanded and she swore she could feel heat emanating from him, too. "I—I really could use your help." She paused to clear her suddenly dry throat. "Could you spare me a few hours of your time?"

"Hours?" That got both of those dark eyebrows arching.

She didn't dare tug his arm and forcibly try and move him down the stairs. She didn't dare touch him at all. She was straddling a dangerous line between frankness . . . and awareness. So she started moving down the stairs on her own and prayed he followed her. "One or two is all I need, promise."

"You're quite free with your promises."

She knew from the proximity of his voice that he was right behind her. It was as alarming as it was relieving. She didn't even want to think about trying to control her reaction to him in the confines of her tiny rental car. "I don't make them if I can't keep them," she tossed over her shoulder, wishing she felt as casual as she sounded.

"That remains to be seen."

She ducked under another ladder and stepped over a dropcloth, winding her way toward the rear of the house. "My car is right over there," she said as they stepped outside.

"We'll take mine."

She turned to find him striding off toward a detached stone building. She had to hurry to keep up with him. "You don't have to do that. I don't mind driving, and that way you don't have to waste gas."

He was already bending to the task of manually hauling up the garage door, which didn't budge easily. He had to put some muscle into it, every ripple of which Erin quite shamelessly observed.

He grunted as he dragged the paneled door upward. "Might as well make something positive out of this debacle."

Erin didn't argue further. If it got them out of there, she would ride on a hay wagon pulled by mules. Still, no one was more surprised than she was when he lifted the door to reveal a sleekly stunning, midnight blue Jaguar convertible. "Wow."

Dylan propped his hands on his hips. "I know," he said, without the least bit of smugness. "That's exactly what I said when I first laid eyes on her." He brushed at the dust with his sleeve and plucked at a few leaves that had blown in. "Hullo, darling, missed me, have you?"

Erin did a double take. The man scowled more often than not, and any humor she'd ascribe to him would be sardonic at best. At no time had she ever thought him capable of that low, purring tone. She instantly folded her arms across her chest. "I take it you don't drive her much?"

"No. With all the work here, I take the lorry, as I'm usually hauling things about. Hasn't been much reason to do any pleasure cruising for . . . well, for longer than I care to admit."

In her experience, he was either direct, defensive, or wary. And always commanding. So it caught at her, that thread of vulnerability in his tone. "Was this the car you drove when you lived in the city?"

"One of them, aye." He answered almost absently, his attention more on the car as he continued to pluck leaves and brush off the fine layer of dust. "'Tis the only one I kept."

She didn't know what to make of him now. He was less Great Scot, and more . . . normal. And all the more appealing. She walked around the other side of the car. The more room she could put between them the better. "Can we put the top down?"

When he didn't immediately answer she looked up to find him studying her, rather than his beloved sports car.

"What?" she asked, trying not to fidget under his steady regard. "I just thought you could use a little fun, that's all. I figured you bought a convertible for a reason, so we might as well, right?"

"Aye," he said, but he made no move to get into the car or take the top off, or anything else for that matter. "What exactly is it you need my help with?"

She really wanted to be on the road and some distance away from the house before she answered that, but his implacable expression forced her to opt out of that little plan. He'd been lethal enough to her libido when barefoot, wearing paint-spattered jeans. Standing there all intense and enigmatic, framed by his prowling roadster, only intensified things. If that were possible. She smiled. And kept her arms crossed firmly in front of her. "Fantasy dates."

To her amazement and delight, his lips twitched into a hint of a smile, and a bit of a sparkle finally entered those dark gray eyes of his. "I should know by now to expect only the unexpected from you." He slid into the car and reached across the seat to pop her door open, then released the locks on the canvas top and swiftly tucked it away in the space provided behind their seats. A second later the engine purred to life. Apparently living in the middle of nowhere had its perks. He'd left the key dangling in the ignition.

"Are you coming?"

Loaded question, she thought, then quickly tucked herself into the low slung passenger seat before he changed his mind, or took off without her. She buckled in and slid her sunglasses on.

"Fantasy dates," he repeated as he eased the car out of the garage.

She risked a glance at him. He wasn't exactly smiling, but there was a distinct air of amusement about him. "Yes."

"A little fun, indeed," he murmured.

Any reply she might have made was lost on her sudden gasp as he floored the gas pedal and sent the little sports car rocketing down the rear drive. When she looked at him again, he was grinning. And a fiercer thing she'd never witnessed in her entire life.

Dear God, she'd unleashed a monster.

Chapter 7

It felt impossibly good to have the warmth of the sun on his face, the wind snatching at his hair, the open road in front of him. It had been a long time, far too long, since he'd indulged in spending even a minute's worth of time on something as frivolous as racing his car through the countryside. Longer still since he'd had company by his side.

Of course, only a fool would believe this was anything other than a business meeting dressed up as a spontaneous outing. Erin's claim that she needed his help was merely a sham to get him away from her people. What she might not have factored in was that he also had her away from her people now. He might have relinquished some of his power over Glenshire, but Erin and the entire production staff would soon learn that he wasn't going to simply turn a blind eye. They might have him contractually bound, but he planned to use every advantage he did have, and push for whatever more he might claim.

Now that he had Erin's undivided attention, he had every intention of making her understand why he should personally oversee the work they were doing. In this case, there was no better restoration consultant than him. But as Glenshire receded quickly from view, he found himself in no immediate hurry to bring it up. Instead, he let the chaos he'd left behind stay behind him and allowed himself a few moments to enjoy the fleeting sense of freedom. It would all bloody well be there waiting for him when he got back.

His thoughts wandered instead to his road trip companion. From the few conversations they'd had over the past couple of days, it was clear she knew a great deal more about him than he knew about her. Which wasn't saying much, since, other than knowing her name and what she did for a living, he knew pretty much nothing. Of course, what she knew of him was mostly information that had been filtered through either his brothers or the villagers, and therefore probably a bit skewed. Then again, in their brief acquaintance, she'd proven herself to be disconcertingly perceptive where he was concerned. It surprised him to discover he was somewhat curious about what conclusions she'd drawn, between the village gossip and their personal interaction.

"So, what exactly is a fantasy date?" he asked, choosing a far safer topic. She'd invaded quite a bit of his personal space. Maybe it was time to turn the tables a little. See how she felt being the focus of the conversation. Not that he personally cared to know more about her, of course. It was merely defensive strategy. "And whose fantasy is it? His? Hers?" He paused a moment. "Yours?" He risked a brief glance her way before returning his attention to the winding mountain road.

The car hugged the curves like a woman reunited with her long lost lover . . . and he was willing to let that embrace continue for as long as he could manage it. God, this felt bloody fantastic. Erin wasn't looking particularly alarmed by the speed with which he was tackling the mountain track, but she did look somewhat surprised by his conversational gambit.

His lips curved a little. Good. He hated being so predictable. "I'm assuming this is something to do with your Prince Charming and his ever-so-lucky brides-to-be?"

"What makes you say it like that?" With the top down, she had to raise her voice a little, but it carried easily through the sound of the wind. But then, she was direct in everything she did.

He rather liked that about her. Or admired the trait, anyway. They were business partners at best, so it didn't much matter what he thought of her outside that arrangement. It's not like he'd demanded she be his liaison because of any personal interest he was entertaining. He'd only insisted on dealing with her to exact some sort of compromise from her personally. Seeing as it was her discovery of Glenbuie, and by extension, Glenshire, that had turned his life upside down, it seemed only fair to shake hers up a little, too.

"Well, I can see the attraction from Prince Charming's perspective," Dylan said, downshifting as the sports car took a particularly tight turn. "What man would turn down the chance to wine and dine a dozen beautiful women?"

Erin surprised him by laughing. "You, I'm betting."

Again, her insight, even if she were joking, was a little disconcerting. He'd do well not to underestimate her. "Perhaps. Then again, at a different time in my life, I might have taken the chance." Realizing he'd handed her an opening into his personal life, he quickly added, "But I simply meant he doesn't exactly have the tough assignment. The women all have to compete for the attention of one man, whereas all he has to do is pick the one he fancies most out of the pack."

"Since when have you become a student of reality television dating shows?" she teased.

"Since they took over my life. Literally."

She smiled, nodded. "Fair enough. Well, the guy usually thinks like you do, that it'll be easy. Trust me, he'll learn very quickly that he has the harder job by far."

"How so? Because he has to be the bad guy and eliminate the other eleven? The women know going in that only one will be chosen, right? They're all adults. They might be upset at having their telly time cut short, but surely none of them are personally devastated by his rejection? They can't possibly know him well enough to have their hearts truly broken."

"You'd be surprised."

"I doubt it. But go ahead, illuminate things for me."

From the corner of his eye, he saw her shift in her seat to give him her full attention. And it surprised him to realize he wasn't just making small talk. Not that he gave two wanks about some ridiculous American program, but he found he was interested in hearing what she had to say on the matter.

"The show might seem unrealistic in terms of developing a true and lasting relationship because the dynamics are so out of the normal realm. And yes, the fact that there are cameras recording their every snip of dialogue and every action and reaction can make some of them behave less than naturally, but trust me, that all goes away pretty quickly. It's one of the reasons we mount so many cameras, so as to have as few visible production people present as possible."

"To enhance that false sense of intimacy."

"Partly false. Sure, they are being put up in a fancy place, with no jobs to worry about, no bills to pay, and their only focus being developing a relationship with each other. In that way, it's not reality. But the flip side of that is that they are all living under the same roof for an extended period of time, with no other distractions. They will all spend an enormous amount of time together, so naturally things can and do move along at an accelerated pace. The intimacy factor is quite real."

"I still say he has the royal flush. A bloke stuck in a manor home with nothing better to do but let twelve lovelies dote on his every word? Nay, my heart isna bleedin' for him."

She snorted. "Men."

He had to fight the urge to laugh. "I imagine he might have to contend with one or two cat fights along the way, though. A dozen birds on a mission to land one lucky lad is just asking for trouble."

"I'd love to argue that point with you, but unfortunately I can't. You are right about that. The boxed in atmosphere does tend to enhance the competitive natures of some of the contestants."

"Only natural. But do they want to win for the sake of the win? What if they get to know the guy and aren't interested in him? Can they opt out?"

"Yes, they can, of course."

He glanced her way. "Aye, but do they? That's my question." He watched her shift in her seat. "No, they don't, I'll wager. It becomes something of a sport then, or about ego and pride. Because everyone back home is watching. So it's no' all quite the storybook affair you're painting it to be."

"Not for all of them it's not, no," she answered honestly, "but the point I was making was that it does end up being exactly that for our prince and the woman he falls for . . . and who falls for him."

"What with all the fighting and bitching going on, and the cameras going every second of every day, and them being flung into these over-the-top romantic fantasy dates or what not . . . I don't see where anything real can come of it. Are ye tellin' me he really falls for her? Or for the illusion of this great romance he's been presented with, with none of those pesky real world complications that will come along shortly after? It's more fantasy than reality, it has to be."

"When you spend that many hours with someone, even a group of someones, you're going to get to know them far more quickly, and far more intimately—and I'm not talking physically, per se—than you would in a regular, real-world dating situation. In those cases, you're usually showing the best of yourself, being on your best date behavior, at least until you decide if a relationship is going to develop, then you let down your walls a bit, let the real you shine through. These couples might be given a reprieve from the day to day, real world issues other couples have to contend with, but being that they're around each other all the time, the whole 'date behavior' thing vanishes far more quickly. No one can keep up that front twenty-four/seven, no matter how hard they try. You get to see the real person beneath the perfectly applied date makeup, the perfect date hair, and the perfect date clothes pretty much right off."

"Then it's more a miracle that he chooses any of them, in that case."

She pretended to swat his arm. "Very funny. Trust me, they get to see the real him, too."

"Sounds like they're all in for it, then."

"They are. Why do you think it makes such fascinating television? And you're right, it's not easy for the women to be in a situation where they're all competing for the attention and hopeful affections of one man. And yes, some of their reasons for being there are less than altruistic, or become less so as the contest progresses and their competitive natures kick in. But, in general, for the ones that truly become involved anyway, they're more equipped to better handle the situation than the guy is."

"You mean they're far more willing to strap on the

old ball and chain than he is. Not exactly a shocking bit of news there, now is it?"

"So cynical," she chided.

"Just realistic."

"Then you'd be surprised to know it's quite the opposite."

Dylan glanced over at her. "I find that hard to believe."

"Which just proves my point."

"You're saying these Prince Charmings of yours are really in a mad rush to tie themselves down to just one lass?"

"Men apply for the show because they're ready to settle down, and most of them actually mean it. But they all tend to think like you do, which, broad generalization here, is typical of the breed standard."

"Thanks. I think."

"You're welcome," she said with exaggerated sweetness and a bat of eyelashes.

His lips curved again, and he realized he was actually enjoying himself. She was a piece of work, Erin MacGregor was. Certainly not like any of the local lasses, this Yank.

"In that respect, you're right, they come on the show thinking, 'All these gorgeous women are here for me? Woo hoo! Score!'"

"Aye," he said, nodding. "My point exactly. And why not? 'Tis true, is it no'?" He caught her smug grin from the corner of his eye.

"It can be, and I'm not saying they're against the idea that something long term could come from the adventure, either," she told him, "but more often than not, they really believe that regardless of how things go, they're in full control, calling all the shots. That they'll decide if and when they want to feel something for someone." She shook her head. "And they never see it coming. Until it's too late, of course."

"You're saying he always falls then?"

"That's exactly what I'm saying."

"Well, assuming you've hand picked the lot of them based on his taste, it's no' surprising he'll find himself attracted to some of them."

"I'm not talking about attraction. Of course there is attraction, usually with more than one of the women. We do carefully select the contestants hoping for exactly those kinds of sparks to fly."

"So you're saying the poor bloke actually loses his heart then? Wants the commitment, the whole ball of wax? After such a short run?"

"Why is that so hard to believe?" She said it more rhetorically, as if asking all men to respond, but Dylan took it upon himself to be Everyman.

"Falling in lust, that I can see," he said. "But under such a contrived situation, it just seems as if they might mean well, and even think they're madly in love, but surely when the cameras stop rolling and they reenter the land of the living, breathing, normal lot of us, they come to their senses and realize it was all a kind of emotional illusion. Rather like a holiday fling then, isn't it? Those don't tend to hold up under the harsh examination of real world pressures and stresses."

She laughed. "Says the man who lives in an ancestral mansion on the outskirts of nowhere."

He nodded readily, enjoying her easy directness. Too many people had tiptoed around him for too long, which he'd have said he didn't care one way or the other about. But this felt good. Almost too good. "Touché," he said, his quick concession surprising her, if her raised eyebrows were any indication. "But I was a city lad for a long period of time. I think I know whereof I speak."

Erin started to say something, then apparently thought better of it.

"What?" he asked, already aware it was not her nature to censor herself. Nor, he found, did he want her to.

"Nothing. It's none of my business anyway."

"Since when would that stop you?"

She looked indignant for a moment, her mouth opening, then shutting, then her lips quirked in an endearingly rueful smile as she sat up a little straighter in her seat. "Sometimes it stops me."

He should let well enough alone. The last thing he wanted was her poking about in his personal life any more than she already had. Maybe it was her willingness to see herself clearly, even when the view wasn't entirely flattering. Whatever the case, instead of shutting up and focusing on the road as he should have, and steering the conversation back to her television show romances, he said, "Tell me, anyway. What inappropriate, none-of-your-business remark were you going to make? I've already signed your contract. You don't have to worry about nacking me off now."

"It was nothing really," she insisted. When he shot her a come-on-now look, she shrugged. "Okay, okay. I was just going to say that most of the time you were in the city, you were married, so you weren't exactly a guy on the prowl. But I understand you're a widower, so I thought better of going there, that's all."

She'd said it as matter-of-factly as possible, as if to spare any inadvertent poking at tender spots that she could. So that made it surprisingly easy to respond in kind. "It's been a few years now. I'm through the worst of it. Despite what they'd have you think in town."

He felt her looking at him then, and while it was a little uncomfortable, it wasn't as irritating or intrusive as he'd have expected. Maybe because she didn't know him, and therefore didn't really have any preconceived ideas on what he'd probably felt then, or what she thought he should be feeling now. Unlike every other person in the village, she had no direct, personal knowledge of his life here as a child, no knowledge of his life in the city, and certainly nothing of Maribel, or the supposed fairy-tale marriage that had swept him away from Glenbuie and his chiefly clan duties.

"They care about you," she said. "It's kind of sweet, actually. I'd think it would be nice to know I mattered like that, and to so many. Although I can imagine for you it probably feels a little suffocating."

She really was the most disconcerting sort. But she went on before he could frame a reply, which was just as well because he was suddenly feeling quite revealed. And he hadn't yet said a word.

"Do you miss city life? I mean, not specifically the life you had there with—with, well, you know what I mean. I just meant the overall idea of living in the city, versus living out here. Brodie mentioned you left here pretty young, so you obviously wanted to get out and see the world, which a lot of kids in your position would, I think. Being tucked away out here, as well as the burden placed upon you by your birth."

He nodded. There wasn't anything else to say. It was like she could see inside his head. And he found himself intensely curious as to what she'd ferret out next.

"Was it hard to come back to the slower, bucolic way of life? Where everybody knows your business? And you had to take on the family responsibility and the clan leader role, too." She shook her head and laughed as she waved off her questions. "Never mind. Stupid questions. Of course it wasn't easy. And I'm really putting you on the spot. I'm sorry."

"I don't mind," he said, more stunned than anyone that he meant it.

Early on he'd been too raw to discuss his reasons for coming home with anyone. Later, he'd tried to broach the subject with his brothers, but even though they knew him better than most, he'd been gone a long time, and they were more village-oriented and grounded in Chisholm clan life than he was. As different as each of them were, of the four brothers, he was the true changeling. And at that time, none of them were married or seriously involved. He doubted they'd really understood his reasons for leaving, but the fairy-tale marriage that kept him from coming home again after graduation had smoothed over most of that. They wanted the happily-ever-after for him, as much as they wanted it for themselves. It was the only story that made it okay for him to abandon his birthright.

People forgave a lot for love.

It was a story he'd wanted to believe in, too. So how to tell them it wasn't the fairy tale that had kept him away? Or that it hadn't been much of a fairy tale after all? Just a tragic end. Especially now that his brothers had found their own happily-ever-afters? It had seemed easier to leave them to their beliefs. Cowardly, perhaps. But he could live with that. After all, that was far down on his list of sins.

But now, here, with Erin, he was finally free to express himself honestly and directly, without fear of recrimination or misunderstanding. The opportunity was tantalizing. Almost a relief of sorts. "And you're right," he said. "Initially I wasn't particularly happy to come back to Glenbuie or Glenshire. It was a responsibility I had borne for a very long time, and one, I suppose, I knew I couldn't avoid forever, though I was giving that a pretty good shot."

"What—if you don't mind my asking, what happened to your parents? How old were you when you became next in line, so to speak?"

"They died when I was ten. Car accident. Our grandfather, Finny, raised the four of us. Tristan was barely out of his nappies. But my brothers were more invested in following family traditions than I was. They love Glenbuie, always have, and are truly devoted to this way of life. After I left, I did my best to contribute my share from afar, but I knew it wasn't enough. After Maribel died, the decision to come home was simpler." Though not exactly simple, he thought. Not simple at all.

"And everyone was happy to have you back? No recriminations for being gone so long?"

"I was welcomed home with open arms. I felt a bit guilty about that." Something he'd never spoken aloud until just that moment. But it was okay with Erin. She was . . . safe.

"Why guilty? Do you think you'd have eventually come back anyway, even if the tragedy hadn't occurred?"

It was a question he'd asked himself more than once. "I don't know," he replied honestly. "I suppose if my presence here were required in lieu of actually losing our ancestral property, I'd have figured something out."

"Which isn't really a yes," she said, kindly, but with that little eyebrow arch that added a little ribbing nudge.

"No, I suppose it isn't. But it's the truth."

"Was it because you loved the city that much, or hated it here?"

"Yes," he responded, sending her a short glance, catching her dry smile in response. "It's more complicated than that, though."

"I'm sure it is. Your wife . . . she was a city girl, right?"

"What do you know of Maribel?"

Erin shrugged. "Just what I picked up in town. You're quite the topic, you know. The Great Scot."

He flushed a little at the unasked-for moniker. "Aye, much as it pains me."

"Well, I learned that you met in university, were head over heels in love with her, and stayed in the city after graduating and marrying because she was from a bigwig family who—"

"Bigwig?"

"Sorry, I'm not insulting her, I promise. Important, high society. I'm not sure what your term is for that. Posh?"

Dylan's mouth curved and he didn't fight it this time. "Yes, you could say that about the Leightons. And then some."

"So . . . you stayed in the city for her. But I'm guessing you also stayed for yourself. Hence the guilt?"

He glanced at her, no longer focused on the thrill of the drive, going more on autopilot at this point, having traveled this track often enough to manage it in his sleep if he had to. "Aye," he said, the honest answer easier than he'd thought it'd have been. "Not that she'd have agreed to come home with me if I'd chosen that path, but that was a decision she'd never have to make and she knew that when she married me. She's no' to blame for my avoiding my clan obligations. That decision was mine."

"But because she was in your life, because you were in love, people here sort of forgave you for staying away."

He kept his gaze firmly on the road. "Aye," he said at length.

"So, after . . . you know, did you feel like you had to come back then? Were you ever tempted to just strike out for new territory, start completely over again some place completely fresh?"

"Quite the curious sort, aren't you?"

"I'm sorry," she said, immediately and sincerely contrite. She settled back in her seat again. "You said you didn't mind, but I'm probably poking too much. You should have just told me to shut up."

"I would have if it had bothered me. I think you know me well enough by now to know that much."

She laughed lightly. "True. It's just . . . people interest me. Always have. And your life is so different."

There was nothing generic about her life either, he'd bet. And was surprised to realize he wanted to know more about her. "To answer your question, no, it didn't occur to me to strike out. It was easy enough to leave Glenbuie at the tender age of seventeen, but dinnae confuse that with thinking it was easy for me to put off my role here, put it onto my brothers' shoulders, no matter that they willingly accepted the weight. After Maribel's death, I stayed on in Edinburgh for a short time, but I knew where I'd end up. Life in the city quickly became unbearable for me."

"I can imagine."

"As does everyone else, but it wasnae what people thought. I was forced to confront some truths about myself that weren't so easy to accept. And coming back here made those truths even harder to deal with. But I knew I had no choice but to finally grow up, come home, and take on my due share. Which I have, and am committed to continuing."

"Very noble of you."

He shot her a sideways glance, unsure if there was hidden censure in her seemingly sincere tone. "I certainly make no claim to noble gestures. It was hardly that."

"But you did it, you made the sacrifice. And, from what I can tell, though you're not outwardly enthusiastic in your role as innkeeper, you're doing what you must to make everything work for the best of your family, and the villagers too, I suppose. There has to be some reward in that, a sense of fulfillment."

"Aye, there is. But I wouldn't consider it a sacrifice on my part. I wouldnae return to Edinburgh now, even if my obligations here were to diminish. My reasons for wanting to be in the city, away from here, no longer exist."

She reached across the stick shift and briefly laid her hand on his arm. "I'm sorry," she said, so quietly he barely heard the words over the rush of the wind. "I know you say you've dealt with your loss, but obviously it's changed you pretty profoundly as a person. It might mean good things to the people of Glenbuie, but you did suffer a loss for their gain. I'm sorry for that."

He braked as they approached a turn and let the car roll to a stop near an overlook. He glanced down at her hand, still lightly touching his arm, and tried to remember the last time someone sincerely tried to comfort him, with no other agenda at stake. And the words just sort of tumbled out.

"I didnae come back here grieving the loss of my perfect union. The truths I had to face were about admitting the fact that I'd stayed in a loveless marriage. And no' for any noble reason, as if I believed so deeply in commitment and till death do us part, as I'd told myself for years. I stayed because I knew in my heart it was my only excused escape from contending directly with the burden of my birth. And when I was completely honest with myself, when I truly hit rock bottom, I realized I had probably always known that about my union with Maribel, despite believing myself madly in love in the beginning." He looked up to find her gaze steady on his. "So you see . . . it's everyone in the village who made the sacrifice so I could run off and live this grand life I wanted and thought I was so deserving of. In the end, coming back was the very least I could do. For them. For myself. I'm no' a noble man, Erin. Far from it."

Chapter 8

Erin didn't know what to say to that startling confession. And from the way Dylan suddenly shifted his attention back to the windshield in front of him, he wasn't all that comfortable with it, either.

"So much for being enigmatic," he said.

Erin laughed. He really was quite the paradox. "Oh, I think you still have that one cornered."

He opened his door. "Come on, look at the view."

At the moment, she was perfectly content with a view that contained only Dylan Chisholm, but she realized he probably wanted to be anywhere but trapped inside the small confines of a car, possibly with anyone other than her, so she readily complied.

He gestured toward the railing, then pointed. "That's Glenbuie below."

She was still thinking about what he'd revealed, and, okay, looking at him standing there, all windblown and casually dressed, and finding herself far more intrigued and turned on than she knew she should let herself be, so she was caught completely off guard when she followed the direction of his hand and saw the glorious view sprawled out below. "It's stunning. You can see the whole valley." She edged closer to the rail. "There's the square, the distillery . . ."

"Aye. 'Tis the best view of the village to be had." His voice came from next to her ear, which meant he was standing right behind her.

It sent a shuddery sensation of pleasure through her. She casually crossed her arms in front of her to hide the instant effect it had on her. And also because the contact, even with her own arms, assuaged the ache just a little.

"Beyond the town, those fields on the other side, with the narrow river cutting through them, that is our farming and grazing land." He lifted his hand to point again, grazing her shoulder with his biceps.

She had to drag her attention away from his arm, his hand, his very nice, large hand, the same hand that had gripped her shoulder earlier at the top of the staircase and made her knees go dangerously wobbly . . . Yes, she had to stop looking at him and look at the damn view. If he had any idea where her thoughts were at the moment, he'd likely laugh.

"My youngest brother, Tristan, lives out there." He lowered his arm and rested it on the rail next to her hip, boxing her quite neatly between his very large, imposing body, and the railing in front of her. "Reese's place is back behind the distillery. Brodie lives above the pub still, with Kat, but they're looking to build a home on some of our property west of town."

"It's really quite the legacy," she said, proud that she could form words at all at the moment. Her pulse was thundering and she had to press her thighs together against the rather insistent ache that was building there. No way could Dylan know the ridiculous impact he was having on her senses. He was just playing tour guide, trying to make her forget about what he'd said in the car. "I assume in centuries past, the clan chief was responsible for all of it. Your family took care of the town, the farms, the land, all of it. Wasn't that how it worked?"

"Aye," he said, not putting so much as an inch more distance between them.

She couldn't help it, she turned her head just slightly so she could catch his face from the corner of her eye. He was staring straight ahead, his thoughts perhaps a million miles away. Given the topic of their conversation, it made sense. But it didn't remove the teeny tiny moment of disappointment she felt, confirming what she'd known to be true. Dylan Chisholm wasn't remotely aware of her as a woman. A shame she couldn't say the same about her awareness of him as a man.

She was just deciding how to slither out from between him and the rail without somehow embarrassing herself, when he continued to speak. "It's no' much different now, really. We lease the fields to tenant farmers. The distillery is still the main employer in the village, with the other businesses around the square thriving mostly to support the population that works making whisky."

"So, you still feel somewhat responsible for their welfare? Economically, I mean."

He sighed a little. "Why do you think I agreed to your offer?"

She did turn then. Big mistake. He didn't move right away and her body brushed fully against his. She jerked back, mostly in an instinctive reaction to the hot jolt that went rocking through her on contact, banging her hip against the rail. "Oh!"

She wouldn't have lost her balance, she wouldn't have. Not that time. But it didn't stop Dylan from bracing her hips with his hands and shifting her away from the railing anyway.

"I forgot putting you near a steep drop was a dangerous proposition."

If he only knew. The only thing she was in danger of propositioning at the moment was Dylan. "You startled me. I'm fine, really."

"Really."

Why wasn't he letting her go?

Before she did something extremely foolish, she extricated herself from his grasp. "So, you agreed to the lease because of the villagers?" Her voice was too perky, too . . . just, too. She was striving to be businesslike, but she'd take anything other than breathless. She'd never been the breathless type before.

The corners of his lips quirked and she was instantly entranced. The prospect of getting an actual, honest smile from him tortured her. She wanted one, in the worst way possible, but she didn't think her heart was up to handling it at the moment.

"I told ye, I'm no' a saint. Of course I did it for myself, my family, to help maintain the auld pile. But when I came down to Hagg's that night, it was clear how excited everyone was, and they all made their case for the economic boom it would bring. So it came into consideration. It had to."

"You make it sound like you really don't care, that you're doing it out of obligation, or maybe that leftover guilt. But that's not true, is it? You do care, maybe more than you want to admit." Why was it she couldn't keep her mouth shut around this guy? Who did she think she was? Dr. Phil? "It doesn't matter, really." She waved her hand, ready and willing to dismiss the whole topic, which was totally none of her business. "What matters is that you agreed and everyone wins," she said brightly, thinking it was time to get back in the car, get on with her original plan for the afternoon.

Yeah. Planning fantasy dates. With Dylan. Great.

Why hadn't it occurred to her that getting him to help her find romantic date locations might not be such a great idea? Definitely not clear thinking on her part. A growing problem the more time she spent around him.

"Actually, you're more on track than you know," he said.

She knew better, she did, but she heard herself saying, "I am?"

"There is real value in putting others' needs first, in doing the right thing, even if it's not the thing I'd have chosen for myself alone. I had plenty of years doing exactly that. In the end, it was a hollow achievement, and no' so fulfilling."

She didn't say anything to that. She would have thought he'd had plenty of experience putting others' needs first, what with being married and all. But his declaration in the car, about staying in a loveless marriage so he could hide in the city and avoid his obligations at home still echoed in her mind. Had he really been as self-serving as all that? Sure, he didn't come across as Mr. Happy Innkeeper, but he was literally devoting his entire life to the project.

"Cat got your tongue," he said, at length.

"I'm just . . . processing."

"What part, specifically?"

He was standing in front of her again, only she didn't shrink back this time. Instead she looked up into his face, into those guarded eyes of his. "It's just . . . you strike me as a man who, when he wants something, or believes in something, is very devoted to it, very committed."

"Aye, 'tis true."

"So—" She broke off, shook her head, and this time she did turn away.

A gentle hand on her arm had her turning back. "So, what?" he asked. "No censoring, remember?"

She paused, thinking there was a time for everything

and perhaps now was the time to curb her curiosity about him, for his sake and her own. She had a list longer than her arm of things she needed to be focusing on. Learning more about Dylan Chisholm wasn't on that list.

"Erin."

She sighed. Damn. Her name, with that accent . . . She looked up again. "Okay. You said you stayed in a loveless marriage, but that your reasons for doing so were selfish."

"Aye, they were."

"So the fairy-tale relationship with Maribel—"

"Wasnae much of a fairy tale, I'm sorry to say, for either of us. Perhaps in the beginning, when we were young, quite foolish and headstrong, we believed it to be."

"So . . . you're saying you both . . . fell out of love?"

He nodded. "If we were ever truly in it. She married me to rebel against her parents controlling her every move. I married her because she was the epitome of what I'd dreamed of for the life I knew I was destined to have in the city."

"But you thought you were in love. At some point."

"Oh, aye, quite infatuated we were. But we soon came to realize the infatuation was as much from the rebellion we'd mounted as it was true infatuation with each other."

"So . . . if neither of you loved the other, then why stay together? I mean, you say you did it to keep the fairy-tale premise alive, keep your reason for staying in the city. What about her?"

"Somewhat the same thing, to keep her parents at arms' length. They are excessively wealthy and if given an inch, they tend to take over completely. It was . . . convenient, I guess, for both of us. At the time, if you'd asked me, I would have said we were being quite mature, accepting our limitations and being adult about them."

Erin bit the corner of her lip, then asked the question on the tip of her tongue anyway. "So, did you have an open marriage then?" His immediate look of surprise made her feel inordinately better, which was silly since she wasn't supposed to feel anything where he was concerned. What he did with his life was certainly no business of hers.

"No. We'd have never done that to each other. We had a marriage in full, we had enormous respect for one another, we just weren't madly in love with one another."

"But—"

His lips quirked in that almost smile of his again. "Sex?"

"Well, yeah," she said, swearing she wasn't blushing, but possibly she was, a little bit. Maybe more than a little bit. How sick was it that the idea of him having sex only with his wife was making her hot? Well, the idea of him having sex at all was going to make her hot. Him standing there, breathing, was doing that.

"We knew how to take care of each other. I'll leave it at that."

"It sounds . . ."

"Cold? Clinical? It wasn't. We just . . ." Now he trailed off, then shrugged. "It was what it was. She was on a cruise with some friends of hers in the Mediterranean when . . . when she died. There was a malfunction and the boat essentially blew up. Maribel and the captain were the only ones aboard at the time. Neither survived. I was working insane hours and was out of contact, so the authorities tracked down her parents first." He shifted then, looked at his feet, then out at the view, before looking back at her. "I never quite forgave myself for that. We might not have had the fairy tale, but she deserved better than that from me. She certainly deserved to be protected from them better than I protected her."

"What do you mean? You were next of kin. Didn't you have more legal rights than they did?"

"Technically. But in foreign countries, things can get confused. And her father has deep pockets and knew how to pull strings. To be fair, she was their only child. They were beyond themselves with grief. Maribel was gone and I . . . they handled it like they wanted to . . . and at that point, it was too late to interfere. They had her interred in their family mausoleum. Perhaps I should have fought harder for that, but it was the closest thing to any home she'd have had. We'd never . . . we'd never done anything about that kind of eventuality. Anyway, I tried to stay with them, console them, but they blamed me."

"*How?* You weren't even there."

"Exactly," he said, his tone sardonic, but his expression pained nonetheless. "They were traditionalists. When they weren't nagging us about starting a family, they were begging us to move back into the Leighton manse so they could have what little family they did have around them in their later years. They couldn't understand why we'd take separate vacations, or . . . well, separate anything. They were convinced that had we been together on vacation things would have been different and she wouldn't have died. He trailed off, shook his head. "So I let them do what they needed to do to make peace as best as possible, but I've never really reconciled with the fact that I didn't stand up more for what Maribel would have wanted."

"As you said, she was gone. Her parents are still here." She touched his arm. "You did what you had to do at the time. If she respected you as you say she did, then she'd have understood, right?"

"It's what I tell myself, aye." He let out a short bark of a laugh. "Why in the bloody hell I'm telling you all this I have no blinkin' clue." He gestured to the car. "We're wastin' your valuable time."

Erin turned toward the car, still absorbing everything he'd told her, not sure what to think, or how to feel, then suddenly stopped and turned. He plowed into the back of her, but quickly steadied her with his hands.

"This is becoming quite the pattern with us as well," he said, and the small, but noticeable gleam in his eye made her feel inordinately better.

She hadn't meant to drag him along what had to still be a painful path of memories. "Aye," she said, mocking his accent.

"No' bad," he said, his lips curving a wee bit.

She had an almost unbearable need to make him smile. He might have reconciled himself with his past, and with his future, but something told her he didn't smile nearly enough. "I've a knack for it, dinnae ye ken."

A little bit bigger quirk, almost there. "Why did you turn about?"

"Oh, that." All caught up in that half smile, she'd forgotten. "I just wanted to say I'm sorry. For what you've been through. And for making you relive any of it just to satisfy my curiosity."

"I'm a big lad, Ms. MacGregor. I could have thwarted your questions if I'd wanted to."

"So why didn't you?" The question was out before she thought better of it. But he was inside her personal space again and she didn't think clearly when he was this close. Or in the same room. On the same planet. Whatever.

"You're safe."

"I'm—" *Safe?* Oh joy. That's what every woman

wanted to hear. She felt instantly foolish for entertaining, even for a brief second, that he was feeling some kind of connection to her, as she was beginning to feel with him. Of course he wasn't. She managed a smile, prayed for a casual tone. "Well, if you ever need an ear or a shoulder, I've got two of both."

His hands were resting on her shoulders and he tightened his hold for a brief second. "Thank you." His expression changed, his eyes darkened a bit, and she couldn't for the life of her figure out what he was thinking or feeling. Just when she thought he might say something else, he dropped his hands away and stepped around her, sweeping his arm in front of him toward the car. "Your chariot, miss."

Erin sighed inwardly. Outwardly she gave him a little curtsy. "Thank you, milord."

"Och, dinnae be callin' me that, lass," he retorted with an exaggerated accent that made him sound exactly like the lord of the manor.

She laughed and opened her door before he could do it for her. He had a playful side to him somewhere. It wasn't something she had any business thinking about, much less even consider doing anything about. He was not her project. *Your Prince Charming* was. But there were a couple of fantasy dates to be planned. And the farther away she got him from Glenshire, the more he'd seemed to loosen up. So as long as he wasn't haranguing her about the work crews, or in any apparent hurry to get back, she'd take what help she could get from him. And hey, if it gave him the chance to let his guard down a little and maybe get a much needed break, all the better for both of them. A happy Dylan was in everyone's best interest.

Sure, and that was the only reason she was grinning like a fool as Dylan peeled out of the overlook, spraying gravel behind him.

"Hang on," he said, unnecessarily, as she was gripping the door handle and dashboard, heart in her throat, while he let the car do what it was built to do . . . hug the curves. Tight.

Erin MacGregor, thrill seeker. Who knew? She glanced over at Dylan, who was intently focused on the road, his thoughts his own once again. But he looked like a man on a mission, so she asked, "Do you have a particular destination in mind? Because I was thinking maybe you knew of other nearby villages where there might be something that would suit my—"

"I know just where to take you." He glanced at her briefly, and there was something about the intensity of his gaze, even for that split second, that made her entire body come alive all over again.

I know just where to take you. She swallowed a little sigh. Oh, aye to that. She didn't care where they went, as long as he took her.

She knew she should consider getting herself under control. But she was in a hot sports car, with an even hotter Scot behind the wheel, careening down the side of a mountain, with the sun on her face, the wind in her hair . . . and lust in her heart. She stole another look at him. And had to shift in her seat, press her knees together a little more tightly.

They reached the bottom and the road straightened out as they shot across the valley floor. Low stone walls lined the single track road, with the occasional farming croft and herd of black-faced sheep breaking up the endless sea of brilliant green grass. Not one of the sheep dared to leap in front of them.

She was dying to know where he was taking her, but the silence was companionable if somewhat electric, on her side of it anyway, and it felt good to let someone else be in charge for a change. Like as not, he had no clue what constituted a good date site, but she'd deal with that later. He didn't strike her as being all that romantic-minded, far more the pragmatic sort, given both what she knew of his behavior in person, and the little he'd shared of his past, as well. But he was trying to help. And she was still trying to convince herself that as long as she kept him out of Tommy's hair, she was doing them both a favor.

The valley road eventually became more winding as it sidled along a creek bed. The creek eventually widened into a narrow river, and just before they began climbing into the mountains on the opposite side of the valley, it emptied out into a beautiful loch. The blue sky and sunshine made the water sparkle. "It's gorgeous," she said, finally breaking the comfortable silence.

"Aye." He said nothing else as they began the climb back into the mountains. The Jag didn't tackle the steep ascent with quite the same aggressiveness as their roaring descent earlier, but Erin enjoyed the ride nonetheless. Minutes passed and the foliage blocked the view of the valley floor. Curiosity was finally getting the better of her and she'd just decided to ask him to give her a hint, when he abruptly turned off the main track onto an even narrower road, gravel this time, that took a tightly curved line almost straight up the mountain. Digging her fingers into the leather upholstery, she finally braved a look in his direction. "Wow."

"Almost there."

"Almost where?"

They took another exceedingly tight turn that sent gravel spitting, and the road abruptly dead-ended into a small clearing. A muted roaring sound filled the still midday air. Beyond the small turnaround they were parked in, there was a narrow patch of grass and a skinny stream strewn with boulder sized rocks, wedged between towering stands of pines. "It's lovely, but—"

"Come on," he said, opening his door and getting out.

She slipped off her seat belt and did the same.

"How good are you at hiking?"

Erin looked down at her shoes, which were comfortable lace ups, but far from hiking boots. "Not much on traction," she said, "and I'm kind of fond of these." She glanced at him and smiled in the face of his obvious anticipation. If she didn't know better, she'd swear he was maybe a little excited. Or nervous. Or something. It was that something that made her smile broaden. Whatever on earth could make the Great Scot nervous was something she had to see. "What the hell. I can always buy another pair if I trash these, right?"

He nodded in approval, then gestured for her to go in front of him.

"I don't know where I'm going. Why don't you lead?"

He pointed. "See that trail there, angling off by that split tree trunk? We're headed that way." He stepped up behind her, making her quite aware he was in her personal space again.

Just as she was quite aware she did nothing to move herself out of it, either.

"I'd go first," he added, a teasing note clear in his tone this time, "but ye have this alarming habit of stumbling about. Best I stay behind ye, in case ye need catching."

She shifted just enough to look up at him over her shoulder. His eyes were crinkling at the corners. Probably the sun. But maybe not.

"What?" he asked, making her realize she was staring.

"When was the last time you laughed? Really laughed?" The words were out of her mouth before the thought had even completed itself.

"Far too long ago, I'm certain. I've been busy."

She turned to face him. “Since when did busy and laughter become mutually exclusive?”

“Good point. I have no idea.”

“Before, when you lived in the city, were you happier?”

The question seemed to surprise him. “Since when was happiness measured by laughter?”

“How would you measure it?”

“Fulfillment. Contentment.”

She nodded. “Valid. So, were you? Fulfilled and content?”

“At times. Never completely, but then that’s what provides the drive necessary to fight on, does it not? Are you?”

That gave her pause. She’d poked and prodded him almost since the moment they met. This was the first time she could recall him asking something about her. “No, not completely. But I am happy. Maybe I should have used the word joyful. Are you such a serious man as all that? Or is it life circumstance that has made you so dour?”

“Dour? Dour am I now?”

She merely arched an eyebrow.

He shook his head. “Och, if true, that’s a sad state of affairs then. I’m no’ a dour man, Erin. But perhaps ye have a point about me no’ finding much to be joyful about, not in the sense you mean. But my business has been serious of late. My new life is fulfilling in ways my old life never was. And there is peace in that, which is a good start. The rest will come in time.”

“So you’re saying you’re an optimist.”

“You think me the opposite?”

Now she smiled. “Honestly, I don’t know what to think of you. I guess that’s why I keep badgering you with questions. You aren’t easy to figure out, Dylan Chisholm.”

Amusement did shift into his eyes then, and the resulting gleam was no trick of the sun. She swallowed hard. Perhaps it would be wiser not to provoke the playful side of him after all.

And then he was lifting his hands, pushing back the errant strands of hair the car ride had likely blown into a complete rat's nest around her face. Suddenly painfully aware of her looks, or lack thereof, and at the same time exquisitely aware of his touch, almost to the point of pain, she wanted to shrink away, pretend this moment wasn't happening. Because whatever he was thinking behind those dancing gray eyes of his, no way could it be anything she found herself suddenly hoping, praying, it would be. She didn't attract men like Dylan Chisholm.

Gorgeous, confident, successful men were typically attracted to beauty first, and brains a distant second. Erin was used to falling in the distant second category, okay with it even. When it came to men like the one touching her now, looking at her so intently, well . . . it simply didn't happen. So it had hardly been a problem for her. It would be the epitome of foolishness to allow herself, even for a second, to think this was somehow different.

"I canno' figure you out either, Erin MacGregor," he said, his voice deeper, somewhat rougher, as if . . . as if he were perhaps at least a tiny bit affected by her. Then all rational thought fled, because he was lowering his head toward hers, pressing his fingers into the back of her neck, to tip her face upward to his.

"Ye badger me with yer questions, talk me into abandoning my own home . . ." He lowered his head further until his mouth was hovering just above her own.

He couldn't be, wasn't going to—

"Ye sneak into my dreams, haunt my waking hours. I dinnae understand it. What've ye done to me, lass?"

She haunted his dreams? In a good way? "Dylan—"

He made a guttural noise at the sound of his name that had a little instinctive moan of her own escaping her lips.

"I havena felt a hunger such as this in a very long time. Will ye allow me the pleasure?"

He was asking permission? Did he not realize that a second or two more of his heated whisperings and he could have her naked on the hood of his Jag?

He brushed her lips with his. "Perhaps I havena been the most merry of fellows, but if there has been anything to cause me to want a bit of respite from the endless hours of work, it has been you."

"I thought I made you crazy."

And there it was. The smile she'd been waiting for. It was slow to happen, but as it stole across his face, his entire countenance changed, as if he was lit from within. There was fire there, passion. "Aye, that you do. Yer trouble, Erin, with a capital T. Ye plague me."

"A plague am I," she said, but the intended dry sarcasm was somewhat offset by the breathy quality of her voice.

Which served to widen his smile further. "You have refreshing candor, and a smart mouth. You don't seem to care overly much what I think."

She tipped her head back slightly, to look fully into his eyes. "And that's attractive to you? Hard to believe I'm still single with those lovely attributes."

He rubbed his thumbs along the corners of her mouth, making her shiver at the feeling of his work-roughened fingers on her skin. "Hard." Then he slipped his arms around her waist and brought her fully up against him. "Aye, 'tis that."

She barely had time to register the stunning truth, shocked silent by the rigid proof pressing against her midsection. Then he claimed her mouth with his own and any hope of rational thought fled completely.

The hot thrill of being sheltered against the hard length of his body, feeling his hands on her, his mouth on her, swamped her senses. His kiss was insistent and compellingly seductive. Forceful and inviting. An intoxicating combination she had no hope of resisting. Not that she made any real effort.

Where had this come from?

He slid his hands up her back, into her hair, then tipped her head further back, so he could slant his mouth more fully across hers, take the kiss even deeper. She clutched at his shirt as he slowly seduced her lips apart, then took his sweet time seducing the rest of her mouth. She shifted more tightly against him, as he slid his tongue along hers.

Her hands were caught between them, fisted in his shirt, curled against his chest. Just as she thought maybe she should become a more involved participant in her own seduction, and began sliding her hands up to his shoulders, he was ending the kiss, lifting his head. Quite breathless, she was struck uncharacteristically speechless and, for that moment anyway, could do little more than stare up into his face. Oh, the way he was looking at her. She had to fight like hell to keep her knees from giving away completely. Just once, she wanted to stay balanced around him.

"I've taken advantage," he said, his voice even sexier all rough and raspy like that.

She noted he hadn't offered an apology. Good. "I'm a big lass." Her voice wasn't much more than a croak. She tried to tell herself it was a very alluring croak. "I could have stopped you if I had wanted to."

That light was still there in his eyes. "What a curious pair we are," he said, smoothing his thumbs across her cheek bones.

She'd never get enough of his touch. It was like he'd found her ON switch, and wouldn't take his finger off it. She should step back, gather herself, realign her thoughts. Instead, she said, "Are we?" The question just slipped out. "A pair I mean."

She sighed as he pressed his thumb against her lower lip. Who knew he was such a sensualist? She could get very used to his constant need to touch, stroke, soothe. The needier the better.

"I've no idea what we are," he said. "All I know is that you're no closer to leaving my arms now than a moment ago."

"Is that why you kissed me? To prove a point about attraction?"

His smile was so natural and easy, she couldn't imagine how he'd kept it hidden away so long. "Shh. We're looking at fantasy date locations. Go with it."

She stiffened slightly. So this *was* all some kind of sport? A tweak at what he thought was her silly television show? "So you're just selling your location then?" She scrambled hard to keep up, to not let him know how deeply he'd affected her with that kiss. Hell, even before the kiss. She tried for an admonishing, teasing smile. She'd traveled the world, she could be cosmopolitan about this. "I have to tell you, a gravel lot, no matter how remote and pristine the surrounding forest, is still just a gravel lot."

She couldn't tell if he'd bought her attempt at casual insouciance or not. True, she hadn't made any concerted effort to step away from him. But there was that very real proof that the sparks hadn't been totally one-sided. Of course, that didn't always mean anything with men.

"We're not there yet," he told her, not moving either.

"So why—"

"I got sidetracked."

"Proving a point."

"No." He urged her face closer to his again. "Satisfying curiosity. Something you've been doing all day. Fair is fair, after all."

"Dylan—"

His pupils swallowed up the gray of his eyes at the sound of his name on her lips. Did she really affect him like that? It made her feel powerful and utterly female, or want to, anyway, and he did a lot to make her think she might be, but she was afraid that the instant she gave in to it, the joke would be on her.

Then he tugged her closer and there was that spark, that sizzle. That rock-hard body. "I still have a few questions," he said, his lips brushing hers.

She dug her fingers into his chest, clutching at his shirt once more, wishing like hell she could clutch at her own self control as easily. "Such as?"

He dipped his head and nipped at her chin, making her breath hitch. "Such as, will she kiss me back this time?" Then he took her mouth again, kissing, nibbling, teasing, entering . . . and left it up to her to satisfy his curiosity. And maybe satisfy her own.

Chapter 9

She tasted sweet, like cinnamon and honey. Her lips were so soft, her mouth so inviting. She'd badgered and queried, been honest to a fault, and caring beyond necessity. And he had no business playing with her like this. This hadn't been his intention at all when he'd climbed into the car. How exactly she'd so completely seduced him, he still didn't fully understand.

But whatever slender thread of hope he had of reclaiming his wits, was instantly and quite thoroughly dashed when he heard her make that little grunt of unmistakable need as she nipped at his bottom lip. She urged him closer, then went searching for his tongue with her own. His reaction was swift, urgent, almost primal. He wove his fingers into her hair and shifted her mouth beneath his, so he could take over the kiss, take her.

But she wasn't having any of it. She shifted her mouth to his chin, and murmured, "You said it was my turn."

He grinned against her cheek. He should have known that, even where she was most vulnerable, she'd still be direct about what she wanted. "I said I wanted to know if you'd kiss me back." He teased her earlobe with his teeth, then pressed a hot kiss to the tender spot just below it, making her gasp, and his body twitch. Hard. "You did. After that, all bets were off."

"Hmm," was all she said, then bit his chin.

Not hard, but hard enough to make the fit of his jeans tight to the point of serious discomfort. His heart was pounding and every inch of his body was poised and ready. He felt such an intense rush of excitement, of anticipation, like he hadn't felt in . . . in forever. He should slow down, he knew that, but it felt so damn good. Almost too bloody damn good.

And she wasn't even his type.

Yet he was utterly fascinated. He'd never met anyone like her. She'd been a lovely source of amusement, what with her brash manner and take-no-prisoners conduct, but nothing more. Determined, aye, and smart, but so sublimely unaware of her own appeal, he'd never thought himself truly at risk. Yet, here he was, with a hunger so voracious even he was startled at the power of it.

He'd do well to remember she was also the source of most of his frustration. She'd taken over his entire home, for god's sake, and all but booted him out of it in the doing. Glenshire should be his only concern at the moment, not this overwhelming need he had to know what she tasted like . . . everywhere.

Then she was sliding her hands up the nape of his neck, burying her fingers in his hair, raking her nails along his scalp as she urged him closer still. He was helpless against those throaty whimpers of need, so he opened for her adventurous little tongue, let her tease her way inside his mouth, reveling in the way she tipped his mouth to fit hers, for her own enjoyment and pleasure. Och, but she went after what she wanted and that more than anything sealed his fate.

Then she was sliding her tongue along his, almost sinuously, almost—almost—in a way that spoke of more experience than he'd have attributed to her. It both aroused and disconcerted him. Why should he care what her past experiences were? Maribel hadn't been a virgin when she'd first come to his bed, and neither had he.

He'd spent the night in more than one bed after Maribel's death. Whether it was to numb the pain, punish himself for not being a better husband, punish Maribel for abandoning him, forcing him to rethink his life, his future, his . . . everything, he hadn't known, or much cared at the time. All he'd known was that he'd crawled out of their beds feeling more hollow than when he'd crawled in. And when he'd finally taken his leave of the city, he'd left that pattern of behavior behind as well.

But he didn't feel numb. And he didn't feel hollow. In fact, he couldn't remember feeling more alive, so fully sensate, in a very, very long time.

He claimed Erin's teasing tongue, no longer willing to let her dictate the course, but unwilling to let her withdraw, either. He dueled with her, pulled her up against him so her feet left the ground, allowing him to press himself fully between her thighs, letting her know in no uncertain terms the full extent of what was happening here. Her grunts became moans, her fingers fisted more tightly in his hair. His own groan of need became a growl, as he cupped her buttocks and urged her to wrap her legs around his hips.

She broke their kiss first, but only so she could avail herself of the access to the tender side of his jaw, which she nibbled and nipped her way along quite expertly as he began to feverishly look about for a solid surface to pin her against. Those little whimpering growls were driving him mad. And standing entwined in a parking lot, no matter how tightly she'd wrapped those gloriously strong legs of hers around his waist, was simply not satisfying his hunger.

And then the roaring noise of his own heartbeat was superseded by a louder, more incessant thunder. *Bloody hell yes, that was it!* The tranquil little spot, the wide flat rock, positioned just across the glistening pool, opposite the roaring waterfall he'd brought her here to see, would be the perfect spot to finally feel the full, soft length of her wrap itself around the full, achingly hard length of him.

"Hold on," he instructed her, hitching her hips up higher, swearing under his breath when she rubbed intimately against him.

She murmured something against his throat, but was too busy tracing her tongue along the side of his neck, and nipping his ear lobe, to do more than tighten her ankles around his back as urged. Dear lord she was going to kill him before he could get them down the path. And that was assuming he could walk.

It was amazing, the sort of supernatural powers a man could attain when he hungered for something deeply enough. And oh, he hungered.

He staggered across the small lot, and found more by feel than by sight, the well-worn path that led down to the base of the falls. There was a narrower, ascending trail that snaked off to the right, into the rocks, following the stream upward into the mountains, eventually leading to the head of the falls and a stunning view. He'd had that trail in mind when he'd headed this way.

At the moment, however, he had only one view in mind. Erin. Naked. Splayed on that rock.

"Where are we—?"

"Shh," he murmured, dipping his head to take her mouth again, stumbling half blindly down the path.

She kissed him back, giving all of herself in it,

which moved him as much as it aroused him. It made no sense, this gentle affection that kept rearing its nonsensical head within him. Not that he wasn't a gentle man, or couldn't be, but . . . he didn't know her well enough to stir up those sorts of feelings. This was about pure animal attraction, nothing more.

But she was already sliding her mouth from his, her eyes blinking open, then squinting against the shafts of sunlight that lasered through the tree limbs overhead. "What is that sound?"

"You'll see."

It was as if opening her eyes and speaking had broken some sort of spell. She squirmed lightly against his hold. "You can put me down. I can walk." He thought he heard her add "I think" under her breath, but her squirming was putting his already sorely strained control to the test. And, dammit, he didn't want reality to quite intrude just yet.

Reality. Fantasy.

He was rather wishing they'd never engaged in debating that particular topic.

"Erin—"

"I need—"

They both spoke at the same time, both broke off. Dylan paused on the path, not halfway there yet. Their gazes caught and held for what felt like an interminable moment. Her eyes were a bit unfocused, her lips a little puffy, her cheeks flushed, and her hair, well, was even messier than normal. She looked like a woman who'd been quite enjoying a man's attentions. His. The mere thought of which kept him right on edge. Such an oddly possessive feeling.

And then her lips twitched, before she gave in to a smile that set those heavy-lidded eyes to sparkling once again. He wasn't certain which part of her entranced him more.

"You know this is crazy. What do we think we're doing?" She pushed gently at his shoulders until he very reluctantly let her go, steadying her as she let her feet drop to the ground, before moving just far enough away that they no longer shared any contact.

As disappointed as he was with this sudden turnabout, he found himself smiling in return. "Testing out the fantasy date site, of course. You do seem the sort who likes to be thorough with her work."

She laughed. "Uh, not typically that thorough."

"I wasn't implying that you—"

"No, no, I know that. I—" She broke off, made a short sound of disbelief, then shook her head. "I, uh, will admit I don't normally just throw myself at someone, however."

"I didn't feel jumped," he said. "In fact, if anyone did the throwing, it was me." He heard the disbelief in his own voice, which she clearly picked up on, if her bemused expression was any indication.

"So . . . why did you?"

He tilted his head. "Why did you let me?"

"No fair, I asked first."

"If I knew the answer, I'd tell you."

"That hard to comprehend is it?" She said it with easy self-deprecating humor, but he didn't miss the momentary flicker of vulnerability in her eyes.

He didn't dare allow himself to ponder that rarely seen side of her or why it affected him so. His body was taking its sweet time calming down, and, as it appeared their momentary lapse of judgment was going to be just that, he thought it was probably best to let things . . . subside. Still, he gave her as honest an answer as he could. She'd been nothing less with him. "I could give you a list, but it's still sorting itself out and I've no desire at the moment to poke and prod at it." He held out his hand. "Come on, let me at least show you the site."

Initiating contact with her of any kind at the moment was putting his barely restored control at grave risk, but he tempted fate all the same. He might not fully understand his response to Erin MacGregor, but he wasn't willing to dismiss it entirely out of hand either.

She looked from his extended hand, to his face, then back to his hand.

"It'll suit your needs, promise."

She looked as if she was going to say something, then stopped herself. He hadn't missed the wee bit of sparkle in her eyes.

He wagged a finger. "Uh-uh. None of that. We decided no censoring."

"Yes, but when we made that decision, there wasn't so much at stake."

He raised a brow. "Such as?"

She rolled her eyes. "Please. Don't play coy with me now." She skirted past him and took a few steps farther down the path. She grinned at him over her shoulder. "I was about to say, what makes you so sure you know what my needs are? But I didn't stop myself because of censoring."

He followed her. "So why did you stop then?"

"Because, I'm pretty sure you do."

His body leapt in response, even as he laughed at her easy confession. "Are we talking about the fantasy date for the show?"

A wiggle of her eyebrows was her only response, then she turned around and continued striding down the path.

The roar of the falls grew louder with every step they took. And didn't come close to competing with the roaring sound inside his head as he watched every bounce and roll of her hips. He also made no attempt to catch up. He needed a few moments to process, at least a little bit, what was going on here. And what he wanted to go on next. It was one thing to go with the heat of the moment, then later he could say he'd merely been caught up. Now that he was being given time to think, that excuse would no longer hold up.

Anything he might do now would be deliberate and with intent. So . . . what was his intention where Erin was concerned? She was only here temporarily, so, realistically, it didn't much matter what he might want. Or not want. Any man in his right mind would simply enjoy the moment, take what came his way, and be thankful for it.

He'd never been accused of spending much time in his right mind.

The truth of the matter was, his attentions were engaged. And he was no longer the kind of man who could be cavalier about such things. It had been too long. He'd been through too much. From the outside looking in, this might appear to be the perfect setup for him. A way to get a read on how whole and healthy he truly was these days where matters of the body were concerned. Unfortunately, he couldn't focus on the body without the soul coming along for the ride.

He watched her saunter down the path. Saunter. That was Erin's style. Self-assured, without being cocky. She was no femme fatale in the traditional bombshell sense. She didn't exude sexuality. But she had an innate confidence about her, a true measure of self, a determined sense of purpose, that all combined to overrule her less-than-overt femininity and command attention anyway. So different from the cool, sophisticated, aloof woman who was quite aware of her sexual allure and understood it for the asset it was, whether the arena was professional or personal, and wouldn't dream of leaving such a vital resource untapped.

He understood that woman, knew how to play in her

world, knew what the rules of engagement were, regardless of whether the field of play was a boardroom table, or a down-filled bed.

He had no clue what to make of a woman like Erin. Had no idea what the rule book said, much less the stakes involved. She didn't wield sexuality like a tool. She didn't wield it at all. He couldn't imagine it had ever occurred to her that she even had that particular weapon in her arsenal. She was a woman entirely without artifice. Crafty and canny, yes, but also honest and direct about her intentions, her wants, her desires. With Erin there were no rules other than a call for forthrightness.

And he wanted her so badly he could taste it.

"Oh," she gasped, stopping abruptly at a turn in the path. "Wow."

Dylan stepped up behind her, knowing the exact scene she was gazing upon. Just beyond the turn, the path widened into a clearing that extended all the way to the large pool at the base of the falls. From this side, you could wade directly into the water and swim across the pool to the immense flat rock that sat squarely in the middle of the opposite side, tucked into the base of a sheer mountain wall. Or you could walk a short way downstream, and cross on foot where a heavy rock bed provided a natural bridge to the other side. The trees hid the view up to the top of the falls and Erin walked to the edge of the pool so she could take in as much as she could.

"It's beautiful. Powerful," she added, having to raise her voice a little to be heard over the thundering roar. "Like a place out of time, totally untouched."

He stopped next to her. "It's no' well known, only locals know of it." He pointed to the right of the pool. "That trail leads up to the top of the falls. It's not a difficult climb, takes about half an hour. The view from the top is truly spectacular. If you like the site, you might consider—"

"It's perfect," she said, and he could hear the excitement in her tone, even as he watched her expression change to that determined, all-business one he was coming to know well.

She'd already switched gears back into professional mode. He should be thankful. Relieved. Whatever it was she provoked in him was probably better left unexplored. But that didn't keep him from watching her every move as she set out to explore the immediate area. He caught up with her as she started across the rock bed. Without waiting to be asked, he reached for her elbow and braced her as she took small steps, balancing from one rock to the next. Other than a quick glance in his direction, she said nothing. But she didn't turn down the offer of assistance, either.

Such a pathetic sod, he thought, so happy to have any continued contact with her at all. Clear proof how conflicted he was over what to do about her.

Erin paused just before reaching the other side, but before Dylan could adjust his footing, she made a leap for the bank, jerking him completely off balance when he didn't release her elbow in time.

"Sorry!" she called out as he swore and went splashing into the water.

Fortunately he kept his balance and didn't completely humiliate himself, but his shoes and the legs of his pants were soaked clear through.

"I'm so sorry! I didn't realize you were holding on so tightly."

He sloshed out of the water, up onto the bank next to her. "Not a problem." He glanced at her. "I'm getting used to it."

"Hey, I didn't lose my balance this time. I totally stuck my landing." At his lifted brow, she shook her head. "I take it you don't watch much in the way of gymnastics."

"Can't say that I do."

She smiled and held out her hand. "Come on, we'll go sit on that rock and you can dry out a little." He looked from her hand, to her, and got a raised eyebrow in response. "I didn't hesitate when you offered."

"Yes, you did."

Her lips quirked. "True. But for completely different reasons."

"None of which included being afraid for your safety."

"Oh, I wouldn't say that. In fact—"

He took her hand and tugged her forward, catching her by surprise, but stepping forward just in time to take the brunt of the impact of her body against his, keeping her from stumbling into the water. He wrapped an arm around her waist and held her against him. "You're in no danger with me," he said, looking down into her eyes.

"If you believe that, you sorely underestimate your impact on the fairer sex."

The corners of his mouth kicked up a little. "Really?"

She rolled her eyes at him, but just as he started to lower his head, she pushed free and strode ahead of him, back toward the falls, and the flat rock.

He followed, grinning like a loon, suddenly completely unconcerned with his water-filled shoes and sodden pant legs.

She clambered up onto the rock with more fortitude than grace and scooted across until she was facing the falls, her feet dangling from the other side. He hoisted himself up after her, and slid across until he was in the middle, before unlacing his work boots.

"It is truly a gorgeous spot. You can almost see the top from this side." She glanced over her shoulder. "I really am sorry about getting you wet."

He braced himself and stuck one foot in her direction. "A wee tug if you don't mind."

She shot him a dry look. "And send me tumbling off into the water?"

He gave her his best, Who? Me? look, then waggled his foot. "Give a chap a hand, will you?"

She scrambled to her knees and took hold of his boot, taking no chances and wiggling it free rather than yanking at it. Once she'd gotten that one off, he stuck out the other one, earning another look, but she went at it with the same determination she did everything else.

"Thank you," he said, once she'd freed him of the second one. He peeled off his socks and spread everything out off to the side where the direct summer sun was beaming through the trees.

"Least I could do," she said, then returned to her spot, admiring the falls and the view.

True, he thought with an inward sigh, given he'd already imagined her doing quite a few other things on this very rock. He shook those images free and rolled up his pant legs, before sliding next to her, letting his feet dangle next to hers. She didn't look at him, but continued her study of the area. She didn't scoot away either.

"So," he said, at length, suddenly feeling a wee bit like a naff lad on his first real date. "Do you think this will suit the needs of your Prince Charming?"

"It's not his needs I'm concerned about."

And just like that a certain part of his anatomy stood up and saluted. "Oh?" he managed to choke out, and casually shift a little on the rock to find a bit of comfort . . . and hide his reaction from view. Naff lad, indeed.

She sent him a sideways glance. "I'm fairly certain he'll be so happy with some alone time away from the tension in the house, that he won't care much where he is. Besides, who wouldn't love spending an afternoon here? A romantic picnic, followed by a swim under the falls?"

He held her gaze and the silence grew between them as awareness sprang to life again in her eyes. "Would that appeal to you, then? Are you a romantic?"

"Given what I do for a living, that seems rather obvious." She'd said it easily enough, but there was the telltale shifting of her gaze, away from his and back to the falls.

He'd lay odds she wasn't really seeing anything at the moment. "No' so obvious, I don't think."

There were a few moments of silence, then she said, "Do I come across otherwise? Like someone who doesn't appreciate the romance in life?"

"I didna say that."

She looked directly at him. And he had to fight not to smile. Even when she was put in an uncomfortable situation, she couldn't hide from it for long. Direct confrontation was her style. "So, what are you saying then? I don't strike you as a romantic woman? Just because I don't polish my nails, or wear tight—"

He cut her off with a kiss. To his surprise, she let him. Which was likely why he gentled it almost immediately. For someone with a tart tongue, she tasted remarkably sweet. Like warm morning pastries. Her kisses were the only thing about her that weren't always determined and bold. The gentler he was, the more tentative she became, almost too willing to let him lead. It both aroused him and made him want to do something, anything, to get her to unleash the real Erin here, too.

When he lifted his head, they both had to take a moment or two to gather themselves. He spoke first. "I never said I didn't think you were romantic. I'm surprised you didna accuse me of it. I thought you might laugh when I brought you here."

"Laugh? Why? It's perfect."

"Given our conversations, given what you know of me, I'd have imagined you didn't think I had it in me. To know of such a place, much less consider it a romantic spot."

She cocked her head slightly. "I don't know. You've struck me from the beginning as someone who is passionate about what he believes in, what he wants. You don't shy from commitment, or giving your all. Does that make you a romantic, no. But . . ." She trailed off, dipped her chin and broke eye contact.

He tipped it back up again. "But, what?"

The corner of her mouth twitched. "You'll think I'm as big a sap as the women who come on our show looking for love."

"So?"

She playfully swatted at him.

He smiled. "There's nothing wrong with being a wee bit sappy now and again."

"Well, you don't strike me as the sort to be sappy, or appreciate it in others. But a man who is passionate about anything in his life, is probably, at least at heart, a man who understands the kind of passion I'm talking about, even if he's not the living embodiment of it."

Dylan knew exactly what she meant, and knew that once again, she'd seen something inside him most people didn't. But there was something else in her tone, something . . . personal. "Aye, I'll agree with ye." He caressed the length of her jaw with his fingertips. "But I'm no' so sure if you're talking about me . . . or yourself."

"Hmm," she murmured. "Good point."

His smile was slow, easy. He couldn't recall the last time he'd felt so relaxed, so at peace. "I've been known to make one, once in a great while."

Her smile was equally slow, equally easy. "Have you now?"

He slid his hand around the back of her neck, and tugged her closer, angling his body to press her back until she was lying on the rock beneath him.

"Dylan—"

"Shh."

"We shouldn't—I don't have time to—"

"Just another minute or two," he said quietly. "After all, reality will intrude soon enough, and this moment will pass. Don't we deserve a peek at the fantasy every once in a while, too?" He kissed the side of her neck, then the soft spot just beside her ear, then gently bit her jaw, making her gasp and her hips shift beneath his. It was a dangerous game he played, as his body continued its urgent insistence to go farther.

But entirely worth the risk when she reached for him and pulled his mouth down to hers.

Chapter 10

"Yes, Tommy. No, no I didn't forget about the phone conference at three." Which was a total lie. She'd been so wrapped up in Dylan, she'd completely lost track of time. "Yes, I know, Daisy is helping me with site plans. I know it's not your responsibility to talk to—yes, I'll call her, too, just as soon as—" Erin broke off, scowled at her phone, and continued to listen in barely sustained silence, then her mouth dropped open. "They're coming in a day early? But we're not—yes, I know, I know. Yes, I've got that . . . situation under control." She darted a quick glance at Dylan. Another lie. Probably. He hadn't said a word about his issues with the workers at Glenshire, nor had she. But she was certain that was only a matter of time. "I'm almost there, five minutes."

Dylan already had the car flying along, hugging the tight mountain curves, his attention exclusively on the road. Erin had much preferred the way things were about a half hour ago, when his attentions had been exclusively focused on her.

"I'm sorry," she said to him as she pocketed her cell

phone when Tommy finally finished his latest rant. He'd called twice already, barking instructions and demanding information. It was a miracle they'd gone as long as they had without interruption. It was even more of a miracle that she'd let herself get so far off track. Her schedule was beyond tight and yet there she was, cavorting on a rock beside a waterfall . . .

Sure, she could tell herself she deserved some personal time now and again, and if Tommy hadn't called when he did, who knew what she'd be doing right now? Except that, whatever it was, she imagined it would have involved a lot less clothing. Dammit. "I wouldn't be surprised if we hear from him again before we get back."

"Don't worry about it."

She glanced Dylan's way, then back to the road ahead. He hadn't seemed particularly perturbed by the abrupt end to their impromptu interlude. In fact, it was hard to tell by the set expression on his face what he was thinking. Erin sighed in silence. As fantasy date sites went, Dylan had picked a winner. And thank God she had that much to give Tommy. The problem for Erin, however, was that, as a fantasy date, Dylan had pretty much been a winner, too. So much so, she'd actually let herself believe she could have the fantasy, at least for a few blissful hours. When she damn well knew she had no business thinking about anything but business.

Dylan hadn't said three words to her since they'd left the falls and climbed back in the Jag. Possibly because she'd spent the bulk of that time with her phone stuck to her ear. But possibly he'd also realized, as she had, that it was just as well things hadn't gone any further than that last kiss.

Sure, they were both consenting adults, but getting intimately involved with a client was never a good idea, and where Dylan Chisholm was concerned, most definitely asking for trouble. The things he did to her with hardly more than a smoldering glance were downright illicit and should be illegal. Probably were in a few states back home. He made her want to be reckless and to act with complete and total abandon. Which she'd been well on her way to doing before her cell had decided to play chaperone. And with her schedule? That was a surefire way to end up on the unemployment line.

She told herself their little interval this afternoon was a good thing. A learning experience. She'd been mooning after Dylan to some degree since she'd first laid eyes on him. She'd known even then the infatuation was silly and foolish, even if her attraction hadn't turned out to be wholly one-sided. A fact that still boggled her, but then the man had been holed up in a tumble down manor house in the middle of nowhere for almost two years. Probably anybody new—meaning anyone he hadn't grown up with—would have sparked his flame.

Didn't matter. Today had been proof positive that she couldn't handle anything close to hot sex on a flat rock while simultaneously trying to do her job. She'd blown both the conference call with the network and her meeting with Daisy. Completely out of character for her. And Dylan had been a major distraction even before he'd kissed her. If she'd gotten naked with him? Her mental lecture paused for a brief moment of highly visualized fantasy before she shut it down. Reluctantly. No. No flinging, highland or otherwise. She was definitely not cut out for it.

It was all fine to say she wasn't going to get involved with Dylan because he was a client, but the truth was more problematic than that. She'd known him such a short time, but realized after their talk today during the car ride that she already risked emotional involvement. Yes, Dylan drove her crazy, but she was undeniably intrigued by him. The more she got to know, the more she wanted to know. And that curiosity would only lead her on a path to total job destruction.

The sweaty, highly detailed, exceedingly erotic dreams she had of him every night proved she was already more than just a little invested. And after today? She had to press her knees together against the renewed ache that sprang to life between them. God only knew what lay in store for her when she finally closed her eyes tonight.

But that was between her and her decidedly sex-addicted subconscious. No one had to know about those dreams but her. Maybe she should be thankful for them. After all, they would have to fill the void she couldn't let Dylan fill for real. That she couldn't even let him dare try to fill.

Better for all involved that she'd learned her lesson now, before anybody ended up getting hurt. Namely her. While Dylan was hardly a player, she doubted he was looking for emotional involvement of any kind at the moment. They'd shared a few laughs, a few kisses. Now they'd go back to dealing with real world issues and put this firmly where it belonged. In the realm of a fantasy fairy tale that would never be told.

No harm, no foul.

She leaned back against the head rest. Who was she kidding? Her job required her to spend most of her waking hours thinking about fantasy fairy tales. Would it have killed the gods of fate to let her have just a wee bit of hot Scot sex? Hmm? She would have gotten over it. And Dylan. Eventually.

"Is there a problem?"

His sudden question startled her. "I'm sorry, what?"

"You've sighed quite heavily a few times and I was just wondering if everything was all right."

"No, no—I mean yes. Yes, I'm fine. Just thinking about . . . work." She sat up straighter and risked a brief glance at him. She caught him doing the same with her, but before she could read anything in his eyes, he turned his attention back to the road.

"Is there a problem with the production? You said something to your boss about something happening a day early?"

"Oh. That." Of course he wasn't thinking about her, or worried about her. He was thinking about Glenshire and the precious production crew presently nailing and hammering away at four hundred years of his family heritage. She wasn't going to compete with that. What happened back there by the falls had been a momentary blip out of time for him, too. An aberration caused by long hours, too much stress, and . . . and . . . opportunity. It wasn't like it was going to happen again.

"Aye, that," he echoed.

"It seems the chartered flight bringing the women from London to Edinburgh, flew them all the way to the private strip we're using in Inverness."

"So?"

"So, we had reservations for them and their handlers in Edinburgh for another few days, until filming started. We're not ready to move them into—"

"My house." His jaw was definitely tighter now. His mind was definitely not on getting her naked any longer.

"Yes." She sighed with regret, but forced herself to move past it. "And the hotel in Glenbuie is full with production staff."

"What difference does it make where you put them?"

"Secrecy is key. We don't unveil the names of the contestants until just before the show actually airs. And that's not for four months."

He glanced at her. "Four months? But you said—"

She smiled at him. "Now, don't get your kilt in a

knot. Production is eight weeks. But there is a long post-production time when we actually go through all the hundreds of hours of film and put the show together. We have to decide on the story arcs for each contestant, how much air time to give them, who will fill what role—"

"What do you mean, 'role'? I thought this was unscripted."

"It is. But when you put a group of women under one roof, different personalities surface."

"Such as?"

"Well, there are usually types, you know, like the den mother, the goody-two-shoes, the wild child, the girl next door, the bad girl, the repressed virgin, the girl with her biological clock ticking, the villain—"

"You mean the bitch."

"Pretty much."

He shook his head. "I imagine you putting a dozen women under one roof competing for the attention of one poor sod and they'll all have their try at that role at one point or another."

"Well . . ." He shot her a droll look and she laughingly conceded. "Maybe you have a point."

"I still say it's an unnatural way to find a mate, but it's no' of my concern. What is of my concern is how your men are handling some of the installation work—"

He was just pulling into the courtyard in the rear of Glenshire as he launched into that discussion, which was cut mercifully short when the Jag was immediately swarmed with crewmen and production assistants, all vying for Erin's attention, talking over each other. She raised her hand, and when that didn't work, she let out a shrill whistle. "Hold up, will you? Let me get out of the car, then I'll deal with you one at a time."

She started to open the door when Dylan put his hand on her arm. "Erin."

She looked back at him. "I'm sorry, but things look crazy and—"

"And you'll need to squeeze me into your busy schedule sometime today." He said it in a flat tone that brooked no argument, but which definitely got the attention of several of the assistants standing closest to her door.

She immediately pasted on a professional smile. "Mr. Chisholm, I—"

"I believe I fulfilled some of your needs today," he said, a very wicked gleam leaping to his eyes, clearly not willing to accept her attempt at pasting a professional, business-like face on their outing. "Now I believe it's time you address some of mine."

He topped that off with a knowing grin. Much to the rabid delight, she was sure, of the same gossip-loving staffers. Ruddy bastard. Who'd have thought he had it in him? It would race through the entire staff in less than the time it took her to cross the courtyard. In fact, she turned and caught two staffers tapping away on their BlackBerrys. A direct glare had them both pausing. "Could one of you find Tommy for me?" she asked tightly. "I need to see him right away."

Without waiting, she turned back to Dylan, tight-jawed smile firmly in place, though what he might have seen in her eyes, she wasn't entirely sure. That smile of his . . . well, having become only recently acquainted with it, she wasn't exactly immune to it just yet.

"This evening," he reiterated, before she could say anything. "However late. I'm a night owl."

It was a losing battle to continue this debate here and now. "I'll see what I can do."

He drew his hand down her arm. "See that you do."

She was doing fine until his fingers brushed her skin like that. She shivered. Her throat worked, but her brain didn't. "I—"

"Erin?" Despite his less than dominant stature, Tommy's strident bellow managed to rise above the collective courtyard noise.

Jerked out of her descent into the haze of Dylan lust, she didn't waste any more time and immediately got out of the car, not caring if he saw her scrambling retreat as cowardly. She'd deal with him later. Chances were he just wanted to talk about his concerns with the crew, which she knew he wasn't going to simply forget about anyway. He'd just been playing with her out there because . . . well, because he could. Probably. Most likely. What other reason could he have for willingly and knowingly putting her job in jeopardy by even suggesting there was anything else between them other than a purely business relationship?

What, indeed? her little voice whispered. How did he know he was jeopardizing her job? She hadn't exactly been in any big hurry to stop him out on that rock. If Tommy hadn't called—

Mercifully, it was Tommy who cut her thoughts short.

"Where in the hell have you been?"

He knew exactly where she'd been, so she didn't bother to reiterate. He'd already taken hold of her elbow anyway, and was bodily propelling her through the rapidly dispersing crowd, and toward the rear of the house. The last glimpse Erin had of Dylan was him trying to navigate the Jag toward the garage while a half dozen female production assistants all but draped themselves over his car.

A totally uncalled for stab of jealousy shot through her. "Shouldn't they be working," she muttered, but Tommy was deep into dictator mode and wasn't paying attention to her.

"All twelve of them, MacGregor, tomorrow. Here."

"I thought you said the charter took them to Inverness. I'm sure I can arrange something suitable to house them until we're ready here. Just let me get on the phone and—"

"What's wrong with your neck?"

"What? I beg your pardon, sir?" Her hand flew to her neck.

"It's all rashy. Do you have an illness, MacGregor? Because I'm telling you, we can't afford for you to be anything less than a hundred percent productive. So, don't even think about getting sick. And no more gallivanting about the countryside with the top down. You probably caught . . . something."

"I wasn't gallivanting, sir," she told him. At least not on purpose, anyway. "I was scouting a date location. And I haven't caught anything. Even if I had, it was worth it," she added under her breath.

When Tommy shot her a sharp look, she hurried on. "Worth it because the location is outstanding. Very private, and will need next to no prep on our part. Securing permission will be no problem, either," she assured him, feeling her neck grow more splotchy the longer he stared at her. "Now, about finding rooms in Inverness," she went on brightly, urging him forward now. "I'm sure I can find something discreet that will keep the women entertained but well out of the public eye."

"See that you do. We can't have them down here just yet. This place is a nightmare of reconstruction."

"Precisely why I thought it best to get Dylan, I mean, Mr. Chisholm, off property today, sir." And as soon as the words were out of her mouth, she knew it was precisely the wrong thing to say, if Tommy's immediate renewed interest was any gauge. And it always was.

"Speaking of Mr. Chisholm, I need to talk to you about him."

Erin tensed. Her entire body was probably splotchy by now. She felt like she was sporting a big neon sign over her head, proclaiming, "Yes, I kissed him, and it was pretty fantastic. So what?"

"I—I know he's been a bit of a problem, but don't worry, I have that under control." Boy, she was becoming quite the accomplished liar today, wasn't she? But one way or the other, before the night was over, she vowed she would have Dylan Chisholm under some kind of control. Her determination fueled by the little show he'd put on back there. She wasn't fooled into believing he thought this was all fun and games. Where Glenshire was involved, it was anything but. So whatever his game had been just now, she realized it was because he thought he was gaining leverage to get his way later. In fact, maybe the whole seduction scene out by the rock had been more of the same.

Of course, she'd always thought herself a pretty good judge of character, and everything they'd talked about in the car on the way there led her to believe he was nothing if not direct and sincere, but still—

"MacGregor? Are you listening to anything I'm saying?"

"Yes, sir. Of course." Christ, she really had to get a grip where Dylan was concerned. "I'll—I'll make sure he doesn't get in the way again. I know we're behind schedule and—"

"Get in the way? What the hell are you talking about?"

"The installation crew? I—" *I really wish I'd been paying closer attention*. "I'm sorry."

He waved a hand. "Never mind. Just proves my point anyway."

"Which is?"

"He's got the 'it' factor."

"The what? Who does?" Then a sick ball of dread formed in her stomach. "Dylan? I mean, Mr. Chisholm?"

"Who in the hell else have we been talking about for the past ten minutes? Yes, yes, Mr. Dylan Chisholm. The Great Scot himself." Tommy stopped then and turned so he faced her, grabbing both her forearms in his tight, mad leprechaun grip. His grin was a fierce thing to behold, but not half as scary as his eyebrows, which arched high on his forehead as he shook her arms in his excitement. "I need you to have a talk with our Mr. Chisholm."

Since when had Dylan become "our" anything, Erin wanted to know. Up until right that very second, Dylan had very specifically been *her* problem. And she knew Tommy. He only took credit for anything when it was a good thing. "What about?"

"I've been doing run-throughs all day, blocking out the grand staircase where we'll have our elimination ceremony."

"I thought we agreed it would be best to have those by the fountain out in the front—"

"I changed all of that while you were gallivanting around with our Mr. Chisholm today." He squeezed her arms so tightly she was pretty sure it would be some time before she regained feeling in her hands. "Don't interrupt. All day, all I've heard is chatter about the Great Scot."

Erin frowned. This news did not come as a surprise to her. Tommy's apparent excitement about the problem, however, did.

"Everyone from the food services girl to the cleaning staff is gaga over him."

"I know I promised to keep him out of—did you say gaga?" She'd been so prepared for the complete ass-chewing she was going to get from Tommy due to the delays, she simply couldn't process the sudden direction change Tommy was taking with this. "Gaga?" she repeated.

Tommy gave her a knowing look. "Come now, MacGregor. I know you're not exactly a man-eater, but even you've obviously come under his spell. Which I suppose, in a way, merely underscores my choice. If he can get to you, no woman is safe from his charms."

"Charms?" Since when did Dylan have charms? Well, charms that anybody but her knew about? And what did Tommy mean by that "not exactly a man-eater" crack? He, more than anybody, should be thrilled that she'd devoted her life to her job, thereby avoiding distractions like outside relationships. But that didn't mean she didn't want a relationship, or couldn't get one if she tried. Just because she wasn't the giggling, flirty type who wore form-revealing clothes and sported perfectly plucked eyebrows, did not mean she wasn't interested in men.

She was very tempted to tell Tommy that she had charms, too, and that if he hadn't called earlier, Dylan would have had said charms naked and writhing in pleasure. Luckily for her, he was already talking again. Her job was safe another day.

"Chisholm seems to communicate well with you," Tommy was saying, although she could have done without the "why, I have no idea" tone underscoring the statement. "You've gotten close to him, he listens to you, am I right?"

She'd gotten close to him, yes, she had. Whether that meant Dylan would listen to her now any better than he had before was anybody's guess. But Tommy obviously needed reassuring, so Erin said, "I will be talking to him later. Is there something you want me to bring up?"

"Perfect!" Tommy was grinning broadly now, which was almost scarier than when he scowled. "I knew I could count on you, MacGregor. I'm sure you'll have no problems getting him to agree to be our next Prince Charming. He is just the fresh angle we need to keep things lively and interesting. The Great Scot." He shook her slightly. "My god, ratings gold, I tell you!"

Stunned, she could only gape at him. "You want me to *what*?"

"Honestly, Erin, you need to keep up." And with that they were walking again. And she was Erin now, which meant this really was important to him. "You were able to talk him into giving up control of a four-hundred-year-old house, surely you'll be able to make him see what a wonderful opportunity this is. He is exactly the kind of available bachelor we're looking for, toss in the accent, the ancient history—ooh, do you think he has any royalty in him?"

Erin was still stuck back on square one. "You want Dylan Chisholm to be our next Prince Charming?"

Tommy paused for a second, waving off the phalanx of assistants who rushed toward him the second they stepped through the back door. A thunderhead of furrowed eyebrows threatened to mar his heretofore grinning countenance. "Is there a problem? He is available, is he not?"

Erin swore Tommy flickered his gaze to her pink, razor-burned neck, but she couldn't be absolutely sure. Not that it mattered. Just thinking about it had likely caused her to break out in self conscious hives. "Um, well, I'm not exactly in the position to know about his personal life and—"

Tommy stared her down.

"Yes, as far as I know he is. He's a widower, though, you know, so I don't know if—"

Tommy clapped his hands in glee. "A widower you say? Magnificent!" Not exactly the reaction she was hoping for.

"Maybe for you," she murmured beneath her breath, but at his glare, she cleared her throat and said, "I'm not certain he's ready for a relationship."

"Well, that's even better. How long since his wife passed on?"

"Around two years or so."

Tommy snapped his fingers. "Perfect. And he's kept himself alone here in this house. My god, it just keeps getting better and better. He's ripe for the picking. He'll be irresistible. Oh, the ad campaigns we can run. The marketing will be brilliant. We'll have every corporation in the hemisphere begging for commercial time." He broke off, seemed to refocus, looked her directly in the eye and demanded, "So? What are you waiting for?" He clapped his hands. "Get to it!"

"But the phone conference? And we need to discuss the location I found today."

"Strike while the iron is hot, Erin." Now she was certain he was looking at her neck. "I'm assuming you know a little something about that, eh?"

She was certain she flushed clear to her roots. "Ah, yes. Yes, sir. I'll—I'll get right on him—I mean. Sir." Images of her getting right on top of Dylan flashed immediately to mind. There was a lot of nudity involved. And pistoning hips. She immediately shut the images right back out again. Her cheeks couldn't be any hotter. Dear lord, she hoped she hadn't moaned out loud.

"See that you do. Report back to me later this evening. I'll handle the phone conference."

Panic set in and Erin spoke before she thought better of it. "Shouldn't we finish up the immediate details of the current show before we worry about—"

"Are you telling me you can't handle this assignment? Because I was pretty sure I made it clear that I don't want to wait. You know as well as I do that our bachelorettes are arriving here shortly. Twelve gorgeous women with their clocks ticking and marriage on their mind. Do I have to remind you of what that's like? We want him signed, sealed, and delivered before he gets any ideas about romancing any of this season's castoffs." He flicked a glance at his watch. "Get back to me by ten this evening. I should have a few minutes then. And we can go over your day's agenda as well. I want to hear about this site, and hopefully you'll have lined up the last remaining one by then. Perhaps our newest Prince Charming can suggest another one, eh?" He grinned and patted her on the arm. "I want good news, Erin. Good news." And then he was gone in a swarm of P.A.'s and cell phone chatter.

Leaving Erin standing in his wake, dumbfounded . . . and more than a little aghast at the job that had just been thrust in her lap. "But I just do locations," she said to no one in particular. "I don't do Prince Charming. It's not in my job description."

"Good. Let him get his own lass," came a deep voice just behind her.

She turned to find Dylan standing there. Smiling. Well, she'd soon take care of that. Her heart sank. So much for hot waterfall sex.

"We need to talk," he said, his gaze intent on hers in a way that made her body come immediately to life.

She was going to have to find a way to control that. "Aye," she said, stifling a deep sigh. "That we do."

Chapter 11

Dylan wasn't sure what reaction he'd expected from her, cornering her so soon after that little stunt he'd pulled out in the rear courtyard. But it wasn't the rather gobsmacked expression she was currently sporting.

He glanced in the direction of her recently departed boss. He hadn't overheard any of their conversation, but he'd come down the backstairs in time to see some of the director's facial expressions and gesticulations. The diminutive man looked rather like a despot ruler of the fairy kingdom. But he'd also looked quite delighted. Dylan had been banking on the fact that he'd been happy to hear that Erin had secured another date location. "Are you all right?"

"Define 'all right'," she said, somewhat wearily.

Hmm, so all was not well. Hopefully he hadn't added to that. "Perhaps I can make your load somewhat lighter."

His assurance didn't have the hoped for result either. If anything, she looked more stressed. He plowed on, thinking he could only improve her mood with his news. "I've been upstairs to talk with the work crew, and—"

"Dylan, is there somewhere we can talk?" she asked abruptly. He wasn't even sure she was listening to him. "The office you mentioned earlier today maybe?"

He frowned. "If you'll hear me out, you'll see that your boss no longer has to worry about my getting in the way. I've managed to resolve my differences with the workmen, and without resorting to violence, I might add." She didn't smile at that. She was looking past him. "It seems I even owe you something of an apology. Their work, while at times a bit on the creative side, has been of a higher caliber than I expected and they have shown some ingenuity in dealing with some of the more antiquated materials I feared would be damaged. Although I admit I wasn't happy when I found them up there working away before I'd given the okay."

"I told them to go on," she told him, snapping her attention back to him. "We had contractual rights and we couldn't afford the time loss. I know you're worried—"

"Was worried. Are you even listening to me? We've come to terms, Erin. All is resolved. There were a few adjustments made, but none that we can't both live with. I should have had more faith in your claims, but you'll have to forgive me for being a wee bit overprotective of the auld lass. But all is well that ends without coming to blows, aye?" She didn't smile, or look relieved. She was staring right at him, but her thoughts were clearly on something other than what he was saying.

He waved a hand in front of her face. "Am I getting through? Has something else come up?" He frowned again. "Has there been something damaged?" That would explain her distraction. She was afraid to tell him they'd broken or irreparably harmed something.

"What? No, no, nothing like that. Not that I know of anyway."

"Well, then, what could be the problem? I thought you'd be relieved to hear all is well."

"I am, I am." She took his arm and steered him through the back kitchens, out into the foyer, ducking under ladders, stepping over cables. And studiously avoiding making eye contact with him or anyone else. "I need to discuss something else with you. Office?" she queried, as they headed toward the family wing.

"Through the double doors, down the hall. Fifth door on the right." She was a woman on a mission and he decided it best to let her forge her own path. For the moment anyway.

There was the niggling concern that if she wasn't worried about their work-related issues, then this need to talk might have something to do with the rather non-work related issues that had, er, risen between them earlier that afternoon. But who would know about that except the two of them? Perhaps it hadn't been wise to goad her in front of her coworkers, but he couldn't imagine her getting into any kind of real trouble over such a tiny thing. If anything, he'd assumed the entire crew had been happy to have him and his complaints out of their collective hair for the afternoon.

And it wasn't as if Erin hadn't been accomplishing work-related tasks. Surely her boss wasn't such a stickler that he'd reprimand her for taking a wee bit of time for herself while there. And hell, they'd hardly had any of that before the man had so rudely interrupted them and dragged her back for some meeting or other.

Brief images of the two of them sprawled on the rock flashed through his mind, the thundering falls matching his thundering pulse as he dropped kisses along her jaw, then alongside her neck, before dedicating his attention to the rewarding path downward . . . or it would have been rewarding if her blasted mobile hadn't begun chirping.

Better not to think about that at the moment. He'd spent the ride back to Glenshire trying to sort out just what had happened to him during those few hours he'd spent with her. He hadn't come to any concrete conclusions as yet, but he wasn't a heartless bastard, either. He had no interest in complicating her life. If he had done something to put her job into jeopardy, he would do whatever necessary to set things right.

"This one?" Erin asked, already turning the knob on the door.

"Aye." He reached past her and took the knob, pushing the door open for her. "Let me get the lights."

She stepped past him as he found the wall switch. It took several flickering moments before the lights came on and stayed on. The current wasn't entirely reliable in some parts of the house.

She stopped short and he heard her gasp. "This is some office!" She turned in full circle, her expression one of awe and wonder.

He smiled at that. Clearly she was taking in the two walls of bookcases that extended up to the fourteen foot ceiling, or the pair of imported Italian glass windows bracketing the far wall, or the massive mahogany desk that sat opposite the equally immense inlaid tile fireplace. The fireplace sported a marble frontispiece, above which hung the heavily gilded portrait of his great-great-grandfather Rahnald Chisholm, seated astride his dappled stallion, with his faithful hunting dogs at the ready.

Just as clearly she wasn't seeing the dark brown water stains creasing the buckled linen wallpaper that lined the space between the windows, or the gaping cracks that ran alongside the fireplace where the heavy stone centerpiece had settled more rapidly over the past century or two than the walls on either side of it. Or the ganglion of exposed wires strapped down along the baseboards, the result of his mission to bring the internet to Glenshire.

He motioned to the settee and two high-backed chairs, all grouped facing the fireplace. "Sorry there's no fire to ward off the evening draft. I could start one if you think we've the time." Summer days were long in the highlands, but once the sun dipped toward the horizon, the winds could put a chill into even the warmest rooms in the house. Considering most were somewhat dank and dark even in the zenith of sunlight, an evening fire was commonplace any time of the year.

"No," she said, pacing the length of the room, looking along the shelves at some of the spines. "That won't be necessary."

She had her arms folded across her body as she said this, and he felt a chill in the room that had nothing to do with temperature. "Will you have a seat?"

She took a few more steps, and he thought he saw her gather herself somewhat, before she finally turned to face him.

"Is something wrong?" he asked, because it was clear that there was. "Did you take a bit of flak because of our trek today? Was it anything I did or said that—"

"No, no, it's not that. I mean, yes, Tommy wasn't thrilled with my absence, but I had to scout out locations and I'd have been gone for some period of time whether you'd been with me or not."

He was standing a bit too far away to tell, and the golden glow of the lighting in the room masked it as well, but he wondered if that was a blush stealing into her cheeks. Was she having a hard time suppressing images of their activities earlier this afternoon, as he was? It surprised him how badly he wanted to ask her just that. As if he were some callow schoolboy in need of confirmation of his attraction. "True," he said, walking over to the sideboard. "Can I pour you a drink? Whatever the issue is, you're looking a bit vexed by it."

"Thank you, but I'm fine."

So polite, so reserved. Not his Erin at all.

She walked over to the settee, as if she were going to finally perch somewhere, only to turn back to him again and blurt, "I have a proposition for you."

A slow smile spread across his face. Well, well. This was unexpected. But given the immediate reaction his body had to the news, quite a welcome surprise. "Do ye, now?"

She held his gaze for a moment, then, quite uncharacteristically, broke the connection and looked down at her hands, twisting her fingers together.

It was so unlike her, he immediately crossed the room, taking her hands in his and holding on more firmly when she instinctively tried to pull them away. "If this is about this afternoon . . . I hav'na quite figured out how to feel about it either, but . . ." He paused, and when she didn't look up, he ducked down to catch her gaze, smiling as he did. "Have no fear, lass. I'll no' force my attentions on ye. But if you are interested . . ." He let go of one of her hands and tipped her chin up as he straightened and stepped closer to her, his body brushing fully against hers. "Well, then, I'm open to discussion."

"Dylan, I—"

The words came out roughly, and something about hearing his name, with such emotion, spoken in that flat American accent, did things to him that made absolutely no sense whatsoever. Despite having just sworn that he wouldn't needlessly complicate things, he was dipping his mouth to hers, intent on tasting those parted lips, without even a moment of caution. He captured her mouth boldly this time, remembering her fierce return of his last kiss.

She planted two fists on his chest and he thought she was going to shove him away, but he took the kiss deeper, eliciting a little moan of capitulation from her that set his body instantly on fire. Instead of pushing him away, she dug her fingers into his shirt, then slid them up to his shoulders as he took her fully into his arms.

As capitulations went, she somehow managed to find a way to give in to his demands and make him prisoner to her response at the same time. There was absolutely nothing polished or rehearsed about the way Erin MacGregor kissed. She laid claim to his mouth as if it were her first, and possibly last kiss ever. As if she'd hungered for a very long time, and so she fully intended to feast her fill lest she ever starve again. And he readily admitted that being the focus of such a ravenous appetite shot him right to the edge of restraint.

There was a long groan as she slid her tongue along his, dueling now for control of the kiss, of him, and he distantly realized, as she moved against him, that the groan had come from him. So long, so very, very long, since he'd felt anything like this. This punch to the gut, this hard yank at the very core of those long-suppressed needs completely unleashed them for the first time in far too long, and they threatened to completely consume him. And whatever shred of composure he might have retained, she was systematically dismantling by teasing his tongue, toying with his hair, pulling his tongue into her mouth, then slipping hers into his, not to mention the way she rose onto the tips of her toes, straining to match her hips to his.

He had too much of a height advantage for that, but that was quickly remedied when he lifted her from the floor and backed her slowly up against the shelves, knocking several books off their perch. He left them where they fell and pinned her there. He slid his hands down her sides, over her hips and along the back of her thighs, urging them up so she could wrap her legs around his hips, so he could—"Dear God, there is a heaven," he breathed as he finally settled himself fully between her thighs, making both of them groan in deep satisfaction.

And still it wasn't enough. He wanted to devour her whole. He wanted to strip her naked and have her, right then, right there. Repeatedly and with absolute dedication, until neither of them could breathe much less stand. He couldn't recall, at any point in his life really, feeling such out-of-control lust. Of course, he'd never denied himself for so long, but he'd never truly felt the lack, and taking matters into his own hand on occasion had been enough.

But this . . . this went somehow beyond merely slaking pent up need. He could have done that a dozen times over, twice that, had that been the case. There had been no shortage of offers. He'd never once been tempted.

No . . . this . . . this was insanity. Not of the sort that he'd indulged in shortly after Maribel's death. No, this wasn't anything like that. This was . . . more. More of everything. What should have been a simple slaking of desire suddenly felt anything but simple.

He must have instinctively tensed as that realization sank in, because a second later she was twisting her mouth away from his. "Wait, wait," she said breathlessly.

He didn't want to wait. He wanted all of her, all of this, right now. He'd wanted it to be mindless, immediate, primal. Why the bloody hell had he let his conscience have even a sliver of a toehold at a time like this? He tried to capture her mouth again, but she dodged his kiss.

"We can't do this," Erin gasped, her chest rising and falling against his.

"Oh, but I think we can, and quite brilliantly, if I'm not mistaken." He nipped at her neck, forcibly stomping his conscience flat, unwilling to bring this wild ride to a premature end yet again. He was over-complicating things. This was just good, old-fashioned fun. He traced his tongue along the throbbing vein he found there, deeply gratified when he felt her shudder in response. He moved between her legs.

She whimpered in response, making him harden to the point of pain. She clutched his shirt, pulling him closer even as she said, "Dylan, I can't—"

"Won't."

"I didn't come in here to get all tangled up with you again."

He finally lifted his head and looked down into her eyes. "And yet here we are, tangled up in the very nicest of ways, though there's a bit too much clothing involved for my tastes." His lips twitched to a grin. He hoped it wasn't too feral. He was feeling quite . . . primitive at the moment. "That can be remedied. She's an auld pile to be certain, but there are locks on the doors, and a nice pile of rugs in front of that fireplace. We dinna have to go at it like two rutting beasts, up against a wall." He moved slowly between her legs, feeling her thighs tighten instinctively to hold him right where she needed him. "Although you'd have gotten no complaints from me."

She let out a soft little gasp and her chin dipped slightly as he settled his teeth gently along her collarbone, making her shudder again. "This is crazy," she managed, barely more than a whisper.

"I dinna pretend to understand it, either, Erin. But I'd be a liar if I said I wasn't interested in figuring it out."

"I—I know," she said, the words tight, short now, as he continued having his way with her. "Me, too."

"Perhaps we shouldna ask so many questions, then," he said, leaning back just enough so that he noticed the way her nipples had become two tight little points, thrusting at the confines of her bra and thin shirt, and how badly, oh how very badly he wanted to free them. Lay claim to them, capture them, taste them. Take them.

He shifted her up a bit higher, propping her against the shelves so he could push her shirt up. Intent now on laying siege. His ancestors' blood flowed in his veins, did it not? He tugged at the hem of her cotton shirt. "I want to taste you." No matter what words were coming out of her mouth—and there were none at the moment—there was no masking what he saw in her eyes. She wanted this every bit as badly as he did. "I'm a fair man, Erin, that I am." He pushed her shirt up over her bra. Thin, white, uninspired cotton cups were all that lay between him and sweet bliss. And yet he didn't think he'd ever seen anything quite as sexy as Erin MacGregor, hair in wild spikes about her head, in full dishabille of plain old cotton and khaki. "When I'm through, I'll let you have your way with me, too."

She groaned even as she let out a short laugh. "And here when I first met you I thought you were sober and humorless," she managed, somewhat hoarsely. "Boy, was I wrong."

It was the first of the old Erin he'd heard since they'd entered the room, and his blood sang with pleasure. "Shall I show ye some other bits of me you may have overlooked, then?" He brushed his tongue across one cotton covered nipple. She jerked against him, so he teased her again, just a light flick. "So sweet. I want to taste you, Erin." He ran his tongue along the slight swell filling the bottom of the cup, nudging at the soft elastic edge.

She was grinding against him now, her thighs clenched so tightly around his hips that he no longer needed to support her weight, freeing his hands to be as adventurous as his mouth. Her eyes had drifted shut, her breath coming in short little gasps, and she was no longer denying him anything as he pushed her bra up, freeing her breasts to his avid ministrations. They were neither large nor small, quite average really, as were her little pink nipples. Nothing to send him waltzing so close to the edge of reason. And yet there he danced.

When he didn't immediately touch her, her eyes blinked open. And for the first time he saw a real flash of vulnerability. "I'm—I know I'm not exactly—"

"You're exquisite," he said, and found he meant it. He captured one tight little bud between his lips and was instantly rewarded with that sound that started somewhere deep in her throat, and was almost a growl by the time it came out.

The thought flickered through his mind that while she knew of his somewhat monkish existence, he knew little of her private life. For all he knew, she bedded a new man every week. He hadn't gotten around to delving into her past. Yet.

She's hot and willing, man, and yours for the taking. Don't concern yourself with the rest. Enjoy yourself, but don't lose your mind.

She wriggled against him as he traced his tongue around one rigid tip, then suckled her again, knowing it was far too late for that. He couldn't seem to separate the woman from the act. Nor was he particularly keen to do so. Dangerous path, oh so dangerous, indeed. And yet here he was, nigh to skipping merrily down it. Possibly right to his own destruction.

Well. He'd survived worse, hadn't he?

"Hold on," he instructed, sliding his hands around and up the smooth skin of her back as he spun her away from the bookcase. He wanted more, needed more, and didn't want any constraints getting in his way. He cursed his ancestors for favoring hard, understuffed settees, and highback chairs that were far too narrow for tucking in knees and straddling hips. The carpet won out. This time. It was that or make the dramatic gesture and clear the desk with a broad sweep of his arm. In that split second of indecision, apparently he gave Erin enough of a moment to gather her wits about her.

"Dylan," she said, this time straightening and putting her hands against his shoulders. "Give me a second." Her voice was still rough, a bit reedy with want, but when he caught her gaze he knew reason had reared its ugly, untimely head. "I swear, I'm not a tease, I just—you have this way of—and it makes me so—but I really can't. I want to, don't get me wrong, but there's something—we need to talk."

He paused next to the desk, then finally sat her on the edge and let her unlock her legs from around his waist. She wriggled her bra down. And with more regret than he thought a man was capable of feeling after such a short period of knowing a woman, he did the gentlemanly thing and helped her smooth her shirt into place. Though he had enough rogue in him to stay put between her thighs, if no longer in intimate contact. He wasn't ready to relinquish his entire proximity to her just yet. A man's needs should be allowed to abate a bit, after all. He'd been on quite a ride there. Was enough to make even the sturdiest of blokes a bit weedy.

He allowed her an overly long moment to smooth her clothes back into place and settle her rioting emotions as well. He hadn't been the only one affected there. Finally, however, she did look up into his eyes, and while desire lingered there, he saw that his woman of determination had made her return. Funny thing was, it didn't abate his desire for her one whit. If anything, it kept him rather rigid.

"I'm sorry," she said, holding his gaze directly now, clearly sincere. "I really am." That pronouncement was followed by a dry little laugh. "The opportunity doesn't come along often enough for me to thoughtlessly toy with it, trust me."

"I find that hard to believe," he said. "Meaning, I can't imagine you not making an opportunity whenever you wanted. You're a very determined sort."

She cocked her head slightly. "I'll take that as a compliment, I think."

He nodded. "As it was intended. As to the other, have no fear. I'm no' a callow schoolboy who canno' contain himself." His lips twitched at one corner. "Though you made me feel pretty damn close to it."

She smiled a little then, too. "I—thanks. I shouldn't have let it get out of hand, or led you to believe that I—"

"That you wanted me as much as I wanted you? Was that no' true then?" He knew it was, but wanted her to confirm it, for both their sakes. There would be no guilty recriminations, no regrets, for acting human.

"You know I did. The difference was, I knew that I couldn't—that we couldn't—do . . ." She gestured between them.

"Why? We're both free and unencumbered." His gaze narrowed. "You are unencumbered, are you no'?"

"Of course. I'd never do something like this if I weren't."

"I believe you," he said truthfully. There was no subterfuge or artifice with her. She struck him as the type who would have no patience with that in others, either. Which was why he got straight to the point. "You sound very definite about this, when you obviously wish it could be otherwise. So you'll have to pardon me if I'm a wee bit confused. What is it then? Your boss frowns on your fraternizing with the annoying Scot?"

"Tommy doesn't know anything about . . . this." She said that last word as if she wasn't quite sure what "this" was.

Well, that made two of them. The only difference was, at the moment, he was quite willing to continue onward until they figured that out. Clearly she was not. Perhaps she was being the wiser of the two. He wished he was more enthusiastic about that.

He shifted back slightly, knowing he should move completely away, put some much needed distance between them until they completely cooled off, but there was something he needed to know first. "If your boss isn't hounding you on this, and we're discreet, and I promise not to completely derail your hectic schedule—although, in my defense, can I say that keeping me preoccupied will make everyone else here quite happy—"

Her gaze narrowed. "You said you'd come to terms with the prep work and made peace with the crew."

"I wasn't sure you heard that. You've been somewhat distracted since our meeting again. Although, might I add, I was quite enjoying that last bit of distraction." When her pupils flared a bit, it took enormous restraint not to take hold of her again, plant his mouth on hers and kiss her until she realized that whatever flimsy obstacle she'd erected wouldn't withstand this kind of heat and need. So why not just cave in to the inevitability of it all?

Her words, however, didn't match the look in her eyes. "I assumed that meant you'd be leaving them to their work and wouldn't require further intervention."

He tried a shrug and what he hoped was a charming smile. "A bloke could hope. I rather liked the way you intervened this last time."

He could see she was fighting to maintain some semblance of seriousness, so he rather enjoyed the way the corners of her mouth twitched as she fought the urge to smile. Och, he'd get through to her eventually, that he would.

"Filming starts soon," she was saying, "so you won't be able to wander freely over there, anyway. Besides, you've apparently done enough of that already, or we wouldn't be in this fix."

"What 'fix' is that? And what *we*? What have *we* done to put anything in a fix?"

And suddenly she wasn't looking at him again. *Oh, for god's sake.* How bad could it be? He gripped her chin gently, but firmly enough to tip her gaze upward to meet his own. "It's no' like you to duck an issue."

She lifted an eyebrow as if to question how he felt qualified to make such an assessment. He merely lifted a brow back until she capitulated. He was right and they both knew it. "Out with it."

She held his gaze for a moment, likely just to prove she could, then surprised him by heaving a rather defeated sigh. "Maybe we should have a seat."

"Maybe you should stop beating about the proverbial bush. Your forthrightness was one of the first things I admired about you."

"Tommy wants you to be the next Prince Charming. There. How's that for direct?"

He saw her mouth moving, heard the words that had come out, but surely somewhere in there he'd lost track. Because surely . . . no. He stepped back from her completely then, leaving her to grip the edge of the desk, before sliding off and finally standing on her own two feet.

"I know," she said, sympathetically. "That expression you're wearing probably matched mine when he told me." She shook her head slightly. "That's quite a sales technique I have, huh?" She looked like she was going to take a step toward him, to do what he had no idea. Instead she turned and wandered over to the settee and sank down, burying her head in her hands. "I'm so going to lose my job over this. I should have stayed in London. There are plenty of locations in London. But nooo, I had to prove I could be more creative, shake things up, pump some fresh life into this show." She was muttering to herself, which he found quite endearing.

Or would have, if he wasn't still frozen to the spot, trying to absorb this latest turn of events, and what to say to her. Because it was plainly obvious to them both that hell would freeze over before he'd ever agree to such a ridiculous thing.

A certainty she apparently hadn't shared with her boss. Or if she had, he'd threatened her into asking anyway. Threatened her with her job, it sounded like. Bloody hell. How he had gotten himself in this tangle, he had no idea. And to think he'd believed his life complicated before she'd strolled into it.

Dylan Chisholm, star of an American dating program? Just hearing he'd been asked would be enough to send the entire village into paroxsyms of glee. His brothers would never let him hear the end of it.

Suddenly he needed to take a seat, too. And a very deep breath.

Chapter 12

"He wouldn't even discuss it with me." Erin paced her hotel room, phone pinned to her ear.

"And that was two days ago? When are you going to talk to him again?" Dana queried.

Good question. And thankfully one Tommy hadn't asked her yet. "It's crunch time here and, at the moment, Dylan is staying out of sight, and I'm willing to let him. When are you getting in? I thought you'd be here tonight."

"I got stuck getting out of Orly, so I can't connect and get up there until tomorrow morning. Is there anything you need me to do on the way in?"

"No, but I do have you tied up from the second you set foot in the village, so don't promise your time to anyone else, including Tommy. If he tags you, call me."

"What's up?"

"Due to some . . . personnel problems, we've had to accelerate the preliminary filming schedule. The women will get into town Friday—"

"Friday? Day after tomorrow Friday? But I thought they were all safely tucked away in Inverness until early next week."

"Yeah, well, one of the handlers apparently got drunk and spilled the beans to some guy she was hot for and—"

"Word got out about the women's location." Dana groaned.

"So far it's just the local media speculating on who the women are and why they're there. But it's only a matter of time before someone posts on a bulletin board or someone's blog, then we'll have people snooping around and haunting our every move."

"You don't have to tell me. Tommy must be going ape shit."

"Understatement," Erin answered. "Anyway, bottom line, he wants them here in Glenbuie as fast as possible."

"You sure no one in the village is going to slip up? Just how in hell did you secure all that without Tommy having a major apoplexy?"

"Who said he didn't?" she responded dryly. "The town council here signed a confidentiality agreement. The villagers are all very close and well aware of the sanctions they face if anyone so much as breathes a word during filming."

"I'm guessing it's not hurting any having the entire crew invading the town, spending freely."

"Exactly. Anyway, I've got some locals lined up to keep the women under roof until we officially bring them out to Glenshire on Monday. Tommy's going to start filming the preliminary confessionals at the hotel and do more background filler stuff, so in a way, this helps get us back on schedule, but with all the prep work still going on, we're stretched mighty thin."

"So what else is new?" Dana said, matching Erin's dry tone. "What do you need me to do?"

"Well, here's the thing," Erin said, knowing her assistant wasn't going to be thrilled, but she didn't have a choice. "I need you to help out with those two contestants whose handler was fired."

"Baby-sit the Barbies? Are you kidding me?"

"Now, now. Maybe you got two of the sweet ones. Anyway, it won't be for long, just until we move them into Glenshire."

"I tell you what, I'll trade. You baby-sit and I'll try and convince your hot Scot that he should be our next Prince Charming. That's more my skill set anyway."

"Who said anything about him being hot?"

"Oh please, like Tommy would beg you to sign an ugly guy. Come on, I'm stuck in an airport all night. Dish with me a little. Please?" she wheedled and Dana was a world class wheedler. "Tell me about him."

"There's nothing to tell, except hell will freeze over before he ever agrees to sign on as Prince Charming, which means our asses are on the line here."

Dana ignored her dire warning. "Word is he's intense."

"Word from who? Who have you been talking to?" Erin sighed. Of course there was gossip. Who was she trying to kid?

The crew was, in many ways, like an oversized family unit. A highly dysfunctional family unit who happened to be putting in very long hours under extreme stress and pressure. So, naturally, gossip was one of their main forms of entertainment. Hoisting a few at Brodie's pub and fraternizing with the locals being the other two. Mostly Tommy operated on a don't-ask-don't-tell basis. As long as it wasn't flagrant and nothing came back to bite him in the ass like it had in Inverness, he didn't care what the crew did on their minimal downtime. Of course, this time, with the entire village in on the story, it was far easier for the crew to take advantage. And from what she could tell, boy were they.

Her cheeks heated just a bit. Like she had fat room to talk.

"Never mind," Erin said, not really wanting to know what everyone was saying.

"So? Is he?"

"What? Intense?" Erin had to press her thighs together just thinking about it. "Um, I can see why he comes across that way. He's pretty reclusive. It almost took an act of Parliament to get the use of his house. I can't see him putting himself under a microscope."

There was a pause, then Dana sighed. "Fine, okay. I'll have to drag it out of you later."

"You'll see him for yourself soon enough." Although Erin discovered she'd be perfectly happy if Dylan just stayed hidden for the duration. It was foolish to think she could have kept him anyway, even for the duration of the film shoot. What with all the women coming to town, any interest he had in her would likely have evaporated like so much mist over the moors.

"But then I'll probably have even more questions for you," Dana said. "So, if you're not going to give me hot, insider details, have you figured out what you're going to tell Tommy when he asks why you haven't signed him up?"

"Well, as they say, timing is everything. With the women coming in early, he's been pretty distracted. So that buys me a little time."

"He'll just assume you've taken care of it, like he always does."

"That's what I'm banking on. And I plan to have it taken care of. Soon."

"But you just said—"

"I know what I just said. Tommy has his heart set on a Scottish bachelor for his next Prince Charming. I'll make sure he has one."

"Erin," Dana said, a note of dread in her voice. "He

wants Dylan, and you know how he is when he wants what he wants."

"Yes, I know exactly how he is. I promise, I have it under control." A total lie, but she would have it under control. Just as soon as she figured out who she was going to get to substitute for Dylan. "On the bright side, we'll get to camp out here for the duration. No need to head back to L.A."

"Oh. Right. I hadn't thought of that. But . . . won't it be a little redundant to use Glenshire again? I mean—"

"Well, see, that's going to be my angle. If we get a new guy, we get a new location to go with him."

"Works for me. Surely, in all of Scotland, we can find another hunk with a family castle," Dana said, sounding almost convinced.

"Well, that's where it gets tricky. We don't have the time or resources to go too far afield without tipping Tommy off. And I want to present this whole thing to him as a fait accompli."

"How was he planning on re-using Glenshire anyway? Maybe you can talk him into using Dylan at another location entirely. Then we can scout locations and hunks at the same time."

"Tried that. Tommy has this grand idea of introducing Dylan in a kind of teaser segment at the end of this season's finale, telling the whole backstory of how he actually owns the home in which the series was filmed and is a real life Prince Charming, blah blah blah. He's set on it."

Dana said nothing.

"Details. Don't worry. We'll make it work." Erin felt her palms begin to sweat. "Listen, get some rest and I'll catch up with you tomorrow. Be prepared to hit the ground running."

"Aye, aye, boss."

"And thanks in advance for service above and beyond the call with the whole handler thing."

"Yeah, well, I figure you'll owe me then."

"You're my assistant. I'm pretty sure it's in your job description to do things that don't actually fit your job description."

"True," Dana admitted. "But I know you. You'll feel bad about sticking me with this, because you just know I'm not getting the nice ones, and then you'll end up making it worth my while at some point."

"I just sent you to Paris," Erin reminded her.

Dana let out a deep sigh of contentment. "And did I remember to thank you for that assignment from the bottom of my very, very, very appreciative heart? It was so fantastic, Erin."

Erin smiled, hearing the exact same kind of excitement in her assistant's voice as she felt when she got to scout a new place. "Sounds like *you* owe me."

Dana laughed. "Damn, hoist by my own petard. And yeah, maybe I do. But I found the most magnificent date sites. Nothing cheesy or touristy. You're going to love them, I swear. I even have three back ups that are also to die for. Tommy might even smile."

"You'll be handsomely rewarded if you can pull that off at the moment," she said with a laugh. It occurred to her then how much she did trust Dana, because she had little doubt her assistant was going to come through as promised. Erin took pleasure and a certain kind of pride in seeing someone she'd trained spread her wings a little and do well. "I can't wait to see the dossiers. I knew you were ready, but—"

"Hey, don't thank me. Well, thank me, but you should also thank Jacques. If it wasn't for him . . ." She trailed off, then there was another deep, appreciative sigh.

Erin rolled her eyes. "Don't tell me, you left a string of broken hearts all up and down the Champs Élysées."

"Hey, I was only there for a week."

"Let's just say I have faith in your dedication and ability to focus."

Dana laughed. "Interestingly, that's just what Jacques said."

"I bet," Erin muttered, but she was smiling as she said it.

"So come on," Dana cajoled. "I'll tell you about my hot Frenchman if you tell me about your Great Scot."

"He's not mine." More's the pity, she thought with a sigh. "So there is nothing to tell."

"Uh huh. That's not what I heard."

Sometimes Erin wished her assistant was a little less focused. "Well, with all you've apparently already heard, there's no need for me to cater to your prurient interests, is there?"

"There was prurient stuff? Oh come on!"

"Just get up here safely, okay? We'll talk tomorrow."

"Okay, okay, I fold. For now. Night, boss. Sweet dreams. Sweet, hot dreams," Dana added with a laugh, before signing off.

Erin groaned. Hot dreams, indeed. Like the past two nights hadn't been a scorching marathon replay of their time by the waterfall and in Dylan's library. Only in her dreams, they hadn't stopped. Either time.

She hadn't heard a word from him since he'd abruptly left the library two days ago. Not one measly pink slip demand. Which she'd told herself was a good thing. Except that didn't stop her from thinking about him. Constantly. She kept half expecting him to suddenly pop up out of nowhere as he had before. She'd be doing something totally innocuous, like going over production notes, and, bam, out of the blue, she'd remember how it felt when he put his mouth on her, the way he'd pushed her up against that bookshelf, half tugged off her clothes, flicked his tongue over her oh-so-sensitive nipples . . . and god help her, her entire body would go all hot and wet and needy.

She turned away from the hotel window and stared at her bed. Her big empty down-filled bed. Sweet, hot dreams, indeed. *Thanks, Dana*. "I am so firing you," Erin said into the now dead phone. An empty threat, especially since Erin would be lucky to hold on to her for another season before Tommy promoted her to take on more responsibility anyway.

Or worse, gave her Erin's job when she couldn't produce next season's Prince Charming on a silver platter and got her ass fired. That was the one pink slip she didn't want to see.

She sank down on the side of her bed, then flopped back and stared at the ceiling. She needed a plan, dammit. She needed to talk to Dylan. In this whole crazy mess she'd gotten herself into, he was the only one she felt she could really talk to about any of it. And yet, he'd steered clear of her, which, to her mind, was sending a pretty clear signal that he'd appreciate it if she did the same.

Well, considering it was his demands that had put her square in the middle of this situation in the first place, she figured she had a right to contact him if she needed to. He'd been the one insisting on having her as the go-between. So if she did contact him, she'd be doing so for strictly professional reasons.

And she was so full of shit it wasn't even funny. She wanted to see him again. Hell, she was dying to see him again. All the more reason to lock herself in her room and not come out until filming was over. But she knew he'd be the one person who would listen and perhaps help her figure out a sane, rational approach to solving her problem.

A shame he also *was* her problem.

Just then there came a tap on the door.

Erin groaned and rolled off the bed. It was almost midnight and she'd been up since dawn. If this was one of Tommy's minions with yet another addendum to the schedule, she was going to scream. She peeked through the peephole, only to find Amelia standing on the other side. If Erin wasn't mistaken, she'd been on duty early this morning, too. She threw the latch on the door and opened it. "Hi. You're working late."

Amelia blushed quite prettily. "Aye, mum. Getting some extra hours in so I can have off this Saturday." She smiled. "My boyfriend is to compete for his Gold Clasp in Inverness and I want to go watch him win."

"Gold Clasp?"

She beamed with pride. "Aye, mum. He plays the pipes, ye see. They've a prestigious competition this weekend and only former gold medal winners are eligible for the Clasp. He'll be one of the youngest to ever win it."

"Wow," Erin said, spending a wistful moment thinking how nice it would be to have her life benchmarked by such simple pleasures. "It sounds like he's got a great supporter in you. If he's half as determined to win as you are to see him do it, I don't doubt he'll bring the trophy home."

"Oh, he will, I just know it! I know I'm biased, but no one is as good as my Ian. He's one of the most sought after pipers in the region. I'll bring you one of his CDs if you'd like." She leaned in as if to share a particularly juicy piece of gossip. "He's quite good looking, if I do say so, and I do. Which doesn't hurt his sales any. Girls chase him all over. But his heart belongs to me."

"Sounds to me like he knows a good thing when he sees it."

Her blush deepened, but she gave Erin a saucy wink. "I'd like to think so." She fanned her face with the envelope in her hand, then realized what she was doing and blanched. "Och, I'm so sorry! Here I am disturbin' you so late and now I'm going on about my Ian." She thrust out the small, white envelope. "I would have put it in your box for the morning staff to deliver, but it had a note attached saying deliver immediately. Hope you don't mind the late intrusion. I'd have slipped it beneath your door, but you all seem to keep pretty late hours and I saw your light on, so—"

Erin took the envelope, her mind spinning on Amelia's story. "No, problem, really. Let me ask you, is the bagpipe competition open to the public?"

"Aye, 'tis. It's one of the largest solo competitions in the country, so it's a big draw. I can get you a copy of the notice, we've flyers downstairs, if you'd like."

Erin smiled. "That'd be great. Just hold it at the desk for me. I'll pick it up in the morning."

Amelia beamed. "My pleasure. Is there anythin' else I can get you?"

"No, I'm fine." Erin waved the envelope. "And thanks for this."

Amelia nodded and skipped off before Erin could tip her, but then she'd tried several times since taking up lodging in the hotel, only to be very sweetly rebuffed each and every time. Erin had already determined to do something nice for the girl before she checked out. At the very least, she'd send a note to her boss, detailing what great help she'd been during Erin's stay.

At the moment, however, her thoughts were on bagpipers. Men in kilts. Lots of them. She turned and leaned back against the door, tapping the envelope to her chin. She needed to find a hot Scot. Where better to start than to check out a bunch of studly guys in uniform? And if none of them filled the bill, perhaps they could recommend someone who did.

She was already mentally rearranging her schedule so she could sneak out for a good chunk of the day on Saturday. If this panned out, she was going to owe Amelia a hell of a lot more than a glowing letter to her boss.

All caught up in the hatching stages of her grand plan, she almost forgot about the envelope. It wasn't large and manila, which meant notes from Tommy or someone on staff. It was small, square, and white. She turned it over. There was nothing printed on it, not her name or room number, so it must have been hand delivered.

"Hmm." She wedged a fingertip under one corner and slid it along the sealed edge. There was one single sheet of folded note paper inside. And when she flipped it open, there were two lines scrawled across the middle of the page:

Still in need of that second fantasy date site?
Meet me in the courtyard at midnight.

She turned it over, but that was it. No signature. But her heart had already started its now-familiar tattoo inside her chest. It had to be Dylan. Who else would write this? Who else knew she still had one site location to nail down? Well, Tommy did, as that had been the focal point of his ten minute harangue tonight after their end-of-day production meeting had ended. She looked at the note again. The writing was bold, masculine. But maybe she was just projecting.

"Yeah, projecting your own doom." If it was Dylan, the very last thing she needed to do right now was give the gossip mill anything more to latch on to. Which was the least of the reasons why she had no business meeting him anywhere, at anytime, but certainly not in the middle of the night to head out on god knows what kind of adventure.

She walked over to the window and looked down over the village square. Night had long since fallen, but given that it was early summer, the square was still dotted with more than a few people. The shops were closed, but Hagg's was still ablaze and Erin knew a quick walk around the corner would show the windows of Miss Eleanor's coffee shop still lit with a warm glow. She kept her attention on the square, scanning the couples and the small groupings. She noted a number of the show's staffers as well as a few familiar locals, but Dylan wasn't anywhere to be seen.

Meet me in the courtyard at midnight.

She glanced over at the bedside clock. It was ten to.

It had to be him. She tapped the note against her palm. But why the sudden turn around after the silent treatment for the past two days? She'd told him what was what in the library, he'd listened, then told her no. When she'd tried to discuss it, he'd stood and excused himself, telling her that particular topic wasn't up for discussion. She hadn't heard from him since. Maybe he'd been waiting for her to make the next move.

She looked from the mess of notes and folders scattered on her bed still waiting to be attended to before she could sleep tonight . . . to the door to her room. A midnight rendezvous, huh? She sighed, the romantic in her trying not to swoon, but it did anyway, just a little. He'd phrased the request as a work meeting, but she knew damn well it wouldn't be all business. Or she could hope. And it wasn't like she didn't need to talk to him, anyway, about her idea to find a replacement. If Dana were here, she'd be personally dragging Erin down to the courtyard.

"Wait a minute," she murmured. "What courtyard?" She'd read "courtyard" but had been thinking "village square." Maybe they were one in the same, but none of the locals she knew called it that. He couldn't possibly mean the courtyard behind Glenshire? If he did, then there was no hope as she'd never make it in time.

She crossed to the hotel phone and dialed the desk before she could change her mind.

Amelia's perky voice popped up on the other end. "Yes, Miss MacGregor?"

"Is there a courtyard somewhere off the square?"

"A courtyard, mum? You mean aside from the car park behind the hotel?"

"The rear parking lot?" She'd parked back there when she'd first checked in, but once Tommy had arrived, he'd commandeered it for his own personal use. So she'd gotten used to parking along one of the side streets and walking up to the hotel. The one nice thing about the village being so small, was that pretty much everything was in walking distance. She'd all but forgotten about the little courtyard back there.

"Aye. I dinna know of another. Would you like me to ask about?"

"No, no, that's okay. Thanks." She'd barely hung up when the phone rang again. Assuming it was Amelia calling her back, she scooped it up and said, "It's okay, I know where it is."

"Then why aren't you down here?" came the decidedly masculine, and very familiar voice.

"Dylan."

"Erin."

Maybe it was the amused tone in his voice. Maybe it was the fact that, at the moment, he really was the only one she could talk to. Or maybe it was the way her entire body went on a full, four alarm alert.

"Don't leave without me." She dropped the phone, grabbed her bag, and flew out of the room before common sense could return. Common sense was no fun.

Chapter 13

He'd been sweating. Waiting. And sweating. Truly worried that she might not show up. What the hell was wrong with him anyway? He'd walked out of the library the other night, worked up and worn out. His life was already upside down. And everything that was upside down about it, all circled round to one Erin MacGregor.

Yet, here he sat, in the middle of the night, like a stupid nit, waiting to see if she'd come to him. Or if he was going to have to go in there after her. He'd told himself that steering clear of her was the smart, rational thing to do. But as one day turned into two, then looked to dawn into three, it had started to feel a hell of a lot more like hiding.

When things got complicated, he liked to think he was a take action sort. He'd done that with Glenshire, hadn't he? So it only stood to reason that he would handle this . . . whatever the hell it was he was doing with Erin . . . the same way. Her boss' mad scheme to have him parade about on the telly as their next pig to slaughter was just that, crazy. But he shouldn't hold that against Erin.

All he wanted to hold against Erin was himself. Preferably naked, and on a comfortable surface where he could explore her naked self at his leisure. Maybe if he could do that, he could get his head back on straight and stop thinking about her every damn minute of every damn day. And night. Och, but the nights were about to do him in completely. Which explained why he was sitting in the car park at midnight.

He wasn't sure which was worse, the fantasies his conscious mind dreamed up, or the intensely erotic, highly detailed forays into fantasy his subconscious treated him to the moment he allowed sleep to take him.

It was enough to drive anyone raving starkers. So he was a man with a mission: Get her, take her, get on with life. Only a fool wouldn't act on the chemistry they shared. It was healthy and good to feel something. Anything. Even lust. Not a bad place to start in his book. So he'd slake his curiosity and his hunger while they filmed their little program, then he'd take their money and free promotion, wish Erin godspeed with her next project, and get on with the business of being an innkeeper.

Hell, after this circus, running a bed and breakfast would seem tame by comparison. He was actually looking forward to having only a handful of guests underfoot. Perhaps he should thank Erin for putting his future career in proper perspective for him.

And he would. If she ever got her flat little arse out here.

As if he'd willed her to appear, there came a tap on the passenger side window, followed by her sharp-eyed, gamine face peering in through the glass. He leaned across the seat and popped the door handle.

"Hello, stranger," she said brightly, as she climbed in and settled herself in the bucket seat. As if they hadn't last parted under less than lovely circumstances. As if it was nothing out of the ordinary for her to meet up with a man in the dark of night.

And yet, he'd not only asked it of her, he'd expected her to comply. More fool he, perhaps. Except here she was. Alone with him. By choice. His body stirred at the thought, and he wondered if she had any idea of the motives behind his invitation. If she, too, was hoping this was more personal than business.

The overhead light briefly illuminated her face before she shut the door. She seemed quite at ease, not at all anxious. Perhaps she'd taken his note at face value. A peace offering of sorts, for walking out on her the other day, then avoiding all contact since.

"Your note surprised me," she said, as if reading his thoughts. "I almost didn't come down." Before he could ask, she said, "You might want to sign your notes."

"You receive a lot of midnight invitations, do you?"

She laughed at that. "Only from Tommy, usually involving a crisis that only I can solve, sure to rob me of what little sleep I do get."

He was more relieved by her confirmation than he'd liked to be. He wasn't a jealous sort. Or he never had been. He didn't know what he was now. "Well, hopefully I'll be helping you reduce your workload rather than increase it. I'm sorry about the loss of sleep time."

She lifted a shoulder, as if to say he wasn't to worry about it. "I haven't had a second to breathe the past couple of days, so if this site is viable, you'd really be helping me out. I'd give up more than sleep to get this particular headache resolved. Speaking of which, where have you been hiding out?"

So, she was here for business, then. He'd see about that. "Catching up on paperwork, my investments, and other things I've let go in my haste to complete the construction work for the grand opening. If anything, I've enjoyed the respite."

She shot him a knowing smile. "So it was just coincidence, then, that by holing up in your wing, you'd keep from inadvertently crossing Tommy's path so he didn't hound you about the whole Prince Charming thing."

So, she wasn't going to duck that sticky issue, either, though he'd have been perfectly willing to let her. "There might have been some side benefits, aye."

"Given the flurry of final construction taking place, your restraint has been admirable."

"Ye have no idea," he muttered beneath his breath.

"What?"

"I said, I had an idea. I overheard some chatter that there was concern that the last site hadn't been nailed down. I thought I might be able to help you with that."

"Can I ask why?" She held up a hand. "Not that I'm complaining, mind you, I'm desperate enough at this point I'd take help from any corner."

"I believe I was just insulted."

She laughed. "Sorry, that did come out a bit wrong. It's just, I assumed you'd prefer to steer completely clear of me and my boss, so I'm just . . . surprised, I guess. You certainly don't owe me a thing."

"I know your boss really fancied the idea of signing me on and I suspected my refusal might have left you in a wee bit of a bind. So I thought maybe I could redeem myself and help you get back in his good graces."

She just stared at him. "Really."

He gave her the look right back. "Really." He lifted his hands. "Why is that so hard to believe? I'm not that bad a sort, am I?" She certainly hadn't thought so when she was moaning as he teased her nipples with his tongue, but he thought better of mentioning that at the moment. His body, however, was perfectly content to respond quite fully to the memory.

"Let's just say you haven't been all that motivated to

help me thus far, usually quite the opposite. Getting you to agree to the lease was a battle right off the bat."

"Och, so quickly they forget. Was it not me who helped you secure your other much-needed date site?" His body grew even harder at the reminder, like it needed more taunting memories at the moment.

"Only after I dragged you bodily from the building to get you out of my crew's hair. It was more by default than by design." She shifted a little in her seat, as if suddenly a bit uncomfortable. "And trust me, I've hardly forgotten."

He smiled at that. So, she wasn't quite as unaffected as she seemed.

She caught his smile and quickly added, "But don't get any ideas. Nothing has changed since our, uh, talk in the library."

"Talk."

She gazed at him rather defiantly. "Yes. Talk. Which you bailed out on pretty quickly when it became clear you weren't going to get what you wanted."

"You've no idea what I want," he said. How could she when he didn't know himself? He thought he knew. Hadn't he just told himself he was out here for the express purpose of finishing off what they'd started? Easy to say when he was alone and horny. Only now that she was sitting next to him, he wasn't at all certain that was all he wanted. She confused the hell out of him. But there was one thing he wasn't at all confused about. "If you've come out here tonight thinking to sway me on that whole Prince Charming thing, dinna waste yer breath. I've no' changed my mind on it, nor will I."

"I know that."

Now it was his turn to look a bit wary. "Do you?"

"Yes, I do. I knew going in you'd never agree to anything like that, but with my job on the line, I had to at least try."

He wouldn't have expected anything less of his tenacious lass. Which was why it was so surprising to hear her give up so readily. It was completely ridiculous, but a part of him was curious to know if she'd backed off because, perhaps, she wanted him for herself and had no intentions of sharing him with a bevy of hand-selected beauties. His ego would like to think that was true, of course. But there might have been some other part of him in there wishing the same thing. A part that had nothing to do with ego or thwarted libido. He ignored that part. "And now your job is no longer on the line? You've convinced your boss to look elsewhere?"

She didn't answer. And, he noted, she no longer held his gaze, shifting her own forward, staring through the windshield at the stone wall surrounding the hotel courtyard.

"Erin?"

"Not exactly," she blurted out after a long, silent moment. "But I—I have another plan on how I'm going to handle it and Tommy, so you don't have to feel obligated to do anything for me, okay?" Gone was the casual, unaffected demeanor. Back was his hard-wired, always thinking, highly motivated Erin.

And that right there was the thing about her that captivated him. Things were never dull or complacent with Erin. It was a rare moment indeed where she didn't manage, without even trying, to fully engage him. Never a moment where he wasn't all caught up in her.

He made himself settle back in his own seat. Only his body had no intentions of complying. Bloody hell, but he hadn't spent this much time with a hard-on since he'd been thirteen and discovered there were magazines with undressed women in them. And was obviously what he'd been thinking with when he came up with this plan in the first place.

He abruptly gunned the engine to life. Moving, he needed to be moving. "We are still on for tonight, right?"

She nodded and pulled on her seat belt as he backed out of the narrow parking lot.

"So, what is this plan of yours?" Not that it really mattered, but if he got her talking about that, it would give him time to reassess his real motives here, get a firmer grip on his self control.

"To find Tommy someone else who will fill the bill in your place."

"Which is what, exactly? I'm no' quite clear on why he'd want me in the first place."

"Which is part of your charm."

He barked a laugh. "Charming am I, now?"

"You can be."

He gave her a sideways glance as he steered them out of the village square and headed out in the opposite direction from the way he'd come, heading away from Glenshire toward the mountains on the far side of the valley. "So much the flatterer."

She cast him a sideways look. "Well, you didn't strike me as the type who needed his ego stroked. But I can give you a list if you insist."

Oh, he wanted to be stroked all right, but he politely kept that thought to himself. "I was merely curious. It was a sincere question. I just wondered what this bloke would have to have to appease your boss, is all. It's no' about me."

"Okay, then. He can't be hard on the eyes, owning a crumbling, historic mansion or castle would be a nice bonus, even better if it's set against a stunning landscape. There's the whole accent thing. The tragic past." She glanced at him, as if gauging his response. "I don't know if we could get all that and swing having him be clan chief to a village of people who adore him, but it's on the list. That guy would be quite the romantic figure. When packaged properly anyway."

"I think I've been maligned in there somewhere, but I'm no' entirely certain." He caught her responding smile from the corner of his eye.

"Quite the opposite. You won't be easy to replace. Tommy already has the whole thing laid out in his mind's eye. And he can be pretty dogged about getting what he wants."

"Which explains why he hired you."

"See, I'll take that as a compliment."

He smiled. "As well you should. So, does Tommy know about this substitution you'll be making? Or am I still the target?"

"It'll be easier to persuade him when I can hand him the new guy, all signed up and ready to go." She patted his knee. "Don't worry, somehow, someway, we'll manage to limp along into a new season without you."

He downshifted, then trapped her hand on his knee before she could withdraw it. A quick glance at her showed a fast instant of awareness in her eyes, before she carefully looked away.

"I appreciate your boundless optimism," he said dryly, tracing his fingers along the backs of hers.

She shrugged, vainly attempting to appear unaffected, but he'd felt the fine tremor in her fingers. When she slid her hand from under his and carefully folded her arms across her chest, he had to work to contain a triumphant grin. Unaffected, his white Scottish arse.

"I figured you'd be happy to be off the hook," she said. "I should have it resolved this weekend. I'll be sure to let you know so you won't have to hide anymore."

His lips did curve a bit then. Someone was hiding here, but he didn't think it was him at the moment. "I appreciate that. So, you've prospects then?" he asked, definitely relieved she'd shifted her focus from him in this instance. If she'd promised to find someone else, he trusted she'd do just that.

But then he couldn't help but picture her interviewing those other blokes . . . and wondering if perhaps they would be looking at her and thinking the same thing she had him thinking. Of course, in the end, despite the sparks between them, she'd taken the professional high road. So he could rest easy knowing that even if one of them did strike her fancy, it was doubtful she'd pursue it. If she were inclined that way, she'd be pursuing him then, wouldn't she?

Gah. He really needed to get her naked as soon as possible. All this waiting and wondering was making him over-think things. Surely he'd cease to care so much once he'd gotten his fill of her. All his questions would be answered.

Though he'd have liked to be a wee bit more convinced of that than he was.

"Um, well, I do have a target of opportunity," she answered.

"A 'target of opportunity.' Sounds more like a military drill."

"A well thought out battle strategy never hurt anybody."

He laughed. Something he did with increasing frequency around her. Widower or not, he didn't like to think himself so humorless and severe. But he suspected it had been more true of him than not of late.

"Speaking of which, where are we headed?"

He glanced over at her, as he let the Jag run a little. The single track road they were on wasn't all that windy, nor was it well traveled at any time of the day. As late as it was, they were in little danger of coming abruptly upon a slow moving lorry, or a herd of sheep or cattle blocking their progress. Racing across the valley floor, the full moon lighting his way, his adrenaline surged to match their pace. He enjoyed the rare thrill, the heady rush of excitement, and perhaps a bit of the danger as well. The danger being seated next to him.

"Would you rather it be a surprise or shall I spoil it for you?"

She didn't answer right away, but rather seemed to settle back in her seat and relax a bit more. A quick glance showed her attention was on the moonlit road ahead, and not on him. But then he'd known that. He felt it whenever her gaze was on him. Like a physical caress.

"You did do a pretty good job of picking the last spot," she said, at length. "I suppose I can trust you."

He wondered if there was a hidden meaning in that, but decided there wasn't, as that suited his plans far more. She could certainly beg off once again if she didn't welcome his attentions. But he didn't plan on making it easy for her. "How I've come up in the world," he said dryly.

He felt her look at him now, and caught the smile curving her lips as he downshifted and looked over at her, before starting the climb into the low hills.

"You might not be fully aware of your charms, but you're hardly an innocent," she told him. "Not even close."

"Are you saying I'm a wicked sort, then?"

That made her shift in her seat. "You told me yourself you were no saint. But what I'm saying is you're self-assured."

"You say that like it's a bad thing."

"Not at all. But while I appreciate your assistance, I figure it's probably best not to poke and prod at you too much. You tend to poke and prod back."

He laughed again, because she was quite right. At least where she was concerned. If she only knew the poking and prodding he dreamed of doing with her. Well, he supposed she had a pretty clear idea after their little tryst in his library the other day. "When you decided to come down and meet me, you truly had only business on your mind, then?"

She didn't respond right away. His hands tightened on the steering wheel. He might have been holding his breath.

"Your track record with date sites is stellar," she said at length, once again taking the safe tack.

He'd see how far she'd get with that. "Ah."

"Ah, what?"

"So, that's it then. I'm only to play tour guide?"

"That is what you offered."

He slowed the car on a curve in the road, then braked so he could turn off the main track onto a narrower packed gravel path. It was hardly more than a trail, but it only went about fifty yards, and having been out here once today already, he knew it was traversable in the sports car.

"Where are we?"

He rolled to a stop just before passing the end of a stand of trees that blocked the view of their destination. He released his seat belt and shifted in his seat to look at her fully, waiting for her to return his gaze. When she did, he said, "You were right when you said you could trust me. That has been true since we first met, and remains true now. I've been honest to the point of bluntness from the start, and admire the same in you, more than you might know. So answer me this. A man asks you to meet him at midnight for an adventure and you agree. Is business all that really came to mind when you read my note?"

"You first. Do you really have other intentions this evening?"

He responded by opening the door and climbing

out, circling the back of the car and opening her door. He held out his hand, and after staring up at him for a long moment, she placed her hand in his and let him draw her out of the car. He didn't back away, keeping her in the narrow space between the open door and his body. She didn't shift away. Nor did she move closer.

"You know I wasn't the one who wanted to stop things the other evening. Do you think that has changed?"

"Given the way that meeting ended, and your silence since then, perhaps. Do you think my reasons for stopping have changed?"

"You said yourself that you're going to look elsewhere to find Tommy his next victim. There might be a bit of a muddled line between us, but I see your production team has no problems mixing business with pleasure." His mouth curved at the corners. "I don't think the local lads have stopped beaming in days. Bragging over ales has kept Brodie's tap bent non-stop most every night."

"Be that as it may—"

He stepped a bit closer then. "Do you usually set yourself apart from all that?"

She looked up into his face. "I don't have to. Normally by now I'd be back in L.A., getting ready to head out on a round of preliminary scouting trips for the next season."

"Only this time the next season is here." His smile deepened. "Lucky me."

He saw the desire flare in her eyes. His body responded to it instantly and ardently. This time he didn't try to fight it or control it.

"Dylan—"

He placed a finger over her lips, further surprised to feel the fine tremor and realize it wasn't her lips that were trembling. "Why don't you let me show you the site?"

"So there is a site, it wasn't some ruse to get me alone in the middle of nowhere?" Her eyes danced a little. He liked it when she teased him.

"Oh, there's a site." He grinned. "Not to say it wasn't a ruse, though."

She shook her head, her smile a dry one. But the desire hadn't abated one bit. "So tell me, I don't hear any waterfalls. What could be up here that's best seen at midnight?"

"You'll see. I wanted you to look at it through the same eyes as the couple you're tracking this site for, who will hopefully be experiencing this setting with a bit of romance in their hearts."

Her lips twitched.

"What?" he asked, a wee bit affronted. "I thought we established that, shockingly, perhaps I had a wee bit of romance in my soul. Ye think I dinna appreciate the pleasure of it?"

She shook her head. "No, that's not it. I just—I don't know. Never mind, ignore me. You read me far too well."

He smiled now. "And that's a bad thing?"

"Sometimes," she said archly, but with obvious amusement.

He took her hand. "Come on, walk with me. It's just around the bend, past the trees."

"It?"

"Aye."

She bumped her shoulder into his, but matched his pace. And left her hand in his. "Tease."

"No' yet, but give me some time," he said, his tone never more heartfelt.

Her step faltered.

He turned and tugged her closer, so there was barely a space between them. "I willna lie, Erin. I want you. You know that."

"Yes, but—"

"But I willna take you, that I swear."

She looked confused. "Then why are you—"

He tugged her closer, so her body brushed his and she had to tip her head back to hold his gaze. "No' without your request. I willna do anything unless you ask me to."

Even in the moonlight, he couldn't mistake the way her eyes darkened, or miss the way her throat worked.

He ran the tips of his fingers along the side of her face, and down along the side of her neck. "You're right, I'm no saint, Erin. I could have brought you here in the daylight, no' that it would have made a difference, I suppose. It didn't the last time we were alone. But this is a place meant for moonlight and stars. It's what gives it its romance. And I'm a selfish man. During the day you have so many people pulling you in so many directions. I wanted you to myself. Away from the calamity."

"Away from untimely phone calls?"

"Aye, that, too," he answered honestly. "And it's no' to say I'm not trying to bend things to my favor. I wanted to show you this site, aye, and help you. But of course it wasn't entirely for your benefit, but also about my own. I needed to know . . ." His voice trailed off, suddenly unsure of the words to use.

"Needed to know what?" she asked, sounding a slight bit on edge.

He knew the feeling. He let go of her hand and cupped her face with both palms. "I needed to know what this is about," he said, sliding his fingers into the short wisps of her hair, cupping her head, tilting her mouth up to his.

"What what is about?"

"This." He lowered his lips to hers, surprising even himself, given the voracious hunger she unleashed in him, that he didn't crush his mouth to hers, but took her gently, almost tenderly. He tasted her as if he'd never tasted anything so wondrous in his life, and maybe he hadn't. Slowly, as if he had all night, praying he did, he seduced her mouth, teased her lips apart slowly, before sinking sinfully deep into her mouth. Her groan of pleasure was matched by his own, and he wanted nothing more than to drag her down to the ground right there. His lack of control should have been unnerving, and perhaps it was, but in an exhilarating, life-affirming way that was in equal parts terrifying and addictive.

Only when she lifted her hands to his shoulders, and he felt her body sigh into his, did he force himself to lift his mouth from hers. He wasn't sure if it was to avoid losing what was left of his control so soon . . . or losing what was left of him. Forever.

He leaned his forehead on hers as they both steadied themselves, taking several deep breaths.

"I don't believe I asked for that kiss," she said a bit breathlessly, fake rapprochement in her tone.

"Aye, but ye did. I saw it in your eyes."

"Oh, so that's how it is," she said, amused.

He smiled, but addressed the question seriously. "Maybe I have been out in the countryside too long," he said, his voice barely above a whisper, but clear in the still night air. "All I know is, we didn't feel as if we had finished yet." He tipped her chin up so her eyes met his once again. "And I don't like to leave things unfinished."

She stared at him for a very long time, during which he went through a kaleidoscope of feelings. Most of them unnerving. It mattered more than it should, he knew that. She mattered more than she should. It was time he stopped pretending otherwise.

"It—" She stopped, looked away for a moment, then back to him. "It didn't to me either." Her gaze was beseeching. "I really don't know what to do about this, Dylan. What I do know is that I have a job to do, and I am not savvy enough to juggle a personal life with a professional one when they're so tangled up like this."

"So when do you have a personal life?"

Her short laugh held not a whit of humor. "I guess I don't."

"But you love your job."

"Of course I do," she said automatically, without a second thought. "It's a dream job."

"So that's enough then. Does it fulfill you completely? And remember who you're talking to. A man who gave up his entire life to bury himself in a new one not of his direct choosing. A man only now coming to terms with such things as fulfillment and putting personal needs up against professional obligations, or, in my case, family and ancestral ones. So you canno' bullshit me, Erin."

"Maybe it's not all fulfilling," she confessed. "But I've never had to think about it. If I wonder about it from time to time, and I do, I guess I just figure it would find its own way at some point. I've been busy enough where I haven't really had time to think about it that much. I don't feel like I'm missing out on anything. Or I didn't."

"And now?"

Again, she looked into his eyes. "Now I'm more confused than anything."

"About?"

"You. Me. What it is about me that draws you. Honestly, I'm not typically a real man magnet. Thus the lack of general concern about having a private life, I guess. I've never really been tempted to worry about anything going long term. It's always seemed to sort itself out on its own."

"Because you sort it out, or because it's sorted out for you?"

"Both. Maybe, usually the latter. But possibly because I push it that way. Or my job does it for me." She shook her head and tried to pull away from him, but he was having none of it. "I guess I just choose not to think about it and, to be honest, no one has ever made me want to."

His bravado deserted him then. Which was precisely when he knew he was in way over his head. But before he could find the nerve to ask the question he most wanted an answer to, she took the pressure off him.

"I hardly know you, Dylan. Do you shake me up?" she went on. "Yes. In more ways than I'd like to admit. It would be great to just give in to it, but . . ." Now she trailed off, but quickly rebounded, almost blurting out the rest. "I'm not sure I can keep it in perspective. Okay? There, I said it."

"Ye know me better than most. Perhaps because you only see me as who I am today, and no' the sum of who I've been my whole life." Her lips quirked at that, and he was curious. "What's so amusing? I couldna be more sincere."

"It's just . . . I've thought the same of myself where you're concerned. Not that anybody really looks at me as the sum of my past, not the way they do you. But I guess I carry my past like a chip on my shoulder in my own mind, more than I think I do. And you . . . you knocked it off without even knowing it was there. Scares the bejesus out of me, actually."

He barked a laugh at that. "Join the club, then."

She looked honestly surprised at that. "Me? Scare you?"

He took her face in his palms again, smoothed his thumbs over the corners of her mouth, her cheeks. "Aye, lass. Right down to my toes."

Her breath caught. "Then why not walk away while you had the chance? Why invite me here?"

"Because it's been too long since I let myself feel anything. Something so strong, even fear, seemed worth exploring. Something tepid would be easy to dismiss and perhaps should be. There's nothing tepid about this."

Her eyes widened a bit at that declaration, then she smiled, softly this time, perhaps almost wistfully. It wasn't an expression he'd have equated with her until that moment. "I don't know what can come of it," she said, almost hesitantly, as if not wanting to admit that truth to herself or him. "My life isn't here."

"It is right now."

"But—"

"Ask yourself this. It's what I asked myself before finally sending that note tonight. Which would you rather go through life knowing . . . that you followed your desires, or that you ran from them?"

She sighed a little at that. "I learned at a very early age that desiring something can be a dangerous thing. Not to mention brutal and cruel when the thing you desire most is the one thing denied you. I'm a realist first and foremost."

More layers, he thought, *so much more still to explore*. "Life has taught me much the same. And though I'm no' complainin' on where it's gotten me, at the same time, I'm not so sure I'm willing to define my life that way any longer. Too much of it has been spent fulfilling one obligation or another, however misguided at times. But I know something of regret now. Enough to know to avoid having regret when I can." He held her gaze intently. "And I know I'd regret not doing whatever I could to know more of you, for the time you're here."

Chapter 14

Dylan stepped back before she could say anything, and took her hand. "Come on. Let me show you why I brought you here."

Erin let him lead her away from the car and down the gravel path, grateful for the chance to get her thoughts in order. She wasn't sure what she would have said if he'd pressured her. Her judgment was cloudy at best at the moment. Lost in a fog of hormones and confusion.

If he'd demanded an answer right then and there, she was afraid she might very well have tossed caution to the wind and told him exactly what she wanted for herself. Which was to take whatever Dylan wanted to offer her. Because the one thing she did know was that she wanted him. But while she often got what she wanted when it came to business, it wasn't often Erin had the chance to get what she wanted when it was personal. Mostly because she didn't spend much time wanting anything just for herself.

But Erin hadn't made it this far by going for what she wanted at the expense of going for what was best.

And she wasn't at all certain that what she wanted, in this case, was what was best for her. In fact, she was afraid it was exactly the opposite. She'd been brutally frank when she admitted that she might not be cut out to handle the repercussions of letting herself get emotionally involved with him.

And at the moment, those emotions were running far too high. The danger wasn't so much in trusting him, the real danger lay in trusting herself. Usually Erin managed to do what was best for her by avoiding temptation entirely. In the end, it made things a lot easier.

But then, she'd never been tempted quite like this.

They rounded the bend, past the stand of tall pines, and Dylan drew her to a stop. Caught up in her thoughts, she bumped up against him, then stopped dead when she finally looked up and caught sight of what lay before her. "Whoa." Not exactly the most scintillating or sophisticated response, but accurate in its simplicity. She could only stand there and stare at the stark sprawl of ancient castle ruins laid out before her like so many mammoth building blocks. With jutting walls and crumbling towers, the sheer immensity of it was quite overwhelming. Bathed in the otherworldly glow of the full moon, she felt as if she'd been transported to another time.

"It's . . . there's so much of it. I can't even imagine what it must have looked like when it was whole." It dwarfed Glenshire. They hadn't climbed that far into the hills, but she could see where the position of the main tower would give a pretty good view of the valley they'd just traversed. Or would if the whole tower still stood. She walked along the side of one wall that was little more than rubble now, so she could get a view of what lay beyond. "It just goes on and on."

"Aye, the wall was more an enclosure of sorts. The

tower was connected to the main house, but there were many outbuildings housing the kitchens, the stables, the farrier, the weapons, the guard, and more."

"Almost like a village in and of itself."

"Very much so."

She turned to look at him. "Is this part of your heritage, too?"

He shook his head. "No' directly, no. It was the Fenton stronghold. They were a valued ally and sept of the Chisholm clan for several hundred years." Dylan said, his low, melodic voice carrying easily over the warm night air. "Until they were forced to abandon any hope of keeping it in the family."

"How long ago did they have to give it up?"

"Turn of the last century."

Erin knew that many of the historic properties that were still standing in Scotland and in England couldn't be maintained by the families and were often sold to a trust formed by the British government specifically to help maintain them. The most viable or important were at least partially restored and often opened to the public for tours and such. Many were left to slowly decay. "Who owns it now?"

"We do."

She looked at Dylan in surprise. "But with all you already have to maintain—"

"There's not much to it, in this case, I'm afraid. It's well beyond maintaining. We own the property, we pay the taxes, and my brother, Tristan, and I take turns making certain it's no' vandalized or housing anything or anyone it shouldn't. But beyond that there's not much more to do for it now, I'm afraid."

"Why not sell it to the government then?"

"Because my great-grandfather promised we wouldn't. He was instrumental in its purchase. In addition to being centuries old allies to the Chisholms, the Fentons' last clan chief was a close friend of his. My great-grandfather wanted to save him the final indignity of turning it over to the government and at least keep it in clan lines. It was quite humbling, to say the least, to have to give up direct ownership after more than three centuries."

"I can only imagine," she said, looking back at the ruins. "Actually, that's not true. I really can't imagine. I can't imagine having anything like this to deal with. And that pales in comparison to what you and your brothers had to take on." Not that she hadn't been awed by his responsibilities before, but standing here now, for whatever reason, the enormity of it all struck home. "And here I used to think how much easier my life would have been if only I had family. Maybe I should be careful what I wish for, hm?" She glanced at him, but quickly glanced away when she found his gaze intently on her.

"You said something about not knowing your heritage, or having no heritage to trace, that first morning we met. Where is your family?"

She could sidestep it, or brush it off casually, as she usually did if and when the subject came up. Thankfully those occasions were quite rare. But at that moment, looking at the immensity of the burden that another family had willingly taken on, fought for, likely died for, for hundreds of years . . . it seemed rather disingenuous to pretend that her own circumstances had been difficult in comparison. "I don't have one," she said simply.

"Everyone has family. Historically speaking, anyway."

"In that respect, I suppose I do, but I wouldn't know them if I read about them in a history book or bumped into them on the street. I'm an orphan. I was raised in a state funded home in northern California, outside of San Francisco. My family was whoever happened to be in charge and on staff at the time. There were a few steady faces that would last a few years at a stretch, but, frankly, it was a pretty sucky job. Overworked, underpaid, dealing with a system that was far from perfect and quite often downright depressing. Not to mention kids who were a real handful. I couldn't blame them for leaving. Lord knows I did, the moment I could."

Dylan stepped over a tumble of small rocks, catching up to her, falling into step beside her. She hadn't realized how far they'd wandered along the main wall. The moonlight cast shadows and she had to pick her way carefully.

"How long were you there?" he asked.

She kept her gaze on the rock-strewn path as they continued to walk. "From about four months on. It wasn't all that bad a place, for what it was, but it wasn't all that great, either. I figured out pretty early on that an education was the only chance I had to get out of there and make something of myself. I worked hard, got a sports scholarship to a small college, earned a marketing degree. Never looked back." She paused and looked up at the ruins. "Maybe I should have. But it didn't seem like a history worth preserving, if you know what I mean."

Dylan didn't say anything, just stood beside her. She wondered what he was thinking. A man so overwhelmed by his own history that he'd run off to escape it only to finally grow up, embrace it wholly, and make it his own. She didn't know what he'd think of someone like her, with nothing to lay claim to, nothing to live up—or down—to, nothing to pass along.

"What sport?" he asked, startling her.

She smiled at the unexpected question. "Field hockey."

He glanced at her then and she turned enough to catch his own slight smile. "The one with the wooden clubs?"

"Don't mock me, now," she warned him with a smile. "I was quite good with mine."

"Warning taken," he said, amusement clear in his tone.

He took her hand and continued on down the path. They fell back into an easy silence, both of them keeping their gaze on the rutted moonlit path, neither seemingly in any hurry. His touch alone made her nerve endings tingle with awareness, but at the same time, she felt quite peaceful and relaxed. She liked his silent strength and felt somehow buffeted by it. Funny, as she hadn't realized there was anything in her life she needed to be buffeted from.

Several minutes passed, then he squeezed her hand. "I'm sorry," he said quietly.

She didn't have to ask what he meant. "Thanks," she said. "I like my freedom and my independence just fine, and I think I turned out okay. But I won't lie and say I don't occasionally wonder what it would have been like to have parents, siblings."

"All that time, never adopted?"

She shook her head. "At first I tried. Maybe too hard. Okay, definitely too hard."

His chuckle was low, soothing. "A wee bit intense, were ye? Intimidating at age four. I can well imagine."

She intentionally bumped her arm against his, but didn't so much as knock him off stride. Solid, steady. That was Dylan. "I like to think I was merely precocious."

"Mmm hmm," he hummed. "So what happened?"

"You get passed over enough times, you learn to stop getting your hopes up. Eventually I realized that I was setting myself up for too much disappointment, and life was hard enough, you know? Plus, the older I got, the more clout I had right where I was. I started to realize that maybe it was to my advantage to stay. So, then I made sure I wasn't adopted."

He laughed. "Och, I can only imagine yer methods."

She grinned, feeling a warmth steal through her at

his affectionate teasing. "Well, it's possible I might have been one of those kids I called a handful. Of course, that was open to interpretation. I like to think I was merely headstrong."

He pulled their joined hands to his lips and brushed a kiss along her knuckles.

"What was that for?" she asked, surprised at the tightness the sweet gesture brought to her throat.

"No particular reason." He let their joined hands drop back between them, and kept their easy pace. A minute might have passed, when he added, "Or maybe I just enjoy the idea that, for the moment anyway, you're my headstrong handful."

Her fingers tightened in his for the briefest of moments, the reaction instinctive rather than planned. He squeezed back, but said nothing as they continued their stroll, turning at the end of one wall and heading down the length of another. She noticed, each time silence fell between them, it grew more companionable.

It was odd, considering his touch had her on edge, her body almost hyper aware of his, not to mention the topic under discussion was hardly one she usually enjoyed. And yet, there she was, strolling along, feeling, if not entirely at ease, certainly far less defensive than she usually did when talking about her childhood. Normally she glossed over it with a few dry, self deprecating comments, then quickly changed the subject. It wasn't that she was ashamed of how she'd grown up, far from it. It was what it was. But she'd learned that most people found her personal history fascinating in the same way people couldn't help but rubberneck at the scene of a train wreck. Not the most lovely of situations to put oneself in when one was the train. So she did her best not to.

Only this time, as aware of him as she was sexually, feeling achy and needy and confused . . . at the same time, there was a kind of . . . serenity between them.

She couldn't think of another word to describe it. She felt safe with him. No topic seemed off limits. She knew he wouldn't judge her, much less make her feel like some kind of freak spectacle. Maybe it was his own past, the tough decisions he'd had to make, both in leaving the home of his ancestors . . . and in returning to it. She wasn't entirely sure. All she knew was that he riled her up and managed to somehow be a calming presence all at the same time. And there she was, hand in hand with him. Making no effort to disentangle herself.

From the discussion . . . or from him.

"Did you ever try and trace your history?" he asked. "Do you know anything about your ancestry at all? MacGregor is a common enough name in this part of the world, but perhaps I could help, do some digging on this side of the pond."

She shook her head, though she was touched by the offer. "MacGregor was the name of the apple orchard stamped on the cardboard box I was left in. My first name was scrawled in indelible marker on the tag inside the sleeper I was wearing. For all I know whoever put me in it got it at a garage sale. It wasn't in the best of conditions, so I was told. I guess whoever found me thought they sounded good together."

"Surely there was an effort made to find who had abandoned you?"

"There was the standard investigation, but nothing ever came of it. And yes, I had all kinds of fantasies about who my parents were, what impossibly tragic and ultimately forgivable reason they must have had for leaving me on Crestview's doorstep." She shrugged a little. "Eventually those fantasies gave way to the harsh reality of how the world really worked and I gave them up. I figured my life was what it was and I should be thankful whoever it was at least left me where someone would care for me. I understood how Crestview worked and I was more comfortable and steady dealing with the known, than flinging myself into the unknown. Crestview was all the history I needed."

She squeezed his hand, then stopped and turned to face him with a smile and a little curtsy as they approached the main tower. "So there ye have it, lad, the tragic tale of Erin MacGregor. Would make a good pub song, I'm sure."

Rather than let her go, or worse, give her that look of pity she'd seen far too many times, he did the most perfect thing. He captured both of her hands and tugged her to him, until they were toe to toe, and she had to look up to see into his eyes. The moonlight framed him like a halo, which only leant more power to the words he spoke.

He smiled down at her, a smile that easily reached and lit up his eyes. "No' so tragic, I'm thinkin'," he said, his brogue thicker, his voice easy and sure. "Aye, ye were a wee babe, abandoned on a doorstep, and I'm sure the pub bards could weave quite the tale for you. But if I were writin' the lyric, it wouldna be a tale of woe, but one of triumph." He pulled her closer still and drew their hands together between them. "I admire yer spirit, Erin MacGregor, and I dinna think you'd have thrived the same and become the woman ye are if ye'd taken any other path. So I can hardly find fault in it, now can I?" He pulled her hands to his mouth, dropped an impossibly sweet string of kisses along each bent knuckle. "Because I rather fancy the lass the world made ye into."

It was so unexpected, she couldn't fight the lump that formed in her throat, and she suspected her eyes were a bit glassy as well. No one had ever said anything like that to her, had ever given her that particular gift. Celebrating her adversity rather than pitying her for it. For seeing it much as she'd come to see it herself. Had had to see it, in order to make sense of it, and use it to her advantage.

"Thank you," she said, her voice somewhat gruff. "I—you know," she said, her lips trembling a bit as her mouth widened into a smile and her feelings came tumbling forth, "I rather fancy the bloke you've become, too." She felt her heart swell, maybe teeter a bit as well, but willfully ignored all the danger signs that went along with it. "Imagine that, Dylan Chisholm. Imagine that."

"Come here, Erin MacGregor," he murmured. "And ask me. Please."

"Kiss me," she whispered.

And he did. And it was much like the one before, back by his car. Surprisingly tender, almost reverent. Before, by the waterfall, and in his office, his kisses had been seductive, ardent, almost overwhelmingly sensual. She had so much pent up need at this point she physically ached with it, but rather than disappoint, this kiss brought to life an entirely new kind of ache. The ache to be treated gently and with such sweet affection. Which, perversely, only served to jack up her sexual need for him that much higher. He was a threat to every part of her, and she was already falling, swiftly, and with no safety net in sight. She should be pushing him away, barricading her emotions off, now, while she still had even a slim hope of protecting her heart.

Did he know she was far more vulnerable to this sort of tender invasion? Was he intentionally trying to render her completely helpless?

Then he was sliding his palm along her neck, tipping her mouth to his, taking the kiss deeper. She let him inside her mouth and felt his groan of response vibrate in his throat, felt the urgency increase as his kisses slowly became more demanding, more consuming. And though she hadn't yet decided what her regrets would or wouldn't be with him, it was too late to figure it out now. She gave herself over to it. To him. Fully and completely. It was too rare, this feeling he evoked inside her, too glorious, and too perfectly fulfilling, to toss it aside. And for now, that was guide enough for her heart.

He stumbled from the rutted path and pulled her with him, sinking down on a low part of the ruined outer wall and tugging her down so she straddled his lap.

"Dylan," she murmured against his lips, "we shouldn't disturb—"

"This fortress has withstood greater threats than a couple trysting in the moonlight," he assured her.

She smiled, liking his turn of phrase. "A trysting couple, are we?"

He supported her with an arm around her back, sliding his other hand into her hair as he urged her mouth back to his. "A man can hope."

This time he took her mouth like a man half-starved. And she was torn as to which was more affecting. But there was no time to think, only to feel, as she reveled in the way he claimed her. Thinking it might be fun to do a bit of claiming herself, she was just weaving her fingers into his hair when he wrenched his mouth from hers.

"There—" He had to stop, clear his throat, giving her a little thrill to know she affected him that much. "There was more to this fantasy date than staring at a pile of rocks."

She toyed with his hair, feeling emboldened and more than a little powerful. "I don't recall complaining thus far."

He grinned at that, and the resulting sizzle had her squeezing her knees against his thighs, making her wish she could wrap her legs around his hips instead.

"At the risk of giving ye far too much time to reject me yet again," he started, holding her tightly against him as he stood, then letting her feet drop to the ground. "I've gone to a wee bit of trouble and I'm hopin' to impress you with my rusty romancing skills."

She didn't even try to stifle her grin. "Rusty, huh? Something tells me you probably didn't need much of a reintroduction."

He took her hand and guided her around the base of the tower ruins. "Why you'd think that, I have no idea, but I'll happily allow you the fantasy. As it's likely to last all of a few minutes at best." The far side of the tower still reached several stories up. At the base, there was an archway. If there had once been a door, it was no longer in existence, providing them easy access to the interior. "Mind your head."

Still holding his hand, she ducked in first, then waited for him to follow. "Wow," she said, her eyes easily adjusting to the darker interior, courtesy of the fact that the spire was no longer there and the moonlight poured down into the barren interior. Curving along one wall was a crumbling staircase set into the stone walls of the tower itself. She tipped her head back and followed the line of steps. They wound upward for two full circumferences of the inner tower wall before coming to an abrupt end where the ruined tower walls had crumbled.

Dylan led her to the base of the stairs.

"Really?" she said, following him, but surprised he planned to go up. "But they don't lead anywhere."

He smiled over his shoulder. "Dinna you know there is always more to things than meets the eye?"

Looking into his face, seeing his eyes sparkle, that smile that promised mischief and a few other things that had her muscles clenching even more tightly, she realized she could barely remember the serious, reclusive man she'd first encountered. "Yes," she said, "yes, I do." She inclined her head. "Lead on."

"There's the spirit."

Tightening his hold on her hand, he began the climb. "Stay close to the wall, mind your step. There are some loose stones in a few of them." He glanced down at her. "You're all right with heights?"

"Now you ask?"

He paused, looking suddenly concerned.

"I'm kidding. I'm fine. When I was six, and I needed to be alone, my favorite place to hide out was up on the apex of the roof. I used to sneak up to the custodial closet on the top floor, then climb out through the window and shimmy up the tiles." She sighed a bit wistfully in remembrance. It had been a long time since she'd dredged up any memories of her time at Crestview, and it surprised her a little to discover that she was actually fond of this particular one.

"Ever get caught?"

"I got in trouble a few times for not being where I was supposed to be. Maybe more than a few times," she added when he cast her another dubious look. "But they never figured out where I'd disappeared to. I used to love it up there. The grounds were pretty, clustered with big trees, and the whole place was surrounded by a really high wall. So the view out of any window was limited to our little world. But the peak of the roof was above tree level and wall level. I could see as far as a clear sky would let me. It was very empowering. I vowed that when I got out of there, there would be no more wall between me and the rest of the world. I knew I would find a way to go all the way to the horizon and beyond." She smiled. "And eventually, I did."

"That's how I felt about my visit to the city when I was ten," Dylan said. "There was all this noise and hustle and bustle and people, so many people. I remember being amazed that there were so many cars. More cars than cows or sheep. I felt like I'd discovered the center of the universe. And I knew right then I was not meant to stay in the countryside, no matter what my grandfather told me about my heritage. In fact, the more I was told what I had to do, what I was born to do, the more I grew absolutely certain I wasn't meant to do it."

"Ah, a real rebel."

"More like hard-headed and stubborn."

She continued to trudge up the stone stairs behind him, quite enjoying the view of his backside. "Hey," she teased, "I resemble that remark."

He lightly squeezed her fingers then slowed. "Watch your head here."

She looked up through the open tower top at the moon. "Watch my head on what?"

"On this." Dylan shifted slightly and stepped into what looked like nothing more than a turreted window opening, but turned out to be an alcove.

She ducked her head and squeezed in behind him. They both had to turn sideways to shimmy through the narrow opening to the side of the alcove. "I bet you were awesome at hide and seek," she said, slowly side-stepping through the skinny opening in the thick stone walls.

"Actually, Tristan was the best," Dylan said, grunting a little as he wedged himself into the narrow spot, then pushed himself through. "Wiry little wanker he was, and wily, too. Could squeeze himself into the damnedest places. Often took us hours to find the sod." Dylan carefully helped her through the short passage.

When she popped out on the other side, she immediately plastered her back to the wall behind her. "Oh my god."

"Careful." Dylan braced an arm across her chest until she steadied herself.

She was standing on a narrow precipice of a mostly crumbled turret. With nothing between her and a good two story drop to the ground. "You weren't kidding about the heights thing." Her pulse was thrumming, but it was an exhilarating kind of rush.

"You okay?"

She shot him a grin. "What do you think?"

His expression went all heated and dark, and Erin decided she'd better be a little more careful provoking him. Wonky knees would not be a good thing at the moment. "Right," she managed, earning herself a rather devilish wink. Now her heart was pounding for two reasons.

"Turn slowly," he instructed, helping her to do so until they were both belly to the tower wall. "Follow me." He moved sideways, quite casually, as if they weren't tiptoeing along what amounted to a crumbling, inches wide ledge, on the side of a centuries old castle ruin.

She was all for adventures, and she really did think this was rather exciting, but, all the same, she tightened her hold on his hand just a little anyway. She hadn't done anything wild and crazy like this since . . . well, since the last time the two of them had taken off together. She was beginning to see a pattern. And having a hard time recalling why that was a bad thing. Fun. She was actually having fun.

"Okay, just a bit farther on, up this way."

A series of stone steps curved upward a few yards or so, this time part of the outer, rather than the inner wall.

"Here we are," he said, climbing around to where the tower was connected to the closest main building by a wide, thick stone wall. Or it had been connected at one time. The wall only extended outward about two dozen yards before coming to a crumbled halt. The top of the wall appeared to have once been a walkway, as there were low, crenellated walls on either side that were about chest high. A good portion of those were now gone as well, but enough remained that Erin could visualize how it had once looked.

It was only when Dylan moved forward onto the walkway atop the wall that she saw the rest. Several huge woven blankets had been laid out on the widest expanse, with a couple large pillows arranged on either side. In the center was a large wicker basket and a wick lamp.

He said nothing, but smiled and spread his arm in front of him. "A moonlight feast awaits, milady."

She was so surprised, and so inordinately touched by the effort he'd gone to, she impulsively put her arms around his neck and hugged him. Oddly, considering the rather carnal way they'd entwined themselves now on more than one occasion, when he wrapped his arms around her waist and hugged her back, it felt more intimate than anything they'd done to date.

"How did you get all this up here?"

His eyes gleamed in the moonlight. "Impressed, are you?"

He was so clearly pleased with her reaction, and himself, for that matter, she couldn't bring herself to tease him. "Aye, that I am," she said, in a fair imitation of his brogue. She also didn't have the heart to tell him that, as touching and romantic as it was, dining beneath the stars atop castle ruins, it was unlikely they could use this particular spot in the show. The technical aspects of filming would be a challenge, not to mention the danger to the participants in having them scale crumbling walls and stairs. The legal department would stroke out completely. Not only that, but she'd neglected to mention to Dylan that this particular fantasy date was to be an overnight. And while spending the night at an ancient castle fulfilled most of the fantasy requirements, this one was a bit too ancient to adequately cover the overnight part of the deal.

But she really didn't want to think about work right now. Right now she wanted to pretend that he'd done this all for her, and her alone. That it had nothing to do with her job, that he'd thought of it exclusively for the two of them to enjoy. It was a tantalizing fantasy and she decided she'd earned the right to revel in it for a few hours while the rest of the world slept. No one would be the wiser but her.

He held out his hand, and she ignored the little voice that added that no one could be hurt by this but her, either. She was here. He was here. And their feast awaited. Yes, her heart was dangerously close to being in play. Maybe it already was. But leaving now simply wasn't an option. If there was heartache in her future, she was going to make damn sure she got as much of the good stuff as she could, while she could.

She took Dylan's hand as he guided her onto the blankets and knelt down amongst the pillows alongside of him. Her gaze caught his and held there for a moment out of time. Her heart started to pound, and his hold on her hand tightened.

"Hungry?" he said, his voice going all raspy and deep.

She nodded.

Neither of them even glanced at the basket.

Without saying a word, he shifted the lamp off to the side, but didn't stop to light it. She nudged the basket to the edge of the blankets with her toe. His smile faded, and his eyes darkened. Then he lay back on the pillows and pulled her down on top of him. She didn't hesitate, not for one second. A midnight feast she'd have, she thought as he pushed his fingers into her hair, and tugged her head down to his. He claimed her mouth as he rolled her beneath him.

The good stuff, indeed.

Chapter 15

A bloody hoard of banshees could descend upon them and it wouldn't have stopped him. Aye, he'd planned to woo her with wine and moonlight. They'd have the bottle of wine as an aperitif. Right now the only thing he wanted to sup on, was her.

He was done trying to rationalize or explain it. At the moment he was fully prepared to just give in to the demand of his body and sort out the effect it had on his soul later. It had been far, far, too long, and she tasted far, far too good. Most importantly, she wanted him as badly as he wanted her. That was all that could, or should, matter.

He slanted his mouth over hers, intending on a sweet, selfishly slow seduction that would take as long to finish as his control would allow him. He knew better than to count on more than this moment, more than this night, so he intended to make the most of it. But then she moaned a little, and moved her body beneath his, and reached for him, pulling him down more snugly between her legs as she returned his kiss with a fervor he hadn't expected. She teased her tongue into his mouth, dueling with his, then enticing him into her own. But pulling him deeply inside was akin to striking tinder to dry wood. The resulting flame shot high and fast, and consumed him instantly.

He let her have him, let her take his tongue tightly inside the hot, sweet, softness of her mouth. She suckled him again and again, and every hard inch of him twitched repeatedly in response, wanting the same special treatment from those lips, that mouth. He was pushing himself between her thighs, seeking any relief he could find, not caring how close to the edge he was dancing. It felt incredibly bloody good and he saw no need to deny himself any part of it.

The pleasure of touch, the pleasure of taste, the intoxication of a woman's scent . . . how had he denied himself this for so long? He was already pulling at her shirt, desperate now to bare her skin to his need to taste, touch, consume. His passion was only fed further by her need for the same. He could feel her fingers scrabbling at the back of his shirt, yanking, tugging, wanting him as free and bared to her as he needed her to be to him. He was more than happy to comply.

How many times had he imagined this? Dreamed this? Finally making it a reality, and one that surpassed even his most fervent imaginings. He wanted it to last forever, and he couldn't get inside her fast enough.

He broke off their kiss—causing them both to moan in instinctive disappointment—but only long enough to lean back and drag his shirt off. She did the same with her own. When she went to unclasp her bra in the front, he stopped her. "Me," he said, the word more grunt than anything.

Her gaze met his briefly, but he was intent on one thing and one thing only. Oh, he knew quite well who he was with, but she was already tugging at the waistband of his pants, so he didn't think she'd mind if he didn't stop to have a deep, meaningful conversation with her at that particular moment. There was only one thing he wanted that was deep, and that was every aching inch of him buried in the hot, wet, tightness that he knew was waiting for him, deep inside of her. To that end, they both seemed to be in complete agreement.

"Not much to see," she said, tugging his pants down over his hips now that she'd unbuttoned them.

He'd just sprung open the little plastic catch of her bra—a surprising pale blue silk this time—but paused. "I beg your pardon?" He looked down between them, then back into her eyes.

She laughed. "Not you, dummy. Me." She wriggled her own pants over her hips, then grabbed his hips. "Come here. You can stare later."

Not needing to be asked twice, he managed to fish the condom from his pocket. "Just let me—"

She nipped it from his fingers, then pushed at his shoulders as she hooked a leg around his, rolling him easily to his back.

Caught totally off guard, her little maneuver surprised a laugh out of him as well. He put his hands on her hips, steadying her over him as she went about taking care of business. "Far be it from me to stop a woman on a mission."

But as she straddled him, he found he was incapable of being an inactive bystander. He gripped her hips more tightly and pulled her higher, when she would have pushed immediately down on him. He'd been dying to feast on those nipples of hers again—"Ahhh, god." A deep groan, almost a growl, ripped from his throat when she managed to slide completely down and over him anyway.

His neck arched and his eyes squeezed shut as he felt himself pulled into that magical, wonderful place of intense pleasure. Dear god but it had been a long, bloody long time, hadn't it, then? And then she was leaning over him, bracing her hands on his chest, groaning in pleasure as he pulled her down snugly onto him and began matching her thrust for thrust. Her eyes were shut as she moved on him, seemingly lost in her own world as well. Dylan tipped his own head back and gave himself over to the ride, over to the primal power of being joined in the most visceral of ways. It felt so damn good.

She ground her hips on him and he could feel her quicken, feel her muscles tighten around him, and the idea that she was taking herself to the edge pushed him right to the brink of his. He fought against rolling her to her back, letting her finish, thrusting higher, harder, faster as her muscles convulsed and she came. But he wasn't superhuman, and the moment she began to slump forward, aftershocks rippling through her, twitching him too, still buried deep within her, he rolled her beneath him and pulled her knees up past his hips.

One deep stroke and he was already surging. She gasped, bucked and arched, as he hit all of her highly sensitized spots, rejuvenating the orgasm for a few last precious spasms of pleasure. He milked every one of them for his own shameless enjoyment, until he couldn't hold back a second longer and drove so deeply into her they both shifted upward amongst the blankets and pillows. He roared over the edge, thrusting again and again, until there was nothing left.

He managed, barely, to keep from collapsing heavily on top of her, sliding out and shifting his weight off her to his side, grabbing a napkin to quickly take care of things, then rolling flat to his back as they both lay there, splayed beneath the moon and heavens.

There was only the sound of their heavy breathing as long seconds turned to minutes. Until finally she broke the silence. "Are there really that many stars up there, or am I still delirious?"

He grinned. It wasn't going to be awkward, then. Good. But then he'd known she wasn't looking for anything more than he was. And they'd both definitely gotten what they'd wanted. It was going to be fine. "I'm no' so certain I'm the one to ask," he said, his voice hoarse, gravelly. "I'm a bit obliterated myself." He stretched and took a long, slow breath. Och, but he couldn't remember when he'd last felt so good, so sated. "You sure know how to take it out of a man, Erin, that ye do."

She didn't say anything, but when he rolled his head toward her, he saw she was looking quite relaxed herself, still staring up at the stars. He thought about the wine, the cheese and bread he'd packed in the basket, but he was relaxed to a point beyond lethargy and it felt too sweet to disturb it by trying to summon up something as taxing as motion. Yawning deeply, without much thought other than that she felt too far away, he reached for her and rolled her to his side. She came willingly enough, and he was already mostly asleep as she curled against his side, one leg slung companionably over his. He tucked her head beneath his chin and let sleep overtake him, smiling, thinking this was the smartest thing he'd done in a very long time. No regrets, indeed.

He woke at dawn, the sun barely cresting the horizon and slicing into his closed eyelids. He was initially disoriented, but swiftly realized he was outside, naked . . . and quite alone. The previous evening's activities came rushing instantly to mind, and despite what could be a rather discouraging circumstance, he grinned widely and stretched. The morning air was a bit damp, but warm, and he felt like a sleek cat who'd spent the night sipping the finest of cream.

He did have one regret, and that was that they'd wasted the remainder of the night sleeping, not to mention his carefully packed basket, but there would be another time for that. It was only when he finally pulled himself up to a sitting position, blinking a bit until his vision came into focus, that he realized that the basket had indeed been infiltrated. But she was nowhere to be seen. Hmm. He didn't feel any immediate sense of alarm. He couldn't imagine Erin abandoning him out here. Not only that, most of her clothes were still strewn about the blanket, as were most of his. He grinned and reached for the basket, dragging it closer and fishing out a chunk of bread. He was relaxed, better rested than he'd been in what felt like centuries, and ravenous.

He chewed the chunk of bread and washed it down with a half bottle of sparkling water he'd packed, then pulled on his pants and decided to find out where Erin had gotten off to. He doubted she'd gone far, barefoot and naked.

She wasn't on the remains of connecting wall, and he didn't see her anywhere around the tower, so maybe she'd climbed back down and was wandering the rest of the ruins. He went back that way himself, picking his way, barefoot, over the rocks and pebbles as he wound his way around and inside the castle walls. He wandered across the grass-covered open courtyard and through the archway on the other side, heading toward the far tower and what was left of the abbey. He thought about calling out her name, but it was such a peaceful morning and he felt so damn good, he didn't want to disturb the serenity of his surroundings.

He congratulated himself on how well he was handling this whole thing, how well they both had, in fact. Consenting adults, indeed. All that concern he'd had, trying to analyze things and wondering about her . . . had all been just as he'd thought, a result of him being locked up too long alone in Glenshire. Of course he could handle something as innocuous as a little fling. And who more perfect than Erin? She was intriguingly different, but not the sort to get him all tangled up inside, not for long, anyway. They'd tire of each other eventually, once the newness wore off, which was fine as she wouldn't be about for long. Perfect inside and out, their little liaison. She'd seemed equally content last night. He couldn't have asked for better, really.

And then he entered the side of the abbey that still stood, and found her. Clad in nothing more than his shirt and her panties, she sat on a pile of stone that had once comprised several rows of pews, staring toward what would have been the altar, as a lone ray of morning sun slanted through the gaping hole once filled with stained, leaded glass and now cast in a deep, golden glow. She appeared deep in thought, but that wasn't what stopped him in his tracks.

Bollocks and bloody hell! He was a complete and utter fool, he was. So cocksure and full of himself this morning, with his base needs all handily met. Going on about how smart he'd been to find someone who matched him there, and understood about slaking needs and such. Aye, she'd said it wasn't something she made habit of, but then neither was it for him. But both of them knew there could be nothing more than a rare physical chemistry at play here, right? She'd been worried about juggling things with her job . . . not her heart.

So no one was more surprised than he was to discover, upon seeing her sitting there, her hair a godawful mess, her cheeks pink from the moist dawn air and likely from his beard as well, her knees pulled up to her chest with her arms linked loosely about her legs, showcasing a body that was more functional than feminine . . . that it was his heart that would feel that quickening tug.

His heart doing a dangerous little tango. Where in the bloody hell had that come from he wanted to know?

Safe. Erin MacGregor was safe. That's what he'd known, deep inside. That was what had made last night possible. Hearing about her past, her upbringing—or lack thereof—had only cemented that in his mind. She understood him, understood that life wasn't neat and tidy, knew what it meant to look out for number one and damn the rest. In that respect, she was perfect for him. In that respect.

His gaze lingered on the line of her jaw. A bit too sharply edged. Studied the fingertips that dug into her thighs, none of them sporting so much as a fraction of nail, much less any shiny polish. There were no smudges beneath her eyes, as there was no makeup to smudge. She was a straightforward, no artifice, see-what-you-get woman. Someone he'd never have chosen for himself in the past, but, for this moment in his life, a perfect fit. A perfect temporary fit. Someone to help him bridge old life to new, but bridge only.

So how had he not seen this? How had he not realized, fully, the danger he was truly in? That he'd be the poor juggler . . . not her.

Last night, he'd taken her like a damn rutting beast, sure of the knowledge that she wanted him in exactly that mindless, emotionless way. Nothing to juggle there, aye?

So why did he have to clench his jaw to keep from saying her name? Curl his fingers inward to keep from reaching for her? Force himself to stay out of sight, fighting an almost overwhelming need to go to her, talk to her, make her laugh, see her smile, enjoy everything about her that made her the right woman for him. And not simply for today, but perhaps for all the tomorrows she'd give him?

Bloody, fucking fool.

As if sensing him there, she turned her head. Her smile was immediate, but a bit tentative. "Hey, there."

Pinned, he had to act. Stepping through the abbey arch was both the easiest and hardest step he'd ever taken. He stopped several feet inside the portal. "Hey there, yourself." He suddenly didn't know what to say to her. Far too many emotions were presently battling for dominance for him to be able to sort them all out and handle the moment correctly at the same time. He glanced around. "This was once quite the place," he said, opting to step around the elephant in the room between them. For now. Cowardly though it may be, it was preservation at its most instinctive base. "This part of the fortress was designed by a friar in the fourteenth century, before it belonged to the Fenton clan. More than one of my ancestors was married here."

"I wish I could have seen what it looked like then." If she was hoping for a more substantive or personal discussion, she didn't show it.

In fact, for the first time, he couldn't quite read her at all. It wasn't like her to be enigmatic, and he found he was a bit alarmed by that. It mattered to him, what she was thinking. Scared him a little, too. But he wasn't ready to probe that reaction, either. So he went with relief that she was giving them both some space and was simply thankful for it. "Have you walked more of the place?"

"Some." She slid off her perch, straightening her bare legs and making him instantly ache for her again.

It wasn't just seeing her in his shirt, knowing she was a scrap of panty silk away from being naked beneath him again, if that's what he wanted. What she wanted. The ache so persistently dogging him this morning went far deeper than that.

"There's another tower, in the rear," he managed,

wondering how long she'd let him get away with playing tour guide. Wondering if it would be long enough for him to make sense of the jumble of emotions she'd stirred up inside of him. Just by being herself. "Not as much left of it, but the view just beyond is pretty fantastic." He started to walk in that general direction, but she didn't follow.

"I—I really should be getting back."

He turned, noting the way she scuffed a toe in the grass, the way her fingers were twined together, both of which belied her apparent calm, easy demeanor. Maybe she was confused, too. He didn't have the balls to ask at the moment.

"I didn't want to disturb you," she said, "you were sleeping pretty soundly. So I thought I'd take a bit of a walk. But I have a million things to do and—"

"Right. Sure," he said, his heart squeezing, which told him a great deal right there. "Come on, then. Mind your step."

He waited until she passed by him, back through the arch, and started across the courtyard before falling into step behind her. No pause for a morning kiss, no touch as she walked past him. Nothing more than a bit of a smile, her eyes bright, maybe overly bright.

He'd never felt so lost in a situation. Maybe he should have reached for her, given her some sign, any sign, that last night was more than a rut for him. Except maybe that's all it had been for her. Far be it for him to needlessly complicate something that didn't need complicating. She'd said she didn't think she could juggle, so he should just let her get back to business and be thankful she'd managed to juggle one night with him into her life.

So, why he had an almost overwhelming urge to break something, he had no idea.

She was just far enough ahead of him, that she'd

scaled the outer wall stairs before he could jog close enough to help her. She was at the blanket and tugging on her pants by the time he got there. She scooped up her bra and shirt and turned to face the rising sun as she pulled off his shirt, her back to him.

He hated that she needed the privacy. One thing he'd purely enjoyed about her was her take-no-prisoners style. Yet here she was, almost shyly dressing herself. Had he done that to her? Had he really screwed this up so badly? He watched her, unable to look away, as if he needed to drink in every last vision he might have, store it up somehow. The sun played over her shoulders and arms, burnishing her skin, high-lighting the tips of her wispy hair. She slid on her bra, tugged on her shirt, all with economical grace. He couldn't take his eyes off her. She turned and tossed him his shirt. "Thank you for the loan."

"Anytime," he said, and meant it quite sincerely. The idea that he'd never have her again, never taste her again, never get to truly indulge himself in her—as last night had hardly involved any of that, despite his best intentions—left him feeling quite desolate. Which was ridiculous. Sure, he'd hoped for more than a one-night stand, but nothing more serious than a string of a few more. This aching desperation wasn't acceptable. Yet he had no idea how to switch it off.

She, apparently, hadn't had that particular problem.

She slipped on her shoes and started to fold up the blankets.

He still stood there, barefoot, shirt in hand.

She glanced up at him. "You want to step off that so I can fold it?" If she thought it odd or frustrating that he wasn't in any real hurry to dress and get out of there, she didn't say so. Again, she seemed outwardly calm, and mostly, well, functional was the word that came to mind. Picking up, cleaning up, dressing. He couldn't read what she was thinking or feeling. It drove him crazy.

He stepped back and reached down to grab the basket and lantern and move them aside, nudging a few of the pillows off the blanket, before finally giving up the charade that everything was fine and dandy. "Erin. I—"

"How did you get all this up here, anyway?" she asked, cutting him off. "I still can't believe you went to all this trouble. If you were out to impress, you certainly did." She was talking too fast, sounding too effusive. Erin was direct and enthusiastic, but bubbly was not exactly her typical mien.

So the whole calm demeanor thing was a façade. Good.

He tossed his shirt down and took hold of her arms, pulling her to a stand in front of him. "Aye, I *was* trying to impress," he said, "but I've failed miserably."

She kept that faux sincerity on her face, despite the surprise he'd caught briefly flickering through. "But I just told you that you didn't. I've never had anyone go to such lengths. Of course, I know it was more for the show than for me, and we'll have to talk about that. I don't want you to get your hopes up there, but—"

"Stop."

She abruptly shut up. Which told him volumes more about her state of mind than maybe she'd intended to telegraph. Too bad. He had no problems exploiting it if it meant they got past this farcical behavior.

"Erin." He waited until she looked him in the face. "I'm sorry."

That definitely surprised her. "What on earth for?"

"Last night was—"

"Better for me than for you, apparently." Bright smile gone, she was all practiced defiance now. It irritated the living hell out of him. He wanted his Erin back, not this . . . this . . . automaton.

She tugged her arm free and crouched back down so she could start folding again, only she clearly wasn't paying any attention to what she was doing and just balling things up. A chink in her armor, finally. At least that was a start.

"Maybe I should be the one doing the apologizing," she said, not as calmly as before. Perhaps a bit huffy, in fact.

"Oh, for god's sake." Dylan crouched in front of her, stopping her manic movements by taking both her arms in his grasp. "What is wrong with us this morning?"

"Wrong? What do you mean? I've been perfectly civil. I let you sleep, I'm helping to clean up, complimenting you, what do you want?"

He wanted to shake her. Then throw her down on the blanket and make love to her the way he should have last night, instead of taking her like some beast in full rut. "I want the real Erin back, please."

Her eyebrow arched. "Excuse me?"

He smiled. "Yeah, more like that."

She gave him a disgusted snort, then returned to her hasty packing. "Whatever. I'm sorry to cut all this short, but I really do have to get back."

So . . . could it be that she was avoiding dealing with the same thing he was? Just going about it differently, perhaps. Escape and avoid. Same tactic he'd used in the library. He could tell her it was a waste of time. But he doubted she'd listen.

"I know, and I'll get you back as quickly as I can, but I wanted to talk to you about . . ." He trailed off, realizing he sounded like every lame morning-after guy in history. The was-it-good-for-you guy. He wasn't that bloke, all frail ego, needing reassurance. But that's how it was going to sound to her. He needed a different kind of reassurance altogether. But faced with the exact wording, he was left a bit speechless.

"About what? About last night?"

Of course she'd handle it directly. Why had he worried?

"Well, yes."

"I thought it was pretty obvious we both had a good time, enjoyed each other, unless I'm really that off my—"

"No, no," he hastened to assure her. "I—we both seemed to manage to figure things out well enough, it's just—"

"There's a scintillating review." She said it dryly and without malice, as if she hadn't expected raves. She laid a hand on his arm.

He wondered if she had any idea the instant reaction her mere touch caused in him, or that he was already thinking of how to talk her into staying here for just a wee bit longer.

"If you're worried I was expecting more, don't. We've already gone over our essential incompatibilities. I would have said no if I didn't want things to go where they did, and I know you'd have respected that or I'd have never agreed to come out here with you in the middle of the night in the first place. I have absolutely no regrets." She smiled, and it looked sincere and bright, but he noted it didn't quite reach the depths of her eyes. A beautiful green as always, but not sparkling this fine morning.

He realized he wanted nothing more than to make her eyes sparkle again. It bothered him a great deal that she could look at him, talk about something intimate shared between them, without so much as a glimmer or gleam.

"So, no worries, okay?" She patted his arm, then went back to rolling and gathering blankets.

But he was worried. Worried that he should be vastly relieved by this little chat, and was anything but.

Worried that he wanted her to care more, to expect more, nay, to absolutely demand more from him, and even more worried that perhaps he wouldn't be able to deliver if she did. No' that he wouldn't try. But what if he'd given her his all and she'd still looked at him as she was right now? Very thanks-for-the-toss-time-to-go-mate.

"Tell me then, you never answered me earlier. When you accepted my invitation . . . was it with a thought as to where it might lead?"

She glanced up briefly, then held his gaze when she saw the sincerity of his tone matched his expression. "I think it would be disingenuous to pretend otherwise, but I won't say I expected something to happen."

"You'd have been satisfied then, if we'd gone for a spin, and I'd returned you to your room, safe, sound and—"

"Unravished?" she added, a start of that daring smile sparking back to life. "Part of me would have been disappointed, the rest of me would have convinced that part that it was for the best. To keep from complicating things."

"So no regrets regardless then. As long as things don't get . . . complicated."

Now she didn't even pretend to do busy work. She sat back on her haunches and truly looked at him. "What do you want me to say? What are you angling for here?"

Good question, that. He opted to go with honesty, and see where that took them. "When I set this up, I did have every intention of seducing you."

She merely nodded. "Okay."

"When I left the library earlier this week, my plan was to stay away. Perhaps even make all our lives easier and go bunk with one of my brothers for the duration."

"But?"

He looked at her, truly looked at her. She was everything he'd never wanted in a woman. So why did he all but ache to have her again? Was it the chase? That she wasn't throwing herself at him? "Ye plague me, still, you know that."

Which made her laugh. "Yes, I haven't forgotten the lovely light in which you hold me."

He shook his head. "I heard what you said, that day in the library, about complicating things, juggling obligations, and I agreed with you. So I left, with every intention of keeping that agreement. But I couldn't stop thinking about you. That I had to stay away in order to make it stick, should have told me something right then and there. But no, I told myself it was simply a matter of opening myself up to feeling anything, and you were simply the catalyst of that reawakening."

"I'm feeling more flattered by the second," she said wryly, causing him to hang his head.

"I'm no' conveying my meaning properly." He looked back up. "In the past, my taste has run quite differently, but I'm a very different man now, who perhaps doesna know himself well enough to know what is right for him. I respond to you, for myriad reasons. I grew tired of analyzing them, of trying to make sense of it. It seemed to me the best way to figure things out was to spend more time with you and let it define itself."

"That's up front, and I appreciate that. So I'll respond in kind. I confess I accepted your invitation for much the same reasons." She smiled briefly. "Don't let it go to your head, but ye plague me, too."

"You're getting far too accomplished with that accent," he said, enjoying the return of her warmth as well as her acerbity. There was a sense of security in that.

"It's a skill I picked up growing up. I could mimic

most of the staff, and did a dead-on impression of the head mistress. I figured out early on that I could win friends and influence people by making them laugh."

"Was that your goal then, when you moved to Hollywood? Were you hoping to be a performer?"

"No. I fell into my job entirely by accident. I had just finished my marketing degree and was working for an ad agency in L.A. and . . . long story short, I ended up helping Tommy's then location coordinator after overhearing her trying to work a deal with a maitre d' where I ate lunch. I stepped in, set her up, and it turned out well. Really well in fact. Tommy offered me an assistant's job. It sounded exciting and it was crazy to take the leap, but the promise of travel really grabbed me, so I took a risk and went for it. Then my boss got pregnant and left, and I got her job." She smiled and for the first time her face truly lit up. "Truly a dream come true job."

Her eyes finally sparkled, he thought, and it wasn't for him, but for his number one adversary: her occupation.

Didn't that goddamn well figure.

"You're a lucky lass, then. To have married work and life together in such a blissful union is the best of all rewards." He pushed to a stand, needing to step away from her, this aborted morning, all of it, and reclaim a bit of himself. He'd allowed himself to indulge in the fantasy and look where that had taken him. But perhaps, given his inability to be the juggler, that was for the best, too.

Now it was back to the norm of his life. Cold, harsh reality. One thing was for certain, if he couldn't manage to separate the two in such a short time with her, that certainly cemented the truth that he was no' cut out to court a dozen women as their next leading man. He began to see the truth behind her explanation of why the men in question on her program fancied themselves in love with someone they'd hardly just gotten to know. Constant exposure under extreme circumstances did interesting things to one's perception and logic.

Good thing he'd figured out that he was merely suffering from a cause-and-effect situation and by extracting himself now, he would swiftly return to reason and rational thought.

Now if he could only be certain he'd also have dream free nights, as well.

"Leave the blankets and picnic basket. I'll return for them later. We should be getting you back."

"Are you sure? I can carry the blankets if you can get the basket and lantern." She glanced down at what had been the scene of his planned seduction. "I'm not sure about the pillows."

"Leave it all. I'll bring the basket if you want to snack a bit on the ride back. I've bottled water and bread. The cheese is probably fine. There are some grapes." And oh, the midnight tryst he'd had imagined, exciting all the senses with the crisp taste of fruit, the heady scent of wine . . . He wondered if it would have made a difference in how this morning had turned out, but refused to allow himself to make any more of a fool of himself than he already had by even speculating on that possibility.

She grabbed a plump, square pillow and stood, the not-quite-sparkly smile pasted back on her face. "I really do appreciate all the trouble you went to. I'm sorry we didn't give the feast its proper due."

"It's okay," he said, wondering if his own smile was as noticeably forced as hers was. "Come on." He led the way, needing to leave as much as she did, only perhaps for different reasons. He'd missed the feast. And not the one that included grapes and chunks of cheese. But the feast of Erin. He hadn't even managed to handle that right, for memory's sake.

"I'll drop you round back at the service entrance so you can head in and freshen up a bit and no one will be the wiser."

Hugging the pillow to her chest, she passed him as he gestured for her to take the stairs down first. "Very gallant. I appreciate that, thanks."

Gallant. Hardly. He found himself resisting the urge to apologize all over again. Clearly she didn't feel the lack of romance last night, or hadn't been looking for it in the first place. She'd said all the right things. If he were truly gallant, he'd follow her lead, both figuratively and literally, and let this one night be what it was. A sexual release of pent up need, ne'er to be repeated. He should be thankful he'd gotten that much.

They were halfway back across the valley, the ride spent almost completely in silence, not as companionable as their easy silences of the past. He abruptly pulled off the road and tugged the pillow she still hugged from her arms. No more shields, no more barriers.

"What's wrong?" she said, blinking at him in sleepy surprise, as she'd been half drowsing. She was fully awake now.

"This. It's all wrong."

Before she could ask him to elaborate, he leaned across the center stick and reached for her. She was still getting her senses straight, which was probably why she let him without any attempt to pull away. "Dylan, what are you—"

"Once we get back, the craziness will consume you again. I know that's your world, and you thrive on it. I'm glad we had the night, but I apologized before not because I was disappointed in you, but because I'd wanted it to go differently than it did."

She sat up a little straighter, alert now. "Different how?"

"I wanted all night with you, not such a hurried rush. I knew it might be one night and one night only and I'd meant to make the most of it. And instead—"

"We both reacted to the moment the same way. You didn't see me objecting to that."

"I know. We took the edge off what we'd been building since, well, since—"

"You startled me into almost falling over the railing in front of your house," she said, with a hint of teasing smile. "Or maybe it was later for you. But I wanted you right then."

The confession both poleaxed him, and gave him the exact toehold he needed to finish what he'd once again begun. "I wanted more than that edge removed, Erin. I wanted . . ." He trailed off, not sure what the words were he was looking for. So he showed her. "I wanted this."

He tugged her close and this time when he took her mouth, he claimed it slowly, thoroughly, and completely, seducing her with his tongue, with his lips, with everything he could pour into one, soul-searing kiss . . . until they were both left leaning limply in each other's arms, trying to draw a regular breath and finding only partial success.

"Um . . . wow," she breathed, moments later, her fingers still entwined in his hair, her face pressed into his neck.

He turned his face into her hair. And grinned madly. "Yeah," he murmured. "Exactly."

Chapter 16

Erin was still reeling when Dylan gently disengaged her arms from his neck and tucked the pillow back against her body. A moment later they were spewing gravel as he peeled the little roadster back onto the track and shot them like a bullet across the valley floor.

What in the hell had just happened? She'd had an hour or so of hot, sweaty, wild sex with this man, with him thrusting everything he had into her and taking her screaming over the edge into a violently satisfying orgasm. It had been raw and visceral, exhilarating and staggering, all at the same time.

And yet it hadn't even hinted at the intimacy he'd just shared with her in that one, soul-searing kiss.

She couldn't string coherent thoughts together, much less actual words. She couldn't even bring herself to look over at him. So she simply stared ahead, clutching at the pillow in her lap, wondering what in the hell happened now?

It had cost her everything she had to play the unaffected, one-night-stand girl this morning. Yes, when she'd spied the blankets, the basket, the lantern, the pillows, her little romantic heart had gone pitty-pat. She had visions, albeit brief ones, of them slowly undressing each other in the moonlight, taking the time to explore each other's bodies, making slow, sweet, mind-blowing love to one another as stars shot across the sky overhead. Ah yes, she'd had it all plotted out in under five seconds.

And had quite willingly thrown that scenario right under the bus when he'd grabbed her and pulled her down on top of him. Something about an alpha male like Dylan wanting her, average Erin, so badly he could barely be civil, had been possibly the most exciting thing she'd ever experienced. She had thrown herself completely into the moment, and at him, with great and willing abandon. No complaints on her part.

Then, afterward, when they were lying there, sprawled on their backs, staring sightlessly up at the sky, breathing hard, with big, stupid, satisfied grins on their faces, a little of the romantic in her began to creep back in when he pulled her into his arms. She'd listened to his breathing smooth out as she let sleep claim her as well. There would still be morning, she'd thought. Or perhaps sometime in the middle of the night, they'd wake each other up, start slowly, enjoy each other again, only more lingeringly and with great tenderness, as he'd shown her in those kisses earlier in the evening. Only when she'd opened her eyes again, dawn had been breaking, and Dylan had been sound asleep, his arm still carelessly slung around her. She'd watched him sleep, toying with the idea of waking him up, seeing where the morning might take them. She'd let her fingers do a little exploring, but stopped before she got too bold.

The longer he slept without so much as a murmured whisper or grunt of awareness, the more she started to think. Never a good idea the morning after a night like they'd shared. It had been sex, she'd realized. Raw, passionate, primal sex, but what they'd shared could in no way be construed as personal. And she wanted more. She wanted lovemaking, she wanted him to look into her eyes while he made love to her.

She wanted exactly what she'd been trying to avoid wanting.

Emotional involvement.

Which was when she'd gotten up and slipped on his shirt—so she'd wanted the scent of him on her a little longer, so what?—and wandered a safe distance away. Before she did something truly foolish.

And thus, one-night-stand girl was born. She'd learned early on that the best defense was always an awesome offense. Being the first to rise gave her the distinct advantage of setting the morning-after tone. She could be cool, she could be unaffected, she could be blithely blasé about the fact that not six hours ago she'd had hot monkey sex with this guy. She could if it meant keeping her heart intact, anyway. Because if she let herself want, or wish, or hope, for one teeny tiny second, that things had gone a little differently, she'd be doomed.

She liked Dylan Chisholm. She liked his complexity, his moods, his laughter, his intensity. She appreciated the tough choices he'd faced, and that he wasn't a hundred percent okay with every one he'd made. Who was? She certainly wasn't. She had enormous respect for the choice he'd made now, in coming back and taking on such a monumental task. She'd like to think she'd have done the same, but it was so far outside the realm of any part of her past, she couldn't really know for sure. He made her think about herself, about her life, about the choices she'd made.

But it was the very difference in their paths that held her frozen in that seat, clutching a stupid pillow, instead of reaching for him. She'd been able to divert, intentionally misread, or just plain pretend she didn't understand what he was getting at back at the ruins. She'd expected him to take her nonchalant lead gratefully and go with it. She hadn't expected that maybe he'd woken up with the same confusing swirl of emotions she had. Because to even consider that complicated things in ways she had no hope of handling.

Until just now. When he'd taken matters into his own hands. Taken her into his own hands. And put an indelible stamp on her, so she had no choice but to understand exactly what he was thinking, exactly what he was wanting. And what terrified her most? She was secretly thrilled by it. Totally, want-to-jump-up-and-down, squealing like a Barbie, happy toes, thrilled by it.

She wanted Dylan Chisholm. And, by all that was holy and truly incomprehensible, he seemed to want her too.

So now what in the hell did she do?

Given what had just happened, she doubted Dylan was going to sit idly by and wait for her to set the pace. No, he was going to go after what he wanted. And damn if that didn't make a girl squirm in her seat, in the most pleasurable of ways. She wondered what Dana would say. For about a second. She knew exactly what her assistant would say. *Go for it, you big dummy!*

She sneaked a peek at him from the corner of her eye. The play of muscles in his forearm as he shifted gears. The solid length of his thigh, which she happened to know was perfectly muscled. Restoring a centuries old mansion was apparently better than a regular gym workout. And it could all be hers.

Temporarily.

And for a price.

Given how her secretly mushy heart was currently oozing all over the place, the price tag would be a hefty one. She'd get involved. Okay, more involved. Who was she kidding? And then what? Even if she stayed in

Scotland to do the advance prep work on the next season when everyone went back to California to do the post production on the piles of film from this season, it would only extend her stay here another few months at best.

Just enough time for her to fall well and truly under his spell, before having to say a tragic good-bye.

She was never going to watch Brigadoon again.

Erin came out of her fog in time to notice they were pulling into the service lot behind the hotel. Dammit, she'd wasted all this time mentally fencing with herself and hadn't figured out what she was going to say to him. Fortunately or unfortunately, as it turned out, she didn't have to.

In the service lot were two of the production crew's oversized van rentals. Both of which were spewing out a cluster of gorgeous women in a tumble of hairspray and laughter.

"Oh crap. They're here," Erin muttered.

"What?" Dylan asked distractedly.

Erin sighed and glanced over at him. Yep. Glazed eyes. "You sure you don't want to be on the show?" she asked dryly, while he stared in unabashed awe at the women as they continued to step from the vans. She made a hand gesture like a game show girl. "All this could be yours, Mr. Chisholm," she intoned in her best hostess voice. "Twelve beautiful women, all dying to have you."

She already had her hand on the door. It was for the best, anyway. Took care of her stupid fantasy issues real quick. Now she didn't have to worry what to do. Then Tommy was squeezing himself through the throng and suddenly appearing at her car door, flinging it open and pulling her out. "What is this?" he demanded, tugging the pillow from her arms and tossing it back in the car. "My god, you look like something the cat refused to drag in. Anyway, no time, no time." He clapped his hands. "Listen up. What is this I hear about you taking off this weekend for Inverness?"

"I'm still scouting that last overnight," she said, not really lying through her teeth since she planned to kill two birds while there. "I've got everything covered here, don't worry."

He dramatically gestured behind her. "Well, I think it's quite obvious plans have changed. They're here early and I'm not set up. I need you to—Oh." He broke off when a sudden squeal rose through the cluster of contestants and they both turned to see Dylan swarmed as he got out of the car.

"Is that him!" one woman excitedly squealed, starting a mad rush.

Tommy shot Erin a quick, almost naughty wink. "Well, why didn't you just tell me you were sealing the deal. Bravo."

Before Erin could open her mouth to—well, she wasn't sure, to what. Lie, cover her ass, cover Dylan's ass? Slap Tommy for even insinuating she'd do something like that as part of her job description?

As the women swarmed Dylan, the petty, insecure side of herself reared its vulnerable little head and she decided he could save his own sexy ass. What she couldn't do was let him tell Tommy he wasn't doing the show. Of course, another ten minutes of being pawed by a handful of the most gorgeous women in the world, he might change his mind and solve all their problems.

All but the one that made something inside her chest twinge painfully tight as she was forced to watch them touch his chest, lean on his shoulder, take his arm . . . and she was forced to acknowledge the twinge was rampant jealousy. She wanted to fling herself in front of him and proclaim him off limits, to loudly and definitively state that she and only she had the right to fawn all over him, thank you very much.

At which point they'd all take one look at her and laugh themselves sick. And the worst part is, Dylan might have joined them. Well, no, he wouldn't have, but far worse would be the look of "Sorry, what was I thinking?" he very well might send her way.

Every rejection she ever faced as a child at Crestview came roaring back, as crystal clear as if they'd happened yesterday. Which was completely ridiculous. This had nothing to do with that. That was ancient history she'd long since settled within herself. But it didn't stop the little knot of anguish from forming in her belly anyway.

Then Tommy was in her face again. "God, he is marketing gold. Do I have an eye or what? But we have to get him the hell away from the women before he spoils them for Greg." He clapped his hands again and raised his voice to be heard. "Ladies? Ladies, please, follow your handlers to the rooms we've set aside for you. We'll have people in there to prep you for your first interviews shortly." He turned and shouted. "Sebastian, did we get the hair and makeup people in yet? Where the hell is Tanya?" And whatever else he'd been about to lecture Erin about was lost in the ensuing melee of production assistants, hairdressers, and handlers.

Erin was tugged away in the throng and the last she saw of Dylan, they were prying one particularly clingy contestant from his arm. She ignored the wrenching pang in her gut, telling herself she deserved nothing less for being foolish enough to entertain even for one split second that this was going to end well for her. Maybe she should be thankful. Cut it off dead now, before she got in any deeper.

Yeah, thankful. That was going to take a bit longer to embrace.

"Oh, thank god!" Dana materialized from the craziness and took Erin by both arms. "You're back. Where have you been? I've been paging your room for the past hour." Then she looked past Erin's shoulder. "And who the hell is the rock star over there? My god, you'd think these women had never seen a tall, good looking guy." And then she was looking back at Erin and froze in the act of leaning in to give her a half hug. She leaned back and studied Erin's face, then shifted her gaze to the rapidly disappearing Dylan, then back to Erin. "Oh. My. God. *Him?* Really?" She pulled her glasses out and jammed them on her cute button nose, lifting up on tiptoe to see over the crowd in the lot. "Score."

Erin grabbed her arm and tugged her around the side of one of the parked vans. "We need to talk."

"Sure thing, boss. What's up? Wait, wait, first I have to know one thing." She stared Erin right in the eyes, studied her for a long few seconds, then grinned. "Oh my god, you did, didn't you?" She raised her hand in a high five gesture. "You go, boss."

Erin tugged Dana's hand down and pulled her farther around the corner, away from the insanity. "It doesn't matter. Listen. I need you to go to Inverness this weekend for me."

"But Tommy has me on Barbie Patrol twenty-four-seven." She leaned in and lowered her voice. "And I swear they gave me to this season's psycho-drama-bitch. I kid you not, this woman has at least three personalities living inside her at any given moment. She'll never make it past the first elimination, but mark my words, she'll get her fifteen minutes worth. Ratings gold right there. Tommy is probably peeing his pants just watching her deliver the crazy. But for me? Not as much fun. I could do without so much crazy."

"Good, then you won't mind going to Inverness for two days and scouting guys in kilts for me."

Dana opened her mouth to retort, then snapped it shut

again. A moment later her lips curved and she clasped her hands together under her chin. "You wouldn't tease a jet-lagged, seriously stressed out woman now would you, boss? Because, that would just be cruel."

Erin smiled despite the emotions still roiling around inside of her. This is why she loved Dana. "No, I'm serious. Tommy is having orgasms over Dylan and—"

"Who wouldn't?" Dana sighed. "Oh right. Not you!" She laughed, then immediately stopped when she saw something in Erin's expression. She sobered immediately. "Uh-oh."

"I don't want to talk about it. Not now." And she'd apparently put enough flatness into her voice that, for once, her assistant complied. "And now that Tommy has seen the women react to him, he's probably already calling L.A. I need to find a new Prince Charming like yesterday."

"One better than him? With his own castle?"

"Glenshire isn't a castle, it's—never mind. Yes, that's your mission, Jane Bond. I'm sure you're up to the task. Unless you really have your heart set on Barbie wrangling."

She saluted Erin. "When do I leave?"

"Just as soon as you dive into that mob and keep Tommy away from Dylan. We were swarmed on arrival and I didn't get the chance to instruct Dylan on what to say to our wonderful boss if confronted about the whole contract thing."

"So . . . you arrived together? Just this morning?" She beamed like a proud parent and touched Erin's arm. "My little girl is growing up."

Erin knew better than to think she was going to stifle Dana's enthusiasm for something like this, and only because there was absolute sincere affection lacing her every word, did she not strangle her assistant on the spot. Dana couldn't possibly understand the tangle of raw emotions Erin was going through at the moment.

"Just go do that for me, okay? We'll meet up while your Barbies are getting their first grilling and by then I should have things worked out. I'd like you to leave tomorrow morning, back Sunday nightfall. That gives you two-and-a-half days to find Mr. Perfect. Oh, and you'll be staying in a hotel I want to use for an overnight, so you'll have to do a little meeting with their coordinator."

"Will do." Dana leaned in. "You want I should casually knee him or something? Was he mean to you?"

That was the other reason Erin loved her assistant. She was truly loyal and would defend and protect without question. "No, he was fine. There's nothing to—just keep him away from Tommy until he can get out of here. He'll be heading back to Glenshire just as soon as Tommy gets the women sequestered inside and away from him, I'm sure."

Dana held her gaze for another second and looked like she was going to ask another question. Erin was sure she had at least a couple dozen already on the tip of her tongue.

"Please?" Erin added. "Now?"

"Right. We'll talk later then?"

Erin nodded, though she had no intention of talking about any of it, and scooted her assistant back around the van, then took off the other way, ducking into the kitchen entrance of the hotel, and taking a back flight of service steps up to her floor. She whispered a heartfelt thank you to the merciful gods who allowed her to get all the way upstairs and into her room with the door shut and locked behind her without being seen or stopped by a single soul.

She slumped against the door and let out a long,

heartfelt sigh. By her calculations, she had at least ten minutes to take a shower, change clothes, get her entire emotional state in order, and be back downstairs in time for Tommy to be screaming for her when he remembered he hadn't finished dictating his latest set of orders.

"You look like you've been chased by the hounds of hell."

Erin let out a yelp and leapt away from the door, spinning around with her hand pressed to her chest. Only to discover Dylan's rangy body sprawled in one of the stuffed chairs by the window. "What the—how did you get in here?"

"A very nice hotel employee by the name of Amelia, I think it was, was kind enough to let me in."

"You can't be in here. You—you should head back to Glenshire—"

"And hide out there instead?" His grin was lazy and far too cocky. "I'd much rather hide here."

"Are you kidding? There is no hiding here."

"Aye, I know." He raked his hand through his hair and let out a weary sigh. "Are all American women so aggressive? I was lucky to get out of there with my clothes intact."

"All the more reason to head back to Glenshire. You've created enough stir around here for one day. All we need is for there to be buzz that you're in my room."

"Dinna ye think us turning up just past dawn in my car might have lifted a few brows already?"

It was chaos enough in the courtyard when they arrived. She was hoping no one was really paying attention. Tommy had noticed, but obviously if he thought she was signing Dylan to be his next Prince Charming, he'd give her all the overnights she wanted. An idea immediately popped in her head, and she just as immediately shoved it right back out again. Because as much as she wanted to get out of town for a few days, a trip to Inverness with Dylan would be far more complicated than staying here. The very notion of a few days alone with him made her heart ache. Yep. Very bad idea.

No, she'd let Dana take care of that trip and focus on keeping the peace here for the time being. Which wasn't going to happen if everyone was gossiping about a certain Scot being stashed away in her room.

"If it'll ease yer mind any, I asked Amelia to keep mum about my whereabouts. She seemed more than willing to comply."

Erin silently thanked fate for delivering the one hotel employee who was loyal to her and Dylan in his time of need. If there was a hope of keeping the rumor mill down to a dull roar, Amelia was her only one. "I've got five minutes, maybe ten, then I have to meet Tommy downstairs." And likely deflect a barrage of questions about her progress with Dylan.

Dylan stretched his long legs out and smiled at her. "I thought perhaps I'd avoid the entire mess and camp out here for a bit. I'll be out of the way at Glenshire and out of the way here."

For a man she'd thought entirely too taciturn upon first meeting him, he'd turned into quite the cocky charmer. The very idea of trying to get anything done, knowing he was up here, tangled in her sheets, slumbering the morning away . . . Yeah. She'd be a total loss.

"Why don't I run lookout for you and we'll find a way to sneak you down to your car. I'm sure the women are all tucked away by now, doing their interviews and being briefed on the first day of filming. Tommy really doesn't want to have you in eyesight of them anyway. So you'll be doing us all a favor by heading home.

You'd much rather camp out in your own wing anyway, I'm sure. Or you could let me book you in somewhere else entirely as I wanted to do all along."

He rose with panther-like grace and intent that had her all caught up in staring at him, thereby giving him an edge she couldn't afford. He was standing in front of her before she realized she was cornered. He lifted a finger and traced the line of her jaw. She wanted to think the energetic night they'd shared had dulled her reaction time, but it was more that he had her mesmerized with the look she saw in his eyes.

Desire, yes. But she'd seen that before. Quite clearly, in fact, even with nothing more than moonlight to illuminate him. There was something else there now, something almost . . . playful, and affectionate. And confident. All but proclaiming that now that he'd staked his claim, he wasn't planning on shying away from it. Which robbed her of any hope she had of finding the strength to resist him.

"Dinna make me go, Erin," he said quietly. "You've booted me from my own home, ye've taken over my world. The least ye could do is let me stay in yours for a wee bit." He moved a step closer, let his fingers trace up along her cheek, along the outer shell of her ear, then down along the line of her neck, before slipping slowly along her collar bone. Never did he take his gaze from hers. She couldn't have moved if her life depended on it. And while it might not be her life at stake, her livelihood most certainly was. Considering that was her life, she was in a wee bit of trouble here.

"Dylan, I thought we agreed—"

"That we weren't finished yet." He moved in close now, and her defenses were rattled to the core. He slid his hands down her arms until he covered her hands, tugging them up and placing them on his chest. "I know it's complicated, Erin. And no' convenient or easy. But let me ask you this. When I kissed you in the car . . . did we feel finished to you?"

There was no breaking his gaze. The intensity, the sheer force of his will, was too demanding. There was no subterfuge possible. "It doesn't matter what is or isn't finished," she finally managed, her own voice dropping to a quiet murmur. "This . . . I don't even know what you'd call it, but I told you before, I'm not good at juggling."

"I won't keep you from your work."

"Are you kidding? I'm already too distracted by you."

That was a serious miscalculation on her part, as it brought the most wicked, satisfied grin to his face.

"And I wasn't talking about juggling my job, though that's a major concern. I was talking about . . ." And suddenly she couldn't finish. She'd made herself vulnerable enough to him already. Too vulnerable and far outside her safety zone.

His smile faded and his expression turned quite serious. "I know what you were talking about," he said quietly. "'Tis no' a simple matter for me, either. This is no game for me. If that was all I needed or wanted, I would spend far more time in the village, taking advantage of all the matchmaking schemes being dreamed up on my sorry behalf."

That he wasn't playing around, that he actually thought of this, of her, as something he could be serious about . . . ? Erin shut down that highly terrifying train of thought. But the message didn't reach her mouth in time. "What is this, then? Because you're here, with a world of burden on your shoulders. And I—my world is wherever my job takes me. Here for now, but not for long. I appreciate that we're attracted to each other, and I do wish—"

He suddenly framed her face, more serious than she

could ever remember seeing him. "What do ye wish, Erin? That it were simple, easy? Nothing is. We, more than most, understand and appreciate that."

"I know. I just . . ." She covered his hands and pulled them from her face, holding them tightly for a second, then dropping them and stepping back. It took every scrap of willpower she had. But it was now or never. If he'd pulled her closer, kissed her, she'd be lost with no hope of surfacing in time to save herself. "I want to. I want you. More of you. Maybe all of you. But I have to be realistic."

His lips twisted into a smile, but there was nothing warm in it this time. "Says the woman who makes a living creating fantasy."

"Which is why I understand the difference between the two," she said softly, sadly.

"You said yourself, that despite all the odds, your Prince Charming manages to find the rose amongst the thorns. In a situation that is structured fantasy, it allows the two people to discover the core of what is real between them. You told me this." He took up her hands again, held them between him. "So why don't you believe in what you see happen time and again when it comes to yourself?"

She'd never thought of it that way. But then she'd never had a reason to. So when she answered him, it was with the same blunt honesty she'd given him since the beginning. "Maybe because I don't know how." Her lips curved softly. "You're a lucky man, that you still hold on to that, after all you've been through. Who'd have thought, of the two of us, that I'd be the one with the cynical heart, huh?"

"Erin—"

"Maybe you should reconsider. Maybe you should be the next Prince Charming after all. You're in the perfect place in your life, and you're open to the idea of letting someone in." The idea of hanging around while they set him up with twelve other women, forced to watch while he looked at someone else the way he was looking at her right now stabbed at her heart. Which only cemented her decision. After all, at best, she was temporary anyway.

"Not really," he told her. "I'm overwhelmed by my life almost all the time. These past few weeks of insanity notwithstanding. I didn't want to let anyone in then, and I'm definitely not interested in entertaining a harem now."

"Then why—"

"Why you?" He smiled again, and the twinkle was there, the honest and open affection. Damn him. "I have no idea. I wasn't ready for a woman like you, Erin MacGregor. I would have never been ready. But maybe that's the point. It's not about being ready, but just being willing. Now that you've invaded my hearth and home . . . I'm rather liking you there."

Her heart was pounding. She was dreaming, that was it. She'd come upstairs and lay down for ten minutes instead of showering and she'd obviously fallen asleep and she was dreaming. Dreaming that this gorgeous, complex, fascinating man was standing there proclaiming that she was the one who'd captured his attention. Erin MacGregor.

Obviously dreaming. Or hallucinating.

He'd shrugged off the attentions of twelve gorgeous women to come hide out in her room, to seek her out, to tell her he wanted to spend more time with her, get to know her better . . . and she was turning him down?

Totally hallucinating.

"But I won't be staying," she whispered. Giving voice to the cold, harsh reality of truth.

"I plotted and planned my whole life to get out of here, go to the city. I was convinced that was where I belonged and I manipulated everything around me, to make sure that plan stayed intact. I refused to see what was plainly obvious, stubborn to the end. Then life changed. And I came back here, still unsure if it was where I wanted to be, but I knew it was where I had to be, where I was supposed to be. Now my life is controlled by my ancestry, by my obligation to others. I've gone from over-controlling my life, to having life control me." He lifted their still joined hands and brushed a kiss along the back of her knuckles. "For once, I'd like life to just take care of itself. No planning, no plotting, no analyzing, no worrying about tomorrow. Just let it take its own course."

He made it sound so easy. "I don't have that luxury. I already know my course."

"You'll be here, in Glenbuie, for a while longer. Why not allow yourself to let go of the worry, the fear of what might be? It could end sadly, could end badly, but at least we'd have had the time we did have. Do ye plan to live the rest of your life sealed up tight, so ye don't risk disappointment or heartache?"

"I don't live my life sealed up."

"Don't ye now? If ye dinna let anyone have a say in things, then ye don't have to worry about them letting you down when you've come to depend on them, now do ye?" He pulled her closer, until their bodies touched, once again pressing her hands to his chest. "Ye started yer life with the one person who was supposed to be there for you, no matter what, leavin' ye on a doorstep for strangers to find. But perhaps, just perhaps, you were left with the hopes of finding something better than ye'd have had if she'd kept you. Meaning, sometimes ye have to risk the worst, to get the best. And even a chance at the best, is worth the risk, don't ye think? One thing you're not, Erin, is a coward."

"You don't know that," she said, badly shaken by his

words, far more than she could let on, or even wanted to acknowledge. "You don't know me."

"Then let me."

"Dylan—"

"Come here," he murmured, tugging her close, bending his head to hers. When his lips were brushing hers, he whispered, "You're no' the only one takin' risks here, ye know."

She hadn't wanted to think about that, about his past, about how long he'd been holed up, hiding out from the world. No, he wasn't quite the tragic, grieving hero she'd made him out to be, but he hadn't allowed himself to feel anything for anyone in quite some time either. "Maybe this is just a sign you're ready to rejoin the world," she said, shakily.

"I told myself the same thing."

It surprised her, how much she didn't want him to agree with her. God, she was a perverse creature. "And?"

"And I was just assaulted by a bevy of beautiful women who will no doubt turn every man's head in Glenbuie. Propositioned by a few as well." His lips curled. "You were right about not all of them being here to find true love."

"Did it make you curious?"

"If you mean, curious as to how your poor sod of a Prince will sort through that mess, then yes. Curious as to what it would be like to have them all chasing me for a few fortnights? No." He caught her face in his hands. "If I wanted that kind of attention, I'd be talkin' to your boss right now. Instead, I'm up here, hidin' out in your room. Because while they were pawing at me, all I kept thinking was that I already missed you."

Her breath caught, and her heart slipped even further from her control. *Danger, danger*. "Dylan—"

"I don't proclaim to understand why the heart or mind works the way it does, Erin. You say maybe I'm ready to rejoin the world. I say, maybe I'm just a man who knows what he wants when he sees it. It doesnae make me want to go search the world over. You haven't sparked a hunger in me to go on the prowl." He dipped his head, brushed his lips across hers. "Ye've just sparked a hunger in me for you. Just you."

When he took her mouth this time, she had no defenses left.

"Ye taste good, Miss Erin MacGregor," he murmured against her mouth. "And I didnae get my full of you last night. Aye, I'm a greedy bastard, indeed, because I want more. Much, much more."

She wanted to tell him he could have it all, but some shred of self preservation remained and wouldn't let her put it to words. So she showed him instead, returning his kiss with everything she was feeling, even if she hadn't exactly sorted that out for herself just yet.

His hold tightened for a moment when she responded to him so ardently, then he completely let go, taking her mouth hungrily, almost savagely. If last night had been all about animal lust, this moment between them was all about staking a claim. And maybe, just maybe, she was finally staking one of her own.

Chapter 17

Slow down, slow down, Dylan schooled himself. He'd gone too fast their first time, he'd be damned if he was going to bulldoze his way through this once again. Despite her willing capitulation, he was well aware she still had reservations. Her instincts to protect herself were every bit as strong as his own. And it wasn't that he had no fear in this situation, he had plenty, but for the first time, he was acting on an instinct that was driven purely by his own desires . . . and not what he'd already determined was right for him.

With Maribel, he'd been as driven by possessing who she was, what she would provide for him, as he was by the woman herself. Aye, he'd been but a lad at the time, and she'd surely captivated him on first sight. But he'd long since convinced himself of what it was he wanted, and when she stepped into that campus cafeteria, he'd taken one look at her and put her squarely in that pre-determined slot he'd created just for a woman like her.

This was different. So completely different. He wasn't looking for anyone or anything, and wouldn't know where to begin if he had. His focus in life was entirely elsewhere, and if he'd been asked to describe who he thought might best suit him on this new path he'd undertaken, nowhere on an endless list would he have ever described someone like Erin. It simply wouldn't have occurred to him.

Which was why he knew he had to pursue this. Because maybe you weren't supposed to know until you just *knew*. Last time, all that endless plotting and planning intended to insure his everlasting happiness had only succeeded in getting him long-term discontent. For the first time, his heart was leading the way, no' his head, nor logic, or some kind of other determination of who would be most suitable for him when matched with his current goals.

Of course, there was no guarantee that this wasn't simply an all-new recipe for disaster. She wasn't from here, her life was an ocean away. Hell, she wasn't even sure she wanted him long term. Not, perhaps, in the way he knew he wanted her. They could be horrible for each other. Or they could be the best thing that ever happened. He didn't know, couldn't know. But he wanted to find out. With a determination that was made far less terrifying by the fact that he hadn't felt this alive in a very, very long time.

She was clutching at his shoulders, driving her tongue into his mouth even as he claimed hers for his own. He felt this fierce, almost overwhelming sense of protectiveness, not just of her, but of this fragile new beginning they were creating. He wanted to feed and nourish it, and do nothing that would jeopardize its fledgling roots. And alongside that need grew a fear that no matter what he did, or how well or thoroughly he did it, he might still fail to bring a relationship with her to fruition. Because he wasn't the only one who had a say in it.

He scooped her up against him, their mouths still fused, tongues dueling, chests rising and falling, as he blindly turned them toward her bathroom. He kicked the door open, rousing Erin enough to break their kiss long enough to blink and look around. "There's a bed. Where are you—?"

"You said you had to shower and get back downstairs," Dylan said, pinning her against the wall next to the shower and tracing kisses along the side of her neck as he leaned down to pull the water faucets on and crank them toward hot. He pressed more tightly between her thighs as the room slowly filled with steam and smiled as he framed her face again. "I'm showing you how compatible I can be with your lifestyle."

She arched one eyebrow and looked poised to make a quick retort, but he took her mouth again and all she managed was a long, soft moan as they once again gave themselves over to the demands of their untamable need for one another. He wanted more from her than that, but it was a start. And a damn fine one, he thought, as he tugged her shirt over her head, and yanked his off shortly thereafter. They both shimmied their pants off and he stepped into the shower first, holding out his hand for her to step over the high side of the deep, narrow tub.

"I have no business doing this," she said, even as she took his hand and stepped in next to him.

He blocked the spray with his body until she had a chance to acclimate to the hot steam. "You have every right in the world to a shower before putting in another fourteen-hour day." He took her shoulders and turned her away from him. "You're simply lucky enough to have someone willing to scrub your back. Don't complain."

Whatever she'd been about to say was lost in a long groan of deep satisfaction when he poured a puddle of her scented body wash in his palms and proceeded to lather her up.

"My god, that feels incredibly good."

"Exactly." He massaged her shoulders and ran his thumbs along her spine as she braced her weight on the back wall. Her muscles were tight, the likely result of sleeping on a pile of rocks the night before. He pictured the huge feather bed in her hotel room and wondered what it would take to convince her to let him share it with her tonight.

But all thoughts of sleeping and beds vanished when she arched her back and tossed her head back as he kneaded his way down her spine, thrusting her hips back at him, and . . . onto him. Now he was groaning as he instinctively moved forward, slipping the rigidly hard length of himself between her thighs as he slipped his sudsy palms around her waist and up over her stomach, before closing them around her breasts and taut nipples. She squirmed back against him, panting, and his hips began working without any permission from him, but he was well beyond controlling it.

He leaned over her back, kissed the side of her neck, as he continued his slippery slide between her wet thighs, continued his soapy teasing of her breasts. Dear god, he would go mad with want of her.

She pushed herself back harder, ground on him a bit, whimpering. "Dylan . . ."

He knew exactly what she wanted as he wanted it in the very worst way himself. "I—I canno'."

"Wh—why? Oh," she gasped as he slipped his hands down over her belly and slid his fingers between her thighs.

"I'm afraid I'm no' prepared."

She was jerking against his hand and he could feel her coming close to climax. He could well go there himself without ever being inside her. Dear god, she was so honest in her response to him. What man wouldn't crave this? Crave her?

"I—it's okay," she panted. "Really. I'm . . . oh . . ." she gasped again as he slipped one finger slowly inside her.

He had to bite the inside of his cheek to keep from exploding when her body squeezed tightly around his finger and she started to move on him, her thighs clamped tightly around the part of him he dearly wished was where his finger was at this very fine, torturous moment.

"Pill," she finally managed to gasp. "I'm on the—please! Dylan. It's okay—"

He didn't have to be told twice. He slipped out of her, making them both sigh in regret, then quickly stepped back, allowing the brunt of the shower to cascade over his shoulder and down her back as he lifted her hips slightly. She took him all the way with one thrust, crying out, her back arching deeply, her hands slapping against the tiled wall. He wrapped his arm around her waist, keeping her hips pinned to his for a long, rapturous moment as he simply reveled in the feeling of her holding on to him so tightly, so perfectly.

When he thought he could keep his legs beneath him, trembling as hard as he was, he slid his hands to her hips, and began to move. Thrusting slowly, deeply, both of them grunting, almost growling, as their pace quickened, bodies slapping together as the water pummeled down on them. He went screaming right to the edge and had to force himself to slow down. *Pacing, lad, pacing*. But the feel of her directly against his skin, with not even the flimsiest of barriers between them was almost too much of a perfect thing. When he thought he had a shred of control, he leaned over her back, holding her tight against him with one arm, as he slid his other hand between her thighs again.

"Oh, oh," she cried, as he teased her, holding her tight, moving slowly, deeply.

Only when he felt her begin to convulse did he give himself over to it. As she came, he pumped harder, deeper, pulling her hips back so tightly against him it was all he could do to maintain balance.

And as she continued to shudder through after-shocks, he slid his hands back to her hips and reared up, and let himself loose inside of her. Thrusting hard, fast, deep. She pounded her fists on the tiles, pushed back hard against him, on him, but it was that moment, when she looked over her shoulder at him, her eyes still filled with need, filled with desire, and, in that moment, needing to connect specifically with him, and not simply giving herself to the moment . . . that was what sent him finally soaring over the edge.

And even as he was pumping everything he had into her, he vowed that next time, it would be slow, gentle, and she'd know, without a doubt, who was making love to her with every second they were joined.

He wasn't sure whose knees were wobbling the worst when he finally slid from her. They were both gulping in the thick, steamed air, their breathing labored and raspy. He shifted his back to the wall, leaning all his weight against it as he turned her toward him, cradling her against his chest. They said nothing, just let the hot water caress them, as he held her close, his cheek pressed to the top of her head, her face buried in his shoulder, as they slowly reclaimed control.

But this closeness wasn't enough, and the moment he could, he tipped her face up to him and kissed her. This time it was tender, quiet, more a reverent benediction than an impassioned plea. His heart squeezed almost painfully when she responded in kind. He couldn't remember ever feeling such sweet affection, such honest emotion, for anyone.

There were so many things he wanted to say to her, but, for once, he was wise enough to know it wasn't the time. They were too raw, too confused, too riled up. So he kissed her, and held her, until the water started running cool. "I think our ten minutes are up," he said, smiling when she laughed a little.

"Tommy's probably had a cat and a few litters of kittens by now," she said, then leaned back and looked up into his eyes. "Poor Tommy."

Dylan's smile spread. "Aye." He leaned over and shut off the water, then reached out for several of the hotel towels. She reached for one and he shook his head. He wrapped the towel around her and helped her out of the tub, carelessly wrapping his towel around his hips before joining her. "Let me," he said, when she started to pat herself dry. He winked at her when she just looked at him. "Full service." He didn't give her time to argue, though she seemed pretty willing to let him dry her off.

But when he'd wrapped her in the hotel bathrobe and tugged her close for another kiss, she surprised him by whipping his towel off. "My turn," she said. "Fair's fair."

"I rather like the way your mind works," he told her, then snatched the towel back and wrapped it again around his hips. "However, if you've any prayer whatsoever of getting back to work, you'll leave me to it. Otherwise we're going to find out what it would feel like to make love in that big bed of yours out there."

He saw the emotion immediately leap into her eyes and reveled in it. Aye, so she did want him as he wanted her. Body and soul. His body stirred in response, which, considering the toll taken on it these past twelve hours, was nothing short of miraculous. He shooed her out of the bathroom before he could change his mind. "Off you go. Unless you'd like me to dress you as well."

She looked over her shoulder as she crossed the room toward the wardrobe. "As I can't go downstairs naked, I'm thinking that's not such a good idea."

"Now you're getting the drift." He stayed in the doorway of the bathroom, leaning against the jamb, both enjoying the steamy air behind him . . . and the view in front of him. Aye, he was a lucky, lucky man, indeed.

She toweled her hair dry and he found himself grinning at the messy pile of hair that looked about the same wet as dry. He couldn't imagine her looking any other way.

"What about you?" she asked, as she pulled the clean bra and panties from her drawer. She slipped the panties on, then shrugged out of the top half of the robe, leaving it hanging over the belted waist.

"What about me?" he asked, crossing the room and brushing her hands away as he helped her hook her bra in the back.

"Here I'm all clean and fresh. I'm sorry you have to pull on those same clothes again."

He crossed to her bed and flopped backward, arms crossed behind his head, ankles crossed. "I suppose I'll just have to do without."

"Your towel! You're getting the bed all wet."

To which he simply whipped it off. "There."

"God, what am I to do with you?"

"Have you a few hours? I can give you a detailed list. Or better yet, I can show you."

"Don't you have anything better to do than lay about my room, a kept man?" she teased, clearly expecting that to get a rise out of him.

He stretched luxuriously and rather enjoyed the way she couldn't stop sneaking peeks at him. "You're the one who took over my home and all but booted me out. I think it's only fair you cater to my well-being in the meantime. Besides, I'm beginning to see your point about the owner not being underfoot during filming."

She pulled on a T-shirt and a pair of khakis, then scooped up his damp towel and flung it at him as she crossed the room to stand by the bed. Just out of arms' reach, he noted. "The women scare you that much?"

"They're a formidable lot."

She folded her arms and pretended to be affronted. "And I'm not?"

With lightning fast reflexes, he lunged to his side and snagged her hand, tugging her off balance and onto the bed, sprawled across him. "Oh, you're the most formidable of all," he said, kissing the tip of her nose, delighting in the accompanying frown that earned him.

"Yeah, I can see that. You're completely cowed."

He rolled her beneath him in one swift move, intending to continue their playful banter, but somehow his words turned all serious and earnest. "You have no idea the power you hold over me, Erin MacGregor. None a'tall." He looked down into her eyes, wishing like mad he knew what she was thinking about him. "It might well terrify you if you did."

"I don't scare easily," she said, holding his gaze, searching his eyes.

"No' perhaps when it comes to getting the job done for others." He pushed damp strands of hair from her forehead. "But what of the things you want for yourself? Will ye fight for them as hard? Will ye risk yerself that way?"

"I—" She started strongly, then immediately faltered. "I don't know," she answered, never so honest, her voice more uncertain than he'd ever heard it. "I'd like to think so. I guess I've never really let myself want all that much."

"Hard to disappoint ye, then, aye?"

"Aye," she repeated softly.

Then she reached up and stroked his face, her eyes still searching his, and his entire body trembled at that single, tentative touch. "Let yerself want," he said, the words barely making it past his lips. *Let yerself want me,* he wanted to add, but couldn't make the words form.

"I'm afraid it's too late for that," she whispered. And his heart squeezed painfully until she added, "I already do." Then she tugged his head down and kissed him. So tender, so sweet, so full of want and need, and fear.

And no one was more terrified than he was, to let himself want this much, this big, this deep, knowing full well the chances of him having all that he wanted were slim. Why her? Why now? Had he the wherewithal, he'd have laughed. The gods had certainly not made his life a simple one thus far, so why should he think they'd change his life's path now?

Before they could continue, her mobile phone chirped loudly to life.

He didn't want to let her go, didn't want to let the outside world intrude, until he felt more secure that it wouldn't steal her away from him forever. But of course he had no choice. So he reached across her to her nightstand and handed her phone to her. But he wasn't a Chisholm for nothing. He slipped his weight from her and allowed her the room to talk, but kept his body in contact with hers, stroking lazy circles on her stomach, his leg tangled with hers.

"Hey, Dana," she said, smacking at his hands when he inadvertently hit a ticklish spot by her ribs.

His grin was unrepentant. After all, she wasn't exactly scrambling off the bed. In fact, she made no move to leave his side. Point to him.

"Where are you?" Her assistant's voice squawked through the small phone, causing Erin to hold the phone away from her ear, and allowing Dylan to hear the conversation.

"I had to come up and change clothes," Erin told her.

"I was just there, pounding on your door."

"I—I grabbed a quick shower. I must not have heard you." Erin sent him a warning glare when he started to slide his palm under her shirt. But she didn't make him move it. "I'm on my way down. Right now." That last part was directed toward him.

He merely winked at her. And started kissing the side of her neck.

"Tommy's on the warpath," Dana continued. "The women are sequestered at the moment, readying for their first interviews, but he wants them moved out to Glenshire early. And he's not real keen on me disappearing for a few days, so you might want to take that up with him. I tried to tell him we needed that last location, but at the moment, he's more concerned with keeping the women away from the locals. One local in particular. Who I lost track of when Tommy snagged me, but his car is still here, so he's around somewhere. You might want to get down here."

Dylan chose that moment to nip her earlobe and a small moan escaped Erin's lips.

"Boss? Are you okay?"

"Fine." Erin had to clear her throat. "Just a bit, uh . . . I'll be down in a second. Hold the fort." She quickly disconnected and shifted to glare at him. "I thought you were all about showing me how well you could fit in with my work schedule."

He gave her his best "Who, me?" look, then quite unabashedly pulled her to him and kissed her as if they might be parted for eons, rather than hours. To his immense gratification, she resisted for all of a nanosecond, before kissing him back in kind. When he finally lifted his head, he thought it might be a while before he could wipe what was likely a very smug grin off his face. "Just wanted you to have something to remember me by. You know, so you dinna forget me, up here all alone, naked, hiding from scary, aggressive Yankee women, waiting for you to come rescue me again."

Her lips quirked, then she gave up the fight and laughed. "You're completely shameless."

"If it will get me what I want, aye, that I am."

She pushed at him. "Right now what I want is to get downstairs and keep Tommy from imploding."

He rolled off her, but quite brazenly propped his hands behind his head and stayed sprawled naked across her sheets while she got up and gathered her shoes and fresh socks. "What was that bit about you sending off your assistant for a few days?"

"I still need to find an overnight date location, and in case you have forgotten, I need to find a replacement for you. I was hoping Dana could kill both of those birds with one stone, as it were. But it looks like Tommy is set on getting the women out to Glenshire early." She perched on the edge of the desk chair and slipped on her shoes. "Apparently you got them pretty riled up and he's concerned you've gone and spoiled them for the real Prince Charming."

"They've merely been pent up too long, is all," he said, ignoring the blush of heat that stole into his cheeks.

"Nah, it's the accent. We're suckers for that. It doesn't take much else." She glanced up and he saw the teasing twinkle in her eye.

"Oh, so that's all it is, is it?" He rolled off the bed in one swift move, prompting her to shoot out of her chair, grab her bag, and back quickly toward the door.

"You know," she said hurriedly, "you might want to

consider sneaking out while the women are sequestered, and hightail it back to Glenshire, so you can be safely barricaded into your wing before the squealing horde arrives."

She had one hand on the knob when he trapped her up against the door. "You know, ye might want to consider another plan entirely," he murmured, leaning in to nuzzle her neck.

He wasn't sure which was more intoxicating, their playful, easy banter, or the way she melted the instant he touched her. He'd like to do more of a study. An in depth study.

"What plan is that?" she managed, sighing a little when he lifted his head.

"As I'm an apparent disturbance here, and I'm certain I could be quite a bigger one out at Glenshire were I to put my mind to it, and as your boss seems to need your assistant more than you do, perhaps you could persuade him that the best use of your time would be spent away from here this weekend, doing your research . . . with a certain nuisance Scot in tow. A certain Scot you're trying to persuade to sign on the dotted line for next season." He dropped a kiss on her forehead, then tipped her chin up to look into her eyes. "Just tryin' to help kill those birds for ye, luv."

There was emotion in her green eyes that filled his heart with hope. And helped him ignore the confusion and wariness he also saw there. "Dylan, I—"

He pressed a finger across her lips. He wasn't willing to let her shoot him down so quickly. Now that he'd had the idea, he was quite sold on it. A few days away from the demands of her job might be the only chance he had to convince her that this was something worth pursuing. Something ultimately life-changing.

Which is what it would have to be for her, if he had any chance. If his circumstances were any other than what they were, he'd follow her to the ends of the earth if he thought it was what would make them both happy. But he was locked into a life here in Glenbuie. And to be honest, though the villagers and his brothers could be a meddlesome lot, he'd come to realize that it was something of a comfort to know they were there for him, caring about him. Comforting to know that, unlike Erin, he had a place where he truly belonged. He'd just had to learn that the hard way.

Erin had had plenty of learning things the hard way in her life. And he honestly had no idea if she felt as if she could belong in any one place, or even if she wanted to try. A weekend wasn't much time, but it might be all the time he had. She was something special that he couldn't let slip away without at least fighting for her. And that had been one of the hardest learned lessons of all. Life was too short, too unpredictable, too fragile, to sit around and wait and hope things would change or get better. He was finished with waiting around.

He rubbed his fingertips across her lips, then replaced them with his own. Only this kiss wasn't carnal, or about claiming, or about sex. This kiss was simply about letting her know. He framed her face with his hands, tilted her mouth to his and poured everything he was feeling into that one, slow, sweet kiss. When he lifted his head, he wasn't sure who was more dazed. He had to clear his throat twice before he could form actual words.

"I, uh, there are a few things I need to take care of, at home, if I'm going to be away for a while."

"But—"

It was gratifying that her one word was but little more than a croak itself, but again, he cut her off. "I'll ask one thing of you, and I want you to be dead honest with yourself. And with me."

She nodded, her expression sober.

"While you're figuring this all out, I just want you to think about this. If I walked out that door and never spoke to ye again, hid myself away for the duration, steered clear of all your women and crew, until you were packed up and gone from here, would ye always wonder what might have been if we'd but taken those few days for ourselves?" He pressed a finger across her lips. "Think on this, don't answer me now. It's a lot I'm asking of you, I know that. And you should be sure of your answer. For both our sakes. So I'm putting this out there, as a measure of your importance to me. If ye'd rather forever wonder than find out for certain, then have your boss bring me the papers and I'll sign on for next season."

Her eyes widened in surprise. Which was good considering he'd just shocked the bloody hell out of himself as well. He had absolutely no idea where that had come from, but now that he'd gone and done it, he wasn't back-tracking. Maybe something that shocking would make her really stop and consider what it was he wanted for them. He gained a slight measure of reassurance when he spied a wee bit of jealousy in her eyes at the idea of him devoting himself to a bevy of beauties. It was a promising start, anyway.

Heart pounding hard now, he plowed ahead. "Dinna get me wrong, Erin. I want the chance to know you. And only you. And given even half the chance, I plan on being a single-minded, supremely selfish bastard who will do whatever he can to convince you it's time to be just as supremely selfish about your own life and what you want. And I hope to god what you want is me."

He could feel the cold sweat forming on his brow, but the words continued to pour out of him. He was well and truly in it now, so he might as well go all the way. It was what he was asking of her, after all. "But if ye'd rather go on about your life without taking that risk, then at least let me show you what commitment and real caring can mean. Let me help you with that all important job of yours by making your boss a very happy man." He tried to find an insouciant smile, but it was beyond him. Far too much was at stake here. "Who knows, you could get a raise in pay, or a promotion, boost your dream job to the next level. And maybe I'd find that true love you seem so convinced your show provides." He forced a grin then, though it was more like a baring of teeth. "It would certainly prove your point that the best things happen when you least expect them."

Then he gazed directly into her wide, green eyes, and laid it all on the line. "Although, you've already made a believer out of me."

Chapter 18

Erin was still in a complete dazed fog of confusion as she stumbled her way around the maze of crew and camera cables running up and down the corridors on the second floor of the hotel, in search of Dana. They'd commandeered the entire floor in order to complete the first round of one-on-one tapings with the contestants. This time, the women would each privately confess on camera why she'd decided to come halfway around the world in hopes of meeting the man of her dreams.

Erin didn't want to think about that. While she was proud of the show's success rate with matching couples together, she'd never really fantasized about applying the format to herself. She figured she'd spent more years behind the scenes making it work for everyone else to ever really be able to open herself up to the process. Until today . . .

Today, wandering the halls, hunting down her assistant, she'd gotten glimpses and peeks at the women currently taping, most of them talking about being skeptical of finding that special someone on a television program, but confessing they were secretly hoping they would be the one lucky enough to do so. And for the first time, Erin actually found herself identifying with them. Terrifying, really.

She hadn't come halfway around the world looking for romance, much less love. She'd come here to work. Then up popped Dylan and suddenly everything she thought she knew and understood about herself was all a confused jumble. Falling in love didn't fit in with her life, her career, her . . . anything. Most especially falling for a Scotsman half a world away. It wouldn't work. It couldn't work. "He doesn't fit into my plans."

"What plans?"

Erin whirled around to find Dana right behind her. "There you are. I've been looking for you, and trying to avoid Tommy." She took Dana by the arm and steered her into the nearest empty room. There was a padded armchair and lighting all set up for the next confessional, but no crew or contestants about at the moment. "So, what's going on?" Erin asked. "Why is he moving the women to Glenshire early?"

"What plans?" Dana persisted. "And where were you all morning?"

"I told you, I needed a quick shower so I could feel human again. The schedule has been brutal."

Dana batted her eyelashes. "And would Dylan have been part of this humanizing morning break?"

She was like a dog with a damn bone. "Please," Erin said, thinking she lied pretty convincingly, though she might have had a little problem meeting Dana's eyes.

Apparently that little slip was enough. Dana tilted her head, then a smile broke out across her pretty face. "You dog!" She spontaneously hugged her. "I'm so proud of you."

Erin wasn't exactly a huggy person or much for

spontaneous contact, though she'd certainly enjoyed a great deal of spontaneous contact with Dylan in the past twenty-four hours. Which was entirely different. Still, rather than feel awkward, it felt good and she found herself hugging Dana back. And for reasons completely unbeknownst to her, she began tearing up. In horror, she backed away and dabbed at the corners of her eyes. "An eyelash or something," she murmured.

Dana sobered instantly. "Oh. Wow."

Erin frowned as she blinked hard and pretended to see if she'd gotten that stray eyelash out. It could have been a stray eyelash. Why else would she suddenly get so stupid? "Oh, wow, what?" she grumbled, examining her fingertip to see if she'd removed the offending lash.

"And here I always thought you'd be more suited to it than me, but no, huh?"

"More suited to what? What are you talking about? And why do I care?" Dammit, her eyes wouldn't stop leaking.

Dana put her arm around Erin's shoulders and gave her a friendly squeeze. "Because *I* care, and I realize now you aren't used to anyone caring. Which is why you're not good at flings, Highland or otherwise. But that's okay. I should have known. You really do have a soft, gooey, marshmallowy center, don't you?"

Erin looked at her like she'd sprouted three heads. "What? And since when does everybody think they need to psychoanalyze me, anyway?" She sniffed and wiped one last time at her eyes.

"Everybody? You mean besides me?" The knowing smile returned. "Ah, so he wasn't just interested in getting in your pants, he wants inside your head, too?" She gave her a light shoulder punch. "That's a very good sign, Erin. Very promising. Trust me."

"A very good sign you're both crazy." She threw up

her hand, palm out. "We've got to figure out a way to get Tommy to let you go to Inverness for the weekend. I really need that overnight date site."

"And we need the perfect replacement candidate for next season."

Erin was nodding her head, but that was the other thing that had been eating away at her since she'd left her room. Dylan had offered her the perfect solution to both of her problems. The smart thing to do would be to take him up on it. Then he'd let go of this ridiculous fantasy he'd concocted whereby she was actually someone he could be interested in for the long haul, about, oh, two seconds after he signed on to be the next Prince Charming. Of course she knew he'd just said that to bait her, and that his feelings about starring on a reality dating show had not changed. But they would. Or they could. She'd seen it happen too many times.

She ignored the sick twist in her belly as she was reminded how the women had clamored all over him this morning. And it would only be worse when they really were there for him. The knot tightened up a notch, but she chalked that up to the fact that she'd just been with him an hour ago in the shower. Of course she'd have jealous feelings. Didn't mean she was in love with the guy. Just meant she didn't play well with others.

But if she didn't want him enough to fight for the long haul, then taking what she could get short term wasn't right either. Not fair to him, and not fair to her. Her heart was already taking a beating. Better to let the best Barbie win, right? If she was going to have to handle something, she'd rather handle the heartache now. At least they'd both come away with something. She'd keep her job and he'd get . . . someone who wasn't a big, fat coward. Someone who deserved his dedication and commitment. She rubbed at the center of her chest.

"Earth to Erin," Dana said, waving her hand in front of her boss' face.

Erin immediately snapped to attention, and made her decision in the same instant. She turned her complete attention to Dana, who actually backed up a half step. "I do need the overnight date, but I won't be needing a replacement for Dylan."

Dana frowned. "What are you saying?"

Erin forced a smile. Certainly at some point they would start to feel sincere again. Probably when her body wasn't still tender from the way he'd been buried inside of it a mere hour ago. Not to mention the way he'd kissed her. Had she ever been kissed so tenderly? Had any man ever made her feel so wanted, so desirable, so—

"Boss?"

Erin blinked the images away along with a few last tears. The accompanying tug on her heart wasn't as simple. She'd have to work on that. "We won't need a replacement because Dylan agreed to do it."

Dana's mouth dropped open, then immediately snapped shut. "No way."

"Yes, way. So, one major problem solved anyway." Now if she could just stop feeling like she wanted to throw up.

Dana had to crouch a little to catch Erin's gaze, which was presently on her feet. She'd have to work on that, too.

"But you just told me that you two—"

"No, I didn't. You assumed."

"But . . ." Dana trailed off, then peered even more closely at Erin's face. "I wasn't wrong about that." Her confidence in that statement wasn't quite on par with her usual self-assuredness. "Was I?"

Erin didn't bother to confirm or deny. She was pushing the limits of her ability to hold it together as it was. "It doesn't matter. Bottom line is he'll do it."

Now Dana folded her arms. "What did you do?"

"What do you mean, what did *I* do? Who said *I* did anything?"

A cameraman poked his head in the room at that moment. "I need this room in five."

"No problem," Erin told him, relieved at the timely intrusion. A few more minutes and pit bull Dana would have likely had her babbling all about how confused she was about her feelings for Dylan and before you knew it, she'd be rethinking things all over again and, well—no. She'd made up her mind. It was over. Over before it could really get started. Dylan would be pissed, of course, but she knew that, in the end, it was better for everyone this way. "Come on, we've got to find Tommy and figure out how to open up the schedule a little."

Dana followed her out into the hall and had to skip a little to keep up with Erin's quick pace. "Well, if we don't need a replacement, do we really need to go to Inverness to find the overnight location? Surely there is something around here, some kind of romantic castle or something."

Erin's stride faltered and she stumbled over a cable. Catching herself, she made a point not to look at Dana. She was pretty certain her neck was flaming red as it was. "Nothing suitable, really. Besides, we've got a few other things scheduled for the immediate surroundings. I think it's a good mix and Inverness is a beautiful town with some historic architecture and lovely old hotels. In fact, you know, now that I think about it, maybe I should be the one to go after all." Getting away for a few days right now was exactly what she needed to clear her head, get back on steady ground. Two days without

Tommy in her face. Or Dylan in her bed. Or her shower. Or against the nearest wall.

She really had to stop thinking about that.

"Better for you to stay here and help Tommy with the transition to the Glenshire set."

"Are you sure? Because an hour ago you were set on having me—"

"That was then, this is now. When I tell him we got Dylan for next season, he'll probably let me do just about anything."

"Right." She was still frowning. And staring.

Erin knew Dana only had her best interests at heart and that she only wanted to see her boss happy. Dana would just have to realize that Erin knew what was best, and what was best right now was for her to get the hell out of Brigadoon for awhile so she wouldn't screw things up by second-guessing her decision. She was weak where Dylan was concerned. That was half the problem. All of the problem, maybe. But admitting that was half the battle, right? She simply had to steer clear until she got past this infatuation she had with him, and that he had with her.

Although telling him she was taking him up on his offer would likely take care of that last part.

Then maybe her life would get back to normal. Or at least a normal she could handle. One that didn't turn her emotions upside down and inside out every other second and have her questioning everything she ever knew to be true about herself.

Tommy chose that moment to barge out of one of the rooms, barely stopping before plowing into them. "Perfect! Where the hell have you been?"

Nice to see you, too, Erin thought. "Good news," she said, preempting whatever lecture he'd been about to deliver. "I have Dylan ready to sign for next season."

Tommy's bushy eyebrows lifted and he clapped his hands together. "Fabulous! About time something started going my way. Now, listen—"

"There's one other thing, though," Erin broke in, knowing she had to milk her fifteen seconds of Tommy's goodwill for all it was worth. "I really need to get out to Inverness to scout that last location this weekend. Dana can stay here and help you out with the Barb—I mean the women."

Erin could see Dana shaking her head from the corner of her eye. It had been Dana who had come up with that nickname right after she'd been hired a few seasons back. Erin had given her grief over it from the beginning, telling her one of these days she was going to slip and use it at an inappropriate moment. "She knows the contestants better than I do," Erin added, ignoring Dana's smug smile. "And I'm sure she'll be a great help to you in getting them all settled in over at Glenshire."

Amazingly, her assistant didn't seem to be fighting a case of the snickers now. Erin only felt partially bad in sticking Dana with Barbie Detail. The chance to get away for a short trip and recollect herself was too important to pass up.

To her relief, instead of arguing with her, Tommy bestowed one of his mad leprechaun grins on her.

"You know, that's a great idea." He linked his arm through hers and started moving down the corridor. It was a miracle he'd stood still as long as he had. "I have an even better one. Our Mr. Chisholm has apparently made quite the lasting impression on the ladies. And despite the breadth and depth of the mansion, I am a little concerned with them being distracted by knowing he's anywhere under the same roof. You need to convince him to relocate for the duration of initial filming.

Have him shack up with one of his umpteen brothers or something."

"Three."

"I beg your pardon?"

"There are only three of them, sir, and they're all—"

He waved a hand. "I don't care about the particulars. Just make it happen. You'll have all weekend to convince him."

"I'm not sure he'll be—what? What do you mean, 'all weekend'?"

Tommy stopped as a phalanx of production assistants and crewmen descended upon him as the elevator door opened. He turned to her and took her arms in his hands. "Get him out of here. Take him to Inverness. Leave him there if you have to. Just make sure he's staying anywhere but Glenshire when you return." He released her and patted her shoulders. "We'll talk about the plans for next season when you get back. Good work, Erin. I knew I could count on you!"

He didn't give her a chance to swallow, much less retort. He'd already turned to Dana and snapped his fingers. "You, with me." Then he started barking orders at his crew and they quickly disappeared down the adjoining hall, with Dana sending her a weak wave over her shoulder.

Leaving Erin standing in front of the elevators, scrambling once again to figure out a plan. Well, she'd gotten permission to take the trip to Inverness, which was a good thing. But she wasn't taking Dylan with her. All she had to do there was track him down and tell him she'd already told Tommy he'd agreed to be next season's Prince Charming. She seriously doubted he'd want to have anything to do with her after that. There was still the matter of getting him to relocate for the next month and a half, but, well, first things first.

Absently rubbing the tender spot in the center of her chest, she stepped in the elevator and punched the right number, rehearsing what she was going to say as the lift slowly ascended each floor. He'd be understandably angry, or worse, hurt. Her stomach tightened at the thought, or maybe that was her heart. Then it skipped a beat entirely when it occurred to her he might actually try and get her to change her mind by seducing her.

She could handle the first two. Probably. He'd asked for her honesty, after all. But if he tried that last one . . . well, that's why she'd needed the weekend off in the first place. To build up her resistance. Unfortunately, she didn't have time to build it up before telling him.

She had to jam her key in three times before she could get the door to open. Only to find he'd already vacated the room. Which was a good thing, since her immediate reaction was disappointment, not relief. She missed him.

Not a good sign.

Trying not to think about what had taken place in this room mere hours ago, she quickly stuffed a few things in an overnight bag, grabbed what she could out of the bathroom—while studiously avoiding looking at the shower or the damp towels he'd hung over the curtain rod—then raced back out again. Maybe if she was lucky, Dylan was still somewhere in the village. But if not, she'd head out to Glenshire, deal with him, then get on the road to Inverness. She'd call Dana once she was underway and they could network the site details from there.

Bag in hand, she resolutely marched to the door, but not before giving in and glancing at the rumpled sheets on her bed one last time. Her mind immediately flashed on a very naked, very relaxed Dylan, sprawled on her sheets, coaxing her to join him. A soapy, water-slicked Dylan, tugging her under the hot spray of the shower. She slammed the door shut behind her and almost ran toward the elevator.

Yeah. She definitely needed to sleep someplace else tonight.

She managed to get back downstairs without being waylaid by anyone, and was almost to her car on a side street a block off the square when someone called her name. Dammit. She just wanted to find Dylan, do whatever was necessary to get things over and done with, then get out of town before something else happened to complicate her life.

"Erin!"

She turned to see Daisy MacDonnell jogging across the small lot.

"I've been trying to catch up with you," she said, her ever present smile creasing her lovely face. "You're one busy lady." She glanced at the overnight bag in Erin's hand. "And I can see you're headed out. Listen, I won't keep you long, promise, but if you could spare a few minutes."

Erin pressed her car key deeper into her palm, really wanting to get out of there before Tommy found some other reason to screw up her plans, but the least she owed Daisy for all her help was a minute or two of her time. "Sure. Just let me shove this in the backseat." She stowed the bag and tossed her satchel on the front seat, then turned to face Daisy. "What's up?"

The wind tossed Daisy's hair about and she fought to keep it smooth while she talked. "I know things are crazy for you, but I was hoping to maybe bend your ear for a minute or two at some point before you left town. I was thinking about the help you'd asked for, for the date sites. I understand some of them panned out for you and you'll be using them in the show?"

Erin nodded. "Yes, yes they did. I can't thank you enough."

"Well, actually, maybe you can. You see, I was thinking about ways to capitalize on the fact that the show is filming here. When the time comes, I'm going to be updating the Glenshire website, obviously, along with most of the village sites as well, and I was wondering if I could discuss with you the idea of showcasing some of the date sites featured on the show as a way to boost tourism." She lifted a quick hand. "Of course I wouldn't do that until after it had actually aired. But if we could advertise the idea that our guests could go on the same kinds of fantasy dates as your cast members, well, I thought that might be a fun idea. I wasn't sure who I needed to talk to, so I thought I'd start with you. I was hoping maybe you could share with me some of the other dates you have planned—I'd be sworn to secrecy of course—so I can get a head start on designing the pages for those dates. I know I could wait until the show aired, but I'd like to start advertising them as that happens, really make the most of the exposure, so I'd like some advance time to plan and prep." She finally ran out of breath, and managed a short laugh. "Sorry to gush all this out at you, but—"

"No, no, not a problem. I think it's a great idea, actually, and I don't see where it would be a problem. Let me follow up with my boss and see if there are any specific kinds of things we need to do to make sure no legal toes are stepped on."

Daisy beamed. "Thank you, so much. And if there is anyone I need to talk to, I'll be more than happy to do that. I can even do a mock-up of a page or two so they can see what kind of thing I'm looking to do. I really appreciate your help on this."

"Sure, no problem. I'm heading out of town for a few days, but I'll put it on my list of things to handle as soon as I get back."

"Oh, that's fine. No hurry, really. I just wasn't sure

how long you stayed with the production. I knew you were doing more an advance team kind of thing and I didn't want to miss the chance." She paused for a moment, and there looked like there was something else she was going to say, but instead she stuck her hand out. "Thank you, Erin. I'm glad we had a chance to meet."

Erin shook her hand, and couldn't help but wonder what she'd opted not to ask her. Daisy didn't strike her as someone who backed away from pretty much anything. "My pleasure. And I'm glad we met, too. You made my job a lot easier when I first got here. I appreciate you paving the way with some of the other locals."

"We Yanks have to stick together," she said with a grin.

"Aye, that we do. Well, I need to run." She opened her car door, then glanced back at Daisy. The question came blurting out before she thought it through. "How long have you been here? In Glenbuie, I mean? Was it hard to adapt?"

Daisy tilted her head slightly and gave Erin a considering look. "Not very long, but it seems like I've lived here forever." She laughed. "In a good way. As for fitting in, for all it's a small town and the villagers definitely take care of their own, they were very welcoming to me. But then I had the added benefit of being related to one of their own, so they were predisposed to be kindly toward me, anyway. As for the rest, well, I suppose it would depend on the person, but I was very much ready to make a big change in my life. Of course, I wasn't expecting quite as big a change as I got." She fiddled with the gorgeous engagement ring adorning her hand. The smile that came to her face then could only be described as radiant.

Erin felt an odd little pang in her chest. She'd seen

that look before. Over and over again. Every season, in fact. She'd always been thrilled because she knew that meant the show would be a success. Expressions like the one on Daisy's face meant higher ratings and better market share.

At the moment, however, she wasn't thinking about any of that.

"I've been truly blessed since coming here, so I'm probably a bit biased," she went on. "But I'd already fallen in love with the place, even before I fell in love with Reese, or the rest of the villagers." She looked at Erin, paused for a moment, then abruptly said, "Can I ask why you asked?"

"I'm not sure," Erin said, which wasn't exactly a lie. She really wasn't sure. She'd just finished deciding to end things with Dylan, so there was no reason to be wondering about any of it. "I guess it just intrigued me, the idea that you gave up everything and moved half a world away."

"I didn't have all that much to give up," Daisy told her. "And I knew I was moving toward something important. Because it was finally something I was doing just for me. At that time in my life, that's what really mattered."

"Well, obviously no regrets. Which is great. I'm really happy for you." Erin forced a sunny note into her voice, wanting to get in her car and drive away and pretend she wasn't having this conversation. Because then she wouldn't have to think about Daisy's answers. Or why she'd asked the questions in the first place. "I should be going."

"Right." Daisy stepped back to allow Erin to get in her car. "Thanks again for your help with this."

"No problem." Before Erin pulled the door shut, she glanced back up at Daisy and asked, "By the way, you didn't happen to see Dylan in the village anywhere this morning, did you?"

Daisy shook her head. "I saw him pulling out of here earlier on my way to Miss Eleanor's. From the direction he was heading, I'd say he was going back to Glenshire."

Erin swallowed a sigh of disappointment, even though she'd suspected as much. She really didn't want to have their next conversation on his turf, but apparently she wasn't going to be given that option. It was probably the least she deserved anyway. "Thanks."

Just as Erin went to close the door, Daisy lifted her hand and stopped her. "Wait. I—uh . . ."

Erin waited, shading her eyes against the sun as she looked up expectantly at Daisy.

Daisy fidgeted a little, then said, "I was just wondering, there's a rumor making the rounds. About you and Dylan and, well, is it true you're—?"

"Considering him for an upcoming season?" Erin hurriedly interjected, knowing that was not where Daisy was headed, but knowing it would certainly derail where she was headed.

Which her surprised reaction confirmed. "Are you? Oh! Well. I guess that explains things then." She laughed a little. "You two had been spotted together a few times, and well . . . you know how people are." She smiled reassuringly, then said, "It's just that . . . well, never mind." She shrugged and smiled, as if she wanted to believe it, but Erin could tell she wasn't quite sold on the explanation.

"I'd really appreciate it if you wouldn't say anything, or encourage the talk, either. We're just now starting to film the current season and with the craziness of that, it's best not to add more insanity to the mix. Can I trust you'll keep this between us?" Erin silently swore at her big mouth. She knew better than to do something like that. She'd never once put the show before her personal needs before, but then she rarely had personal needs. Yet, she'd taken one look at Daisy's face and had known full well where she was going with that little talk, and given that she was Dylan's future sister-in-law, Erin really hadn't wanted to go down that particular path. Still, she had no business spilling those particular beans, either. If Tommy found out? She shuddered to think.

"Sure, sure," Daisy assured her, sincere this time.

Erin breathed a small sigh of relief. "We have a lot of wish lists for future seasons," she told her, truthfully, "so don't read anything specific into it. It was just that Dylan and I arrived back this morning right when all of this season's contestants were arriving and they all reacted pretty favorably to your future brother-in-law, and of course, why wouldn't they, right? Well, my boss was right there, and there had already been some talk amongst the crew working out at Glenshire about him, and that put the bee in Tommy's bonnet, and, well . . ." She shrugged and smiled, thinking she'd done a good job of diffusing the situation. But the smile slowly faded as a speculative gleam came back into Daisy's eyes. *What had she just said?* She was mentally reviewing her comments, wishing she'd left well enough alone and not babbled on trying to explain away things that didn't need explaining, when Daisy cocked her head, then abruptly spoke up.

"You know, I know this is totally none of my business, it's just . . . I'm rarely wrong about these things, so I guess I'm a little confused."

Erin really wished she'd closed the door and started up the car. She considered doing that now, but Daisy had her more or less trapped. A trap of Erin's own making, so she had no one to blame but herself. "Wrong about what things?" she asked, knowing she wasn't going to get out of there until Daisy got whatever was really bothering her off her chest. So much for diverting attention away from herself.

"Oh, nothing really, it's just that I was known as something of a matchmaker back in my old life, and I was kind of instrumental in getting Brodie and his wife, Kat, together, after I arrived here in Glenbuie. I guess it's like I said, it's none of my business, but I had the feeling that there might be something other than business discussions going on between you and Dylan." She put up a quick hand to stop Erin from commenting. "I'm not unhappy about that possibility, either. Actually, I was really intrigued by the idea of you two together. I'll even confess that I partly tracked you down this morning for the reason we talked about, but it was also an excuse to get the chance to talk to you a little, and, well, be nosey." She laughed self-consciously. "I guess living in a small village is rubbing off on me. I swear I'm no busybody. But I do care about Dylan a great deal. His brothers have been worried that he's spent too much time boarded up out there in Glenshire cutting himself off from rejoining the rest of the world. They've been pushing him, as brothers do, but they're so grateful he's home to stay, they haven't prodded too much. Not to mention that Dylan isn't exactly all that easily prodded."

For once, Erin managed to wisely say nothing.

"Anyway," Daisy went on quickly, seemingly determined to get this out now that she'd begun, "I've worked with him a little on the website stuff and I share his brothers' concerns. We were thrilled when you were able to talk him into leasing out Glenshire for the television program. Not just because we all thought it was great for the bed and breakfast and for the rest of the village, but having his house overrun with people would force him back to the land of the living. We knew that would happen to some degree when the guests he'd booked started showing up, but this was even better." She grinned. "And it didn't hurt, from his brothers' perspective, that a lot of the people cluttering up the house would be gorgeous women. Men," she added, with an eye roll. "But I'll admit to being a bit curious to seeing how he'd react to all that, too. I hate that he's cut himself off like he has. I know how tragic the circumstances were, but . . . well, anyway. Then we heard you and Dylan had taken off for the day a while back, and we put that together with him coming into town that first night after meeting you, then agreeing to the lease because of you, and, well, of course we were all a bit curious." She put her hand out. "In a good way, I promise." She smiled her friendly smile. "We like you."

Erin found herself smiling back. Daisy had the kind of infectious, bubbly force of nature that was hard to resist. In any other situation, she'd be interested in getting to know Daisy better, maybe developing a friendship. The very notion surprised her. Other than Dana, which was a work relationship that had become a friendship, Erin didn't pursue that avenue. Too complicated. The idea that the town liked her gave her a rare warm fuzzy feeling as well. She liked the villagers, liked Glenbuie. They'd made her feel comfortable here. Or as comfortable as possible, anyway.

Of course, once they found out she was going to spurn Dylan's desire to continue developing a relationship with her, they might not be feeling so friendly toward her. She could only hope that Dylan was a man of his word and would stand by his offer to be the next Prince Charming. If his family and friends saw him making that kind of leap, they couldn't be too angry with her for nudging him in that direction. Maybe they'd realize it had all been for the best and forgive her. Not that it mattered, really. She'd be leaving eventually anyway. The thought had her rubbing at that achey spot on her chest again.

"And then you arrived together this morning," Daisy went on, "and, well, enquiring minds and all that. You can tell me to take a flying leap, and I wouldn't be hurt if you did, it's just . . ." She trailed off for a moment, seeming indecisive, then abruptly blurted out the rest. "You say it's business, but then you light up when his name comes up. And he's not the kind of man to spend time with someone, heck, anyone, these days, if he doesn't have to. If he's with you, it's because he wants to be. Now, I know I'm biased, but for good reason. And all I'm saying is, you could do worse than one of the Chisholm brothers, but not a lot better. They're a determined, loyal, dedicated lot. And very tenacious when they want something."

Tell me something I don't know, Erin thought morosely, feeling worse now than before, which was saying something. Unprepared for Daisy's sudden speech, Erin was caught too offguard to school her expression, and Daisy had obviously seen something of what she was grappling with. So she didn't even try to evade the topic again. "I—I don't know what to tell you, Daisy. It's . . . complicated," she said, deciding on honesty, as much as she could anyway.

"So is Dylan," Daisy said with a smile. "But in a good way, I think." She leaned down and gave Erin a spontaneous hug, then immediately stepped back. "I'm sorry to thrust all that on you like that, and I wouldn't have if I didn't think it was worth at least putting it out there." She shook her head and smiled ruefully. "I've said enough. Too much, probably. But I care about him, we all do. We want to see him happy. And lately? From the glimpses I've seen . . . he is happy. He's like a Dylan I've never met, one his brothers have missed immensely. I just wanted you to know how grateful we are for that. And tell you personally what a lucky woman I think you are. So, whatever happens, thank you, for giving him that much of himself back."

"I'm not even his type," Erin blurted. "He told me so himself." She shut up, shifted her gaze ahead, seeing nothing, feeling far too much. She was going to tape her mouth shut, that's what she was going to do.

Daisy froze in the act of stepping back up on the curb, then turned back to Erin. "Dylan had that all sorted out in his head before, you know. And it didn't serve him too well."

Erin glanced up at Daisy, surprised.

"He thinks we all believe his marriage to Maribel was a match made in heaven. And it's true, the villagers like to think of it as a fairy tale. It plays better, makes them feel good. But his brothers know there was trouble in paradise, or certainly suspected it. They suspected his reasons for staying on were more complicated than he let on. As I said, once a Chisholm is dedicated to something, there's never a more loyal man. Dylan's come home. And he's not the same man he once was. So why he thinks his tastes are the same, I have no idea. If you say he's interested, even thinking you're not his type, then maybe he's finally operating from the heart. I'm sure it's as much a surprise to him as it is to anyone. Don't give up on him just because he might not be clear on what he wants."

Erin snorted before she could stop herself, then groaned inwardly at Daisy's increased interest. "If I get him to sign on with the show, he'll have the chance to meet a variety of potential Ms. Rights. At the very least he'll put himself back out there, give himself a chance to figure out what he does want." She dared to look at Daisy again. "I don't think it can be me. I . . . my life isn't here."

Daisy studied her for a moment, then a hint of a smile crossed her face. “But you’ve thought about it, haven’t you?” She pushed the car door shut, and tapped the roof. “That’s why you asked me, isn’t it? So, think about it some more. A man like him doesn’t come along twice in a lifetime.” Her grin spread. “Trust me, I know whereof I speak. Give him a chance, Erin. Or maybe it’s more about giving yourself one.”

With a wave she walked away, back toward the village square, leaving Erin to pull out of the lot and head toward Glenshire, a hell of a lot more confused than ever.

Chapter 19

Dylan clicked open another window on his computer screen and shuffled through the folders on his desk, all the while keeping the phone pinned between his shoulder and his ear. He punched the intercom button and laid the phone down. "Go ahead and sell that block, Ian," he instructed. "But hold on the other two until I get back to you."

"Are you sure you want to do that, mate? I'm telling you, it's going down and you should strike now—"

"Too risky for my blood at the moment. I'll be in touch next week."

There was a short sigh. "You're no fun, you know that."

Dylan smiled. "I can't afford to be fun." He clicked off and was closing folders when a tap came at the door. Now it was his turn to sigh. He'd been home a few hours and for one reason or another, a production staffer of some rank or position found a reason to intrude on his privacy every other minute. "You say you want me out of sight, then don't keep sending people up here to annoy me."

"Dylan?"

His head shot up, and a grin immediately creased his face. "Erin."

"I'm interrupting." She nodded toward the clutter on his desk as she walked closer.

"No, I'm finished. Just some portfolio business to tend to before heading out." He flipped several folders shut, switched off his monitor, then pushed his chair back and stood. "I'm all yours."

He could see immediately from the set of her shoulders, and her jaw, that she'd spent their time apart girding her defenses yet again, instead of letting them down any further. And he tried not to be discouraged. Or scared. Or both.

He knew he was asking a great deal of her and that her default position was to protect rather than risk. So, rather than give her an opening, he made a preemptive strike. He surprised a squeal out of her by scooping her up in his arms and striding across the rooms of his upper floor apartment. There was the study, which doubled as his office, a living room area, and his bedroom. The latter was his intended destination.

"Dylan, what are you doing?"

"Fulfilling a particular fantasy of mine. One in which you have a recurring starring role. Nightly, in fact."

"What?" She didn't struggle, but she did squirm. "Wait!"

"Keep wriggling like that and our trip might be further delayed," he warned. Any response she might have made went out on a gasp when he landed them both across his massive, centuries old four-poster bed.

He rolled so she was pinned, breathless, half beneath him.

"You know, we can't keep jumping into bed every time we spend five seconds together," she told him, looking more disconcerted than he'd like. Actually, she looked almost . . . scared.

His heart started to pound then, but he shoved away the insecurities rearing their ugly heads. "Ah, but we haven't," he said, fighting to keep the teasing tone to his voice. "In fact, a bed has rarely been involved. I thought to remedy that. I've been sitting there, laboring at my desk, sorely preoccupied by this image I have of you, sprawled here, amongst my linens, in my bed. Lord only knows what I may have traded or bought today. You really are quite a distraction." He brushed at the wispy hair on her forehead. "I must say, however, reality eclipses my imagination. Although I'll admit you were wearing far less the way I pictured it." He plucked at the buttons on her blouse.

She pushed at his hands. "Wait a minute. Dylan. Stop."

He stopped, but left his hand where it rested. He could see she was struggling, and though his instincts told him to keep pushing, not to allow her to hide behind her well structured defenses, he found he couldn't force his attentions on her. Though he wanted to. Badly. It was the only time she seemed to go with her heart and not with her head.

He wanted to do whatever it took to batter down those walls once and for all. But he couldn't if she didn't give him a fighting chance. "Erin, I know this is a lot. And I know it's fast. But I dinna have the luxury of time. I want to make every second count."

Her lips quirked, despite the fact that he saw how hard she was struggling to regain control of the situation. "And that means getting me naked for most of them?"

His own lips curved even as his heart continued to race. "Aye, it did seem a point in both our favors."

She held his gaze, and what he saw there both heartened and scared him. Desire, yes. But also pain. And confusion.

"I need to talk to you," she said quietly. "Only, not like this."

So perhaps he wasn't entirely willing not to use every advantage. He was fighting for his life here. Their potential life. He lowered his mouth to hers. "We'll have hours on the road to Inverness to do nothing but talk, and I promise to be all ears," he murmured. "But perhaps we shouldn't waste such a promising opportunity. We've a little time, surely." He kissed her, half afraid she'd turn her head away. She didn't.

She held still for all of a second, then she sighed, heavily, as if defeated, and all the stiffness went out of her. He pressed the advantage, even though all the warning bells were ringing. She went pliant beneath him, her mouth softening, opening to him, her body accepting the weight of his as he pulled her more fully beneath him.

And damn him for using her helpless attraction to him to his advantage, but if that was his only way to get past her defenses, then it was an advantage he'd press without apology.

"I have pictured you here," he whispered against her lips. "Wanted the scent of you on my pillow, the weight of you on my sheets, pressing against me." He pushed between her legs and she instinctively arched up to meet him. He cursed the barrier of their clothing, but didn't try to undress her again. It was enough, at the moment, that she was willing to admit to herself and him that she wanted him, at least in this way, as desperately as he wanted her.

Her nails dug into his back as she slipped her ankles around his legs and pressed tightly up to meet his slow thrusts. They were both moaning, electrified by the renewed intimate contact, and frustrated at the lack of fulfillment. "I do want you, Erin." He forced himself to lift his head, to meet her gaze, despite knowing it would give her a chance to rally her forces. "But no' just like this. I want the chance to know all of you this intimately. To understand who you are, why you came to be the woman you are, what drives you, what motivates you."

She gazed back into his eyes, taking in his words, offering nothing of her own. For once silent, when he least wanted her to be.

"I know I'm in no position to offer much flexibility in return. But we'll find someone in Inverness this weekend who'll make Tommy happy, give us that extra time, at least, to explore this a bit more. All I'm asking is that you give us that much of a chance."

And, like that, her gaze shuttered. She slipped her legs from his and pushed him, gently, but firmly off her, then quickly rolled to a sitting position, sliding her legs off the side of the bed, keeping her back to him.

He rolled to his side, propped his head on one hand, and waited for her to talk. He'd said enough. Possibly far too much. He wanted what he wanted. Perhaps he should have tempered his pursuit a wee bit, but he hadn't known what else to do. Whatever the case, it was too late now.

"I . . . uh . . ." She paused, cleared her throat. But her voice was still a bit on the raspy side when she finally continued. "I didn't mean to let things go in this direction. I have no defense for that and it was wrong of me. I'm sorry. I just . . . you . . ." She stopped, shook her head, and he thought he saw her shoulders tremble a bit when she took a deep breath. "It's not easy with you, or maybe it's that it's too easy. I should have been stronger. But I'm not yet."

Yet. Dylan's heart squeezed, but he schooled himself to remain just where he was. To allow her to conduct herself without his interference this time. It was, perhaps, the hardest thing he'd ever done.

"I—you—" She broke off, shook her head, dipped her chin, but kept her back squarely to him. "I've never met anyone like you. I'm not exactly sure what to do in this kind of situation. I can't seem to control things like I usually do. And I . . ." She shook her head again, her shoulders lifting and falling, as if she felt somewhat helpless to explain.

He curled his fingers inward against the need to reach for her, to touch her, hold her, support her while she found her words. But he suspected they weren't words he was going to want to hear. And making her endure his touch wouldn't perhaps bring her the solace he intended them to bring, but instead make the burden she seemed to be bearing that much harder to contend with.

In that moment, he came to realize that he truly was falling in love. Because, in the end, rather than press his own case, forge ahead with his own demands, so certain it was what was best for them both . . . he was willing to completely abdicate that position and allow her to have whatever it was that would make her feel settled, secure. Happy. Even if it came at the expense of losing his own happiness.

"I honestly don't know what to do about it. I tried just ignoring my concerns, going with the flow, as it were. Have my little highland fling. You make that very easy. It's easy when we're all caught up in it to pretend there aren't complicating factors, like that we're people with real emotions, emotions that grow and get inevitably tangled and messy. To ignore the reality that the more time I let myself spend with you, the harder it's going to be to go back to my world and let this one become a mere memory. A fond one, perhaps. But maybe a painful one, too." She lifted a shoulder, let it drop. A soft sigh escaped her. "I asked myself if it was worth it, risking the pain or heartache, to have this . . . have you, for whatever time I'm allowed." She finally glanced back at him over her shoulder. "And to be honest with you, I'm already feeling that pain, that heartache, just thinking about the end. And I don't know how to handle that. It's not a choice I've ever had to make."

Dylan slowly sat up and shifted so his back rested amongst the pile of pillows stacked against the head board. He held her gaze, then simply held his hand out to hers. "Come here. Just . . . for now. Please."

Erin's chin quivered, but she finally shifted her weight, reached her hand to his. It was all he could do not to yank her against him, to take her to places he knew only the two of them could reach. Instead, he corralled all of his strength, all of his control, and merely tugged her next to him, tucking her close, her cheek to his chest, and held her there, feeling her pressed against his heartbeat, and wondering just when his entire world had started to collapse.

He held her, stroked her hair, stroked her back, and forced the words he wanted to say to remain unspoken. He'd said too much already and placed an apparent burden on her she was unprepared to carry.

At length, she spoke again. "I came up here today, to tell you I was going to Inverness by myself. And . . . and to take you up on your offer."

His hand stilled on her back. "Which offer was that?"

He felt her hold her breath, her body tensing beneath his touch. "The offer to be our next Prince Charming."

He stilled completely, didn't dare breathe, didn't dare speak.

"I've done nothing but think about this . . . us. And I think it's for the best."

"For the best?" he ground out, suddenly ferociously angry, but somehow managing to keep that at bay.

"I don't think I can do this, get any more involved with you. I wanted this weekend, that time, away. To think, to get my head back on straight. To refocus on my job, my future path. And . . . though I know you won't want to see it that way—putting yourself out there could be the best thing that's ever happened to you. Even if you don't find the perfect person, at least you'll be back in the mix and maybe realize what it is you truly do want."

His control snapped. He tipped her chin up to his, knowing from the alarm that immediately crossed her face that his own expression was likely not a beautiful thing to behold at the moment. "Got it all neatly planned out, have you? You seem to have overlooked one very important, pertinent fact." He lowered his face to hers. "I already know what I truly want." And before he did something truly foolish, he stuck to his vow to give her whatever it was she wanted, released her, and got off the bed.

He stalked from the room, pacing the length of the living room, not daring to look back through the open doorway. He didn't need that particular image burned forever in his brain. Erin sprawled in his bed, her expression one of pain and apology.

He grabbed the duffel he'd packed earlier from its place on the floor. "Have the papers sent over. I'll sign whatever you want. I'll be out at Tristan's for the foreseeable future, so your filming can commence without me underfoot. Have a nice time in Inverness." He did pause then, and he did look back. Erin was standing in the doorway to his bedroom. Perhaps not as painful an image as the one he'd been avoiding, but somehow it packed an equally powerful punch. Her face was pale, and all the life and effervescence he so naturally equated with her was nowhere to be seen. He refused to feel bad for being any part of that. They both had their own realities—and pain—to deal with.

Fantasy time was over.

"I'm sorry," she managed.

"Aye, we're both a sorry lot, aren't we?" And with that he strode out.

"I really dinna want to talk of it, Tris," Dylan informed his youngest brother, who, despite his ready hospitality, was already getting on his last nerve. Perhaps he should have thought twice before deciding to hide out in the midst of his brother's besotted bliss with Bree Sullivan, the absolute love of his life. "I appreciate the use of the room. I think I'll take Jinty here and head out for a walk. Any strays need rounding up?"

Tristan cocked his head. "You, go for a walk?"

Dylan gave the look right back to him. "I've been known to do that on occasion." He shoved out of the kitchen chair and rinsed out the tankard of ale he'd been brooding over for the past half hour.

Tristan's smile was as unabashed as any of his brothers' would be. Clearly they weren't nearly intimidated enough by the fact that he was the eldest and de facto clan chief. Privately, he realized he didn't mind so much. It was far, far better than the eggshells everyone had been tiptoeing on when he'd first arrived back on clan soil.

"I believe ye were about sixteen the last time ye went herding," Tristan recalled. "Annoyed as all hell when Grandpa Finny made ye take me along."

"You always were one for the hillocks. You and your sketch pad and your dreamy vacancy. Couldn't even muster up a decent conversation."

"Well, in my defense, I was, what, eight? I don't believe I got into deep philosophy until at least reaching my prime at ten or eleven."

Dylan found himself fighting a smile. He shoved the chair back and slapped his thigh, calling Tristan's sheepdog to his side. He didn't want to smile, didn't want to feel warmth. He needed the cold, sobering chill of silence right now. "Come on, Jint. Let's get out of here for a bit." He was at the door, looking forward to sorting through his thoughts with nothing but green hills and cloudy skies to contend with, but found himself turning back, and putting to voice the question that had been nagging at him since his arrival. "How did you know?" he asked.

"Know what?"

"About Bree. It was sudden for you."

If Tristan was surprised by the question, he didn't show it. Nor did he look smug at the apparent capitulation. "It was rather sudden for Reese, too, and Daisy—"

Dylan waved a hand. "Daisy might be a transplanted Yank, but she hadn't been here six months before making a bigger mark on this village than her great-aunt did in six decades. Besides, she was here to stay when they met. And Brodie has known Kat his whole life. But you . . . Bree landed here by accident."

Tristan grinned. "Literally, I know." Then his grin tempered a bit, but he asked his question anyway. "How did you know with Maribel? It was a short engagement."

For all he'd proclaimed to be thankful no one dredged up his past, he discovered he was relieved, to some degree, that Tristan felt they'd all come far enough so that he could talk about his past marriage without fear of treading on painful ground. "I was a lad, with foolish ideals, so certain what it was I wanted. I don't think I'll ever know if I fell in love with Maribel for Maribel herself, or for all she represented. So, I ask again, how did you know? She wasn't from here, was likely not to stay here."

Tristan propped his hip against the kitchen table and rolled his tankard of ale between his palms. "You just know. And it didn't matter what her plans were, or mine. It wasn't a planned reaction, neither of us were looking, or even thinking about such a thing. I guess what it came down to was knowing that, after having her here, under my roof for such a short time, I already couldn't imagine the house without her in it." He took a sip, considered for a moment, then caught Dylan's gaze squarely. "Is that how it is with your Yank?"

Caught dead to rights, and considering his own probing, he couldn't dodge the question this time. He let out a short sigh. "Aye. I believe so."

Tristan's grin was instant and quite exultant. "Well, what in the hell are ye doin' out here, man? Go and get her!"

Dylan swore under his breath. "Dinna ye think I'd be doing just that if I thought she'd have me?"

"Turned ye down flat, did she? Perhaps I'll have to find my way into the village after all. Meet this paragon of virtue who can resist the Great Scot."

Dylan swore. "Stop that, will ye?"

"You undersell yourself." Then Tristan turned serious. "So why is it, ye think, that she's no' interested? Is it the complication of having a job and a life an ocean away? Or is it your grumpy and dour demeanor?"

Dylan just shot him a look. "Glad you find this all so very amusing." But his shoulders slumped as he sank against the door frame. Jinty, taking the cue, sighed and settled herself at Dylan's feet. "I canno' believe she doesnae feel what I do. It's there in her eyes, Tris. And she's all but admitted her feelings run strong. But, aye, her life and her path take her elsewhere. And I'm committed here, with no plans to go running off again. Not even for this."

Tristan's eyes widened at that last part. "But you say if it weren't for that, ye might?"

"Dinna ye worry, I'm done with my selfish pursuit of—"

He waved his hand. "No, no, I know that. I was gauging your feelings, is all. And given your dedication to Glenshire, to all the village, that's saying something." He put his ale down and stepped closer. "So what can we do to help?"

"We?"

Tristan nodded. "Me, Bree, all of us. We're family, Dylan. We'll do whatever—"

He shook his head. "I appreciate the offer. I do." And he found he meant it. Instead of being alarmed or annoyed at the proposed interference, as he typically would have been, he was truly touched. Not that he'd ever doubted his family's loyalty. They'd always been there for each other, but this was immediate and unquestioning, and that meant something to him. "It's no' something I can change, I'm afraid. I canno' make her want me enough to take such a leap of faith."

"Life offers no promises, but there is always the promise of hope."

Dylan smiled faintly. "No one knows that better than she does. Life hasn't handed her too many promises. She's made her own way and she's attached to the security of her independence. I can't promise her anything better."

"Aye, but you can. You're a loyal man, dedicated. Surely she sees that. She'd be gaining so much and giving up so little, to my way of thinking."

"I'm no' so sure of that. If we were to pursue this and fail, for me, life would continue on much as before, albeit a great deal more dimly. For her, there would be no going back to what was, but having to forge something all new, all over again. I'd never forgive myself if she'd felt coerced into being with me in the first place. I canno' fight against her unwillingness to take the risk, as I appreciate and understand it. Especially as I canno' make the same sacrifice for her."

Tristan sighed deeply as well. "'Tis a fair shame then. I've no' heard you speak with such passion since . . . well, to be honest, since you left here and headed off to university. And I was a wee lad then. Perhaps then you were runnin' away as much as runnin' toward something, and that passion was bound in the thrill of the unknown. So it speaks doubly that you sound as you do, a man full grown, with the lessons of life having left their mark upon you."

Dylan did smile then. "You might have been a late bloomer, Tris, but ye've got the philosophic bent now, that ye do."

Tristan smiled as well, and a handsome color flushed his cheeks at his brother's teasing praise. "I'm just a fool in love and I want everyone to be as ridiculously foolish so I feel less conspicuous with it." He sobered a bit, and added. "And I hate to see you sit idly by with no way to fight for what ye want."

"I tried all I knew to do. I don't know what else there is but to let her have her way. I've put on more pressure than I should have, in hopes of wearing down her defenses. Instead, I think I only pushed her to reinforce them as rapidly as she could."

"How much longer is she here?"

"She's off to Inverness for the weekend. We were to go together, but—"

"So go, anyway."

"No, she specifically asked that I not. She wanted the time apart."

"That she needed the time away from you in order to garner her defenses against what she feels for you is proof that she's not at ease with her decision, either."

"Perhaps. But it's all for naught anyway. I've given her my word on another matter that more or less puts a stop to things all together."

"What matter?"

"They're looking to set their next season here in Scotland as well, and—"

"So she'll be staying on, then? Brilliant! You'll have more time with—"

Dylan shook his head. "No, ye see, her boss is pushing her for a specific site and person to fill the role, and her job more or less depended on it. She was going to Inverness initially to find a location for this current season, and to find a leading man for the next. Only now she won't have to."

Tristan looked confused for a second, then the light dawned and he groaned and rubbed a hand over his face. "Tell me ye didna do what I think ye did?"

Dylan couldn't even hold his gaze. He'd be a laughingstock with his brothers at the very least. Och, well, there was naught to be done for it now. "Aye, but I did. I thought to force her hand, make her realize that perhaps there was more between us than she'd allow herself to admit. I delivered an ultimatum of sorts."

Tristan swore. "What the hell is wrong wi' ye?" He dropped down into the kitchen chair and kicked his legs out in front of him, appearing to be torn between swearing . . . and laughing. "Och, you're well and truly in the deep end of it now. But in case ye were still wonderin', to go and do something like that is proof positive your heart is no longer your own."

Dylan trudged across the room and dropped heavily back into his chair, downing the dregs of his brother's ale in one swallow. "I have no earthly idea what I was thinking. I should have just shut the door in her face the day we first met."

"Dylan Chisholm, the next American heartthrob." A snicker finally escaped him.

Dylan scowled at him. "Don't start."

"Reese and Brodie—"

"I said, don't start."

But it was simply too delicious a topic. "The villagers, however, will probably throw you a feast and a parade. Will they cast any Scottish women, or all Americans?"

"I haven't a clue, nor do I care," Dylan stated flatly. "That's the least of my concerns at the moment."

Tristan's shoulders shook and he finally dipped his chin and waved his hand apologetically. "I'm sorry, but I simply have to get it out of my system. I canno' see you doing it."

"I gave my word."

Perhaps it was the bit of despair he detected even in his own words that had Tristan lifting his gaze. "You haven't signed anything yet, have you?"

"No, but I promised."

"I'm no' saying you should go back on your word. I'm just saying all is not lost as yet. Do you know where she went in Inverness? Where she's staying?"

He shook his head. "What of it, Tristan? I willnae continue to force my attentions where they aren't wanted."

"Sounds like they're wanted almost too much if she has to run away from ye to keep from submitting to them. There must be someone who would know where she is."

"Her assistant, Dana, likely knows, but you're not hearing me—"

"No, it's you who does not listen to me." Tristan leaned across the table. "You've got years of life on me, and not all of them treated you kindly. All I know is that I'd do anything to keep what I have with Bree. It's worth that much. Erin's stay here on our bonny shores is brief, but she's no' gone yet. Dinnae waste that precious time. Fight for what you want, for what you think is possible. I mean, come on man, what have ye got to lose?"

Dylan laughed without humor. "To be rejected time and again by the same woman? I have been fighting. I do have some pride, ye know. I'd like to keep at least a wee bit of it intact."

"Och, then ye can't be truly in love after all. Don't ye know pride is the first thing ye must swallow?"

"I think I've swallowed my fair share." Dylan pushed back from the table and stood once again. Jinty lifted her head with renewed hope and let out a little whine.

"He won't be going for a walk with ye today, my faithful," Tristan informed his four-legged companion. He stood as well and looked Dylan once more in the eye. "He has a drive to make."

"Leave it be, Tristan," Dylan told him.

But when he walked through the door, he didn't take the dog with him.

Chapter 20

"You're in *Greece?*"

Erin held the phone away from her ear at Dana's shriek. "Yes, I am."

"But you can't be in Greece," she flatly insisted. "You have to be in Inverness."

"I have to be where Tommy sends me. I'm guessing you haven't heard the latest."

"I'm in Barbie Hell at the moment. I'm supposed to be an assistant to the location coordinator, but I'm spending all my time and considerable talents keeping this season's contestants from jumping the locals. You'd think these women had never heard an accent before."

"Oh, like you didn't enjoy your Frenchman?"

"Fine, fine, but I was in Paris *working*. I wasn't there as a contestant hopeful to hook up with Prince Charming. I was a free agent. Or at the very least a reasonable one," she added dryly. "But we're not talking about me. What's going on?"

"Short version is Tommy apparently pitched Dylan

as our next Prince Charming to the network suits a few days ago—"

"Before he agreed to sign?"

"Tommy has faith, what can I say."

"What if you'd gone through on the original plan to find a replacement and the suits were all gaga over Dylan?"

"I didn't know he was pitching him already. But it doesn't matter."

"It matters to Dylan, I'm sure."

Dana seemed rather incensed about the whole thing. More than Erin would have thought. "It's all moot, because the suits didn't go for him. Well, not Dylan per se, but the idea of shooting back-to-back episodes in Scotland didn't go over well, especially since this one hasn't even filmed yet, and apparently reports are leaking out about the wayward behavior of some of our ladies, and I use that term very loosely."

"Loose is closer to being the key word there," Dana said dryly. "I don't know what casting was snorting when they made this season's selections. Anyway, go on, go on."

"So, a bit of panic apparently set in and they decided to play it safe rather than wait on how this season would pan out, then be stuck here if things didn't go as well as initially hoped for. Tommy left a message for me when I arrived in Inverness telling me he wanted me to let Dylan out of the agreement and grab a flight to Greece."

"Why Greece? Or does that even matter, at this point?"

"It seems that one of the network execs has this contact via his wife's family or something, with some Greek shipping tycoon. Said tycoon has a very single son and heir who is apparently a big playboy—"

"Just what we need, a man who won't commit."

"I have no idea what's what at this point, other than I'm supposed to meet him and see if we can get him interested. His mother is a big fan of the show or something. I don't know."

"Since when did you become talent scout instead of location scout?"

"I'll be doing plenty of both, trust me. Who knows, I guess the work I did in getting Dylan and Glenshire upped my street cred or something."

"So when did you leave Inverness?"

"I didn't even finish unpacking. I went straight to the airport. I got into Mykonos about an hour ago. I'm sorry I didn't have time to call you sooner. I figured someone had filled you in."

"No, no. No one filled me in," she said, her tone rather subdued now. "Although I really wish someone had."

"Don't worry. I have all the contact information for Inverness. I was supposed to meet with the events coordinator at the hotel I checked into. It's perfect, trust me. It would be better to go there in person, but no way is Tommy sparing you now, so you'll have to do it via phone. I trust you."

"No, it's not that. I mean, thanks, yes, I'll take care of it, it's . . . what did you tell Dylan?"

"I couldn't get ahold of him, so I—I left him a message. Don't worry, he really didn't want to sign on. He only did it because—never mind. Trust me, I'm sure he was relieved to hear his services won't be needed."

"You just left a message? You didn't talk to him?"

Erin stared out of her hotel room at the stunning coastline of Mykonos and the white yachts bobbing in gorgeous blue water below. It was one of the most beautiful places she'd ever seen. And later today, she'd be out there on the water, in one of those yachts. Probably the biggest one.

So it made no sense, this feeling of abject loneliness that had dogged her since she'd gotten on the flight in Scotland. Normally she'd be thrilled to be away from the craziness of production getting under way, mercifully cast back out into the world to do what she did best.

"Erin?"

She dragged her attention back to the present. "It was probably for the best. We'd already said our goodbyes." So to speak. Erin pressed her forehead against the warm glass. The sun felt good. It was the only thing that felt good at the moment.

"That's what you think," Dana muttered.

At least that's what Erin thought she'd said. "Why are you suddenly so worried about Dylan?" Her conversation with Daisy came to mind, as it had during her entire drive to Inverness and the two flights it had taken to get to the island. Now Dana was being morose. "What was between us is done and now we'll move on. I mean, we already have. He was going to be our Prince Charming, for god's sake. That should tell you something."

There was a long silence on the other end of the phone.

Erin straightened away from the window and turned her back on the dazzling scenery. She gripped the phone a little more tightly. "Is there something you're not telling me?"

"That he was willing to do that for you when he didn't want to should have told you all you needed to know."

"What, that he was willing to force himself to submit to the very willing attentions of a dozen beautiful women? Please!"

"Come on, Erin. It's me, Dana, you're talking to. You know as well as I do that if such a private person as he was willing to go on national television with cameras following his every move and do anything with anyone, when the only person he really wants to be with—" She broke off and, for once, held her tongue.

"Dana," Erin started, then paused, and finally blew out a long sigh. Dana was right, she wasn't used to having people care about her, and it was clear Dana was just trying to be a good friend. "And here I thought I was the closet romantic. The closet is getting pretty damn crowded." She tried for dry amusement, but her suddenly tight throat betrayed her.

"I guess I thought . . . if you could have seen . . . he's just so . . ."

"Dana, I know you just want the perfect happy ending for me. But we're on two totally different paths. He's committed to his life in Glenbuie and my job takes me all over the place. I mean, yesterday I was in Scotland, today I'm standing in a hotel room on Mykonos."

"But that's just it. It's just a job, Erin."

Her eyes widened at that. "It's my life."

"And what's wrong with that statement? I know you're very good at what you do, hell, I want to *be* you when I grow up. Only I plan on having a life along with my job."

"Good luck with that in this business. And you know damn well why we do this. We get to see the world, do things that most people would kill to get to see or do."

"We also get to work insane hours, get bitched at on a routine basis, and get jerked all over the globe on a moment's notice. It's exciting, sure, for a while. But then what? You want to be doing this when you're sixty? What about friends, family, falling in love?"

"My family is you guys."

"I rest my case." She tried for the joke, but given the direction of their conversation, it fell flat. "At some point don't you picture yourself more settled? Married? Or at least sharing your life with someone? When does that happen? I'm not saying you should be worried about it, you're young, but when something does come along like this, doesn't it at least make you think about your future?"

Erin didn't answer right away, so Dana plunged ahead.

"Your job is great, why do you think I want it? But, ultimately, it is what it is, it's not a springboard to something else. Once I'm you, that's it. It's such a great opportunity and now is the time for me to be footloose and fancy free, but eventually I'm going to want more from the life part of my life. I love the job, but I don't plan on doing it forever. I can't do it forever and have what I ultimately want, which isn't to grow old alone. Haven't you thought about that?"

No, Erin very purposely hadn't. And Dana was right, there was nowhere to go from her position, unless she wanted to shift gears completely and get into a different phase of production. But it was specifically the crazy hours, the constant change of scenery, the constant demands of her job, that she loved most. It kept her . . . occupied. And needed. But let her retain her precious independence.

"Dana, I appreciate that you care. I do," she said, meaning it more than Dana could possibly know. "But I've got to get off here and do some research about this guy before I meet him later.

"Erin, there's something you need to know about—"

There was a knock at her hotel door. "Listen, I gotta run, someone's at the door. I'll send you all the contact info for the Inverness site and we'll catch up later, I promise." She hung up and crossed the room, knowing she should feel guilty for putting Dana off, but she was in self-preservation mode at the moment. She would make it up to Dana later.

She opened the door to find a young, good-looking Greek hotel employee smiling at her with impossibly white teeth.

"*Kalimera*, Miss MacGregor. Message for you." He proffered a creamy white envelope sporting a gold hotel seal.

Quite a change from the Glenbuie hotel, she thought, thanking him as she took the message. Very five star. But then the network was trying to impress a billionaire's son. And there was some matter of the wife of the executive also owning stock in this hotel. Bottom line, Erin was being put up in very posh digs for the duration of her stay, where she could wine and dine if necessary.

Tommy had even hinted that the Proussalidis might invite her to be a guest on their yacht for her stay in Greece, as well. Hard to complain about the working conditions when you were sitting on a multi-million dollar boat. She fished in her pocket and came up with a few euros and offered them to the bellman. "*Efharisto*," she told him, using her entire knowledge of the Greek language, obtained on the way in from the airport from her driver.

"No problem," he assured in heavily accented English.

This should have made her smile, she thought as she closed the door behind him. Instead, she couldn't help but think how much more she'd enjoyed the homey atmosphere at the hotel in Glenbuie. With Amelia and the cheerful skip in her step, almost admonishing Erin for wanting to tip her. Which reminded her, she had to contact the hotel and touch base with the manager and make sure she praised Amelia's job performance. She owed her that at the very least.

Erin wandered over to the low round table and fat, cushioned chairs arranged in front of the amazing floor-to-ceiling windows of her top floor suite, and sank into the nearest one as she flipped the envelope open. She scanned the short note. A driver from the Proussalidi family would be picking her up at five o'clock and she'd be dining aboard the *Anastasia* this evening.

She tossed the note down and leaned back in her chair and closed her eyes. *Who wouldn't love this job*? she asked herself. Dining with billionaires, staying in all the finest hotels. She was lucky. So very lucky.

"So why aren't I happy?" she asked the room at large. Hearing the question out loud only served to underscore her discontent, not dilute it.

Because the answer was swift and undeniable. She wasn't happy because she was sitting on this fabulous island alone. She'd always done her job alone and had been quite content with that setup. Now, a couple of jaunts with Dylan later, and suddenly she felt lonely without him? She forced herself to get up and shake off the ennui that had descended over her like a heavy cloak the minute she'd driven away from Glenshire yesterday. She'd get a shower, put on something fresh, and by the time the first round of drinks were served on board the *Anastasia*, she'd be back in the zone again.

But instead of rushing off to the shower, she picked up the invitation and fingered the edge of the heavy vellum cardstock, remembering the last note that was hand-delivered to her, inviting her on a midnight adventure to a pile of ancient rocks in the middle of nowhere. Shouldn't even compete with a multi-million dollar yacht.

She sighed and tossed the note back on the table. But it trumped it. Hands down. God, she missed him. She didn't want to be in stupid Greece, getting ready for a stupid meeting on a stupid yacht where she'd have to be on like a game show hostess on crack if she had a prayer of closing the deal for Tommy.

She wanted to be back in Glenshire. With Dylan.

Only what in the hell would she do there?

She hadn't dared even let herself think about that when she had the chance. *Because you wanted it too damn bad.* Now? Now she couldn't stop thinking about it, about how she might have made it work if only she'd let herself even contemplate such a thing. Now that she'd gone and destroyed any chance she had even to try. But what would she have done if she'd stayed in Glenbuie? Seeing Dylan wasn't a full time job. She'd have gone crazy from boredom. It couldn't possibly have worked.

And yet the more she tried to convince herself of that, the more her brain kept circling around the puzzle, picking at it, refusing to let it go. Which was making her crazy since she couldn't damn well do anything about it now anyway. Even if she had a solution. Which she didn't. So why in the bloody hell couldn't she stop thinking about it and concentrate on her goddamn job instead?

She should be going over her location list, feeling the rush of being at a new site, getting to explore a part of the world she'd never seen before. Getting revved up over the thrill of the hunt for the perfect site—and then she went perfectly still as an idea popped into her mind. The conversation she'd had with Daisy played back through her mind, specifically the first part. God, had that only been yesterday?

Her mind was spinning now, and once hatched, the idea quickly took on a life of its own until she was digging through her satchel for a pen and paper to start taking down notes. Not that it mattered of course. She'd already blown it. But she couldn't seem to stop writing. In fact, it was only when the phone buzzed alerting her to the fact that her driver was there to take her to the *Anastasia* that she realized how much time had passed. She'd never even gotten a shower, much less changed her clothes. Or looked over her notes on the Proussalidis.

She looked down at the notes she had made . . . reams of them, in fact. And not one of them was about her meeting with Andrae Proussalidi. Not one of them about her job. Her current job, anyway.

She was torturing herself, doing this. But tell that to the excitement presently coursing through her. Along with a very healthy dose of solid fear. But fear meant she was rational, right? Fear meant she was actually thinking this through clearly. Only an idiot wouldn't be terrified out of her mind, considering the leap she was contemplating making.

The room phone buzzed again. The desk with another reminder. The Proussalidi driver was waiting.

She shoved her notes in her satchel and got up to look at herself in the mirror. She half-heartedly pushed at the matted wisps that passed for her current jet-lagged hairstyle, then shrugged. "Well, perhaps I won't have to work up the nerve to quit. Andrae will take one look at me and run screaming, then Tommy will fire me instead."

She flipped open her suitcase, her heart threatening to pound straight through her chest wall, but not at the prospect of insulting the Proussalidi family with her less than professional appearance. *Was she really thinking of doing what she was thinking of doing?*

And what if Dylan rejected her out of hand? She could hardly blame him. She'd been nothing if not completely inconsistent with him, and topped it off by insulting his sincerely expressed commitment to wanting a relationship with her by asking him to throw himself at twelve other women. "Could you be any more of a complete idiot?"

She swore as she frantically dug through her suitcase, but everything in it was more horribly wrinkled than the trousers and cotton shirt she was already wearing and there was no time to fire up the iron. She made a half-assed attempt to fluff her hair, dabbed at the smudges beneath her eyes from total lack of sleep since leaving Glenbuie, then hastily grabbed some shorts and a T-shirt from her suitcase and stuffed them in her satchel. She could beg a delayed flight and appeal to the generosity of her host and perhaps he'd allow her to change clothes and freshen up on board. It was the best game plan she could come up with and she let herself out of the room before she could second guess herself any further.

If only she'd shown a fraction of that courage with Dylan. But the more she thought about her plan, her germ of an idea, the harder her heart pounded. Not only in fear. Yes, he could totally throw her offer straight back in her face. But now, now she had to try. "Nothing like making it as hard on yourself as possible," she muttered. So what else was new? But maybe she'd had to leave him to realize what she was giving up. And hell, she hadn't even lasted a day before she was scrambling for some way, any way, to make things work so she could go back, so she could stay. That had to count for something, right?

Maybe he'd understand that she just had to figure things out in her own screwed up way, but that now she knew. Now she understood what he meant about regretting not trying more than regretting failing. She already didn't have him. So what did she have to lose now? Her heart dropped further and she forced herself not to think that way, not to get discouraged. He had to give her another chance. Didn't he?

Sorely distracted by her internal debate, she barely nodded at the driver the hotel concierge pointed out to her, and climbed in the back of the sleek black limo that sat idling curbside, waiting for her. She thought it was a shame that she couldn't really enjoy the luxury, and absently wished she'd been able to send Dana in her place. She smiled a little at that. Dana said she wanted to be Erin when she grew up? Well, she was going to get her chance sooner than she thought.

Mind still reeling with a jumble of thoughts, ideas, and plans, she dug through her bag for her pad and pen and continued to jot down notes. It was only when the limo took a rather steep turn that she glanced up from her plotting . . . and noticed they were not heading toward the water. In fact, when she swiveled around, she couldn't see the water at all. She leaned forward and rapped on the glass partition. "Shouldn't we be heading toward the sea?" she shouted, looking around for the button that would lower the privacy screen.

Her driver didn't turn around, but a speaker crackled to life and a deep voice filled the back seat area. "Relax, mum. We'll arrive at our destination shortly."

Well, she thought, settling back in her seat, her attention already drawn half back to her notes. Maybe they had to go down the coast a bit to the Proussalidis' yacht club or something. She really hadn't thought to ask exactly where the *Anastasia* was moored, and given the number of boats she'd seen dotting the Aegean Sea, it could be miles from the hotel.

She'd picked up her pen and was tapping it on the pad of paper, when the driver's words echoed in her mind. *Mum?*

Her gaze flew to the privacy screen, but all she could see were a pair of broad shoulders and the back of a dark driver's cap. She supposed it wasn't unheard of that her driver could be British. Actually, he'd sounded like a Scot.

Erin sighed and pressed a hand against her stomach. She was obviously just projecting her terror over what might happen when she went back. Her stomach was in knots, just thinking about what she would say to him. She forced her attention back to her note pad and turned to a clean sheet. She still had a job to do, and she needed to formulate a plan of attack for the afternoon. She'd never been so unprepared.

Tapping her pen on the paper, she had the oddest urge to tap on the glass partition again. She just wanted to hear him speak. It made no sense, but it was like she needed to hear that familiar accent. It grounded her in a way, reminded her of . . . She cut off that thought. Of course it reminded her of Dylan, but the first word that had come to mind was home. She missed him, but she missed Glenbuie, too. She missed the village, the people she'd come to know. She'd never felt so embraced before and now, being back out here on her own again, it made her feel a little more . . . bereft.

She flipped the pages back, skimmed over the notes upon notes she'd made, and her adrenaline punched in again. Could she really do this? What would Daisy think? And what about Dylan? Would he be able to trust her? Trust that she wouldn't change her mind, that once decided on a course of action, she was as committed as he was?

A million thoughts were still running through her mind and she'd yet to make one note about her meeting with Andrae, when the limo turned up a wide, curving driveway. Erin looked out the window. They were up in the hills now. If she looked out the back window, she could see through the trees and buildings scattered in staggered relief below to a hint of the sparkling sea beyond. But unless the Proussalidis had a really, really big backyard pool, they were definitely nowhere near a yacht club, much less a yacht.

The house that came into view was stunning, but more villa than mansion. Small and tasteful, and very private. Tommy had said Andrae was a renowned playboy.

Perhaps he'd thought to entertain Erin in a more intimate setting? She sighed and slumped back a little in her seat, suddenly a bit more content with the fact that she hadn't wasted time figuring out how she was going to impress the young billionaire-to-be. If this was what she thought it was, he'd be lucky to escape without a knee to the groin. She only hoped Tommy wouldn't lose his job, too. If he thought that just because she'd developed a close relationship with Dylan, that she had a different set of standards when it came to being "convincing," well then Andrae and Tommy were about to get a whole new understanding of Erin's personal code of conduct.

Getting more incensed by the minute, she shoved her notepad back in her bag, took a deep breath, and set her shoulders squarely. She always went into these things prepared for battle. Just not of this particular kind. "Ah well, what a way to go out, huh?" she murmured, and reached for the door before the driver could come around. He looked to be a big guy, she thought, tugging on the handle, maybe she should ask him to accompany her inside. Just in case.

The door opened from the outside and she climbed out, only to have the driver block her from moving forward. She stepped to the side, but he didn't move so she was forced to shade her eyes against the sun and look up into his face. "Excuse me, but—"

He pulled off his hat. "Hullo, Erin."

Erin blinked against the sun spots that had obviously impaired her vision. Either that or it was true that if you wished for something badly enough, you really could make it appear in front of you. "Dylan?"

Chapter 21

"Aye. Dinnae be angry with me, but I—"

"Angry? What are you doing here? You're in Greece."

He'd never been more terrified in his life, and yet she managed to make his lips twitch. "Aye, I still recall the flight. That last leg was a wee bit bumpy for my tastes, but then I'm no' much of a flyer."

"But . . . how?"

"I booked a ticket, just like everyone else."

"Dylan—"

He took a deep breath and began the hardest conversation of his life. "I went to Inverness. Just missed you." Och, but he missed her. It hadn't even been much more than twenty-four hours and it felt like a bleedin' lifetime. But then he hadn't known if or when he'd ever see her again.

"So . . . you followed me all the way to Greece? And what's with the driver's uniform? Why didn't you just contact me at the hotel?"

"It was sort of a last minute inspiration," he said, his cheeks warming. He still didn't know quite what had come over him. "I—I got your itinerary and made it to the hotel—"

"Wait, got my itinerary from . . . ?"

He ducked his chin. "I'd rather not put anyone else on your hunting list. Suffice to say, they only had your best interests—"

"*They?*"

He was handling this quite badly. But then, he'd never been compelled to fly halfway across Europe after the woman of his heart. "I made it to your hotel and was planning to ring you, then I saw the Proussalidis' driver, and—"

"Wait, so you're not driving for them? What am I saying, of course you're not." She looked past him at the villa. "So whose . . . ?" She waved her hand in the general direction of the house.

"I saw the driver, realized you were on your way out to the yacht, and I . . . well, I guess I kind of panicked." He half laughed, though it came out as more of a gargle. Why in bloody hell had he talked himself into doing such a crazed stunt as this? She had to think he was daft. Hell, *he* thought he was daft.

"You. Panicked," she said, deadpan, or in complete disbelief.

He crushed the driver's cap in his hands. "I—I sort of pretended to be your assistant and told him you'd come down with a dreadful stomach ailment on the flight over. I suspect you'll return to your hotel later to find a very expensive floral bouquet or perhaps a gift basket, or both. I told them you'd be in touch as soon as you were feeling better."

"Wait, you sabotaged my meeting with Andrae?"

He felt a little tic pulse in his temple, just hearing her say his name. He'd never once in his life, not ever, felt so much as a twinge of jealousy. But the very idea of her jet-setting off with another man, not to mention one due to inherit billions, even if it was work related . . . "Let's say I just . . . delayed it. Slightly." He leaned forward and lowered his voice. "I should add, you might want to do a bit of research on the chap. I think perhaps he tries a bit too hard to establish himself as a fan of the lassies, if you know what I mean. I believe his interest in appearing on your program is so he can convince dear old dad of his, shall we say, viability."

"Are you saying Andrae Proussalidi is—?" She waved a hand. "Never mind. I don't care about him at the moment. At the moment I want to know why you followed me all the way to Greece. And where did you get the uniform? And the car for that matter? Are you even licensed to drive here? You're supposed to be in Scotland."

She was babbling. She never babbled. It gave him the first toehold on a ladder of hope.

"Fear is a great motivator," he said, in way of explaining his brief change in occupation. "As to the mother land, I'm no' umbilically attached, you know. I am allowed to leave the place. Long as I head back in due time. At the moment, I am quite free of it, as a band of very loud, very, shall we say, determined ladies have invaded my home."

"But the expense of flying, Glenshire, you should—"

"Sometimes the risky investment is recommended. I considered this an investment in hope. Something I thought I could stand to put a wee bit more faith in myself."

She opened her mouth, then closed it again. She didn't look exactly angry, nor did she appear overjoyed to see him, mostly she appeared stunned. He could have told her it was a feeling he shared. No one was more surprised than he to be standing in this exact spot, dressed as he was. Hoping with all his heart it was worth the potential humiliation, already knowing he'd have done far more if it meant getting her to listen to him one last time. Tristan was right. Pride was the first thing you swallow.

"So . . . the villa? I'm guessing not the Proussalidis' either? Are we trespassing? Why not just talk to me?"

"Well, there is investing in hope, and there is banking the odds in your favor. I wasn't planning on any of it. Except the villa. That I did plan. As a back up. Of sorts. I wanted—needed . . . I didn't want you on Tommy's or your network's ground, so to speak. I wanted someplace neutral."

"There are other hotels in Mykonos."

"I know. My brother, Tristan, is engaged to—"

"Bree Sullivan, the famous author, I know." Her eyes widened. "This is hers?"

"No, but a friend of a friend. She thought it might—"

"Wait." Erin put up her hand. "Bree knows you're here? Someone else gave you my itinerary. Not Dana, because she didn't know until a few hours ago, so—" She must have spied something in his expression. "Dana?"

"No' about Greece, but Inverness . . . I do confess."

"And Tristan. And . . . who else?"

"Pretty much the entire village," he said, and surprised himself by the pride he took in saying so. "They want what's best for me, and I think they agree what's best for me is you. I've come to realize how fortunate I truly am to have so many people around with my best interests at heart. I'm more blessed than I ever allowed myself to believe." He dared step a bit closer. "They've come to care for ye, too, Erin. The lot of them. You've made quite the impact on the folk of Glenbuie. But none so much as myself."

He finally put the twisted drivers' cap out of its misery and tossed it on the roof of the car so he could reach for her. He tentatively took hold of her arms and slid down to join his hands with hers. "When word came that I was released from my promise to you, about appearing on the program, and I knew you'd well and truly be leaving me, leaving Scotland, for good . . . I was already on my way to Inverness. I couldnae let you go without taking one last chance to talk to you, to see if there was a way, any way, to convince you to give us, give me, a chance." He drew their joined hands up between them. "I kept thinking of the way you looked at me. It's no' only a physical thing with us. You have to know that, too. And I'm well aware what it is I'm asking. And that despite the villa and my jet setting off after you, I am a man of modest means, saddled with enormous responsibility, and tied irrevocably to my homeland and my people. I canno' compete with the life of adventure you lead. But . . . I'd humbly like to say that—"

She interrupted his stumbling speech by placing her fingers across his lips. He had to fight the urge to grab hold of them, press them against his lips, and keep them there.

"Dylan . . ." she started, then stopped. She closed her eyes briefly, then opened them again, and he could scarcely believe what he thought he saw in their sparkling green depths. Fear, yes. Desire, certainly. And, if he was perhaps the luckiest man alive, that elusive spark of hope. "I haven't stopped thinking about you from the moment I drove away from Glenshire. I've rejected, out of hand, and out of fear, perhaps one of the best things that's ever happened to me. It's . . . it's hard not to cling to what I know, to what I've built for myself. Only I realized, with perhaps the help of people who do care about me, that maybe I've done that at the expense of allowing myself any real freedom. For someone who considers the world her oyster, I'm somewhat trapped by my own circumstance, in a life that must be lived solo.

"I've been solo pretty much since day one. So I clung to a life that suited that, where I'd never have to trust in someone else not to abandon me, or the world we created together. It's why I never allowed myself to be adopted. Better to be self-reliant, then you always know where you stand. And I like this life, yes. I'm lucky, very lucky, to have had the chance to see the world, to do what I do. But I've never really let myself think about what I might want beyond that life. A life lived exclusively for work, devoid of putting down any real kind of roots. Where you have to learn to trust, both in those around you, to want to keep you there . . . and in your own ability to want it badly enough to stay. Long term. Forever, even. It's not that I have to travel, it's merely the thing I do. I know there's more to the world than traveling through it. And . . . and . . ." Her voice was a little shaky at that point, and her eyes grew a bit glassy.

Dylan was fairly certain his heart had stopped somewhere during her little speech. Was she truly working up to saying what he, in his wildest hopes, hadn't dared to allow himself to believe she might say? "Erin, I'll ask no promises of ye. I know it would mean an absence from your work, and I'm no' certain what that would mean, in your ability to go back to it at some later time, but—"

"I—I spent most of my trip here, and all of the afternoon, working on a plan. It's why I looked like I just rolled out of my suitcase. I was supposed to be researching Andrae." She paused. "Is he really . . . you know?"

Dylan lifted a shoulder. He shouldn't have stooped so low, but he was a desperate man. "A plan?" he prompted.

"Yes, a plan. For me. I—I needed to know, to have

some kind of idea, of what I would do, you know . . . were I to stay and . . . see."

"And see."

She nodded, then swallowed hard. "Yes," she said, lifting her gaze to his. "And see. I know I'd need a purpose, beyond just discovering what I might have with . . . with you."

Suddenly his heart, which couldn't have been beating at all, thundered to life. He had to work very hard not to squeeze the life out of her hands, still held in his own. "And . . . ?" he choked out.

"Daisy was the one, actually, who gave me the seed of an idea."

"Daisy?"

Erin nodded. "I think she'll support it. She . . . she wants you to be happy, and I think if she thinks I might be a part of that, she'd help me—"

"I'm certain she will," he said, believing it, even though he had no idea what she was talking about.

"I thought maybe I'd put my talents to use as an excursion coordinator. For the bed and breakfast mainly, but maybe also set up shop in the village. A tourist center and day trip sort of thing. The show will bring people to the village, and if Daisy and I promote it properly, I think I can turn it into a business. I know I can boost the revenue for Glenshire at the very least, and—"

"So . . . are ye comin' back wi' me, then?" he blurted, unable to hold his tongue another second. "My heart's about to pound out of my chest and—"

Her smile was slow, but certain. Her shining eyes held his as she blinked away a bit of sheen glossing them over. And then she nodded. "Aye. That was my plan. As soon as I took care of business here, I was going to come back. If you'll have me. I'm not an easy woman, Dylan. And I have no idea how I'll handle—"

The rest was cut off with a fierce hug.

He spun her around and around, making her squeal, then scooped her up in his arms as they both laughed like loons and turned blindly toward the villa. “If we’re going to start something, we’re going tae start it properly,” he said, groping above the ledge of the door for the key and finding it where it was promised to be.

“I can walk,” she started.

“Aye, but ye feel too damn good in my arms.” He pushed the door open and had a brief vision of a sunshine-filled room accented in lemon yellow and navy blue tile, and filled with white furniture. At the moment, nothing could compete with the vision in his arms. “Indulge me,” he told her, as he strode through the small villa, finding the stairs, and climbing upward to where he’d been told the master suite awaited.

She looped her arms around his neck. “I’m noticing a pattern.”

“Complaining?”

She pressed her lips against the side of his neck. “No,” she said with a deep, heartfelt sigh, punctuating the word with another kiss. “Not at all.” She teased her way along his jaw until he thought he’d go mad not to have her mouth under his.

Two doors he tried, then three. Discovering a closet, an office and a bathroom. “Dammit, where is the bloody bedroom?”

Erin was taking full advantage of his fruitless search. She ran her fingertips up the back of his neck, toyed with his hair, and bit his chin. “Dylan,” she murmured against his ear.

And just like that he turned her toward the nearest stretch of wall and pinned her tightly between it and his body. She wrapped her legs around his hips and he buried himself fully there, making them both gasp in pleasure as he captured her mouth and plundered it deeply.

"I canno' seem to get my fill of you," he breathed, when he could, running kisses along her cheek, down to the ticking pulse that beat at the side of her neck.

"Good," she responded, and dragged his mouth back to hers.

His body roared to life and she tightened her thighs and pulled him closer still. He loved how she was such a match for him, not simply compliant to his needs but meeting them fully and head on, unafraid to reach for what she wanted as well.

He lifted his head, touched her cheek, needing to look into her eyes, needing to be certain she knew what this was, wanting to see that in her eyes as well.

She instantly grinned at him.

"What?"

"You look almost . . . piratical."

"Do I now?" He nipped at her chin, making her gasp. "I do feel as if I'm plundering a treasure."

She sighed. "Would you think me terribly shallow if I told you that your accent drives me crazy with lust."

"No," he said, actually liking that admission a great deal. "But I'm no' above using that tidbit of knowledge to my greatest advantage in the future."

"Darn," she said, her lips curving into an even more delectable smile. "Poor me." She kissed him, softly, and quite sweetly, surprising him with the sudden bit of tenderness.

It jolted him and tugged hard at his heart. "Och, Erin," he murmured. "You undo me."

"Aye," she agreed, "and you me. Tell me that part again," she whispered against his cheek.

He turned his face, caught her gaze. "What part would that be?"

Her arms tightened slightly around his neck and he felt the tension in her fingertips as they dug into his scalp. "The part with the word future in it."

And his heart slipped the rest of the way out of his control. Without saying a word, he gathered her close and found the right damn door. The platform bed was massive and dominated the room. It could have been a cot for all he cared. Or a blanket on a ruined castle wall. But he wanted to feel all of her against all of him when he said what he had to say.

He let her feet slip to the floor beside the bed and slowly, almost reverently undressed her. She didn't shy away, nor did she stand proudly, she was merely herself. He'd seen her body, but this was somehow different. A more deliberate baring. As if they were baring souls along with their skin. He reverently kissed the skin he was revealing. Along her shoulder, down her narrow collar bone. He stripped her bra off, and took a great amount of time paying homage to her breasts, and their rosy tips. She was gasping, small moans issuing from her lips, balancing her weight when her knees threatened to buckle by bracing her hands on his shoulders. But she said nothing, allowing him to continue his reverent journey.

He sank to his knees, trailing kisses along the center line of her torso, running his palms along the swell of her waist. He slipped her pants open and gently pushed them down her legs. She kicked free of her shoes, then her pants, leaving herself standing in front of him in only the thinnest of cotton panties.

"Have you the least idea of how completely ravishing you are?" he whispered as he pressed a kiss against her navel.

That elicited a choked laugh from her.

He looked up and her hands came to rest in his hair, caressing his face, as she gazed down at him. "You make me feel ravishing," she said, her cheeks stained a bright pink.

"To me, you're this amazing adventure of discovery.

I'll never tire of this journey, Erin." And with that he turned his face to her, and caught the elastic band of her panties in his teeth. As he tugged downward, she tensed a bit. And he paused just long enough to look up and wink. "Pirate, eh?" he said, between clenched teeth.

And she laughed.

And he knew he'd found his forever.

He turned and tumbled her back onto the bed, then pushed her up until she was in the center of the sea of soft, plush comforter. Then he slid back down to where he'd been a moment ago. Teasing his finger along her panty line, as he dropped a trail of light kisses along her inner thigh. She whimpered softly, and arched into him. And his body leapt in response.

But this time, his control came more easily, if still at a cost. He'd have a lifetime of getting to know her now, so he could take her fast, take her slow, it mattered not. What mattered was that this felt like the first time for them. And in many ways, it was. The first time when it was a promise of something more to come, and not simply a slaking of need. He wanted her to know that, to feel that, too.

He kissed the panel of cotton covering her and was rewarded with the damp musk of her. He was so hard he thought he might come right then and there, and he pressed his hips hard into the mattress, trying to assuage the driving need he had to bury himself to the hilt inside of her. She moved beneath him, urging him on, and he slowly peeled her panties down, replacing cotton with his lips, and when he finally had them free of her legs, with his tongue.

She pushed hard against him, at the first feel of his tongue and mouth where she most needed it. Hands came down to fist in his hair, as he continued his sweet assault. He could feel her begin to gather beneath him and knew he was driving her to the brink. Giving her pleasure, knowing he could drive her there as she drove him so effortlessly, filled him with enormous satisfaction . . . and made him desperately wish he'd stripped his clothes off when he'd removed hers.

Her fingers tightened in his hair and she was bucking against him. "Dylan, oh . . . my . . ."

He teased her, flicking his tongue over her, then slid one finger deep inside of her. He wasn't sure who groaned more loudly. So hot, so tight, so ready for him. He was grinding his hips against the bed now, throbbing to be released from the ever tightening restraint of his pants. She began pumping against him more insistently . . . so he slowly slid another finger in. And she keened loudly as she bore down . . . and came gloriously beneath him. Shuddering, jolting, pistoning, and noisy with it, her climax was every bit as honest and direct as she was in all parts of her life. Nothing delicate and simpering about her.

Grinning, he slid his fingers free as she still twitched, kissing the inside of her thigh, then working his way up her body, pausing for a rather long and delightful interlude at the tips of her breasts. She wasn't having any of it, of course, tugging him up rather insistently.

"Dylan," she demanded, wrapping her ankles around his, trying to drag him up higher onto her body, her hips arching off the bed as her body sought his, needing greater fulfillment than a mere orgasm could give her.

Och, but he knew that better than anyone.

"I rather seem to have too many clothes on," he murmured against the side of her neck.

And instantly found himself on his back. When the shock subsided, he found himself laughing.

"Amusing, is it?" she said. "Torturing a puir lassie like me?" She all but attacked his white shirt and dark trousers.

"You have a rather piratical gleam of your own there, you know."

"Aye, matey," she said, making him laugh again with her ridiculous accents. She wiggled her eyebrows. "But I'll have you know, I take my prisoners."

He flung his arms outward, opening himself more fully to her than he had to anyone, in ways she, perhaps, could not know. But he did. And she would.

After all, they had time. Blessed, wonderful, precious time. Something he knew better than to ever take for granted.

"Don't bother being gentle with me. I can take it," he told her. He wiggled a bit and she gasped, still twitching, still needy for him after her climax. He laughed, thinking he could hardly remember a time now when that hadn't been such a natural part of his day.

"You take pleasure in my discomfort, do you?" she teased.

"Oh, I believe I'm the one suffering at the moment," he said, then gulped when she got to his zipper, which was strained beyond belief.

"Why, yes," she said, sliding down his body until she straddled his legs. "I can see that." She leaned in, and his hips involuntarily pumped off the bed. He twitched hard inside the restricted confines of his trousers.

She was naked and completely free within herself, her hair standing almost on end, like any good pirate queen. And dear god he'd never seen anything lovelier. Was it honestly true she could be his?

"I'll free the prisoner," she told him, "but I warn you, I'll be keeping quite a close watch on him."

He wanted to say something equally teasing, but the very sight of her tugging down his zipper and freeing him to her lips, her tongue, had him digging his fingers into the mattress for all he was worth. He'd never last if she took him into her mouth. And time they might have, but this time . . . this time . . .

Once free of trouser and shoes, he reached for her and swiftly pulled her beneath him.

"Hey," she protested, "no fair."

"Pirates don't play fair," he told her, making her laugh.

And the teasing left him then, and that sweet, aching tenderness filled him instead as he settled between her legs. "You can and most certainly will have your way with me, and often, I'm sure," he told her, stroking the hair from her face. "After all, you've had your way with me almost from the moment we met."

Her lips curved slightly. "This is true."

He smiled briefly, looking into her eyes, then tracing the lines of her face with his gaze. "I'm no' so certain how I came to be such a lucky, fortunate soul," he said. "But I've learned no' to question fate, to appreciate the now, as there might never be a tomorrow. It's why I couldnae stay behind in Glenbuie if I thought there might still be any chance to have something worthwhile with you. Erin, you ask about the future . . . and . . . I don't want to imagine mine without you in it. It's that simple. And that complicated."

"When I got to Greece," she said softly, "Hell, when I drove away from Glenshire toward Inverness, it was the first time I'd left a place and felt sad, rather than relieved. I felt a belonging there, in Glenshire and the village, that, I guess, didn't make sense to me. It's hard for me to trust that, but mostly, I think, because I never gave myself a chance to. Maybe it's that I'm afraid, not that the place won't hold me, won't keep me, but that I won't measure up." She stroked his face, ran her fingers over his lips. "When I got here on Mykonos, and looked at this magnificent place, instead of enjoying the view, I felt . . . lonely. In just those few trips we took together, I learned how much more fun it is to share that enjoyment, that feeling of discovery, with someone else. With someone who appreciates it, and me, in that special way you can't just forge from nothing. And I missed you. Terribly."

His throat tightened. "Och, but you have my heart, Erin. You must know that. I know this won't be easy for you, but I swear I—"

She lifted her head and placed the sweetest of kisses on his lips to silence him. "That, I think, is the part that scares me most. Because, once decided, this, in some ways, is almost ridiculously easy. Being with you feels like the most natural thing in the world. And I ache to go back to Glenbuie, to see the familiar faces, people who smile when they see me, just because I'm me, and not because I work for them or with them. The true challenge, it turns out, was never seeing you again, never having that feeling of fitting in somewhere, after having felt all of it with you."

"You'll come home with me, then, Erin MacGregor?"

She settled herself beneath him and held him tightly, as she pulled him slowly, deeply, into her body, smiling up into his eyes as he pushed himself fully inside her. They both sucked in a deep breath, their gazes locked as he held himself there. She moved then, and he moved with her, long, slow, deep strokes, each one met with a slow thrust of her hips.

"I already am home, Dylan Chisholm." She pulled his mouth to hers. "I already am."

Have you tried Donna Kauffman's
Black Sheep series?
It starts with
THE BLACK SHEEP AND THE PRINCESS . . .

They're the black sheep—the bad boys every good girl wants to have hold her, touch her, take her, love her. But being bad never felt so good . . .

"I have some spare beer, if you're interested . . ."

I'd know that voice anywhere, and every time I hear it, it makes me sweat. Not that well-bred heiresses are supposed to sweat, but if you saw Donovan MacLeod, trust me, you'd need a change of clothes, too. It's been eighteen years, but he's got the same cocky swagger, silver-gray eyes, shaggy hair, and that sexy smile that promises a whole lot of trouble. Not that I'll ever find out because he loathes me—thinks I'm some spoiled princess. So, there's something I've just got to ask . . .

"Why are you here, Donovan?"

The lady asked a question, she deserves an answer. Well, Kate Sutherland, how about, I've fantasized about you for eighteen years? Or, I wanted to remember how it feels to need a cold shower every time you flick that perfect blond hair out of your blue eyes? Or, Why don't you come over here and let me show you, baby? Yeah, good answers, but I'll stick with the first one—I came back to help, because I think you're in for some trouble. My bad-boy gut says you're gonna need me—in more ways than one . . .

Then it's THE BLACK SHEEP AND THE HIDDEN BEAUTY . . .

They're back—the boys you go out looking for precisely because your mother warned you not to—the bad boys every good girl needs at least once, if not twice . . .

Raphael "Rafe" Santiago may have left the streets years ago, but the street has never left him. A rough childhood in the Bronx taught him never to let his guard down, to keep everything in order, and always to trust that little voice in his gut that tells him when someone's got something to hide. Horse trainer Elena Caulfield, is definitely hiding something, and Rafe intends to find out what it is and take care of it—his way.

But his way wasn't supposed to include feeling an intense attraction to the tomboyish Elena. With her mud-caked boots, quiet strength, and gentle manner, she's nothing like the flashy, seductive, overtly feminine women Rafe usually beds. The closer he gets to her, the harder it is to control that fiery passion he's worked hard to keep cooled, the kind that can catch a man off guard and leave him open to danger—because whatever secret Elena's protecting, it's big . . . and worth killing for. Because when you're from the Bronx, you take care of what you love—or die trying . . .

And last but not least, THE BLACK SHEEP AND THE ENGLISH ROSE . . .

Finn Dalton is the black sheep of his privileged family—because he's always trying to do the right thing. But do good guys let bad girls go free? Ask British heiress Felicity Trent. Finn should have called the cops when he caught Felicity with a fortune in stolen jewels. But after the hot night they'd shared, betraying her meant he'd never have her again. Two years later, he discovers Felicity scantily clad and handcuffed to a bed in a posh Manhattan hotel room. Finn has three choices. Turn Felicity in. Turn her loose. Or turn her on . . .

Finn Dalton is bad boy personified. Felicity Trent should know; she's a bad girl herself. But for Felicity, life as a jewel thief is almost as seductive as Finn is—and that's dangerous. Because for a girl like her one night is all she needs to get what she wants, anything more means trouble. Now, with both of them after the same thing—the rarest of treasures—who gets there first might be the last thing they want . . .

And keep an eye out for Donna's new book,
LET ME IN,
coming in March 2009 . . .

"I always found you to be an attractive woman, Tate."

Alarm filled her. But it didn't come close to matching the rush of . . . what? Anticipation? Surely, she didn't want him to acknowledge, much less act on the other kind of tension that was swirling around them.

"But, even in the most extreme situations, I never once considered doing what I can't seem to stop thinking about doing now."

She was the one hallucinating now, that was it. He was still in the bathroom and she'd come into the kitchen to get soup, and had somehow fallen down a rabbit hole or something, because surely he was not standing right in front of her, saying what she thought he was saying. It was wild enough that she was having any thoughts in his general direction, but at least she had the excuse of being retired and no longer the sharp professional.

He was still team leader, actively on the job. And the only person who'd been even more the consummate professional during their years working together than she'd been. All work, no wink. That was Derek Cole. No ever. With her, or anyone else. At least not that anyone had ever known. CJ had made it her favorite topic o conversation on more than one occasion. So, if he eve had . . . flung, he'd been remarkably discreet about it which was saying something around people whose jol it was to know every damn thing. It was another aspec of his character that she'd admired. So, what the hel was this?

When she finally found her voice, it was damnably shaky. "You're injured, and recently injected with Goc knows what, so—"

"It's not the drugs talking, Tate."

"Well, it doesn't sound like you talking, either. A least not the you I worked for. We've got enough tc deal with, without—"

"Oh, I know. Believe me. I came down the hall jus now to see if I could sit in here and eat some soup. Nc ulterior motives. No skulking intended. Then I hea you commenting on my—"

"Must you repeat it?"

His lips quirked a little then. "See?"

"See what?"

"How is it I missed this?" he asked, sounding sin cerely perplexed.

"Missed what?"

"You."

He was looking at her like he'd just discoverec something amazing, and couldn't quite believe it.

"I'm the same me, I've—"

"No. You're not. I always admired your capable, nc nonsense work ethic. You and CJ were the best agents ever had. Which, considering the talent I had assem bled, is a high, but deserved compliment. I said befor hat I found you attractive. I did. And do. But I always iewed that through the filter of being your team leader, ooking at that as simply another attribute you possessed o be executed professionally where and when best de-loyed."

"Just because I don't work for you now—"

"It's not just that. You're . . . more you now. Still verything you were, but there's so much more. I'm eeing the rest of you, probably the you you've always een, but who I never had the pleasure of meeting. You're ry, sharp, outspoken, and surprisingly sarcastic."

"You're right, the professional filter is off, but maybe 'm not who I was before, either. I'm leading a very lifferent life now. I'll pull it back together, focus, find ny professional balance once again, but only because I ave to. And believe me, no one is more motivated to et through this and make it go away as quickly as pos-ible. To make you go away," she added, truthfully. "To et back to the life I earned, the life I deserve. The life *need*, Derek." If there was a quiet pleading in her one, she wasn't going to apologize for it. Things were omplicated enough without this sudden revelation rom him. Especially considering she'd been thinking ery similar things about him.

Which, if he hadn't known before, he did now, given er comment about his lack of clothing. Now he knew he was noticing him, too.

Which meant one of them had to get their act to-ether, and get it together real quick. He moved closer nd leaned his weight against the counter, along with he walking stick, so he could lift his free hand.

"Derek—" She broke off when he lightly brushed is fingertips across her cheek. His touch was gentler han she'd expected. She should be smacking his hand way, not wanting to lean into the unanticipated warmth she found there. She didn't need nurturing, c caretaking, but that's not what the look in his eyes wa telegraphing. What she saw there was bold, unwavering, unapologetic want.

And what he wanted, was her.